ON THE BORDER OF
BELONGING

Bruce and Iwana -
Hope you enjoy reading
my fantasy of what it was like
for our Czech mothers!
Betty Whiting

BETTY WHITING

ISBN 979-8-218-13220-0

Published by Lulu.com

Cover design and interior layout by Pete Tolton

Cover Photo "Some Things I Always Knew" by Jean Albus

Author Photo by Paul Whiting

Photos used by permission

For more information or to order books: bettywhiting@bresnan.net

For my mother,

Louise Pospisil Leuthold

What is your life?

For you are a mist that appears

for a little while and then vanishes.

James 4:14b, NRSV Bible

Contents

ON THE BORDER OF
BELONGING

Prologue

BILLINGS, MONTANA, AUGUST 14, 2002

*You don't have to be somebody different to be important. You're
important in your own right.*

MICHELLE OBAMA (1964-)

Louisa lay in a fetal position, her forehead pressed against the
wooden slats on the back of the sofa bed in the Alzheimer's
Unit. Sarah thought her mother looked pretty with her white hair
matching the fuzzy yarn of the fraying white sweater thrown across
her shoulders. Sarah slowly lay down beside her and stroked her hair.
By accident she touched the welt behind Louisa's ear where the bullet
had lodged. Sarah flinched, but Louisa didn't move.

Sarah spoke softly. "Mom, it's Sarah," giving her a little hug. "I'm
here for you." Because that remark sounded lame, she added, "I love
you." No response. "You've been brave. We'll rest together." A little
later she added, "You fell out of bed. Are you feeling any pain?"

With the slightest movement, Louisa moved her head in a no.
Relieved that her mother had heard her and responded, Sarah rubbed
her back. Their roles had reversed becoming confused in the last few
years. Sometimes Louisa called her "Mom" or told others that her
sister had come to visit her.

Sarah started quietly singing songs, like Louisa had done for
her when she was a child—some of her dad's favorites—"Que sera,
sera," "Out Where the West Begins," and "Home on the Range."

15

Louisa straightened her legs moving out of her fetal position, drawing away from Sarah.

Sarah wondered about her mom's medical condition after falling out of bed. Another mini-stroke? Should she arrange for her mother to go to the hospital? That seemed to be what the administrator, Ms. Grimm, wanted when she had called earlier. But Louisa's living will said no extraordinary care, just pain relief. Her mom screaming in pain in the hospital emergency room before her hip surgery six months ago echoed in Sarah's mind. Sarah was grateful her mom seemed to have no pain at the moment.

How serious is this? Do I need to call Roger? Sarah was thinking how expensive it would be for him to fly from Seattle for no reason. It's amazing how long Louisa has kept on living after Dad died. Sarah sighed. This lengthy farewell is taking its toll on us with her needing so much attention, first from Peter before he died, and now from me. Oh Lordy, help me remember the good times and figure out how to deal with the present.

Louisa rolled over on her back, but she kept her eyes closed and didn't say a word. Her beautiful hair with its usual waves and curls was now bushy, cut too short by the nursing home staff. Sarah gently touched her cheeks, wrinkled but oh so soft, like the leaf of a potted violet. Sweet, bow-shaped lips invited a kiss and her small, pert nose was the envy of everyone in the family who had inherited Dad's big honker. Sarah traced her mom's features, telling her she was beautiful and Louisa nodded.

A Certified Nursing Assistant came in. "Louisa, do you want to sit up in the chair? We'll help you." Louisa moved her arms up, singling her compliance. The CNA and Sarah helped her sit up in the bed, lifting her feet over the edge. While the CNA pulled the recliner nearer the bed, Sarah gently rubbed lotion onto Louisa's dry, gnarled toes that long ago had been badly frost bitten. Then

Sarah pulled on socks and slippers. Still, Sarah smiled to herself, the frostbite could not have been too big a problem for Louisa because she danced most of her life.

Another CNA came in and together they lifted Louisa to her recliner with the help of a strap around her waist. Louisa had gotten a bit heavy-set in her later years. Louisa sat quietly in the chair with her head down, her eyes still closed. The CNAs left and Sarah started worrying. Did I forget to get Mom's meds? I'm supposed to remember everything for her now that she has no memory. Surely, Ms. Grimm would have records and remind me. Wouldn't she? I wish Peter hadn't died. He and Mom had such a great connection. He did a great job taking care of her. I've neglected my mother! But Mom didn't seem to like me after I grew up and there were times I didn't like her. Sarah rationalized her lack of dutiful attention.

A medical intern came in with Ms. Grimm and checked Louisa's heart with a stethoscope, checked her pulse, and felt her arms, neck, and legs, checking for breaks from her fall out of bed. He nodded at Sarah as if she were to do something.

Sarah bent down in front of Louisa. "Mom, can you open your eyes? Can you see me?" Louisa's eyelids flew open and her brown eyes pierced Sarah whose eyes widened in surprise.

"Your hair's a mess," Louisa announced. Sarah laughed in embarrassment and straightened.

"Welcome back, Mom!" This is the Louisa I know, Sarah thought.

The intern looked into Louisa's eyes with a light and turned to Sarah.

"I don't see anything wrong. No broken bones. Her heart sounds steady now. Her lungs are clear. She's breathing normally."

"You'll tell the story, won't you?" Louisa asked the intern, and all at once she reached out grabbing his arm and squeezing hard.

He glanced at Sarah quizzically, as if to ask what is she talking about? "Sure," he said, patting her gripping hand.

Then her dark eyes looked directly into Sarah's eyes. "You'll tell the story, won't you? You won't forget to tell the story?" She sounded desperate.

"What story, Mom? What story?" Sarah replied softly, trying to remember some recent story Louisa had told her.

"You'll tell the story!" Louisa frantically looked at the intern and then back at Sarah. "Tell the story!" she demanded.

Sarah wanted to reassure her, to calm her down, but also to find out what she was talking about. "Sure, Mom, but what story?"

"The fire." Louisa's eyes were looking into the corners of the room seeing something the rest were not seeing.

Her mom was given to hysteria. Sarah was eager to avoid a scene. She spoke confidently. "Yes, Mom, we'll tell the story. Don't worry." Sarah took a deep breath, trying not to think about what she was committing herself to doing. "I'll tell the story." Louisa seemed to relax.

The intern and the staff left them alone. Sarah, fearful of her mom screaming about something, sat down and took her hand, the blue veins protruding in the white, leathery wrist and hands. Those hands were once brown and strong. Sarah had an image of Louisa squatting over her flowers, digging into the dirt, pulling up an iris root. Moving over a few inches, she'd reset the root, patting down the dirt around the strands. Sarah started talking to her about those flower beds, about the prairie flowers she'd transplanted: the Montana bitterroot, lupine, larkspur, sweet rockets, and Indian paintbrush. She reminded her of the raspberry bushes she planted. And of the birds she knew and loved: the song of the Meadowlark, the crow's caw, and the Morning Dove's coo. Louisa had a sweet smile on her face and she remained calm. Her eyes were closed again.

Ms. Grimm, a business type who Sarah didn't know except from a few telephone conversations, came in. Peter had made all the business arrangements with her so Sarah had never gotten acquainted with

18

her. Grimm is a good name for her, Sarah thought. I wonder if she ever smiles. I wonder if she has a husband or children.

Grimm tried to get Louisa to sip some water, but Mom pursed her lips tightly together. Grimm put a straw into the glass and firmly placed the tip between Mom's lips determined to get some fluids into her. Mom spit out the end of the straw. Grimm abruptly stood straight, slightly nodding her head. Sarah wondered if Grimm didn't like her mother. That was possible. Sarah felt sympathy for her weakened mother.

"I'll stay with her," Sarah whispered. Grimm raised her eyebrows as she looked at Sarah for the first time that day. Sarah couldn't tell if Grimm was surprised she was staying or was she giving her permission to stay? Would Grimm prefer to have her leave? Irritation boiled up in Sarah as she would like to have some guidance. What did the Alzheimer's Unit want from her? The supervisor turned her back and walked out.

Sarah picked up her mother's phone and called her office. "Diane, I won't be back this afternoon. My mother is not doing well. I'm sorry to leave you there alone on your first day of work. How are you doing?" Diane had started that morning as an intern in their non-profit.

"Don't worry," Diane assured her. "I've been reading the policies you gave me. A couple phone calls came in, but nothing important. I took messages and they're on your desk. I hope your mom will be okay."

Sarah sighed with relief. This intern was going to work out. "Thanks, Diane. I appreciate your concern."

The afternoon sun moved slowly down, warming Louisa's room. Sarah stepped out into the air conditioned hallway for a moment, but it seemed cozier to be beside her mother. It was a pleasant day being with Louisa not saying anything or even moving, just the two of them being present to each other. Sarah explored the room and looked through her mother's meager belongings.

What remained in the closet were ill-fitting clothes. "I should have helped you get rid of these old clothes," Sarah confessed, speaking quietly. "You always loved to dress well. Look, here's that dress Peter wore in the Sisters' Act. And he gave you the dress! I need to buy you some new clothes!"

In the bedside table, Sarah found oddities: a broken necklace chain with an old-fashioned cameo, a ring with the gem missing, a Bible falling apart, a small folded piece of white cotton material that had yellowed with age in a plastic bag, a faded Chicago World's Fair ticket to some dancer program, and a filled out dance card from some ocean liner cruise. Sarah asked what meaning each of them had, but Louisa never responded. In an envelope was a small pencil drawing of a cat with MJ, 1962 on the back. Michael. And on the wall, were Louisa's two favorite photos: the Taj Mahal and Ronald Reagan in a cowboy hat. The last couple of years Louisa had been telling her guests that Ronald Reagan was her husband. In many ways Reagan did look like Adam. Overall, though, there was not much to signify a long life.

The sun was nearly down when a pleasant, round-faced, young CNA, offered Louisa some water unsuccessfully. Then Sarah helped the CNA slip the new blue cotton nightgown Sarah had bought recently for her mom over her head. At least I did one thing right, Sarah thought, a new nightgown! She buttoned the tiny buttons in the front and pressed the lace down around the neckline as the CNA straightened the bed covers.

The young helper remarked, "Your mom is very pretty." Sarah smiled as her mother nodded her head. "Of course, I'm pretty," Louisa seemed to say.

"Thank you for your help," Sarah said to the aide. Tears were forming in Sarah's eyes. "And for being so kind." The CNA lightly patted her arm before she left.

Sarah noticed blotchy, brown spots appearing on Louisa's neck and arms. What in the world does that mean? Louisa then turned on her side, her face toward the wall in the position that Sarah first found her that morning. Sarah pulled the sheet and light blanket over her shoulders.

"Goodnight, Mom. I love you." And I do, Sarah thought, no matter how unkind you were at times. Sarah sat down in the chair next to the bed, wondering what to do next. Louisa hadn't eaten all day and neither had Sarah and she realized that she was hungry. She found a granola bar and the apple in her purse that she had planned on eating at the office for lunch. Slowly, thoughtfully, she chewed on the apple, considering the evening ahead. She decided to stay the night. It didn't feel right to leave.

Sarah called her husband letting him know she would not be home. She had stayed with Louisa before in other nursing homes, but not in this facility so she didn't know what their arrangements were. Louisa had a couch in her room with a pillow and her old winter bathrobe would serve as a cover. Sarah figured she would be okay. It would do.

Watching Louisa's quiet breathing, Sarah daydreamed about her mother's life. I always thought she was smart enough and assertive enough to be the president of the United States, Sarah thought. She had so much passion and ability. She was just born a half-century too soon.

Sarah pulled a novel from her purse. Slow going at first, the plot eventually became more complex and Sarah was soon lost in the book. Something interrupted her, a slight sound, perhaps. She noticed it was black outside. Glancing at her wristwatch, she was surprised that it was nearly eleven.

Sarah went to Louisa and bent to check on her. She didn't appear to be breathing! Sarah put her hand on her back. There was no rise and fall. She leaned down to put her hand and then her ear by Louisa's nose and mouth. No air, no breath could be discerned. Sarah felt for pulse on her neck and on her wrist. Nothing. Sarah sat down on the bed, feeling suspended in timelessness.

"Mom, can you hear me?" Sarah asked, knowing she could not.

Gently, Sarah lay down by Louisa and reached her arm around her, holding her, having one last snuggle, and waiting to see if life returned. In her deepest being, Sarah had known all along, that this day was to be the end.

"You did really well, Mom," Sarah said out loud. "You did just right. This is a good way to go." Sarah felt a sadness but also a sense of peace and release. Louisa had fought for life for so long, too long. It was time to go. In some ways, Sarah felt happy for Louisa.

Sarah rose and hurried down the hall to the office. It now felt like an emergency. There were things to be done. "I think she's gone. I'm sure Mom is gone," Sarah repeated in a cracked voice to Grimm who apparently had come back after her supper. Grimm didn't turn from the tall metal cabinet where she stood, sorting through files.

"I'll be there in a minute," she replied.

Almost running, Sarah went back to the room, thinking I must not leave Mom alone. When she got there, she was nervous, wondering what she was expected to do. She sat on the bed and leaned over to give Louisa a kiss and then held her hand. It seemed like a long time passed before Ms. Grimm came and felt for a pulse. She stood, said "Yes" and then left the room. It dawned on Sarah that Grimm came back to work that night because she knew Louisa would die. She knew. She knew! And she put in this extra time for us. Grimm was here when she was needed.

Very soon, too soon, there were sirens and lights flashing from a police car outside Louisa's window. Two police personnel, one a woman with a clip board, came in. They started asking questions.

"Were you here when she died?" "Exactly when did she die?" "Was anyone else here?" "What did she die from?" That last question stopped Sarah.

"Old age? She was 93," Sarah responded. The room was quiet. They were still looking at her, not writing down the response. It wasn't the right answer. They were waiting for another. Do they think I killed her? Sarah wondered. The lights from the cop car outside the window kept swinging around and around, blue and red, blue and red, blue and red, making Sarah dizzy.

"Natural causes?" Sarah answered tentatively. She looked at Grimm for help but as usual, Grimm wasn't looking at her. "She had Alzheimer's," Sarah said rather lamely. Golly. What did she die from? I don't know. She wanted to die. She was ready to die. She willed herself to die. No other reason. "She did a good job of dying," Sarah wanted to shout. Two men with white jackets came in with a gurney.

"Do you suppose you could shut off the strobe light?" Sarah asked the policewoman. "There are people in this complex who are trying to sleep." And the light is giving me a headache Sarah wanted to add.

"Oh. Yes." The policewoman went out. Men in white jackets zipped Louisa into a bag and put her on the gurney in seconds, before Sarah was ready to have her locked out of her sight.

"Which mortuary are you using?" one asked.

"Michelotti's," Sarah answered automatically. Her dad had determined the mortuary and the grave site. Sarah felt grateful for his decisions, made a decade before this moment.

Louisa was wheeled down the hall followed by the second policeman. Ms. Grimm left. All at once Sarah remained alone. She wasn't ready to leave. Sarah sat down on the couch to collect her thoughts. Everything had happened so quickly. A slow day and then horrific activity.

The young Latina aide came in and started removing the bed sheets. "Oh, I didn't know you were here," she said to Sarah.

"That's fine. It's good to see you." Sarah took a deep breath. "What were those brown spots Mom had all over her body?" Sarah asked the CNA.

"They're natural. Many people have them before they die. Their bodies are shutting down."

"So you and Ms. Grimm knew Mom was going to die?"

The CNA straightened up from the bed and looked at Sarah with gentle brown eyes. Full of caring, maybe even tears, she softly replied, "Yes. You didn't know?"

"There's a lot I don't know about, about dying." Very softly Sarah added, "And about living."

The aide, looking capable and strong and yet so young, stood erect before her with the dirty sheets in her arms. "We live each day the best we can. And then we die." A lump came into Sarah's throat. "That's all any of us can do," the youth quietly added. Sarah wanted to look longer into her deep brown velvet eyes, to hold and understand some profound thought. But she, too, like the others, was gone quickly down the hall.

Sarah slowly walked out of the nursing home, the door with its automatic power pushing her out and locking behind her. Weeks before, she had memorized the code she needed to get into the facility. Now she could forget it. She was leaving, walking away from that solid barrier for the last time, never, never having to go into a locked unit again to see her mother, her life source, shriveling up from an incurable disease of brain exhaustion.

The sky was black. With the entryway lights on, Sarah couldn't see the stars. And now Sarah thought Mom is part of that bigger Universe. Sarah wanted to see the Universe Louisa had entered. Sarah drove home by way of Zimmerman Trail, winding up to the top of the rims. She pulled over to look at the lights of Billings below and the stars above, the earthly community blending into ether heavens. She stepped out of the car to breathe better. A soft, warm breeze dried her sweat, and she could feel the heat of the earth lifting as dirt started to cool down. Good old Montana. I love living here. Sarah stretched out her arms in gratitude. Mom gave me this gift, my life here. Tears quickly came. She pulled out Kleenex and moved to sit on the granite stone balustrade which blocked the parking area from the rims. The city lights below and the stars above blurred together, life and death commingling.

Oh God, help me. This passing is hard. What does it mean? Sarah prayed. Every life has value. Is not every life precious? Even Mom's life. She wants me to tell her story. I think that's what she was telling me. Oh, Lordy, I don't want to do it. It'll be difficult. I can't remember half of what she told me. What fire was she remembering? And her life was boring. . . Okay, so not any more boring than my own. I admit that, God. And I wasn't a good daughter. Tears were choking Sarah. I was mean to Mom. I ignored her, avoided her for years. My siblings did a better job of tolerating her, caring for her. Mom had a special bond with Peter. They loved each other! Why did Peter have to die before Mom and leave me with this? I want to hate you both. I hate you; I love you. Huge sobs wracked Sarah's body. It took several minutes for the emotions to subside. Eventually, the mist from tears covering her eyes vanished and she could look at the city where the lights were clear once again. She could see. She could start the journey home.

Already Sarah missed her. Not the ill woman from the last couple decades, but the vibrant, exciting, loving woman she once knew. She longed for the mother she experienced as a child. Maybe I could write, Sarah concluded. Maybe I could tell her story. Can I do that for her? Isn't that what she asked me to do? Is this, then, the meaning of the

25

moment? Every life has meaning. If there's meaning in Mom's life, there's meaning in mine. Perhaps, her story is my story and a clue to the meaning of every life.

At home, Sarah undressed and crawled quietly into bed beside her husband. He reached his arm over and she curled into his arm.

"You're home sooner than I thought," he mumbled half-asleep.

"She died." Sarah held her breath for a moment; then she whispered, "Mom died. Louisa is gone."

"Mmm," and he squeezed her tighter and then relaxed as he fell back into sleep. So that's what's left, a soft murmur acknowledging a long life.

Baptized By Fire

ROSS FORK CREEK, MONTANA 1915

There was a little girl, who had a little curl
Right in the middle of her forehead,
And when she was good, she was very, very good,
But when she was bad she was horrid.

HENRY WADSWORTH LONGFELLOW (1807-1882)

The match lit easily. The flame flared up and bit her finger. Louisa tried to take the match in her other hand, but instead the fire dropped to the ground. Louisa watched a white circle grow on her finger where the fire had burned her. She sucked her finger, jumping up and down in a circle dance. Then she saw the red tongues of fire eating the dried grass. Louisa grabbed the stick she had been playing with and fiercely beat on the orange blaze, her heart pounding. The ignited vegetation spread. Louisa pulled off her sun-bonnet and swat at the ever increasing sharp-toothed red mouth that was eating slowly toward the barn where they lived. Smoke swirled around her. Louisa started coughing. She couldn't breathe. Oh, oh, oh, I'm dying. Smoke covered her, burning her eyes. I'm going blind!

With tears streaming down her cheeks, Louisa turned and ran. In the twilight, she bumped into the hay wagon and pulled herself into it, totally out of breath. I've done something terrible, something evil. I'm a very bad girl. Louisa sucked on her burnt finger trying to stop the throbbing pain, trying to put out the flames in her mind.

Exhausted, she buried herself in the scattered hay pulling her dress over her cut and bruised bare feet. In short, shallow gasps, Louisa sobbed as smoke covered her.

Much later, maybe she had even fallen asleep, Louisa heard Papa calling for her in Czech, "Louisa, Louisa, Kde jsi? Where are you?" Louisa's eyes flew open, wide awake and aware of danger. The sun had set and darkness now hid her. She buried herself deeper into the hay. Maybe Papa won't find me. Her heart was thumping loudly. Maybe I'll have a heart attack and die. Louisa wiggled further into the hay. She heard Papa stop at the side of the wagon.

"Louisa, come out. I know you are under the hay." Alois continued in the Czech language that they spoke at home.

Louisa heard the Mormon crickets from the creek, and off in the distance, her brothers were calling her name. Accidentally, she moved and the wagon made a slight creaking sound.

"Louisa!" her father sharply cried out. She sat up quickly, hay falling around her. Tears welled up and she let out a sobbing yelp.

"Papa, I was afraid. I'm sorry. I'm truly sorry. Don't spank me." Louisa, too, spoke Czech. She had not talked at all when she was small, confused by the English her siblings spoke having learned it at school, and the language of her parents. Now, she understood some English but in this emotional moment spoke Czech.

"You're a very naughty girl," he said. "Worse, you were foolish and I don't raise foolish children. Now get down here."

Louisa scooted to the end of the wagon. Her father lifted her down and brushed off the hay from her hair and dress holding firmly onto her arm so she wouldn't run. Then he reached into his back pocket for a hanky and wiped the snot running from Louisa's nose. He put the hanky back into his pocket and squatted to look squarely at her.

Even in the dark, Louisa saw the anger but also the concern in his dark eyes. I don't think he's going to give me a licking, she thought, but maybe something worse! Her eyes widened at the thought.

"What were you thinking, child?" Alois asked, not unkindly. Louisa thought hard. What was I thinking? And what is the right answer for him? I don't want to feel the willow branch on my hind end.

Louisa stood very tall and proper. "I was sparementing," she said in English. It was a new word for her; a word she had recently learned from her brother, Alvin. She continued in Czech, "I wanted to see how matches worked. I'm truly sorry, Papa, that I started a fire. . . . Did, did the shed burn down?" She twisted her body to see if she could see if the shed still stood. It had been a very big fire before she had run away. She remembered dark red flames rising up around her.

Alois sighed and stood, but kept his hand around her upper arm.

"Boys," he yelled loudly. "I found her." He marched her toward the barn where they were living while the house was being built. Her brothers ran in from where they had been searching in the coulee and the trees along the creek. Papa held onto her upper arm as he led her through the barn door and into the light of the kerosene lamp on the board table. He set Louisa down at her usual spot on the bench at the middle of the table, where the light surrounded her.

"Don't move," her father commanded her.

Louisa folded her hands in her lap and stared at them intently. Her burnt finger still throbbed, so she squeezed it. She could hear her father pouring water into the basin to wash his blackened hands and face and her mother carefully setting the dried dishes on a shelf above the workbench. Her sister Irene rocked and sang softly to the baby. I wish I could be more like Irene, Louisa thought. She's good, always helping Mama, cooking, cleaning, and taking care of Baby Victoria. Then, Louisa sharply realized what she really thought. That's no fun!

"Sit down, boys," Papa said as her brothers came in from the dark. Richard closed the door and sat down to the right of Papa's chair

29

and across from Alvin. Oh no, a Janochek family meeting, Louisa thought, I'm going to get it now. Louisa shut her eyes tightly, trying not to cry. She pushed her thumbnail into the palm of her undamaged hand. Sometimes, physical pain distracted her from emotional pain. The burn on her finger didn't hurt enough right now.

Her mother took Victoria from Irene and sat in her place at the end of the table, opening her dress to nurse. I wish Mama would look at me, smile at me, and let me know everything will be all right. Irene picked up her embroidery and sat by their mother. Helen slipped into her place on the bench between Richard and Walter across from Louisa.

Papa took the Czech Bible down from the shelf and opened it in front of him. He carefully took his glasses out of their case and wrapped the wires around his ears.

Solemnly, slowly he enunsiated, "Přísloví 23:13 Nepřipustí-li dítě neopravení, protože kdybys ho porazil prutem, nezemře."

Louisa's eyes widen. She'd heard this scripture before. Proverbs 23:13. Withhold not correction from the child for if thou beatest him with the rod, he shall not die. Louisa pushed her thumbnail more firmly into the palm of her hand. Now I'm really going to get it. Papa looked over the rims of his glasses at her. Not able to return his gaze, she concentrated on her clenched hands. He let the words soak in. In the silence, Louisa could hear Victoria nuzzling and slurping at Mama's breast.

"Louisa, let's hear your story." Alois' voice had softened.

"I'm very, very sorry that I started a fire." No one spoke. Louisa sighed. Papa wants something more. "I saw Richard using matches and I wanted to try, too." More silence. Louisa looked at Mama, but Catherine was looking down at Victoria.

They all hate me! Louisa's eyes started filling with tears. I refuse to cry. She squeezed her eyes shut and made the tears dissolve back into themselves. Then she looked at Papa. He watched her, waiting.

"The flame came quickly and it burned my finger, so I dropped the match and then the grass started on fire and the fire grew big and there was smoke and a terrible smell and I kept trying, beating at it, but I couldn't put it out and I couldn't breathe and I was frightened and I ran away from the fire." She said it all very fast and nearly in one breath as she slipped English words in with Czech. She then took a deep breath. "What burned?" she asked hesitantly. The images of the bright, red fire against the graying sky and the sounds of her brothers shouting and racing around the wagon of straw where she had hidden clouded her mind.

"How old were you, Richard, when I showed you how to light a fire with matches?" Papa asked.

"About 8 or 9."

"How old are you, Louisa?"

"You know I'm 6, Papa."

"And you thought you could do something dangerous by yourself with no one teaching you or watching you."

I'm smart, she thought. I can learn to do things on my own. Instead, she said, "I didn't think about it."

"You don't think. You don't think." Alois hit the wooden slab with his fist; the bang made all of them sit up straighter. "Louisa, tell me what might have happened tonight from your little experiment."

Louisa thought. "The shed, the grass, the lumber pile." She paused before she admitted, "all of them might have burned." He was still looking at her. He wants something more, but what?

"The new house wouldn't burn. It has rock on the bottom," Louisa defended herself and then she remembered, "Oh. Yes, there's wood above the rock. It could have burned," she admitted.

"What about where we now sit?"

"The barn has a dirt floor and concrete on the side. . . and. . . oh, it has wood above the concrete. Yes, Papa, the barn where we live

31

could have burned." Louisa looked around at her family. They were all looking at her.

"I could have burned everything," she said in a very small voice.

"Yes, you could have burned everything," her father responded in clear English like a judge. The precious grandfather clock clicked in the silence. The lantern at the center of the table sputtered and Helen adjusted the wick.

He went on. "Louisa, if the wind had been blowing, you could have started a prairie fire that could have spread for miles, burning all the grass and trees that the animals need to live."

Papa had said it slowly, solemnly. He kept looking at her wondering what he could do or say to help this beautiful, little namesake of his grow up to be a good citizen. Her brothers and sisters were looking at her, Alvin with a smirk on his face. Only her mother looked away, into a corner of the darkened room.

Louisa put her hands on the table and carefully studied each fingernail. She could no longer face her family. I have been very bad and everyone thinks I am evil. I was bad! I love birds and animals. I didn't mean to kill them. I love my family! They're looking down at me in a mean way. They hate me. I don't belong here. I'll have to run away. That's what I'll do. I'll find another home. But where can I go? Louisa finally looked at Papa.

"Louisa, next time you want to try something new, come to your mother or me." Louisa looked into her father's eyes and saw he had tears starting to seep out of the corner of his eyes.

"Oh, yes, Papa," she quickly agreed. Papa still cares for me!

"Thanks to Richard, Walter, and Alvin, they put your fire out. And they yelled for help. Why didn't you yell for help, Louisa?" he asked kindly.

"I don't know, Papa. The fire scared me. I couldn't breathe. I couldn't yell. I just wanted to hide. I knew I had done something horrible." Louisa cried now, sobbing. "I'm awful, Papa. I'm sorry I'm naughty. I'm sorry I'm bad." He let her cry. No one said anything or reached out to touch her. She cried even harder. Finally the flow of tears slowed to sniffling.

"You have done foolish things before – flipping off the tree trunk above the creek and cracking your head on the rock below was probably the worst. Leaving the corral gate open so the horse got out; feeding the cow fresh alfalfa so she bloated. Let's see, what am I forgetting?"

"Burning a frog in the oven," Alvin said with a grin.

"Nearly strangling the kitty with a string," Helen cried out.

"Spilling water on my math book," Walter complained.

"That's enough!" Papa raised his hand and then looked at Louisa, studying her, shaking his head, wondering how he could discipline her without destroying her spirit. Louisa had stopped crying and met his gaze calmly.

"To be free, Louisa, you must learn boundaries." Silence reigned once more. "You need to learn that you belong to a family, a community. I can't have you destroying yourself, our family, or the animals. For the next few months, you cannot be by yourself. One of us will be with you every minute of the day and night." Alois sadly opened the Bible once more.

"Žalmů 51:11. Nezamítej mne od tváři své, a Ducha svatého svého neodjímej ode mne."

Richard softly repeated in English, "Psalm 51:11."

"What does this Scripture mean to you, Louisa?" Papa asked her.

"To stay close to the holy spirit. To have it in me. I had a wrong spirit, but now I'll wipe it away and have a good spirit inside." Louisa had become an actress raising her voice dramatically on the last phrase, swinging her arm in a big circle wiping away the evil and back to touch her chest with the good spirit. Alois wanted to smile at her histrionics.

"Good." He put his glasses in its case. "You'll have quiet time every morning and evening, Louisa, to meditate on having a right spirit in you. You'll sit on the stool by the stove with your face to the wall."

Then Alois turned his attention to the rest of his family. "Thank you, boys, for your help tonight. Let's check to make sure there are no live sparks out there before washing up and going to bed." He got up and set a small stool by the cold stove. "Louisa, turn your head to the wall. Irene, please stay at the table and keep an eye on Louisa. It's time for bed for you, Helen. It's been a long day."

Louisa moved over to sit in the dark shadows, a place that would become very familiar.

A few days later, they were quietly eating dinner together at the same board table when Alois Janochek announced, "The public school starts on Monday. I'm pleased with your progress, Alvin, Walter, Irene, and Helen. Get your shoes polished and make sure you have clean clothes. The Janochek family will be a proud family with educated children. Richard and Louisa, you'll stay home and work on the house with me, but the rest of you can walk to the school house and learn new lessons."

"But Papa, I'm old enough to go to school, too. Aren't I, Mama?" Louisa asked as she looked for help from her mother.

"You're old enough, but not responsible enough, Louisa," her father replied. "You'll stay and work with Richard and me until I know I can trust you."

"Papa, I promise I will not do anything 'cept what the teacher tells me to do."

"I'm glad you're thinking about doing the right thing, Louisa, but I need to see your good behavior for myself."

Louisa started to reply. Alois held up his hand. "No arguing, Louisa. I've made up my mind."

Louisa envied her older brothers and sisters as they started for school very early several mornings later. Irene gave Louisa a hug and whispered, "Louisa, just be a good girl and you'll be with us in no time."

"I'll be so far behind the others in my class. I'll never catch up. I'll never learn to speak English," Louisa complained in Czech.

"You're smart, Louisa. You'll be ahead of everyone in short order. I'll talk to you in English." Irene said in English.

"Děkuji," Louisa responded. Then, in English, "Thank you."

Irene kissed her cheek and Helen squeezed her hand. Then Irene and Helen ran to catch up with Alvin and Walter who were already walking up the road to school. Louisa waved at their backs despairingly. I'll never be good enough, she thought. Papa says I've got to create myself anew. How do I do that? She looked across the burned grass in front of her to the dried grass further out by the side of the road and onto the prairie. She imagined herself riding in a painted cart, no, an actual gold carriage.

Jsem pani mama. I'm a grand lady riding in a fine carriage with golden ornaments and velvet-covered seats pulled with two black horses, no, white horses with plumed headdresses. Louisa waved to the peasants on each side of her carriage. Dressed in fine clothes with a feather in her broad brimmed hat, she nodded kindly to the folk beside the road who loved her.

"Louisa," Papa yelled at her. Startled, Louisa ran back to her father. "You're to move this stack of boards, carrying one board at a time, up the front stairs to Richard. Be careful you don't bang the boards on anything or drag them in the dirt. Your mother will be watching you. When you've finished taking all the boards to Richard, report to me. I'll be working on the concrete steps on the other side of the house. Do you understand?"

"Yes, Papa." There were a lot of boards stacked in the pile. Louisa sighed and put on the big, stiff, work gloves her father had handed her. The insides of the gloves were rough and much too big for her small hands. She stood tall.

Jsem pani mama. I'm a grand lady with fine leather gloves. I'm a grand lady who walks ever so carefully as I carry golden boards to the prince in the castle. Louisa picked up a board, heavier than she thought it would be, and carefully maneuvered the rough board up the temporary stairway to her brother.

#Metoo

MOORE, OCTOBER 1924

To the daring belongs the future.

Emma Goldman (1869-1940)

"Jan-o-chek, Jan-o-chek, Jan-o-chek, Jan-o-chek," the crowd roared in a solid rhythm, stomping on the bleachers. How I wish the shouting were for me, but of course they're rooting for Helen, Louisa thought as she dribbled the ball across the gymnasium floor at Moore High School. Even though Louisa had been told she was "cute as a button," she knew the bloomers looked better on her sister, Helen, who was taller and thinner than Louisa. And Louisa admitted to herself, Helen is a better shot.

With the score tied, if Moore High School didn't make another shot within the next 15 seconds, the basketball game would go into overtime. Louisa had an uncanny ability to see play openings, so the coach had her control the ball. The team from Hobson knew Helen was the top scorer and they were double guarding Helen. Louisa slowed the basketball game down, weaving from one side of the court to the other, looking like she didn't have a care in the world. The fans were yelling at Louisa to do something! They were counting down the seconds: 13, 12, 11, 10, 9 . . . Louisa heard the count.

The Hobson team didn't know Louisa and Helen had secret signals. Not even the Moore coach knew all of their gestures. Louisa moved slowly down the center of the court, tilted her head to the left, and Helen came back up the left side away from the team's hoop with the Hobson guards following her, everyone expecting Louisa to pass the ball to her. Louisa picked up speed, turning away from Helen, and charging quickly down the right side toward the Moore forward in the corner who wasn't being guarded at all.

The crowd roared in anger and fear, now expecting Louisa to pass the ball to the forward, who was not a good shot. "No, No," the gymnasium roared. The Hobson guards ran back toward the potential shooter, leaving Helen in the open. Helen quickly, lithely moved down the center toward the basket. Louisa without even looking at Helen tossed the ball up over the arm of the opposing team and into the arms of Helen who with a small jump had the ball into the hoop just before the buzzer rang. Moore won. Of course!

The Moore fans exploded with frenzied joy, descending from the stands and surrounding Helen. It was Helen's last home game because she was graduating in the spring. A couple boys lifted her onto their shoulders. "Jan-o-chek, Jan-o-chek, Jan-o-chek." Cheering filled the gymnasium. Louisa loved the way Helen coyly smiled and waved to the crowd from her throne on top of the two boys who had lifted her up. She was the queen! Louisa smiled at Helen and in return had a nod from her. Louisa grabbed a towel from the bench and dabbed the sweat off her brow and neck.

"Nice play, Louisa," the coach shouted at her across the noise. Louisa nodded. It feels good to know the coach recognizes I helped win the game! Louisa smiled to herself.

"Hey, Louisa, do you want to go to Crystal Lake for the party?" her brother, Alvin, yelled down to her from the bleacher.

"You know Papa won't let me go," Louisa shouted back.

"Ask him." Alvin had graduated two years earlier and worked at the garage in town. He owned a car he'd fixed! He was big on partying.

"Tell Pop you can go with me. I'll watch out for you. Helen's coming with Hank in my car, too."

"Yeah," Louisa responded, not excitedly. She knew it would be a wild gathering. She was cooling down from the game and felt a shiver up her back. The party might be fun. And I'm 15, she thought. Maybe it's time to figure out how the rest of the world lives. And I'd like to celebrate with the team.

Louisa found her parents visiting with friends at the entrance to the gymnasium. "Papa, may I go to the celebration at Crystal Lake tonight with Alvin? Helen and Hank are going with him."

Alois Janochek looked at his wife. Catherine gave an imperceptible nod. "All right. But you have potatoes to dig tomorrow at 7 a.m.," he said.

"I'll be there. Thanks."

Louisa ran excitedly to the locker room to get out of her basketball uniform and to get a shower. The team was frenetic with the victory. With one shower in their locker room, they splashed water at each other and soon the benches and floor were wet. Someone had hid the towels. Louisa laughed with the other team members as she washed, fought for the single towel, and then put on warm clothes, safely dry in her locker.

Helen and her boyfriend, Hank, climbed into the rumble seat of Alvin's car and wrapped up in a blanket. It was a mild fall evening, but it would be chilly riding out to Crystal Lake, nearly an hour from town in the Big Snowies. A bonfire would greet them and Louisa also knew there would be plenty of beer.

At the bonfire, they roasted sausages, drank, and sang songs. Louisa relaxed by Helen and Hank where she felt safe. Alvin sat down next to her with a tin cup of beer. Alvin always seemed to know where to buy home-made brew.

"Here, Sis," Alvin said. "Time you tried some beer. Or have you already sipped from Pa's cupboard?" Irritated, Louisa took a big swallow from his cup. She had always enjoyed sucking the foam off of Papa's home-made beer.

"Yuck," she said. "It tastes awful!" A real beer was not as tasty as the foam had been.

Alvin laughed. "You'll get used to it, and like it. I dare you to have another gulp."

He left her then with the cup of beer and a friend of Alvin's who she barely knew sat down beside her.

"You were great tonight, Louisa," Charles said. "You knew what to do to win. Your strategy worked." Louisa breathed in the dark night air with satisfaction. She took a big gulp from the tin cup to show how sophisticated she was. It was great to be acknowledged for her basketball skill. She felt a tingling in her face and arms as the beer quickly went to her head.

"Let's walk down by the lake where we can see the stars," Charles suggested. That sounded good to Louisa. Couples were hugging and smooching around the fire, including Hank and Helen. She could see Alvin and other men drinking whiskey out of pint jars by one of the cars. It would be good to get away from this craziness and go for a walk.

As they strolled along the lake's edge, they paused often while Louisa pointed out constellations. She was surprised he didn't know even the obvious ones, like the Big Dipper. "Now can you see the Little Dipper pouring into the Big Dipper?" she asked him. "At the end of the handle is the North Star. That star never moves, so at night, you can always know where North is. You'll never get lost," she told him. "My favorite constellation is Orion, the hunter. See the three stars? That's his belt. Over to the right is Cassiopeia—kind of a flat W."

Louisa could tell he was bored. What do we talk about? Do we have anything in common? He works at the garage with Alvin. Why did he ask me to walk down here? She turned away from him, watching the moon reflecting with shimmers of light on the dark water. Stunningly beautiful. The lake was low at the end of summer but the pine trees around it made it majestic and magical. Louisa closed her eyes and breathed the pine fragrance in deeply.

Smoothly, Charles' arm went around her waist and he pulled her toward him. Before she realized what was happening, one hand was behind her head and he was kissing her with his tongue in her mouth. His other hand went up her skirt and into her panties where he squeezed her buttocks. He pulled her tightly against him. Her heart pounded in panic. She felt the swelling in his pants as he pressed against her. His movements were so quick Louisa wasn't prepared. She struggled to pull back away from him and to twist her head, but he was stronger than she was.

God, help me! She wanted to scream, but his mouth covered hers. He started to press her down onto the sandy beach. As he tilted, in one desperate move, Louisa bit down hard on his tongue, and with all the strength she had, she drew her knee up as sharply as she could into his groin, pushing with all her arm's might against his chest. His hold loosened as he fell clumsily toward the ground. With the relaxing of his grasp, she stamped her heel into the arch of his foot and spun away out of his reach. She took off running. She could hear him calling, "Hey, Louisa, I didn't mean anything." She ran even faster.

How could I have been so stupid? Why didn't I see this coming? I can see the moves for a basketball play, but I can't see a sexual assault in motion?

As she neared the bonfire, she slowed down and caught her breath. She quickly spotted Alvin and went to him.

"We're going home," she announced to him. She was breathing hard.

"Louisa, relax. Enjoy yourself. We have plenty of time."

"HOME. NOW." There was a shrill, sharp edge to her tone, almost frantic, even though it was spoken softly.

Alvin slowly straightened up. He shrugged his shoulders at his friends and grinned. They laughed. Louisa found Helen and Hank wrapped in the blanket by the fire.

Louisa knelt down and told her sister, "Helen, we need to go home." Helen heard the urgency in Louisa's voice.

"Do you mind, Hank?" Helen turned and asked her boyfriend. Louisa felt a wave of irritation. Why does she have to ask <u>his</u> permission?

"It's fine with me. It's been a long day." Hank worked at the grocery store. He had graduated last May and was trying to earn enough money to marry Helen after she graduated in the spring.

Then Louisa saw Charles with his arm around Alvin in the circle of older boys. The guys were all laughing. A fire of anger ran through her body. How dare they make fun of her. Louisa jumped up yanking on Helen's blanket.

"Let's go!" she blurted out.

It was quiet in the car on the way home. Alvin finally said, "You know, Louisa, you're a pain in the butt. We could have stayed at least another hour. Didn't you know how to handle Charles?"

"Alvin. You're the pain. You set me up with Charles, didn't you? Well, from now on, let me choose my own boyfriends. You and Charles are disgusting. And if you complain anymore, I'm telling Papa you were drinking hard liquor tonight."

At dawn, Louisa was happy to be digging potatoes with her mother. Louisa shoved the spade deep into the dirt, loosening the soil. Her mother pulled up the plant and Victoria helped her mother pull the potatoes from the roots and put them into buckets. Louisa emptied the buckets into the wheelbarrow and when it was full, she pushed it down to the root cellar where she carefully upended the wheelbarrow and stacked up the potatoes. Helen was in the house, doing the morning chores, washing clothes, and preparing lunch.

Each woman chose her favorite tasks, and over the years, they had developed a natural rhythm to their work routines. The steady, familiar movement was calming, reassuring.

What a horrible night, Louisa thought as she dug each hill. I hate boys. They're sickening. How can Helen stand Hank? Well, maybe he's different. He's okay. Hank's polite.

Half-way through the morning, Victoria told her mother she was hungry and begged to go to the house.

"You may go and get an apple, but you need to help Helen hang out the wash. Then come back here." Victoria looked at Louisa for support, but Louisa shook her head. They stood up for each other, but not all the time. Louisa didn't want to upset her mother this morning.

Louisa and her mother rested for a moment on the edge of the partially filled wheelbarrow and sipped water from their jug.

"Mama, do you love Papa?"

"What a question!" Silence followed. Louisa turned and looked at her mother directly.

"Well?" Louisa asked. Catherine was looking down at the dirt.

"Love means something different at your age than it does to someone my age," her mother responded. Then she looked intently at Louisa. "Do you have a love interest, Louisa?"

"No way. I hate boys," Louisa answered firmly.

Her mother raised her eyebrow and responded slowly. "Did something happen last night?"

Mama's too smart, Louisa thought. She knows.

"Nothing important." I can't tell her! I don't want her to know how stupid I was. Still, there's stuff I need to know. "Tell me, Mama. Tell me how love changes as you grow older."

Louisa remained quiet, waiting. Her mother never talked much or long. Finally, Catherine responded, "Love was not something we discussed or thought about when I was your age. With 10 sisters and my father unable to support us, marriage was a way of surviving. Love didn't enter into it." Catherine felt trapped in this conversation. She couldn't tell a 15 year old that she wished she had never married and even now if she had an opportunity, she'd leave. She proceeded carefully. "You, however, have choices. Now women can get good paying jobs to support themselves."

"But Momma, people do fall in love. Look at Helen and Hank."

"Yes, they have a physical yearning for each other, a passion that's hard to control when you're young." Charles felt something I didn't, Louisa thought. Her mother went on, "All I ask of you girls is that you marry first before you enter into a physical relationship. You need to respect your partner. Marriage is built on understanding each other, not one sudden emotion." Louisa nodded thinking, I can see that. Hank respects Helen.

"Do you respect Papa?" Louisa asked, remembering the times he had shouted at her and how he'd hit the table with his fist when angry.

Catherine sighed. "Yes, what Alois Janochek says for us to do is the right thing for us to do. I respect his decisions."

"And you love Papa, now?" Louisa asked.

"Louisa, honestly!" Catherine turned away from Louisa, frowning. She had never had this kind of conversation with anyone! Catherine looked across the potato field studying the gray sky. It acted like it wanted to rain. They needed to get the potatoes dug before it rained hard or snowed.

Louisa tapped her foot on a dirt clump waiting for a response while Catherine wondered how much more she could say, thinking Louisa's the smartest one of the lot. Even smarter than Irene, who's a teacher. Catherine pondered. Louisa could do something with her life. Catherine shook her head. She knew this was a critical conversation. She spoke slowly, trying to choose her words carefully as she gave one of the longest speeches she'd ever given in her life. "Your papa is a good carpenter. He's built four houses here and several others in Kansas. He has supported us and that's not always easy. I appreciate his skill. But no one is perfect. He drinks too much beer. He yells too much. I'm sorry he left the farm for Richard to run, but Alois likes living in town. I try to be a good wife and mother. But you have choices, Louisa," Catherine emphasized turning to her. "You have opportunities I didn't have. Take your time." She paused and then added, "And I don't ever want to hear that I criticized your father in any way."

Louisa nodded. "And so you love him?" Catherine stood up from the wheelbarrow, straightening her back to get the kinks out of her spine, chortling back a bitter laugh. She looked at the rows of potato stocks ahead of them, and started moving toward the next clump. Louisa gently tugged at her mother's skirt. Catherine looked back at Louisa.

"Oh, Louisa, I've lived with him, raised you children, and worked for you all my life. Isn't that enough?" Catherine glanced at her wrinkled, dry, darkened skin above her work gloves and below her shirt sleeve. There wasn't enough money for store-bought skin cream which she would love to have.

Louisa could barely hear her mother as they walked to the next potato hill, "Never really thought about it." The conversation was over.

On Monday morning, Louisa admired the violets in the bay window as she waited for her friend, Cecilia, to walk to school. Papa built the bay window for Mama's plants. Maybe that's love, doing things for each other. Louisa was drawn to the soft leaves on the violets. Her mother had warned her a dozen times not to touch the leaves, but she was still tempted. The plant with deep purple flowers was her favorite, although she also admired the pink one. Mama has a gift for growing things. I wonder if I'll be able to do what she has done. Maybe it's her love that helps things grow.

Cecilia with red bows in her braided hair came into view below the window. Louisa waved, grabbed her books, and shouted, "Bye, Mama," as she walked out the back door. Louisa caught up to Cecilia as they walked on the train rails on their way to school.

"Everyone says you ran away from Charles Friday night," Cecilia said, looking slyly at Louisa.

"Yep."

"Don't you like him?" Cecilia was jumping rhythmically off and on the train tracks.

"How could I like or not like him? I don't know him," Louisa answered carefully. She wasn't going to feed the gossip that might be going around.

"So, it's all right, if someone else... you know...

"Oh, Ceci, be sure you know what you're doing. Sure, if you like him, he's all yours. But Ceci," Louisa stopped and pulled on her friend's jacket to stop her, "the man you marry should respect you. Find someone who respects you. Like my brother, Richard. I think he likes you."

Cecilia looked at Louisa with surprise. "You're different, Louisa." There was a moment of silence. "Richard's old."

"Well, he won't be too old for you in a couple years when we graduate." Louisa defended her eldest brother whom she liked a lot. They started walking on the rails again.

"Are you going to get married when we graduate?" her friend asked.

"Well, oh, sure, later on, but I want to do something with my life first." Louisa had been thinking hard about her mother's comment about having choices.

"Like what?"

Louisa looked down the track. She could stay on the tracks, her destiny laid out one boring tie at a time, or she could take a side rail, stop at an interesting spot, or go on to a new place. "I'm thinking of becoming a teacher or a nurse. Maybe live in a big town. Wouldn't you like to do that, Ceci?"

Cecilia stepped off the iron railing and walked on the wooden planks and gravel, thinking. "How do you get to be a nurse?"

"I don't know, but we can find out. Hospitals train you." Louisa was excited.

"I'm not as smart as you, Louisa. I don't think I can do that."

"Sure, you could. If you want to do it, you can do it. I want to do something different!"

"I don't know," Cecilia looked at her friend in wonder. "It costs a lot to go to college or business school."

"Yes, I know, and Papa has told me he has no money to help Helen or me to go on to college. But he gave Richard a good deal on the ranch and helped Irene with her teacher's certificate. I think I'll write to Irene and see if she could save enough from teaching to loan me some money when I graduate." Alvin couldn't loan me any money, she was thinking. He spends it all on automobiles and liquor. And Walter has no extra money, studying engineering at Bozeman and getting married.

"You're lucky you have someone to ask." Cecilia looked down at her scuffed, worn shoes. "Marrying someone who can work and earn money may be easier."

"I'm lucky to have Irene as a sister. She's smart. But, Ceci, you remember reading about Elnora Comstock in 'A Girl of the Limberlost'? Elnora collected moths and butterflies and sold them to get money to go to school. We can find something around here to earn money, if we really want to go on to college or nurses' training."

Louisa looked at the weeds by the rails with a new perspective. We aren't near a swamp like the girl in the book, but maybe the weeds could be ground up and used as medicines or maybe they could be woven into baskets. Or could I paint birds and sell the paintings?

Louisa's imagination started whirling. She would find a way to earn money for college.

Cecilia sighed and shook her head. "It was a great story, but it's a story. It's fiction," Ceci replied.

"Didn't the novel encourage you, though? Look how Elnora ended up marrying Phillip! He was a prince of a guy. Wasn't that exciting?"

"Oh, Louisa, you're always dreaming."

Louisa was sad her friend wasn't more interested in new adventures. She had loved reading about Elnora wandering into the Limberlost swamp and tracking down special specimens of leaves, flowers, grasses, and moths. Louisa stopped for a minute and looked realistically at Moore. Not much, just a dusty street. Very few trees or buildings. Not like Lewistown. Still, Moore had a grocery where Hank worked, the garage where Alvin worked, the granary, a hardware store, and pool hall. I wonder what Chicago is like or Seattle or San Francisco. What would it be like to walk between tall buildings on sidewalks? I want to see those places. Louisa looked back down the track.

"I'll race you on the rails, Ceci. First one to the school boundary is a princess." Cecilia laughed at Louisa's fantasy. But she started walking rapidly on the rails. Louisa put her books on her head to give her a better balance. I am a beautiful tightrope walker with lions down below me. Everyone's amazed when I dance to the end of the rope. The lions below growl in disappointment. Jsem pani mama. I'm a grand lady on a tightrope with danger on all sides.

Louisa was laughing by the time they got to the schoolyard. She let Ceci win. Louisa snapped tall dry grass and braided it into a crown for Ceci, tucking the crown into Ceci's braids.

"After successful careers, you and I are going to marry princes," Louisa proclaimed to her friend. "You're a beautiful princess, Ceci. Never forget that."

Through Suffering Comes Endurance
GREAT FALLS, OCTOBER 1926

Character cannot be developed in ease and quiet. Only through experience of trial and suffering can the soul be strengthened, vision cleared, ambition inspired and success achieved.

HELEN KELLER (1880-1968)

Louisa shook out her nurse's blue uniform and carefully hung it on a hanger in her dorm room before slipping into a housecoat. She picked up her white apron with a sliver of soap and walked down the hall to the bathroom. A cold draft of air hit Louisa as she opened the door. Virginia sat by the open window smoking a cigarette.

"Gosh, you gave me start!" Virginia exclaimed. "I thought you were the "Sup" doing one of her searches." Virginia looked at Louisa in annoyance and then took a big drag on her cigarette and dramatically blew the smoke in circles out the window.

"Sorry." Louisa quietly closed the door and walked to the basin. She poured water into the bowl and started scrubbing out the stains from her nurse's apron. I can never do anything right, Louisa thought. What does Virginia have against me? She acts superior, but she's only two years older than me. Maybe being 17 is too young to be in nurses' training with hardened, older women! Louisa laughed at herself.

Why can't I make friends? Some of the nurses are plain mean, like Joe Jacobs. We could be friends because we're different from the

49

other nurses, Joe being the only male and me being younger than the others. Instead, Joe's always criticizing me. Why me? Nursing sure is competitive. A lot is demanded from us, to do everything orderly, perfectly. And these nurses are tough—smokers and drinkers—but also physically and emotionally strong. Maybe they drink because we see horrible things. It hardens us.

Virginia drew long, deep breaths on her cigarette, playing with little circles of smoke as they went out the window. Cigarette smoking was forbidden in the nurses' quarters.

"Louisa, do you want to go to the Rainbow Hotel with us tonight?" Louisa looked at Virginia with surprise. Virginia went on. "There's a new band playing. There'll probably be lots of cowboys. Maybe you know some of them, since they're in town for Charlie Russell's funeral and they're from the Judith Gap area where you're from."

Louisa hesitated. Is that why she's asking me? Does she think I can introduce her to a fellow? I need to make an effort, though. The supervisor told me I'm not cooperating enough. And, who knows, maybe Virginia is trying to be nice to me!

"Sure, why not? What time?"

A few hours later, Louisa was laughing with Roy, a cowboy from Guilford who knew her brother, Richard, from a cattle roundup out of the Little Belts. Roy led her in a two-step to "Angeline, the Baker," a fiddle tune that Louisa especially enjoyed. She loved the new dance steps and was having a great time. They found a seat at a table and Louisa was cognizant of the fact that Roy pulled out the chair for her. A gentleman! But then Roy offered her a little bit of bootleg whiskey for their water glasses. Well maybe not! Louisa laughingly replied she'd stick with water.

"I want to show you something." Roy pulled out a piece of paper from his pocket and carefully unfolded it. On it was a pencil line drawing of a cowboy on a bucking horse. "Charlie Russell gave it to me," he confided. Their heads together, they studied the scrap of paper.

"See the buffalo skull in the corner? That's Charlie's way of signing his art. Charlie was some painter. We're sure gonna miss him." After a little pause, he added, "I'd like to be an artist."

Louisa looked at Roy appreciatively. This is his secret passion! He's sharing his dream to me. She felt honored that he'd share this intimacy with her! Louisa took her time before she responded, bending her head over the pencil marks, studying them in detail.

"It's a great drawing, Roy. Charlie really knew how to make a picture come alive with action. Look at the arch on that horse. It'd be exciting to be able to draw that well. I bet you could learn," she assured him. "Do you sketch?"

"Sure, I try. But not like Charlie. He was always drawing, even while on horseback. Out in a rainstorm, he'd be hunched over in his slicker drawing something he observed—a deer or an elk." Roy beamed a big smile of appreciation back at Louisa. He carefully folded the paper and put it back in his wallet.

I wonder if I could draw, Louisa asked herself. What's my passion? She knew Charlie had been obsessed with making art when a teenager. Maybe it's too late for me to start. I wonder if a person needs to be pulled into special careers early in life or if you can begin a new venture at any time. What am I to do? I'm not sure nursing is my ticket. Where do I belong?

Virginia sat down beside Louisa. "You need to care for Esther," Virginia whispered into her ear. "She's drinking too much." Louisa turned around to see Esther sitting alone, her head on her arms sprawled on a small table, her skirt up to her thighs. "Watch out for her," Virginia stated, bumping her elbow under Louisa's arm.

"Well, hello," Virginia said changing to a charming tone, looking alluringly across Louisa at Roy, as if seeing him for the first time.

51

Louisa sighed, recognizing the end of a pleasant evening. "Virginia, this is Roy Coombs. Roy, this is Virginia Barker." Virginia started talking across Louisa to Roy, her voice deep and her eyes wide, focused on Roy. Roy seemed interested.

Louisa turned to study Esther. This is bad, Louisa thought. Other nurses didn't seem to be concerned; they were dancing or talking to men at tables. One of Esther's arms fell off the table and she looked like she was about to fall off her chair. Louisa became alert. This is why I'm here.

"Roy, it was good to meet you." Louisa stood and moved out of her chair. Virginia slipped into the vacated seat.

Roy stood and took Louisa's hand for a brief moment. "I enjoyed talking with you, Louisa," he said politely as he gently squeezed her hand. Then he turned his attention back to Virginia.

"I'll try to walk Esther home," Louisa whispered to Virginia.

"Good girl," Virginia replied condescendingly.

Silently, Louisa responded. Right, that's me, the good girl. Patiently, Louisa wiped Esther's face with a cool, wet napkin and had her sip water until she started gaining control over her movements.

"Let's go home, Esther," Louisa finally said. Louisa put on her own coat and then helped Esther into her coat. Calmly with assurance, Louisa steadied Esther as they made their way out of the bar. Underneath, Louisa was frightened as they began the slow, unsteady walk up the hill toward the hospital. God, let her live. Don't let her die on me. Why do people do this to themselves? Esther is normally a sensible person. Will she realize how close to death she has been? Can she imagine how stupid and ugly she looked at the hotel bar? And why am I not affected with this craving for alcohol? Is it because I've seen what it does to Papa and Alvin?

The next morning Louisa was glad she had left the party and was in bed before midnight. She felt good when she got up. Later she saw

52

Esther having coffee in the breakfast room. Esther said "fine" when Louisa asked how she was doing. Esther didn't seem to remember anything including Louisa. So be it! I'm glad to see her alive!

Louisa was on the hospital floor early and the morning rounds went quickly and easily. She helped with a discharge. It didn't even bother her when Joe remade the bed she had just made, telling her the sheets weren't tight enough. Being able to send people home always made Louisa feel good and no grouch like Joe could disturb that satisfaction. Later in the afternoon, she hummed as she carefully read the labels and put medicines into the right places in the closet next to the administrator's office.

Bang! Louisa was startled and straightened up to listen intently. That sounded like a gun! She quickly stepped out of the medicine closet and into the hallway. Looking into the administrator's office, Louisa was startled to see Miss Jones, the director of the hospital nursing program, slumped over on her side, leaning on her desk. Red blood (is it blood?) spurt down her white uniform.

Louisa slammed the medicine closet door shut and ran into the office to help Miss Jones. When she reached the desk, she heard the office door slowly shut. Behind the door was Joe with a gun in his hand, pointing it at Louisa's head.

Oh, my God, he's gonna kill me! As she dived beneath the desk, next to Miss Jones' chair to seek protection, she heard the click. The gun didn't discharge! Louisa's thoughts were racing as she curled herself as small as possible in the opening under the wooden desk. Joe, go away. Go away. What are you doing? Am I going to die? Is Miss Jones dead? Why, Joe, why? Her thoughts were whirling. Oh, I'm crazy to try to hide in this little space. Joe knows I'm here. Maybe he'll just go away. I can't run now. What else can I do? Oh please, dear God, please make Joe leave. Her heart and mind were racing.

She squeezed herself more tightly into a small ball hoping she'd disappear. The pattern of the tile beneath the desk froze her mind. Black and white hexagons swirled before her. She heard his steps. Abruptly, her head was yanked back as Joe pulled her by her hair. Louisa clenched her teeth and pulled against his grasp as the pistol shot went off. He then slammed her head against the floor and left.

Louisa heard Joe's heavy steps running down the hall as she pulled herself out of her cubby hole. I'm alive! Her head pounded in pain. Red spots were flying around her. Blood dripped from her mouth and onto her blue uniform. I have to catch Joe and call the police! I can't let him get away. All the doors in the hallway were shut as she stumbled toward the nurses' station. She saw Joe turn and run down the stairs. I have to stop him! Louisa could hardly breathe when she saw the Superintendent rise up from behind the nurses' counter.

"Thop him!" Louisa cried. "We've got to thop him."

"Slow down, Louisa, I've called the police."

Louisa felt a wheelchair being shoved against the back of her legs. She collapsed into the chair and blackness whirled around her. After that, she periodically saw bright lights, but mostly she kept seeing the black-white tile pattern from beneath the desk. Someone screamed at one point and then Louisa realized it must have been herself. Blackness surrounded her.

When she opened her eyes, she lay in bed and Mama held her hand, calmly looking at her, gently smoothing back her hair from her forehead.

"Ma...ma, how?..." It hurt to talk. Her head throbbed and she closed her eyes. She tried to think. Where am I? What's going on?

Catherine slowly explained. "You've been shot. You're in the hospital as a patient." Her mother's cool hand on her forehead and cheek felt wonderful.

"Hm, you're here," Louisa murmered.

"The hospital was able to reach Hank at the grocery store last night. Hank and Helen came to the house and told us what happened. Alois wanted me to come be with you. I came on the mail truck from Moore early this morning."The slow, soft speech of her mother soothed her. Louisa concentrated on the information, gradually absorbing it.

"Joe?"

"The man who shot you?" Louisa nodded and then winched with pain. Bad idea to move my head. "He was arrested and is in jail."

"Mith Jone?"

"I'm sorry. They think she died immediately."

Virginia came in briskly. "I see you're awake. Can you sit up, Louisa?" Oh, my gosh, I can't let her know how much it hurts to move. Louisa pushed her arms into the bed and tried to lift her shoulders without moving her head as Virginia shoved pillows behind her back. Pain shot through her shoulders and neck. I wish Virginia were gentler, Louisa thought.

"Here, drink some water." Virginia handed her a glass and then went on to the next bed in the 8-bed ward. Louisa sighed. Virginia's a cold, efficient machine.

The water felt good as it cooled her throat on the way down. It was hard to swallow, though. Water was going down her chin and her mother gently patted it away with her handkerchief. Louisa felt her teeth with her tongue and tried to find which teeth were missing.

Virginia was back in a few minutes. "Do you think you can stand up to go to the john?" Louisa slowly sat up and slid her feet to the side of the bed. Her mother put on her slippers. Virginia steadied her as she stood and then helped her down the aisle between the beds to the room with the toilet at the end of the ward. Who would have thought I'd be a patient using the toilet after cleaning it only yesterday?

55

Her mother was crocheting a hem on a hanky when Louisa returned. After Catherine helped Louisa back in bed, she quietly told her, "The police and maybe an attorney want you to tell them everything you know. Do you think you'll be up to that after lunch?" Louisa nodded. Zounds, my head hurts.

"Where. . . bullet go?" she painfully asked her mother.

"It went through your mouth to the back of your neck. God was with you." Her mother reached into her bag and pulled out a white envelope with a small bulge. "Here's the bullet. From the doctor, but you'll probably have to give it to the police. He removed it from your neck, back of your ear." Louisa felt her throat and the bandages that were under her left ear.

"Oh, Louisa, we're lucky you're alive. I'm grateful to God for sparing you." Her mother dabbed tears off her cheeks and then squeezed Louisa's hand. Gosh, Mama doesn't show emotion much. I must be in bad shape. Her mind wandered to all the times her mother washed out the dirt from wounds and put on bandages. And the times she'd plaster them with mustard when they had colds.

"But thith coth, coth." Louisa frowned. She couldn't say costs. It's great to be alive, but our family can't afford this.

"The superintendent told me the hospital wouldn't charge us for your care. And they'll help with the cost of a checkup with a dentist. You'll be back to nursing in no time."

Louisa lay quietly, thinking, thinking deeply. What does my heart tell me? Regardless of the time I've spent here, regardless of the money I owe Irene, is nursing what I really want?

"Mama, nurth no more." Her mother sat quietly, looking toward the windows. "Want to go home."

Catherine slowly let out her breath, looked at Louisa and gently patted her hand. "We have to think about what your father might say." Catherine saw her daughter's face cloud over.

"Oh, Mama." Louisa sighed. She could feel her mother's anxiety, caught between her concerns for her daughter and wanting to do what was right by her husband. Always Papa. We have to do what Papa wants. Well, I don't like nursing and I'm quitting whether he likes it or not. It didn't cost him anything. It's Irene that should be upset with me, wasting her money. But Irene would want me to do whatever makes me happy. Maybe I'll try teaching, like Irene.

"Mama, let me come home. 'Til Chrithmuth."

Her mother leaned over and kissed her cheek. "It'll work out, Louisa. You've always found a way. You're the strong one in the family." Oh, Mama, I don't want to be strong anymore. Just hold me. Let me be little again. Let me come home and be a child. I'm tired of being grown up.

That afternoon, the Superintendent came in with a policeman and a man in a suit and tie. He was introduced as the county prosecutor. They stood by Louisa's bed, the prosecutor writing down everything that was said on a notepad. Louisa, in her lisping manner, told them what she had heard and seen.

"Did you actually see who shot Karen Jones?" asked the prosecutor.

Louisa gingerly, slowly shook her head no. It hurt her neck. "No."

"Did you see who shot you?"

"Yeth. Joe Jacob."

"How many minutes do you think passed from the time you heard the first shot and when you were in the office?"

"'Bout 5 thecoundth." Louisa held up 5 fingers. "I wath 5 thepth away."

The Superintendent explained. "I showed you where Louisa was when she heard the shot. It's about 5 steps into the office. Five seconds is about right."

"You are certain Joe Jacob shot Miss Jones?" the prosecutor asked.

"Yeth," Louisa nodded.

"Did Joe have a reason for shooting anyone?"

Louisa paused to think before she answered, "Joe wathn't happy." The questions were making her tired and her head really hurt now. It was hard to think, but she had a radical thought. I'm like Joe! He didn't like being here just like me! He didn't like the nurses or the administrators either!

"Did he have a reason for shooting you?"

Louisa shrugged. "He knew I knew he thot Mith Jone." Or maybe he didn't like me.

"We'll call you onto the stand during the trial, Miss Janochek. You need to keep us informed as to where you are living."

"Moore," Louisa answered.

The Superintendent looked at her with a questioning glance. Mama gave the men their home address and they left.

The Superintendent stayed to talk to Louisa. "I know this has been a horrible experience for you, Louisa, but the doctor thought you could be back working on the floor within a few days. You'll heal quickly. We need you back at your station. There might not be time for you to go home."

"I'm not a nurth. I'm quittin'."

The Superintendent's face became red. Was she angry, or embarrassed? Louisa couldn't tell. Louisa closed her eyes and the Superintendent turned abruptly and left.

Louisa lay back, breathing deeply, filled with relief. It was over. She wouldn't have to be with people who didn't like her and where she didn't belong. I escaped death. But where do I belong? Just take me home, Mama. Take me home. Louisa fell into a deep sleep mumbling, Jesm pani mama.

Growth in Grace

BILLINGS, 1927-1928

What we most need is the prayer of fervent desire for growth in grace, expressed in patience, meekness, love and good deeds.

MARY BAKER EDDY (1821-1910)

Louisa stepped down from the train and followed the other passengers into the Billings depot. The tall ceiling and open space resembled a cathedral. People brushed by her as they rushed out the depot doors to the train platform. Families waited inside on benches, their suitcases blocking the sitting area. Luggage was stacked up on carts with wheels. Louisa enjoyed the bustling excitement.

Whooee, Billings must be larger than Great Falls. Can I fit in? Do I belong here? How do I find the college? First things first. Act confident. Let's find the hotel Richard recommended.

Louisa, holding tightly to her cloth luggage bag, made her way across the cavernous lobby and out to the front steps on Montana Avenue. She paused, took a deep breath, and looked around. Shops lined the street and were still lit up for business even though it was already evening. More cars than she had imagined were parked along the avenue. She spotted the Rex Hotel across the street on the corner. I hope I can get a room for the night. Her stomach turned over. It was the first time she had to get lodging in a commercial facility. With a straight back and a crisp step, Louisa carried her bag into the hotel

59

and asked the clerk for a room. She signed the register, gave him $1.50, and he gave her the key. That was easy!

"Can you give me directions to the Eastern Montana State Normal College?" she asked slowly and precisely.

"Two blocks west, then 3 blocks north on 27th. They're using one of the old bank buildings downtown. There's a sign in the window."

"Thank you." She turned away from the counter slowly. Which way is west? It was too dark and she was too tired to get her bearings tonight, but she'd see where the sun was in the morning. She heard the clinking of plates and sound of voices beyond the hotel lobby and for a second wished she had the money to eat in a restaurant. But maybe it's connected to a prohibition bar, something she wanted to avoid. Louisa walked up the stairs and down the hallway, looking for the number the clerk gave her. The key turned easily. Thank goodness. The room was small, but clean. She locked the door behind her. I'm safe!

Louisa took off her hat and coat, poured water into the basin, washed and wiped her face and hands with the linen towel. She lifted the lace curtain and peeked out the window onto the street. It seemed quiet below on the side street that her room faced. She sat down on the chair by the small table beneath the window and folded her hands. She had never felt so alone.

Her mind wandered over the last few months. Life seemed much more important, very real, after her "accident" as she called her near-death experience. It took several months for the dentist to fix her teeth, but she could now smile without feeling exposed. People told her, though, that she didn't act as happy as before. In her heart, she still loved life, learning, being with friends and her family. But she had changed: more cautious, maybe more frightened, or maybe just more realistic. More grown up?

The judge sentenced Joe to 40 years in the state prison. Louisa was afraid of what would happen whenever Joe would be released. No one else testified against Joe. The gun shot frightened everyone and for their own safety, they closed their doors to the hallway. The superintendent, who heard the shot and the running footsteps, claimed she did not see who went by her desk because she was concentrating on calling the police. The police did not find the gun. Joe, however, still dressed in his nurse uniform, was located running in distress from the hospital. When the police stopped him, he was confused and frightened at the same time. They took him in for further questioning. After the police talked to Louisa the next day, Joe was charged with murder and assault with a weapon. Joe protested that he didn't remember having a gun, nor did he confess to any killing.

Louisa didn't hate Joe. In fact, she felt sympathy for him, because she, too, had been struggling against the institutional practices and the nurses' attitudes at the hospital. During most of the trial, Joe sat beside a lawyer with his head in his hands, rubbing his red hair which stood out in all directions.

The prosecutor asked her, "Do you see the person who shot you?"

"Yes."

"Could you point that person out to the rest of us?"

Louisa looked at Joe and he looked up at her, daring her, angry but also pleading. His prison clothes were too big for him and the shoulder insets hung down on his thin arms. Louisa felt his agony and hesitated. How I wish I could wave a magic wand and this horror would disappear, that we could erase the past and I wouldn't have to send Joe to a dark prison or death. A tear started down her cheek. Then she sat up straighter. Louisa pointed at Joe.

"I'm sorry, Joe," she whispered softly. Only the judge could hear her.

"Tell us, in your words, how it happened," the prosecutor asked her.

Louisa carefully described the scene and the entire episode calmly and clearly.

"Why do you think the suspect shot you?"

"Objection your honor," Joe's attorney exclaimed. "It calls for speculation on the part of the witness."

"Let me reframe the question," the prosecutor replied. "Why were you in Karen Jones' office?"

"I ran in when I heard a gunshot. From the hallway, I saw Miss Jones leaning over her desk, bleeding and needing help."

"When did you see the suspect?"

"I was by the desk when I heard the door start to close. I turned and Joe was standing behind the door with a gun pointing at me. He knew that I knew that he had shot Miss Jones."

The defense attorney quickly stood up saying, "I object, your honor. This witness has no way of knowing what my client was thinking."

"Sustained," the judge agreed. "The jury will disregard the witness' last sentence."

There were a lot more questions. She had a terrific memory for details, and she tried very hard not to embellish, her favorite daydreaming activity.

If she hadn't testified, he may have gotten off completely because there was no other solid evidence against him. On the other hand, if there had been further evidence against him, he might have been given a death sentence. It was a hanging offense. Louisa was glad that didn't happen. To kill someone for killing someone to keep people from killing didn't make any sense to Louisa. Still, she hoped the prison would help Joe and he would not be thinking about killing her for the next 40 years.

She poured herself a glass of water from the pitcher and removed from her bag the sandwich her mother had carefully wrapped in brown paper. Neatly, she spread out the brown wrapper and took a bite of homemade sausage and sauerkraut on the thick slabs of rye bread. Tears welled up. Oh, Mama, how I love your cooking. I miss you and Papa and Victoria.

Tomorrow will be exciting. Papa gave me $40! And Irene was willing to loan me more money. After Christmas, the Moore High School principal had asked Louisa to assist in chemistry and biology classes, sciences she had learned at the Great Falls hospital. Louisa was able to repay Irene the money she had borrowed for nurses' training. More importantly, Louisa learned that teaching others inspired her. All in all, everything was working out.

Too tired to read that evening, Louisa put on her flannel nightgown and pulled out her new journal. With a charcoal pencil, she sketched the street scene she had seen as she stepped out of the depot. The Rex Hotel and the cars in the street weren't difficult, but she had trouble with the people. How do you get people looking like they are in motion? Charlie could do it, with a bronco rider having an arm swinging in the air. She couldn't get it right. She climbed in bed and soon fell asleep to the sound of the train whistles.

Early the next morning, Louisa found about ten women waiting for the Normal College office to open. All were eager to start the teaching certificate program from this newly established college. Louisa joined into the conversations around her. Most of the women were from Billings and working in business offices before deciding to register at the college to become a teacher.

"I just hope I don't have to go to some rural school to teach hayseeds," one of the women said.

"I assure you it isn't bad," Louisa responded.

"Where are you from?" a young woman with long dark hair asked Louisa. The women listened respectively to her teaching experiences at Moore.

Louisa learned that her questioner, Mable Lester, had grown up in Billings and worked part-time at a radio station! How amazing to meet someone in the radio business! And Louisa loved her loose hair style with its waves.

"I listened to KDYS in Great Falls on a crystal set," Louise excitedly told her new acquaintance. "I loved the news reports and the dance music. It must be fun to work at a radio station," Louisa enthused.

Mable laughed. "I'm mostly typing letters, filing, and answering the telephone. It's not much different from any other office. I'm so busy I'm not even aware most of the time of what's being broadcast."

"I'd really appreciate the opportunity to visit the station and see what it's like. Would that be possible?"

"I'm sure a visit could be arranged. I'll ask my supervisor tonight at work." Louisa grasped Mable's hand and squeezed it with joy. Louisa felt she had found a friend in Mable, someone with interests in new technologies and the modern world.

The registrar arrived and invited the women into the reception area. She explained, "We're delighted to welcome you as the first class of education students at Eastern Montana State Normal College. We expect to have 100 students registered before classes begin tomorrow."

Louisa's heart raced. One hundred students! Such a large class and all of them will be very intelligent since they are studying to be teachers.

As Louisa looked at the form the registrar handed out, she started ruminating on her identity. A hayseed! So that's what they think of people from Moore. Louisa laughed to herself. Janochek. Lots of Czech people around Lewistown but maybe not many here. A Czech hayseed in new fallow ground. She firmly, proudly filled out the form: Louisa Janochek, Moore, Montana. She quickly copied out her schedule into her journal and went to the registrar's desk.

"Do you know anyone who would exchange board and room for my cleaning, cooking, and caring for children?"

A few minutes later, Louisa walked down 3rd Avenue to look for the house on Division that belonged to George Lewis. The commercial businesses petered out after a couple blocks from 27th.

Then a large Catholic Church, St. Patrick the sign said, rose to a great height on the south side of the street. I'm tempted to take a few minutes and peek inside. I bet it's beautiful. Maybe I'll be Catholic, she thought. Papa and Mama were Catholic back in Kansas. They gave it up when they came to Montana. I think because Papa didn't like the priests demanding tithes. Or maybe because Papa was supposed to be a priest, being the eldest, and he preferred marrying Momma.

Then there were houses, trees, and a Baptist Church a couple blocks later. I think I'm more apt to be a Baptist. It might be fun to be dunked in water and have my sins washed away. I wonder if the water turns dirty as the sins rinse off.

And then, my, oh, my, what a mansion. Oh my goodness. She took a couple more steps and stopped in amazement. The registrar told her to look for a three-story red sandstone home. This building looked big enough to be a high school or a hospital. Can this be the George Lewis residence?

Louisa studied the rough texture of the walls, the steep roof with pointed arches above the third story windows, the way the front butted out a bit from the rest of the house, the rounded archway above the large entry doors. It was much too ornate to be a school or a hospital. A really fine architect designed this building. I wonder if they'll allow a foreign sounding person like Louisa Janochek into the hallway, let alone to work in this place.

Louisa took a deep breath, picked up her bag, walked resolutely across the street, and up the stairs. She knocked firmly on the huge door. A maid in a black dress and white collar answered the knock. Maybe 45 or 50 years old, lines were starting to form around her eyes and mouth, but she looked friendly.

"I'm from Eastern Montana State Normal College and have come to see about a position with Mrs. Lewis."

"Yes, she's expecting you. Could you please come around to the back door?" The maid was factual, but not unkind.

Louisa turned red; she felt humbled, a bit humiliated. Of course, a worker wouldn't walk in the front door. Oh well, I'll learn. The maid opened the back door for her and asked her to leave her bag in the entryway. Then Louisa was ushered into the largest kitchen she had ever seen. The floor had speckled tiles; the stove was shiny white with a black grill area and metal sheeting hanging above the grill. White cupboards lined the walls. A giant double sink with faucets filled one wall. A large, white-tiled counter dominated the center of the room—waist high. It wasn't a table. It was a workspace. Everything was shiny white and sparkling clean. The maid waited quietly as Louisa gazed at the marvel before her, her eyes wide in amazement. This is a kitchen fit for a king's palace.

The maid cleared her throat. "Your name, my dear?" she asked kindly. Louisa was startled back to reality.

"Louisa...Janochek." She said the last name softly. Louisa made a small curtsy to the maid. The maid smiled.

"Please follow me, Miss Louisa." The maid went through a door into a narrow pantry. Glass panes on the pantry cupboards allowed Louisa to see delicate glasses and dishware. Then they entered an elaborate dining area already set for lunch with crystal, napkins, and plates of fine porcelain with flowers painted on them. Louisa stepped a little lighter. The maid led her into an adjoining sitting room, and then into a garden room, really a greenhouse, moving ahead much too quickly for Louisa to see everything she wanted to see. Louisa walked crisply to keep up.

"Mrs. Lewis, here is Miss Louisa Janochek, the young lady from the Eastern Montana Normal School."

A graying, buxom woman turned from a painting easel. Her eyes were sparkling. "Please forgive me for not standing, Louisa, but as you

66

see we would have paint scattered hither and yon and Bertha would not approve of us. Please come closer. Bertha, could you place a chair for Louisa here beside me so we can have our little chat?"

Mrs. Lewis turned back to Louisa. "Would you care for some tea?" Without waiting for an answer, she went on, "Bertha, please bring us tea and a scone or two."

"What do you think of my painting, Louisa?" Louisa had only a minute to look at it before Mrs. Lewis asked, "Do you like art?"

"Oh, yes. I saw a pencil drawing by Charlie Russell that a friend had. I liked it very much." I'm not going to tell her about my own feeble attempts!

"Well, that is something. Nancy made him quite famous in Saint Louis. His paintings will continue to be worth a good deal. My own simple watercolors cannot compare."

"I like your colors, Mrs. Lewis. And the way you blend colors together, making the images seem fuzzy and touchable. How do you do that? The painting reminds me of my mother's pansies."

"What a very nice compliment." Mrs. Lewis studied Louisa for a minute. Louisa kept her head up and her eyes on the painting. Mrs. Lewis cleaned her brush in the water and laid it on the cloth. The very large, sparkling rings on her fingers distracted Louisa. Mrs. Lewis daintily wiped her hands on the small towel next to the paints, signaling that they now needed to get to business.

"Where were you raised?"

"Moore, Montana."

"And how does your mother feel about your coming to Billings and starting to study at a college that's just opening its doors?"

"My family is very pleased for me. However, they don't have the means to provide for me, so I must find employment. I need a room and board in exchange for work." There it is out. Please let her like me enough to offer me a job.

Bertha came in with a tray of tea and scones and set them on a side table.

"Please move the easel and paint table to the corner, Bertha."

Mrs. Lewis rose and removed her painting apron. Her white blouse with tiny buttons up her throat had ruffles and her dark maroon skirt had a sheen glistening like taffeta. She moved to the chair by the side table, motioning Louisa to follow her. They were sitting at one end of a very pretty room with plants growing up the walls and some cascading down the side of the table. Mama would love this room. What are these exotic flowers? I've never seen half of them. I'll need to borrow a botany book and figure out their names.

"Tell me a little about yourself. What kind of work do you like to do?"

"I'm very good with plants and working in the fields. I'm a hard worker." I hope planting and digging potatoes will transfer to caring for hothouse plants. "I have cooked for the family and, of course, I know how to clean." It doesn't sound like much. What about my nurse's training? "I have taken care of newborn babies and their mothers."

Mrs. Lewis sighed. "Unfortunately, we have no babies. I wish we did. Our three oldest children are young adults. None have children. But we still have Isabella, our eight year old. I hope you might help her with her school lessons."

"I'd be delighted. I taught classes this past year as a substitute and of course I'm training to be a teacher. I'd be happy to tutor her, as well as any work you need done, Mrs. Lewis."

They talked about specific jobs Louisa could do. Then Mrs. Lewis said, "I haven't been totally honest with you, Louisa." Louisa blanched. Does she know I haven't been honest with her? Do I need to tell her about the shooting at Great Falls? What would she make of it?

Mrs. Lewis continued. "Mr. Lewis is on the public school board, and then he was influential in getting the private Poly Technical

School here. He wanted me to hire a Normal College student so he could question you about your classes and the new college. Would it bother you to discuss your school program with him?"

"It will be a pleasure. I'll be happy to have him interested in my classes." What a relief that Mrs. Lewis' concern was only to do the bidding of her husband.

A young man about Louisa's age walked into the greenhouse and Louisa automatically stood as if in the presence of a prince. Oooh, he's so good-looking. He wore a nautical navy-blue jacket with brass buttons and a white shirt and red tie. He had a thatch of brown hair and blue-gray eyes. Is he in the military? I wonder what he's like. Louisa had a hard time keeping her eyes lowered and off of him.

"Mother, are you still painting? You promised a bit of piano music before lunch today." He said it in a slightly accusatory manner, as if his mother only existed to please him.

Mrs. Lewis chuckled. "This is our irreverent son, Arthur. Arthur, meet Louisa, a student at our new teacher's college. She'll be working here." Louisa held out her hand, not sure what was proper in this situation, but he dutifully squeezed the tips of her fingers in a perfunctory manner, barely looking at her.

"I'm happy to meet you, Arthur," Louisa politely said as she made a little curtsy.

"Come on, Mother. I haven't much time," was his response as he walked out of the room.

"Ah, and here is our precious Isabella, home from school for lunch." Isabella leaned stiffly toward her mother so Mrs. Lewis could give her daughter a light peck on her cheek.

"This is Miss Louisa, your new tutor." Louisa looked into dark blue, almost violet eyes, distant and guarded. Louisa felt she was entering a troubled cavern in those eyes. With her blonde, curly hair, and her cotton dress ending in several tiers of ruffles, Isabella looked like she had stepped out of a store window. Isabella did a quick little nod and turned her back on Louisa.

"Where do you go to school, Isabella?" Louisa asked.

"Broadwater Elementary. Third Grade," Isabella answered quickly, still facing away.

"May I walk back to school with you after lunch?" Louisa asked. "I'm learning my way around Billings." Isabella simply shrugged.

"That's a fine idea," Mrs. Lewis said as Isabella skipped out of the room.

"Louisa, you will find Bertha in the kitchen. She'll get you started serving lunch and show you to your room later. You may tell Bertha, we'll be in the music room when she is ready to serve."

Louisa lowered her head with a grateful nod to Mrs. Lewis. "Thank you for the job opportunity and for the lovely visit." As Louisa walked out of the room, she saw Arthur and Isabella in the hallway waiting for their mother, but they turned away from Louisa when they saw her. These children are something else, Louisa thought. I wonder if I'm going to be able to relate to them.

The Broadwater School was about five blocks west. Isabella walked rapidly with dainty, little steps. Louisa easily kept pace, with her slow, long country strides. To dispel the child's cool demeanor and to try to break through to her new pupil, Louisa gently commented on the pine trees and plants along the path.

"Do you see the blue jay, Isabella? I've never seen blue jays in Montana before. That's a very lucky omen for us." Isabella stopped to look for the bird. When she saw it, she gasped a little "Ah, ah." When it flew away, she looked at Louisa, a long, studied look, as if to say, "So you do know something." Her violet eyes lit up for one second. A connection. Maybe she'll learn to trust me, Louisa thought.

"I'd like to visit your school and meet your teacher, Isabella. I'm studying to be a teacher. Would you please let me know if there's an

70

opportunity to visit?" Isabella nodded. "Would you mind if I visited your class?" Isabella shrugged and then peeked at Louisa through her long lashes.

"Mother never visited the school," she stated flatly. Louisa wasn't sure of the tone. Was it a disappointing acknowledgment that her mother hadn't cared that much or was it an accusation indicating that Louisa didn't need to bother?

"Well, I would like to visit." Louisa waited a minute for a response. With none, she said, "I'll see you at home after school." Louisa wanted to give her a hug, but instead turned back toward the mansion.

In the middle of the afternoon, after setting the table for supper, Louisa climbed the back stairwell to her tiny third story room at the west end of the house and looked out at the properties behind the mansion. Below her was the carriage house, now the garage for cars. Another big, beautiful house sat just beyond the Lewis's house. She saw a grassy area, maybe a park several blocks away. Beyond that it looked like fields. The Christian Science Church where Mrs. Lewis was a reader was out of sight, but Louisa looked forward to attending Wednesday evening and Sunday morning services with her and Isabella. There's much to do and learn here. What a joy to hear Mrs. Lewis play the piano. And Bertha says one of the older daughters plays a harp! That's amazing. A harp! I've never seen one or heard one.

What a great place to live. A mansion, almost a castle! But I'm not a grand lady. I'm a tutor. Even a servant. Nevertheless, a very lucky servant.

Louisa fell into a smooth routine, helping Isabella get ready for school and then going to her college classes. Isabella was bright but prone to daydreaming. Louisa wanted to help Isabella find pleasure in learning and encouraged Isabella to find ways to incorporate her fantasies into the data to be memorized for school. Mrs. Lewis expected

Isabella to excel without all the imaginative games. Somehow, trying to satisfy both women, Isabella managed to succeed and make progress in her studies.

Louisa helped Bertha with the household laundry, cleaning, and baking. And she served the evening meal. Louisa checked out the Emily Post book on etiquette from the public library and followed the instructions for setting the table and waiting on the family. Folding napkins into different patterns and creating flower arrangements became Louisa's specialties.

College classes challenged Louisa. Bright but prone to daydreaming herself, Louisa progressed by taking careful notes and talking about the class notes with her classmates. She liked Mable, especially. One day, Louisa told her friend Mable about an idea for a weekly education program for the radio station. She spoke about Mr. Lewis wanting to know more about the Normal Education College.

"People might like to know what's going on at the two colleges. I'm sure Mr. Lewis would be happy to talk about Poly Tech and we could ask Dr. McMillan to speak about the classes at Normal. Maybe we could ask students or professors to do readings. Wouldn't it be great to have a 15 minute or half-hour radio program on education?"

Mable was intrigued. "What a wonderful idea for a local information program! I'll make an appointment for you to meet the station manager. If you start working at the station, we'd be able to see each other more often!"

In no time, Louisa found herself assisting with an educational format for the station. Programming relied on local professionals which Louisa helped recruit. Besides college professors, high school teachers wanted to talk about their sports, drama, and music events. Some weeks the program floundered, but more and more people tuned in to hear the "Billings Education Report." Louisa felt fulfilled helping others learn about new educational opportunities and activities.

After elementary school adjourned for the summer, Louisa and Isabella went for picnics as well as reading and working on math. Louisa taught Isabella to swim and roller skate. Louisa was young enough herself to enjoy the activities of her charge and Isabella's playmates. That fall, the children in the neighborhood played in piles of leaves and Louisa jumped in with them. Isabella lost her aloofness and started jumping and running in the leaves with the others. Later that winter, they went ice skating on a nearby frozen pond nearly every weekend. Isabella, imitating Louisa, started inventing games and soon Isabella had friends.

Throughout that year, Mrs. Lewis insisted that Louisa and Isabella attend the Christian Science Church with her Wednesday evenings and Sunday mornings. Mrs. Lewis was the 1st reader and one of the main supporters of the church.

One early spring Sunday morning, Louisa and Isabella sat near the back of the church where the sun shone in from the high upper windows. They kept their coats on because the church did not start its furnace even though it was cool inside. As the readings went on from the podium, Isabella was swinging her feet, hitting the underside of the pew in front of them, and disturbing the woman sitting there. Louisa gently put her hand on Isabella's knee, stopping her from kicking.

Standing on the front platform, Mrs. Lewis read, her voice strong and husky, from 1 John 3: 1-3. "Behold, what manner of love the Father hath bestowed upon us, that we should be called the sons of God: therefore the world knoweth us not, because it knew him not. Beloved, now are we the sons of God and it doth not yet appear what we shall be: but we know that, when he shall appear, we shall be like him; for we shall see him as he is. And every man that hath this hope in him purifieth himself, even as he is pure."

The world knoweth us not. That's the truth, Louisa thought. I have an essence, a spirit, which no one else knows. *It doth not yet appear what we shall be.* What shall I be? Certainly, I won't be a *son of God.* Louisa giggled to herself. Purify thyself, Louisa, purify thyself. Remember Papa's instructions from Psalms 51: create in me a clean heart.

Louisa pulled a hanky from her handbag and wiped Isabella's snotty nose. Isabella started coughing as the 2nd Reader commenced with "Keys to the Scripture" by Mary Baker Eddy. Louisa covered Isabella's coughing with her hanky. What on earth is wrong with this child? Normally, Isabella could sit quietly, but today she was squirming.

"I'll take you to the park this afternoon if you can just be still until the end of the service," Louisa whispered into Isabella's ear. Peace reigned briefly as the sun lit the side wall, white and pure. A few minutes later, the organist played "Postlude in G Major" by George Frederick Handel. Louisa and Isabella slipped out of the pew and down the steps to the entrance of the church with its Greek columns. The sun shone above them, the spring sunshine with its gentle warmth cajoling the trees to open their budding leaves. Louisa buttoned Isabella's coat as Isabella coughed into her face.

"What's the matter, Isabella? Are you sick?"

"You know Momma doesn't believe in physical illness. I can't be sick," Isabella insisted.

Because the readers used a side entrance, they met Mrs. Lewis at the corner of the church. Mrs. Lewis took Isabella's hand and they walked down the sidewalk toward the mansion, Louisa dutifully trailing behind them, humming the postlude in her mind, thinking of the organist who was a fantastic musician. She enjoyed hearing him play the organ at the Babcock Theatre, improvising to the silent movies. Very creative. How can he anticipate when the horses will turn and run? Or when something spooky is going to happen?

Louisa learned music from Mrs. Lewis and at the college. In music class they wrote out music staffs and made a music booklet of children's songs to use when they started teaching. She had bound it with a pink ribbon. I can even sing on tune. Imagine that. But the world would not like to *knoweth* me as a soloist. I'm really looking forward to teaching music to children, though. I know I can do it.

The cook had prepared chicken and noodles with biscuits for Sunday dinner. It came naturally now to Louisa to pour water and coffee from the right and to serve plates from the left. With two additional couples as guests along with the two older daughters at home, one with her husband, Louisa had to step a bit more quickly to get everyone served in a timely manner. Arthur surreptitiously patted her fanny as she served him dessert. She quickly backed away. Honestly, he needs to learn manners. I am not "his little servant girl" as he rudely calls me. Sakra, I have half a mind to pour hot coffee into his lap. Louisa noticed that Isabella was playing with her food and not eating. Mr. and Mrs. Lewis seemed totally unaware of their two younger children's shenanigans.

After dinner, Louisa served more coffee to the adults in the parlor and quickly helped Bertha wash and wipe the dishes. Then she ran up to Isabella's room on the second floor where she was playing with her dolls.

"Would you like to walk over to Pioneer Park? The sun is out. It should be warm enough," Louisa said.

"Oh goody, let's go," Isabella replied. She had already taken off her Sunday frock and put on a simple, broadcloth skirt and sweater.

"I'll go change and be right down," Louisa told her.

Soon they were running down the path to the park. Periodically, Isabella stopped and coughed.

"What's going on? Are you feeling okay?" Louisa asked. "You aren't acting like your normal self."

"I'm not of this world," Isabella replied.

"You hear too much Scripture!" Louisa laughed. "Of course, you are of this world. I can touch you." And Louisa poked her. "You are here with me in Billings, Montana, Western U.S.A., Earth, Universe."

"You forgot North America, Western Hemisphere," Isabella responded.

"Absolutely true, Bella. The student is beyond the teacher. Let's go see if there are tadpoles in the creek." Louisa turned to walk down to the little stream flowing through the park. Isabella followed slowly. Louisa waited for her and then put her arms around her as they looked into the rippling water. The melting snow ran in little crevices between dried grasses into the creek. Dead branches held water back in a little pond where they had seen tadpoles in the past.

"Run little river so clear. April and sunshine are here," Louisa sang a little children's song she had learned at the college.

"It's been a lot of fun to be with you, Louisa. I'm glad you came to tutor me," Isabella announced.

"Why, thank you, Bella. It's thoughtful of you to tell me. But you sound serious."

"I mean it. This has been the best year of my life."

Louisa gave Isabella a hug. As they stood together, Isabella reached up and started scratching her neck. Louisa pulled away Isabella's coat collar and looked closely at Isabella's neck. A rash ran from the back of her ear, down around her neck, and into her throat area. Louisa opened Isabella's coat and the top of her sweater and blouse. A blotch of red dots covered Isabella's chest. Louisa buttoned her sweater and coat shut and felt her forehead. She has a fever. Louisa stood and gently hugged Isabella to her again. In the silence, the creek gurgled. They could hear children laughing near-by. What am I to do? I can't ignore the fact that Isabella is sick. She needs care.

"Isabella, you have the measles. We have to go home and you need to get into bed."

"All right." A quiet moment ensued. In the distance, a crow called his caw, caw, caw. "Do you have to tell Mother?"

"Yes." I can't say straight out that Isabella has the measles. Mrs. Lewis will reject such a diagnosis. Louisa pondered.

"You know she won't believe you," Isabella stated.

"She'll see the evidence for herself and make her own decisions." Most likely it'll include a decision to fire me.

Louisa held Isabella a little longer, smelling the moist, spring dirt, listening to the splashing in the water pond a few feet beyond them, fearful of what lay ahead. It has been a good year. She took Isabella's hand and solemnly they trudged back to the mansion.

Louisa quickly had Isabella in a clean nightgown and into bed with the shades pulled down on the windows.

"Try not to scratch, Isabella," Louisa said as she paused at the door. "I'll be right back." Then she ran down the stairs to the kitchen for baking soda, a bowl, and a soft cloth. She filled a pitcher with drinking water and added a clean glass to the tray.

"What's happening? Why do you need these things?" Bertha asked.

"Bertha, have the guests left?"

"Yes."

"Could you ask Mrs. Lewis to come to Isabella's room?" Louisa responded. And she quickly walked up the back stairwell to the second floor before Bertha could ask anything more.

Upstairs, Louisa dampened the cloth, dipped it into the soda, making a little paste, and lightly dabbed it on Isabella's rash.

"That feels good," Isabella sighed.

"What have you done to my precious baby?" Mrs. Lewis loudly entered, sounding frantic. Arthur followed her with a smirk on his face. Why does he have to be here? Louisa wondered. I suppose he's here for the amusement he'll experience in the explosion which most certainly will come.

"Isabella is resting." Louisa calmly answered.

"Is she tired?"

"Yes."

Mrs. Lewis opened the curtains and then stood at the edge of the bed, taking Isabella's hand in her own, looking at her closely. Arthur stood at the foot of the bed, watching the interactions between the women, grinning at what he knew would soon be happening. Louisa closed her eyes so she didn't have to see his delight in her discomfort. Why does he need to be here gloating? They both were anticipating Mrs. Lewis's response.

"What is it, baby? What has happened?" Mrs. Lewis asked Isabella who had also closed her eyes. And then Mrs. Lewis saw the soda. "What's this?" she asked angrily of Louisa.

"It's baking soda, from the kitchen," Louisa answered calmly, looking right at her. Mrs. Lewis frowned, shaking her head at Louisa.

"Then it should remain in the kitchen."

"It feels good, Mother. It's for the rash." Isabella pulled her nightgown open, consequently Mrs. Lewis could see the small red mass of bumps scattered across her chest, neck, and creeping up her throat onto her face.

"Good God. What have you done to her?" Mrs. Lewis turned to Louisa.

"Isabella has the measles," Louisa stated quietly but firmly.

"Not my child! Disease does not exist in this household," Mrs. Lewis exclaimed. A dead, fearful silence reigned. "Louisa, you are no longer welcome in this house. You are to leave. Now. I never want to see you again."

Louisa's heart sank. A red blush suffused across Louisa's face. She wanted to turn and run, but when she looked into the purple irises of Isabella's now wide-open eyes, she knew she had to take a stand on her behalf. I may never see those beautiful violet eyes again, but I'm not going to abandon Bella without helping her as much as I can. Louisa smiled slightly and Isabella smiled back at her.

"May I please speak to you in the hallway, Mrs. Lewis?" Louisa asked politely.

"What on earth for? I have nothing more to say."

"Not about me. About Isabella." Louisa turned and walked out the bedroom door, hoping Mrs. Lewis would follow. Miraculously, after a moment, she did.

The six bedrooms on the second floor opened onto a large open area. Louisa walked across to the doorway where the back spiral staircase ran from the basement up to the servants' rooms on the third floor. Louisa hoped Isabella and Arthur wouldn't be able to hear the conversation that might turn nasty. Mrs. Lewis stood stiffly a couple feet away from Louisa as if it were Louisa who was diseased. Her mouth pursed with self-righteous indignation, she glared at Louisa.

Louisa gave her report clearly and calmly. "Isabella has the measles, with a runny nose, fever, congestion, and cough. She's not eating and she's weak. The room needs to be darkened; otherwise the light may damage her eyes. Damp soda will help keep her from scratching herself as she could scar herself by scratching. With rest and lots of liquids, she should be fine within a week or ten days. Measles are contagious at the beginning, so I'd recommend no one else, including other family members, be allowed to visit her for a few days."

Mrs. Lewis tapped her foot, looking down at the floor. "By what authority do you speak?"

Louisa sighed. "I was a nursing student for nine months in Great Falls with three months in the children's unit. I saw several children with measles. One child eventually contracted pneumonia and died. Another developed encephalitis, but these outcomes are rare. However, if Isabella is not better in a day or two, I suggest you call a doctor."

Mrs. Lewis was silent. Louisa didn't know if she had heard or if she had understood. What a strange belief to think we're only spiritual and not of the material world, with ailments and pains imagined and not part of our essence. Only the Spirit is real to Mrs. Lewis. I almost believed it myself. I'd like to believe it. But still, children contract measles. Isabella is sick. Illness and pain exist in this world. A few seconds passed. I can see Mrs. Lewis will not bend.

"Thank you, Mrs. Lewis, for the year. I love Isabella and fully enjoyed the opportunity to be with her and to serve you. I'll be gone within the hour." Louisa opened the door to the staircase and ran up to her small bedroom.

Her few articles of clothing easily fit into the bag she had brought from home. She removed the sheets from her cot and carefully folded them at the end of the bed. Then she took her maid's uniform from the peg, folded it, and placed it on top of the sheets. Louisa put on her coat and wrapped her books in her winter shawl, knotting it so she had a handle to carry the books easily. Tears flooded her eyes; she could scarcely see what she was doing. Louisa was furious. Mrs. Lewis is wrong. Isabella needs care. Grand ladies are not always so grand!

"Do you have some place to go?" Arthur stood at the doorway.

Louisa straightened from bending over her cot but didn't turn around as she didn't want Arthur to see her tears or how angry she was. "I'm sure Mable will take me in until I get another job." Louisa turned her mind to her immediate future. If the college doesn't have another place that needs a student to work for room and board, perhaps I could work as a student nurse at the new Deaconess hospital. Louisa sighed. It isn't work I really want to do. But I do have skills and resources. Maybe the radio station will hire me for a few hours. Louisa picked up her bundle of books and turned around thinking of the hike to Mable's house.

"May I give you a lift to Mable's place?"

Louisa looked at Arthur in surprise. Can I trust him? Or is he truly trying to be kind?

"What would your mother say?"

"She sent me to help you. She told me to tell you she'll give you a good reference for a new job." Louisa looked down at the floor, puzzled by this information. He went on. "Mother liked you a lot. You're a good worker. But she can't go back on her principles or her religious beliefs. However, you'll be happy to know she pulled the drapes shut." And he gave a little sarcastic laugh. "That was some scene!"

Louisa turned away again so he wouldn't see the tears welling up once again in her eyes. Taking a deep breath, she stepped over to her bedside table and picked up an object. She rubbed it for a minute before she turned and handed it to Arthur.

"Give this to Isabella for me. Tell her to hold on tight, to remember our happy days."

"What is it?"

"It's a Moss agate we found by the Yellowstone River." Arthur nodded solemnly and put the rock into his pocket.

"Here, give me your books and your bag." Louisa handed them to Arthur. She picked up her purse and the folded linens to take to the basement laundry room and followed Arthur out the door. At the head of the stairs, he turned in the darkening late afternoon gloom. He didn't want her to leave thinking ill of him. "Louisa, you've been swell. I apologize for teasing you."

Louisa nodded. "Thanks, that's decent of you" and then before he could turn, she said, "Wait a minute, please." She swallowed hard and looked through the shadows. Hesitantly, quietly, she said, "Arthur." A moment of silence. He looked at her, waiting.

She wanted to say, "I like you and your family a lot. But just because someone comes from a poor family doesn't mean they are stupid or have low moral values. I wish you could have respected me, seen me as a friend, as an equal. I'm not just a Czech hayseed from Moore." Arthur continued to stare at her without moving. She sighed. Louisa couldn't say it. She wasn't brave enough.

Instead she just said, "I'm hoping that someday, all people can respect each other."

"Yes," he agreed, nodding his head. "But probably not in Billings in 1928." Louisa realized he heard her hidden meaning when his eyes turned dark and in a low mumble he added, "I doubt you'll ever be my equal, Louisa." He turned away and bounded down the circular stairway.

Louisa held onto the cold, smooth, wooden banister with one hand as she slowly followed him. Its solid beauty felt refreshing under her bare hand. She loved wood, both in nature and its beauty in functional furnishings. Reminding her of her papa's constructions, it gave her strength. She straightened her back and held up her head. Her deflated spirits rose a bit as she stepped down the stairway in a stately fashion holding onto the dirty linens and her purse. I've learned a lot in this mansion, she thought. She tried her old mantra. Jsem pani mama. I'm a grand lady. A couple tears rolled down her cheeks.

More Than Survival

ROSS FORK CREEK, WINTER 1930

My mission in life is not merely to survive, but to thrive and to do so with some passion, some compassion, some humor and some style.

MAYA ANGELOU (1928-2014)

The frosted windowpane left one small corner clear for Louisa to see outside where a curtain of heavy snow was falling. The empty coal bin beside the now cold potbelly stove convinced her that remaining in the schoolhouse was not an option. She could try to break up the wooden desks, but she didn't have an axe. Destruction of school property didn't appeal to her. And she wasn't going to burn books! Louisa pulled the blanket around her more tightly. She shivered even though she had on her warmest clothes, coat, hat, socks, and gloves. She was certain the temperature was below 0 degrees Fahrenheit, probably lower.

The day before, late in the afternoon on Saturday, Louisa had noticed the dark clouds gathering in the north. At that time she considered walking out: she should have gone. Hoping it was a cold front that would pass quickly, she opted to stay because she wasn't keen on the idea of walking through the darkening, cold night to reach Richard and Ceci's house. Around midnight, the wind woke Louisa as it howled around the school building. She huddled deeper into her covers in her cot in the attached teacher's room. She knew immediately that she was in trouble. Food and coal, normally delivered on Monday when the children came for classes, would not arrive this week. A good Montana blizzard kept everyone indoors for days. There would be no school this week.

She pondered, do I stay here and freeze to death, or... do I walk the five miles to the home place, and freeze to death on the way? Big choice! There was no choice. It's now or never. She pushed hard to open the door with snow already drifted against it. Once she pushed opened the door, she then struggled to shut it to keep snow from the classroom.

Her first step away from the school stairs left her breathless, but she knew she needed to move as fast as she could. Stupid. Stupid. Stupid. Idiot. Idiot. Idiot. Louisa was furious at herself. Snow swirled around her. Louisa couldn't see two inches in front of her. Oh, God, please don't let the wind shift directions. If the wind changes, I'll miss a direct path to Richard and Ceci. I don't want to take the time to follow the fence line and go around by the road. It'd take another hour. Just keep the wind on my left shoulder and don't let it change directions. I can't afford to make a mistake. These horrid winter storms always come from the northeast and this one is a doozie.

She remembered days at the farm when they couldn't get the grain shed door closed. Then, she thought of the many times when ice and snow came up the inside their bedroom wall. Tears welled up as she remembered neighbors, a mother and two children, who died in a blizzard. God, get me through this. Stop my mind from thinking the worst.

Instead, she turned her mind to the balmy Friday afternoon, two days ago, when the school children went home. The Pospisils invited her to their home for the weekend. Why didn't I leave with them on Friday? At that time with the sun brightly shining and the week's snow nearly melted, I relished a walk and reading a good novel. A quiet time to restore my soul. And I don't like to depend on others. She laughed at herself. I have a false notion that I can take care of myself. Yeah, sure. This is a lesson for me. I knew I didn't have extra coal and I'd be without heat by Sunday night. Now, I have a solitary stomp through a blizzard. Am I crazy or what!

Her teeth already hurt. She could feel the cold in her neck where the bullet had lodged. Here I am freezing to death and Joe is in a nice, warm prison in Deer Lodge. Well, Joe, maybe you're cold, too, and have bedbugs in your cell! Even so, Joe, you're better off at this moment than I am. Why am I still frightened of you? If I make it through this storm alive, I promise that I'll somehow face my fear of you.

Her mind then turned to the dance the night before the shooting. I wonder where Roy Coombs is and if he became an artist. He's the most decent man I've ever met. I wonder if I'll meet a man I can respect and love. It was kind of Roy to take the time to write to me and tell me how sorry he was that I had been shot after he read it in the paper.

And then there is Arthur in his fancy house listening to harp music! I could be there now by the open fire listening to angelic music. I sure messed up that opportunity. Still, Arthur is arrogant and mean. I hope he feels a draft of cold air running up his back wherever he is at this minute! His engagement to a wealthy woman from Boston was in the paper. I should be decent and send him a congratulatory note, if I make it out. Isabella must have recovered okay as she was mentioned as a family member.

I wonder if Mable is having as much trouble in her first year teaching job at Flarety Flats. I thought it'd be easier to return here to my first school after getting my teaching certificate than to a totally different school, but was I ever wrong. They know me far too well. "Familiarity breeds contempt" is a truism. Golly, they can't even keep the coal bin filled and it's not that far to the Roundup coal mine.

Fortunately, my sisters are doing well. I'm grateful to Irene for helping me financially and now she's married to an apple farmer! I hope to pass her generosity on and help Victoria, whatever she decides to do. Helen and Hank are doing great at the grocery store. Ceci and Richard. . .oh, I hope I can make it to the home place. They'll help me.

Then she remembered Alvin and his buddy, Charles. They left Montana for the riches of California. The family rarely heard from Alvin. As far as the family knew, Alvin had never gotten over his fancy for liquor and gambling.

And then there's Walter giving his life to the church, taking care of God's people, preaching and using his engineering skills to rebuild churches.

Louisa's mind kept wandering from one memory to the next. I'm still not sure what my life task is. Just getting through a day is difficult. Maybe now my life is over. Is this all that was to be for Louisa Janochek? Not really accomplishing much at all. Drifting like the snow.

Louisa plodded along, one step after another, concentrating on moving through the storm. How long have I been out here, an hour or two? I have to be half-way there. There has to be a rise in the land soon. Am I lost? My toes tingle; they're frostbitten for sure. Could I have missed the hill above the house? Think! To the east is a road and a fence line. To the west, open prairie. Oh God, let me not be wandering west. It's 20 miles to the curve where the highway bends back north. To the north is more prairie, miles and miles of open land, it must be about a hundred miles before the Missouri River. If the wind swept around and I've turned north, I'll never see anyone ever again. Think, Louisa, think. Am I going in the right direction?

Oh God, help me find the home place. Don't let me die out here. I'm tired and I want to go home. Turn to your left, Louisa, find the fence, or find the hill. Oh yeah, take me home, take me home. I'm going crazy. Just keep walking. As long as I'm moving, there's hope.

86

Keep a'walkin', walkin', walkin'. Oh please, God, turn me in the right direction. Go down, Moses, to Egypt land. Keep my legs moving. Yes, think of desert and warmth and sun. The snow is so heavy. I'm so tired. Maybe I should take off the blanket. It's wet, a weight on my back, but it gives me comfort. I'm tired. Maybe I could lie down under the blanket and take a nap. I'm tired. I could cover up and sleep for a little while, and then be strong enough to go on. I'm going to die. I can't make it. Just a few more steps and I'll take a nap.

The snow looks soft. But lying down, I'll die. Don't lie down, Louisa, you'll die. Lie and die. Lie and die. I have to keep moving, even one tiny step, one more tiny step. One more. One more.

The wind built drifts in the low areas with snow deeper there than on the side of the hill. In the summer, saline seep formed a small, marshy lake, but now the bottomland was deep in snow. Louisa was moving through the middle of that basin, the snow past her knees in places. Then she felt the land shift. With each step, she was climbing.

What? She stumbled. Oh my gosh, I think I'm going up a hill. Can it be? Can it be our hill? Oh, it's hard, harder walking up hill. She shrugged off the blanket. It was too heavy. She took determined steps forward. My legs feel like wooden sticks, like I'm walking on stilts. Hard to move them. The wind is cold, my cheeks are burning. Icicles hung from her hat, covering her eyes. I can't see. I have to see. Maybe I'll be able to see the roof of the house and barn if I can get to the top of this hill. Another voice said, are you kidding yourself, Louisa? You can't see anything in this storm.

Her breath slowed and she could no longer get a good breath of air and fill out her lungs. Each breath hurt her lungs. Her heart pounded fast and hard. Her muscles felt weak; each step took tremendous energy.

My feet feel warm. I wonder if that means they are actually warmer or if I've reached another level of frostbite. No way of knowing until I get over this hill and down the other side to Richard's and Ceci's. I can do it. I must do it. Do I see something... something dark, maybe the corrals and buildings? No, it's all tricks. Just keep moving, one foot in front of the other. Up, and down, up and down. Don't think. Concentrate on one foot at a time. I'm going to make it. Just keep movin', movin', movin'. My mind's numb, my body's numb, I can't think, I can't feel. One more step. Another.

Louisa stumbled on the front step and hit the door with her shoulder. Her fingers were too stiff, too frozen to open the door. I'm so tired. Please open the door, Richard.

"Richard!" she yelled and with the last bit of energy, she hit against the door with her elbow and shoulder.

The door swung open. "Ceil, Pa, it's Louisa!" Louisa collapsed into the arms of her brother. He lifted her and carried her across the entry and set her on a chair in the kitchen. Alois was there instantly. He unwrapped her knitted scarf, packed with ice around her neck and shoulders, pulled off her cap, and unbuttoned her coat, a sheet of snow falling around her as he worked.

"Get a basin of cool water, Ceil. And do you have a flannel nightgown we could put on her? Richard, add more wood to the stove. And then lay out pillows and blankets by it."

Alois kept his attention on Louisa, a bundle of melting ice and snow.

"What the hell are you doing out in this storm?" Alois was furious at this unthinking daughter. Once again this child he loved dearly had risked her life. Would she never learn?

"Papa?" Louisa could scarcely speak. "You're here?" She tried to take another breath. Her lungs hurt. She tried to look at him but everything looked hazy.

Alois carefully removed her leather boots and pulled off the wet layers of leggings and stockings. He held back a gasp. This is bad. His anger dissolved into concern. He cradled her feet in his hands

88

and then plunged them into the basin of cool water that Cecilia had brought.

"I came late yesterday to help Richard get the cows into the corral when I saw the storm clouds. What were you doing, walking in this blizzard, you foolish child?" he asked in a more gentle tone.

Cecilia helped him as they removed her sweaters, dress, and camisole, all wet from sweat and snow, and then they slipped on Cecilia's flannel nightgown and sweater. Richard lifted Louisa onto a short stool by the stove. They helped her put frostbitten hands into the basin of water with her feet, the toes now swollen like sausages.

Cecilia knelt and put her hands on Louisa's cheeks which were turning blue. Cecilia looked into Louisa's eyes, but Louisa's pupils were unable to focus. Tears came into Cecilia's eyes.

"Is she blind?" Cecilia whispered to Alois.

"Could be, looking at that white-out and icy glare. Let's hope it's temporary. Can you warm up some of that good chicken broth of yours, Cecilia?"

After a few minutes, Richard lifted Louisa to the nest he had built by the potbelly stove in the living room. He gently laid her on the bedding. Alois pulled the stool to the stove and placed a pillow on top. He gently patted her hands and feet dry. He put her feet on the cushioned stool and covered them with a soft blanket. Next he put her hands across her belly and tightened a blanket around her.

"Papa, my feet and hands itch."

"That's good. You have feeling. But leave them alone."

"Can't. I've gotta scratch."

"Stop! No scratching." Alois knelt beside her, holding her hands flat on her chest, pulling the blanket more tightly around her. "Richard, get a pillow or something soft to put between her legs so she can't rub them together. And do you have woolen socks and mittens? And where's that tit balm we use for cows?" Richard came back with socks, mittens, and a pillow which he eased between her feet and legs. With an approving nod from Alois, Richard gently squeezed balm between her toes and carefully pulled his own big wool socks over her feet. Alois put balm on her hands and then put the woolen mittens on.

"I gotta scratch!" Louisa cried.

"No," Papa answered firmly. "You lay still."

"I gotta rub my feet, Papa." Richard reached down to firmly hold her legs.

"No, you'll damage your skin. You mustn't rub. Let it heal on its own. Richard, keep holding her legs."

Louisa tried to roll back and forth but her father and brother held her flat. She was heaving, "It hurts. It hurts." Her voice rose in a low scream. "I can't stand it. Papa, the pain. It hurts. It hurts!"

"Here, bite on this washcloth. It'll pass. Bite down." He kept talking as she kept panting and moaning. "The blood is rushing to your toes, to your fingers. Ceil, get another blanket. Oh, Louisa, it'll pass, it'll pass. The pain will pass." Then he whispered, "I pray the pain will pass. God, help us. Don't let her lose her toes, her fingers."

"Oh, thank you, Ceil. Here, take a sip of broth, Louisa. No, you can't hold the cup. Your hands are too stiff. I'll hold it for you." He lifted her head up and let her drink. "Sip, my zelinka, sip away on good broth that will give you strength and will warm you. Oh, my little one, what were you doing in this storm? Richard, put another pillow behind her back. Another sip. Now rest, Louisa." He was talking to himself more than to Louisa. Moments passed.

"Papa, I couldn't stay. No coal. Not enough food. The storm. I would have frozen to death out there." Tears started to run down her cheeks. He patted her cheeks with the washrag.

"Louisa, we thought you had gone to the Pospisils. If I had known you were at the school house we would have come for you.

But you're safe now." He paused. It was hard for him to admit. "You did the right thing."

"It hurts so much, Papa. It hurts!" She was shouting again.

"It'll pass. Give your body time." He spoke in a soothing tone. "Relax. Slow down." He gave her more broth. "Drink, drink, Louisa. You need the nourishment." God, don't let her lose her fingers or toes, he prayed. We thawed her out as quickly as we could. "Put more wood in the stove, Richard." I need to get her mind on something else.

"Now rest and I'll tell you a story. I'll talk and you can go to sleep." Alois set the cup down and leaned against the wall next to the potbelly stove. He kept one arm over Louisa's hands, so she couldn't start rubbing. Louisa's eyes were slowly closing. She was exhausted.

The family settled into a more normal Sunday routine. Cecilia laid a small blanket down by Alois and told Raymond, their 2-year old, to sit by Grandpa. All this time, the little boy had been sitting on the floor by the couch, holding his teddy bear, sucking his thumb, and watching the adults, puzzled by the past hour's commotion. Raymond waddled over to sit on his blanket. He patted his teddy bear and laid his head on Alois's knee.

They were ready for one of Alois's tales. Richard went to his chair and picked up the reins he had been working on, rubbing lard into the leather to make them more pliable. Their baby girl had been sleeping in a bassinet by the kitchen doorway, but now she awoke and started crying. Cecilia picked her up and sat in the nearby rocker to rock her and to nurse.

"While you rest, I'll tell you the story of Joseph and Beta Navrat, your Mama's parents who lived in Prague. Oh, such a city. Imagine, Louisa, walking down cobblestone streets." Louisa's mind followed his words. She could see a pretty country lane leading into the city. Oooh, now the tan road turns to a dark yellow. The path is golden as she steps onto the city's shiny cobblestones.

"Prague has tall, stone buildings with columns, porticos and ornaments," Alois said. Louisa rolled her head. She saw white, shiny buildings with gargoyles and a blue sky peeking through the rooftops. It was bright and hurt her eyes.

"And there, right in front of us is Navrat's Shoppe, a clothing store with the finest clothes you can imagine. It's a big brick store, three stories high, with windows on the first and second floors, real glass panes. On the main floor, your grandfather, yes, your mother's father owned this marvelous clothing store. Joseph Navrat had gorgeous gowns of silk and cotton with flounces and ruffles, of all colors and textures. Can you imagine, Louisa, all those fancy dresses, you in silk, Ceil in rayon with lace covering your arms?"

Louisa could see ladies in fancy dresses and big, floppy hats entering the store. The women are tall and thin, very stately and beautiful. Their movements are graceful. I love Prague and Grandpa's clothing store.

All at once, "No, Papa!" Louisa cried out, shaking her head back and forth. "No, no fancy dresses." Her heart was pounding hard. The story wasn't going right. I'm not a grand lady. I see, I see, what do I see, a little child near the store's entrance, a little girl, an orphan, with a dirty face in ragged clothes. She needs warm clothes, sturdy clothes, not silk.

Alois gently patted Louisa's arms, not understanding her distress, and calmly went on. "On one side of the store were fine wool suits with vests and coats with brass buttons for the men." Just like Arthur's navy-colored jacket with brass buttons, Louisa remembered as Alois went on. "Oh yes, there were beaver hats for the men and felt hats for the women with ostrich feathers. Beautiful clothes." Just imagining these fine clothes made Alois, Raymond, and Cecilia yearn for those better days before the stock market dropped. Even wealthy people were scrambling to make it through the year.

"Your grandfather had many employees. On the second floor of the Navrat Shoppe, big tables were used for cutting out the suits and the dresses, and there were four very fine treadle sewing machines, can you imagine four machines! Grandpa Navrat was wealthy, with skilled tailors designing and sewing these fashions that were for sale only in Prague. The big windows let light into the work area, allowing the tailors to make the tiniest stitches."

"A wooden stairway from the sewing area ran up to the third floor where Grandpa Joseph and Grandma Beta lived with their six girls." He paused. Little Raymond was falling asleep. Alois lifted his arm from Louisa who was resting quietly, and fondly rubbed Raymond's tummy.

"Joseph and Beta's first child was a boy, but he died at birth." He paused as he thought how grateful he was to have Raymond as a grandson. "The next six were girls, beautiful girls, always dressed in the finest clothes of the day. Your Mama was the ninth daughter in the 11 girls they had, but Mama was born later, when they were in Kansas."

"In Prague one night, there was a great fire, and the fire swept through the clothing store." Louisa started breathing hard. The little child on the street was cold. She lit a match and dropped it. Just like I did when I was little. "Grandpa Joseph and Grandma Beta and their six girls, a couple in their arms as they were babies, rushed down the wooden stairway to the street before the fire could burn the stairs and block their way to safety. The fire was huge and not to be stopped." Louisa felt the fire rush up her feet and into her whole body. She was aflame in the heat of the fire. While she had been extremely cold an hour ago, she now sweltered. Sweat ran off her forehead. The pain in her head, hands, and toes turned to a burning sensation.

"The fire burned all the stores on that street in Prague, all of the Navrat Shoppe's clothing inventory, the sewing machines, the bolts of cloth, and the furniture in their third story home. Grandpa Joseph was left with nothing. Once a wealthy merchant, he now had no assets. That's why he came to America with his family and his father. They settled in Kansas. That is where I met your mother, the most beautiful of the 11 Navrat sisters."

Louisa was in a dazed state, her body hot, her mind in turmoil. "As you see, Louisa, you are from a strong family, a member who can survive no matter what the circumstance. Maybe you'll fashion beautiful dresses, be a tailor, and sell handsome clothes like your grandfather."

"No, Papa, no beautiful dresses, no . . . no." Her head rocked back and forth. Her voice was trailing off into troubled sleep with a nightmare. She saw herself as the little waif accidently setting fire to her grandfather's shoppe, a child who needed help. Grand ladies in fancy clothes aren't saving children! Louisa rolled back and forth, shaking her head. I dropped the match! The fire's huge. I can't put it out. I'm very tired. I can't breathe. I'm sorry. I cause so much trouble, always trouble. Give me a clean spirit.

Louisa saw the snow cover the ruffian who had started the fire. Help the little child! Just a small beggar needing to get warm! Tears were leaking out of Louisa's eyes. Where's the grand lady to help? Alois watched Louisa and wondered about her disturbed dreaming. He patted her gently, humming a Czech lullaby.

Louisa's wet clothes steaming on the bench by the door gave off a wool smell blending with the fragrance of the burning cedar in the stove. The wind howled outside the house, making the room a cozy, warm center within the storm. As Louisa fell into a deep slumber, Alois gently moved Raymond off his lap and covered him with a corner of the blanket as the boy also slept. Alois stretched out his legs.

"And we lived happily ever after," he ended his story tenderly, hoping that, indeed, all his children would survive the terrors of this world and the fears in their hearts. Mother Nature can be cruel and we never know what might happen to us.

"Why is Louisa having trouble, Papa Alois?" Cecilia asked. "She's smart and beautiful, but life doesn't seem to be turning out very well for her. Why doesn't she get married, like Helen and me? Maybe life would be easier for her."

"She'll get married someday. She's on her own path, Ceil," Alois finally answered. Richard looked up at his father and they smiled at each other with a shared understanding. "Louisa's curious about the world. It's hard to understand her. But there's a place for her."

Alois pulled out his pipe from his shirt pocket and packed it with tobacco. Standing up he stretched out his back and then bent over to tuck the blankets around Louisa. He lit his pipe with a small ember from the stove and pulled a chair near the warmth of the stove.

The lamp flickered and Richard leaned over to raise the wick.

Cecilia spoke quietly. "I remember how much she loved the play our senior class put on: *Seven Keys to Baldpate*. It was a mystery with seven different personalities coming together into an abandoned hotel. Louisa loved acting out the mystery. She loved playing each one of the roles, pretending she was all seven men and women. She was able to see things differently than the rest of us."

"You've been a good friend to Louisa. Don't give up on her," Alois responded. Cecilia then remembered the good advice Louisa had given her about finding a man who respected her, a man who loved her. She was lucky to have married Louisa's brother, Richard.

"I wish I could help her like she has helped me," Cecilia replied.

"You helped her a good deal today. You and Richard were here to save her life. But Louisa will find her own way. Look, she found her way out of that blizzard," Alois shook his head in amazement.

Richard pondered for a couple minutes, clearing his voice. Then he spoke up. "You know Louisa lives in another world, a world of castles and princes. She's smart enough to not let it out very often, but she's been a grand lady ever since she was a little girl. Ain't that right, Pa? And maybe someday she will be a velkou pani, a grand lady. From her response tonight, though, it won't be in the fashion industry! She was pretty adamant saying 'No' to pretty dresses." Richard chuckled. As they sat quietly, Richard mused, "I wonder why no fancy dresses? Louisa loves dresses."

The blizzard lasted another three days while Louisa recovered, warmed by the fire in the potbelly stove and the love of her family.

Born to Love

MUELLER HOME AND SCHOOL, STILLWATER COUNTY, SEPTEMBER 1930

We are all born for love. It is the principle of existence and its only end.

<small>BENJAMIN DISRAELI (1804-1881)</small>

"Whooee!" Louisa laughed and leaned onto Karl's arm for a brief second. Karl swung her around and they took a couple of two-steps left, then a couple of two-steps right, and then eight steps down the center of the floor. Karl whirled her in a circle and they started back up the side of the hall, swaying with a two-step on one side, then on the other. The quick rhythm left Louisa breathing heavily. *I can't let this 15 year-old kid think I'm an old lady.* Louisa kicked her calf-length skirt out on one side and then the other side before Karl twirled her in a circle for the end of the dance. Everyone clapped heartily and the fiddler took his bow.

"I'm not used to these long skirts!" she exclaimed. *I have to have some excuse for not keeping up with him! I love my new dress with its lacy V neckline and the flared skirt that Mable and I found on sale at Hart-Albin's. Even Grandpa Navrat would be proud of me!*

"Ah, the cost of bein' fashionable," Karl teased. Hemlines had fallen to mid-calf within the last year, along with the stock prices. "I kin tell ya' I've heard the men complainin'. They miss the short skirts and seeing knees."

"Honestly, Karl. What would your mom say to that!" Louisa glanced over to where Anna, Karl's mother, stood visiting with the women.

"She'd laugh and agree with me."

Louisa nodded with appreciation. "Your mother's great. I'm glad I can stay with you folks." She'd moved in with the Muellers the previous Sunday and started teaching the next day at the Mueller School just a quarter mile up the hill from the house. It was an easy walk and she had no more worries about freezing in an isolated schoolhouse! To stay in the home of Senator John Mueller was a privilege. I'll learn a lot, Louisa thought. She looked at Karl thinking about how much fun it'll be to have this lanky, rusty-haired, teen as an adopted kid-brother for the year. Karl and his parents had invited her to come with them for the fall festival dance at the Wheat Basin community hall.

"You add a bit of spice for us, too. Oops, here ya go, Louisa. I told ya I wouldn't see ya much." Karl saw his friend, Adam, approaching. "Remember, we have to leave after midnight supper for the milkin' at 4 a.m. Don't get yourself lost with a boyfriend." Karl acts like he's my father! Louisa mused. Karl turned her around to greet his friend. "This, Louisa, is Adam Martin. Adam, meet the new school marm, Louisa Janochek."

"Mighty glad to make your acquaintance, Miss Louisa." Adam executed an elegant, low bow. Louisa's eyes widened. As Adam straightened to his full height, he brushed his thick, straight blonde hair back from his forehead. His very blue eyes pierced through her dark brown ones into her heart, and it gave a jump.

"My, what fine manners, Mr. Martin," Louisa teased, lightly, trying to recover her balance. Adam Martin. Acts like a prince, but doesn't look like royalty in his plaid cotton shirt, dungarees, and boots.

Adam elbowed Karl. "See, what you can learn from me?" The music started and Adam held his hand out to Louisa. "The next dance. May I have the honor?"

"You may indeed." His rough, strong hand led her to the middle of the floor and she was swept into another Texas two-step with this very energetic cowboy. Immediately after, the band transitioned into a lovely, slow waltz, and without missing a beat, Adam swung Louisa into his arms, holding her more closely than she thought proper. But I like it! With his firm hand on her waist, guiding her smoothly around the floor, she relaxed and followed his graceful moves. He was a good dancer. She slid her hand up his arm to his shoulder and held onto him a bit more tightly to balance her weight. Her heart which had been racing from the two-step, now raced for a different reason. She became dizzy as she breathed in the musky, masculine smell which arose from Adam's chest. What a great feeling of warmth and peace.

"You're a mighty fine dancer, Louisa." Adam gently released her from his arms as the music faded away.

"Well, I'm a Bohemian gypsy. Polkas and waltzes are in our blood." Why am I being silly? Or do I want to be clear from the beginning of who I am?

"And that explains the beautiful shade of rose on your olive colored cheeks." Before other young men could get up their nerve to ask the new schoolteacher for a dance, Adam quickly led her to his parents who were ending their dance near Anna and John Mueller. He introduced his parents to her, Mary and Henry Martin.

Mary lightly held Louisa's right hand between her own two hands for a moment. "We're happy you're here, Louisa." Mary's friendly, round face had smile wrinkles and Louisa felt drawn to hug her, although she prudently resisted. Henry was an older, slightly smaller version of Adam with the same sky blue eyes. Both of them had straight, blonde hair, although Henry's hair was thinning at the sides and the top.

Henry added, "Yes, indeed, we welcome you to our community."

Louisa smiled as she responded, "Thank you. I'm looking forward to the school year." What lovely people. I really like Adam's parents, she thought. They're so friendly.

One more dance with Adam and then others swept Louisa away. Every young man there wanted at least one chance to dance with the teacher. She did not sit out a dance the entire evening. This evening was the most fun she'd had in a long time.

The next morning when she woke in the dark, she raised her arms above her head and stretched, wiggling her toes and her fingers, straightening out her back, and squeezing her backsides. She thought of the evening and how lovely it was to be admired and appreciated.

The Mueller kitchen noise brought her to full alertness and she jumped up to dress quickly in a housedress. Gosh, I'm way too late. What will they think of me? She ran her comb through her short, curly hair, splashed water from the basin onto her face, dried off with the rough towel, and hurried to the kitchen.

"Good morning, Louisa. Did you enjoy the dance at Wheat Basin?" Anna asked from the stove where she was cooking about four dishes all at once.

"I certainly did. A wonderful band and lots of young people."

"I'm glad you're getting acquainted with the neighbors."

"And lots of children! Some of my students were there, sliding on the cornmeal in the corners of the dance floor. And how can babies sleep in the side room when it's so noisy?"

Anna laughed. "Oh, they get used to the music. Here, would you mind running the cream separator while I mix up the biscuits?"

"Glad to. My goodness, you have buckets and buckets of milk."

"Twenty milk cows."

"I didn't realize you had so many cows and such a big dairy business." Nothing like the one milk cow our Janochek family had to feed us kids. Louisa concentrated on the task as she turned the crank of the separator watching the milk go into tall buckets and the cream

100

into jars. Carefully, she filled several quart jars with beautiful, rich cream and moved clean milk containers to catch the skim milk. Karl came in the back door with two more buckets of milk.

"'Mornin', sleepy-head." He acknowledged Louisa's presence as he put cheesecloth across a clean steel container and carefully poured the two buckets of milk through the cheesecloth. Hair from the cows and the slightest amount of dirt remained on the cheesecloth.

"Looks like you're learnin' the mornin' routine," he said. Karl picked up an eight gallon steel container full of milk and went out the door. By the time he got back, Louisa had finished skimming the cream from the buckets of whole milk. Karl put the quart jars of cream into a wicker basket.

"How strong are ya, Louisa? Kin ya carry the wicker basket?" He lifted the precious cargo filled with cream from the floor and placed it in her hands. He looked at her and she nodded. Opening the door, he picked up an eight gallon steel container of skimmed milk, and when Louisa stepped outside, he kicked the door shut.

The sun was rising as they walked down the path to the spring house. Branches from gooseberry bushes that she couldn't see in the morning shadows caught on Louisa's skirt and tore it a bit. Karl stepped onto a couple of flat stones in front of the spring house, bent down into the rock-walled shed covering the spring, and set the steel container of milk into the cool spring water beside other containers. He then took the basket of cream jars from Louisa, rested it on a flat rock, and together they lifted the jars of cream onto a rock ledge where the water came just below the edge of the lids.

"Here," he said, "start stirrin' the cream to keep it cool." He handed her two thin wooden spoons. I'll be back."

It was cool in the spring house and she wished she had a sweater. The sun started to show through a hole in the east end and she could begin to see what was inside the dark shed. There were a couple of ropes on a wooden beam that ran across the backside of the spring house. They must hang meat here, she thought. I wonder if there are snakes or mice. Louisa looked into the dark corners. Is there a rat watching me? A muskrat or a beaver? No reason to fear for rattlers. Only water snakes would like it this wet.

"Can you move over, Louisa?" Karl had two long spoons for himself and after he set another steel container into the cool spring water, he started stirring two milk containers, one with each hand. "We'll be finished in no time."

"You do this every day." Louisa said it as a fact, not a question.

"Every day. Twice a day. Cows don't take vacations."

"You like it." Again Louisa said it as a given fact.

"Sure do. Nothin' like it," Karl responded.

Louisa thought awhile about the chores she had as a youngster. She remembered the hours of picking potato bugs from under the leaves and putting them into the kerosene in the bottom of a jar. I hated working with the hot sun burning through my shirt as the jar filled with sticky, yucky muck with its nauseating smell. I don't want to offend him, but chores on a farm are tedious, even disgusting.

"Doesn't it get boring, day after day?"

"Seems like it might. To me every day is different. Every sunrise, every sunset has a unique feel. I love the barnyard smell while milking. Layin' my head on the cow's flank, the sound of the squish, squish, squish as I milk. Just like a dance, Louisa."

Stirring is a bit like a dance, too, she thought. Swing your ladies round and round, now to the left, now to the right. Very meditative. Very soothing. But forever? Spending your whole life milking cows and stirring cream?

"Wouldn't you like to get a high school diploma? Maybe go to college like your brothers and sister did?"

"Naw. Everybody's got a gift. Start stirrin' the other cream jars, Louisa."

Louisa stood for a moment, stretching her legs before moving to the new jars. Golly, what does he mean? She looked into the face of this freckled kid for some answer.

"So, Karl, tell me about your gift."

Karl became the teacher. "What do you think you're doing right this minute?"

"Stirring cream."

"To what end?" He sounded like a professor or preacher.

"To cool it down. To keep the cream from souring."

Karl's folksy drawl had turned into a crisp, precise lecture. "Yes, cool it as quickly as possible, so it's the sweetest milk and cream in the county when we deliver it to the Laurel creamery tomorrow morning. I," (he pointed to his chest proudly) "with Pa's cows, of course, provide something essential for Montanans. The cows get treated to hay, corn mash, and barley straw. We keep them away from onions and skunkweed. Cows are happy. Customers are happy. We're happy. My gift is working with animals. With nature. I'm a dairyman and a farmer, Louisa. A good one."

Louisa raised her eyebrows as she studied Karl. There's a lot below the surface, she thought. He respects animals as much as people!

"And even though I'm just a punk farm kid, I get to dance with the fancy school marm, first thing." Karl was back to his teasing. "Until Adam takes over."

"Unhuh, and what's Adam's gift?" Louisa asked her young philosopher.

"Adam's like me, Louisa. He skipped school to help his dad farm." Louisa's heart sank. In that moment, she realized she had been attracted to Adam. She had really liked him, enjoyed her moments with him. But not even a high school diploma? She wanted something more. What good is a farmer's wife? Not much of a life. She thought of Ceci who worked hard. Really hard, physical work. Instantly, she realized she was a snob like Arthur Lewis. Ranchers need knowledge to be successful, facts not always taught in school. All people have gifts as Karl said. Each path is to be respected.

Karl carefully screwed the lids onto the jars of cream and put lids on the milk containers leaving them to stay cool in the spring house.

"We're done. That was fast. Thanks for your help, Louisa. Let me show you the barn real quick before we have some of Ma's biscuits and eggs." He's a really good kid, Louisa thought. I hope he stays as sweet as his cream.

The barn had two 12-foot tall rock foundations, flat rocks laid on top of each other without mortar which surprised Louisa.

"My dad is a great building constructor, but I don't think I've ever seen a 12 foot rock wall without cement holding the rock. How did Mr. Mueller do it?"

"Pa came from Switzerland where he built rock walls as a boy. He's good at it all right."

About ten feet separated the foundations on each side of the barn from the outer wood wall. Thick boards nailed together rose from the top of the rock foundations to support a tall roof between them which was the hay loft. Twelve stanchions ran down the length of the barn on each side.

"See, Louisa, I climb up this ladder to the hay loft and throw hay down to the cows." He did what he was telling her he did and pitched hay into the head of each stanchion. He shouted down to her from the hayloft as he worked his way down the building. "Each cow knows her place and comes in to eat. As quick as a bunny, I push each of the vertical boards over, the top horizontal board falls with the notch holding the first board so the cow's head is caught while she eats her hay. Pretty slick. Then I grab a three-legged stool and start milking away. Pa and I each milk 10 cows. Sometimes I beat him!"

A mewing in the corner attracted Louisa's attention and she saw a couple of cats. "I give the cats a few squirts of milk, too," Karl said. Then he disappeared as he tossed hay down from the loft into the stanchions on the other side of the barn to be ready for the evening milking.

Louisa shook her head in amazement. My dad is a carpenter and a builder, but I've never seen anything like this. Almost like a cathedral.

Karl climbed down the ladder from the loft and answered as if he had heard her speak. "It's a skill, all right, to pile up those rocks straight and sturdy. I don't have it, but Pa knew how to do it. The bottom of the silo is a circle of rock, too. Come on, Louisa, I'm hungry for breakfast and then we gotta get ready for church."

After breakfast, John and Anna Mueller, with Karl and Louisa, headed back to Wheat Basin for the community church service, potluck lunch, and baseball game. "We get in as much gossiping as we can before winter hits," Senator Mueller said as the auto started down the dirt road. Louisa laughed at his light-hearted sarcasm. This family is different. They're smart and still down to earth.

The Wheat Basin community hall where they had danced was swept and clean. Who had stayed here in the early morning to clean the hall up after the dance? It really does look like a church now with a cross in front, a podium for the preacher, a communion table, chairs strictly lined up in straight rows. This is an amazing community I've gotten myself into. The same lady pounding out polkas and dance rhythms last night is playing sweet hymns.

Adam sat down beside her. Louisa blushed and sat a little taller. "Glad to see you again, Louisa."

Louisa glanced at him and replied, "It's good to see you, too, Adam."

"The preacher's late. He comes from Absarokee twice a month. Have you heard Pastor Bowman before?"

"No, I haven't had the pleasure."

"He's a Methodist. We're a community church, with people from different Protestant denominations. Do you have a particular denomination?" Louisa took a deep breath. Is this a test? I dare not tell him that the only church I've attended regularly is Christian Scientists. And it probably wouldn't be good to tell him that Papa left the Catholic Church to marry Mama and not become a priest like his family wanted.

"Papa read scripture to us, but we didn't get to church often." That sounds safe, she thought.

Adam accepted her statement of her scanty religious background and started explaining the order of the service. She casually questioned him about details of singing, saying the creed, and taking communion as if she had done it all her life and just wanted to make sure that this religious ceremony was like those she had attended.

Golly, what am I getting into here? I like Adam's sincere attempt to help me, but where is this leading? When the pastor arrived, the congregation grew quiet. Anna Mueller was sitting on the other side of Louisa. Louisa watched her closely and followed her every move, including walking down the aisle and taking communion in the same way Anna did.

After worship, men quickly removed the first row of chairs and set up long tables beside the communion table. Women brought out baskets and pans full of marvelous food from the cars and spread it out on the tables. Louisa helped Anna set out chicken, a pot of beans, rolls, three apple pies and gallons of milk. When did she have time to do all that cooking? Was it this morning? The pastor intoned a blessing and Adam moved in by Louisa as people lined up to eat. Adam suggested they eat together outside on the shady side of the hall. He grabbed a blanket from a bench and spread it out over the weedy grass. Several young people were standing in the shade, but Louisa was drawn to a thin, young woman who held a baby.

Adam introduced them. "Louisa, this is Ella May Robideau. Ella May, Louisa is the school teacher at Mueller school."

"What a cute baby," Louisa said to Mrs. Robideau. My gosh, he's little! "When was he born?" Louisa set her plate down on the blanket and folded the little knit cap back so she could see his face more clearly.

"Two weeks ago." Ella May smiled sweetly and shyly.

"May I hold him? What's his name?"

"Matthew."

"Matthew is just adorable." Louisa looked up desperately at Adam for help as she wondered how this young mother was able to nurse. She's way too thin.

"May we get you a plate of food and some milk?" Louisa asked. Adam saw the anxious look in Louisa's eyes and understood immediately.

"I'll be right back with a plate of food for you," he said over the top of Ella May's "I couldn't possibly impose upon you." But Adam was gone.

When he returned with a huge plate of food and a glass of milk for Ella May, the two women were sitting on the blanket, their backs against the wall with Louisa holding Matthew.

"Burping between nursing helps keep babies from having gas and stomach aches," Louisa calmly explained. "And see how I'm holding my hand under his neck. Matthew's too little to hold his head up. But just you wait; he'll be able to roll over in no time—as long as you get plenty to eat so he'll be strong. I'll hold Matthew while you eat."

Adam studied Louisa. She seemed at ease with a newborn. "Where did you learn so much about babies?" he asked.

"I worked in a hospital nursery with newborns for three months. It was one of my favorite jobs, but it didn't work out in the end."

A softball tossed out by one of the little school boys, who had finished eating, rolled near and Adam lobbed the ball back to them.

"Are you here with someone besides Matthew, Ella May?" Louisa asked.

"Frank is over there by the wagons. He's visiting with his friends," she spoke hesitantly. "He's in the dark shirt."

Louisa could see an older, bearded man uplift a flask to his lips. Golly, how did this sweet young girl end up with him? She looked over at Adam, but he just gnawed away on his chicken leg. Honestly, can't he see there's a problem here?

"Adam, do you know Frank?" Louisa asked.

"Oh, yeah, you folks lease the Larson section, don't you?"

"Yes, Frank's a hard worker," Ella May responded. She wasn't going to reveal much. She reached out to take Matthew back from Louisa.

"Are you new here?" Louisa asked.

"A while back." Ella May had closed down. Louisa sighed and ate her lunch. There's a story here, but I'm not going to hear it today.

The afternoon passed quickly. Adam played first base for Valley Creek. Karl was in the field for them. Frank Robideau played for Wheat Basin. In general, the Valley Creek players were bigger and stronger. Louisa learned that many of the Wheat Basin young men were clerks or garage mechanics. They didn't have the brawn of the farm boys from Valley Creek. The young men from the farms and ranches are much stronger and better looking, Louisa thought. Especially, Adam. I love that body, God forgive me. Valley Creek won. They almost always won. But it didn't matter. Everyone loved the game. It was a great day. And the Muellers were home in time for the evening milking.

That next week Louisa was reading to the first and second graders at the Mueller school, when she heard a car on the road. It stopped in front of the school. Louisa opened the school door to see Adam step out of the passenger side.

Louisa asked one of the older students working on their

multiplication tables to read to the early grade students while she went to see what was happening.

A cool, dusty, fall wind hit her as she stepped outside. She reached back in the entryway to the peg where her shawl hung. With the shawl wrapped around her shoulders, she walked down the path to meet Adam.

"Hello, Louisa," he said with a smile in his eyes as he greeted her. Then Adam turned serious. "Last night my uncle died in California and my folks have asked me to go to Los Angeles to help Aunt Margaret, my mom's sister. I'll work in the automobile shop until my aunt can figure out what to do. My dad is taking me in to Columbus to catch the train."

Louisa's shoulders sank in dismay as her stomach turned over. She looked at the clouds floating high above his head trying to steady herself. She took a deep breath and replied, "I'm sorry for your family." She realized she was going to miss him. It had been fun to be with him over the weekend.

He was quiet, his clear blue eyes studying her. Her heart beat hard and fast. He'll be gone! She may never see him again. Louisa reached out toward him, raising her hands from her side, opening them in a questioning gesture. Adam put his arm around her shoulders to protect her from the wind and drew her closer. She felt an electric current run up her arm. Feeling unbalanced, she leaned onto his chest. Sandy grit got into her eyes and she started blinking. Louisa closed her eyes for a brief moment. Oh dear, I need to get some composure.

"Louisa, we barely know each other. We just met, but I feel close to you." His words went to the core of her being. He paused, looking at her. He swallowed. He was looking for a sign, a signal. Louisa nodded. I feel a close connection to you, too, Adam. But I cannot say it. Adam reached into his jean pocket.

"Louisa, I wanted to give you something to remember me while

I'm gone." He opened a small box and inside was a cameo, a lovely Grecian woman in white profile embedded in an amber oval. "It's a special necklace that my mother's sister, Aunt Corena, owned. She taught school here, too, before she died in the flu epidemic in 1919. My mom gave it to me to give to you. I want you to wear it to remember me." Louisa was amazed. Mary liked her enough to give her son an heirloom to give to her?

"I'm hoping you'll wear it as a promise that you won't marry someone else before I return and we can get better acquainted."

Louisa's dark brown eyes filled with tears. He's very sweet, quaint and proper. It's like a fairy tale. Adam is a prince. He's good. But I'm so, so, so not like him. I can't make this kind of promise, can I? I don't want to be a farmer's wife! I want to do something with my life. But can I pass up Adam's proposal? Not a marriage proposal but a deep friendship promise. Is this feeling I'm feeling. . . love?

She blinked her eyes to stave off the tears. Then she looked into those questioning, deep blue eyes and felt herself sinking into them.

"Oh, Adam, I may never marry. I'm not sure I'm the marrying type. There's so much I want to experience." She had found her ground. "I can promise you that I will not marry before you return, but I may not be the one for you. I don't want to mislead you."

Adam relaxed and smiled broadly. "Louisa, that's good enough for me. Please wear the cameo to remember me. I'll write to you when I get to California. Have a good time while I'm gone. Go to dances. Enjoy life. But if you have any inclination of marrying someone else, you'll write and tell me, won't you? I'll be back in half a second to persuade you otherwise."

Louisa laughed at that pronouncement. "Adam, I won't marry before you see me again." They looked into each other's eyes, sealing the promise. He drew her gently to his chest and kissed her. An electric tingle went through her whole body. Yes, this is what love feels like.

Stepping back, Adam pressed the box with the cameo necklace into her left hand and then took her right hand in his and kissed it. Like a knight in shining armor. Where did this farm boy learn courtly manners?

"Take care of yourself, Louisa," he said softly. "You mean a lot to me." Then Adam abruptly turned and walked to the car with his easy, lanky stride. Before he stepped into the passenger side, he gave her a little salute.

Louise stood stunned, feeling the grit of wind and sand. Clutching the little box to her bosom, she raised her hand to wave a slow good-bye. It was hard to breathe. She watched as the car turned around and went down the road until it disappeared into a dot. He's a terrific person. But is he the prince?

Hungering for the Beautiful and Good
MOORE, MAY 26-27, 1933

*It seems to me we can never give up longing and
wishing while we are thoroughly alive. There are
certain things we believe to be beautiful and good, and
we must hunger after them.*

GEORGE ELIOT (1819-1880) ENGLAND

Helen ran the comb through Louisa's hair and admired the bounce
of the waves. She fluffed up the ends of the silky brown curls
and gently pushed a hairpin to hold the hair back from her face and
up from her neck. The scar below Louisa's ear momentarily shocked
Helen. She removed the hairpin letting a wave fall back around Louisa's cheek bone and ear, covering the marred skin.

"You're lucky to have such beautiful hair," Helen told her sister.

"Thanks." Always enjoying a compliment, Louisa looked up from
the magazine she was leafing through and smiled at her sister. I'm not
telling Helen that Mable and I tried one of those heated permanent
wave machines last week in Billings. Helen might not approve. She's
frugal with her money. Guess she has to be.

Helen placed the ring of flowers with the veil attached onto Louisa's forehead and then put two hairpins on each side of her head to
hold the simple hairpiece in place letting the waves of Louisa's hair
curve down her neck.

"It'll never stay put if there's wind," Louisa worried.

"Just keep your hand on it until you get into the church," Helen advised as she put a couple more hairpins into the flower ring. Louisa turned in her chair and looked at her sister.

"Oh, Helen, what am I doing? All of this fuss just for a honeymoon trip to Chicago."

Helen laughed. "It's a lot more than that, Silly! You're getting married! You know you love Adam. He's handsome, smart, and a hard worker. Comes from a great family. What more could you want? He's a great catch."

"Well, money would be handy. Look at the picture of this wedding in D.C., Helen. Look at the baby roses, dozens in the bridal bouquet. I adore the hat the maid of honor is wearing with its cute little brim and feather in the side. Don't you love the way she has it tilted down over one eye? Wouldn't you like to wear something smart like that? And look at the yards of silk in both dresses with all the flounces and that long train. Men in white pants, and black and white dress shoes. What I wouldn't give for a wedding like that!"

Helen sighed thinking how Louisa always wanted something more, something grand. Helen leaned over Louisa to finger the cameo necklace on the gold chain that hung around Louisa's neck.

"What could be finer than a gift of love like this one that Adam gave you. You know what love is. More than lace and baby roses. Have you forgotten how important the bond of marriage is?"

Louisa raised her eyebrow and turned ever so slightly away from her sister. A marriage should be financially stable, she worried. It took me three years to save $100 from teaching and Adam spent his savings going to Detroit to work in an auto factory to get a new car after his year in California. A honeymoon to Chicago and then we're broke. Is this a good way to start a marriage?

Helen studied her sister's profile as Louisa looked again at the photograph of the marvelous wedding couple and their attendants. Helen tried again. "You could have had a wedding like that. You and

Adam have chosen to go to the World's Fair instead." Louisa nodded in agreement.

Louisa remembered how much fun she and Mable had driving Richard's car out to see Irene and her family in Washington. What a terrific experience seeing Glacier Park and crossing the Rockies. I love to travel and see new sights. I want to see Chicago! Traveling with Adam is one of the reasons I decided to marry him. He wants to see the world as much as I do. I hate to give up teaching, but I also don't want to be an old-maid school teacher the rest of my life. Choices! A career or marriage. Can't have both.

Helen continued. "Besides, a wedding like that in your magazine wouldn't fit here."

Louisa laughed at Helen's remark. "Of course, you're right. Can you imagine fancy clothes in Moore? We'd be the laughing stock of the county." Still, I'd love to walk down that aisle with a flowing gown as queen of the Universe. Isn't that what a wedding is all about? Being a gorgeous creature, something so beautiful you're out of this world? A grand lady! Instead I'm a country schoolteacher marrying a farmer. Louisa closed the magazine with a sigh. I'm so confused at times. I don't know what I want.

As if reading Louisa's thoughts, Helen said, "You're a beautiful bride, Louisa, and lucky to marry Adam." Helen glanced at the clock by their parents' bed and stood up.

"Do you have Papa's Bible and Mama's handkerchief for the wedding ceremony?" Helen hovered nervously over Louisa knowing it was time to go to the church.

Louisa was not to be rushed. Am I doing the right thing? Louisa asked herself one more time. What do I want from life? Travel, yes. A good marriage, but golly, not to be stuck out on the prairie. I'm scared to death of having babies out there. And enough money not to worry! Crops were good last year, Adam was able to save money working for his father and he assured me we have enough to get married and go to Chicago. But what about this summer and the next? It doesn't always rain at the right time in Montana. I wish I didn't love Adam so much. Love clouds my mind! I can't think straight. Am I falling into a hole I can't get out of? Am I going to end up like every other woman I know? I want to be special, not just a housewife.

Louisa picked up her father's Bible which was on the stand beside her parent's bed. "Yes, I have the wedding things right here." The Bible fell open naturally to the center page where all the births and marriages were recorded.

"Look, Helen, Papa already wrote in 'Adam Martin' and today's date by my name and birthdate." Louisa turned and looked with wide eyes at her sister. "It's written in INK!"

Helen looked over Louisa's shoulder. She saw her own name a few lines above Louisa with her husband's name, Hank Elliot. "I'm glad he's recording everything."

"But we were planning on getting married yesterday on Adam's birthday! Papa was so sure we would do what he wanted and get married today!"

"Today's better, Louisa. It was easier for everyone to come on Saturday." Helen tried to get her sister focused on something else. "It was exciting this morning to greet Senator and Mrs. Mueller and your future in-laws, the Martins. Golly, I like Adam's mom a lot! She's very gracious."

"Yes, Mary's kind, and like Mama helping you having babies, she'll help me. Were you scared. . . having babies?" Louisa asked hesitantly.

"It's been easy for me. With Hank at the grocery store, I know everyone in Moore! They help me." Helen doesn't understand, Louisa thought. Having a baby is not a community event. Or is it?

A car horn tooted. Helen looked out the small window. "Oh, there's Karl in Senator Mueller's car to pick us up. Let's see if

Mama is finished with the table and we'll ride over to the Methodist Church together."

"We could walk." I could clear my mind, Louisa thought.

"Not on your wedding day! A bride needs to arrive in style! I really like Karl. Do you think we could get Victoria matched up with Karl?"

Louisa laughed at her sister as they headed down the stairs. "You can be the family matchmaker!"

As the sisters came downstairs, Catherine straightened from arranging her best silverware and linen napkins on the dining room table for the reception following the wedding. She hoped her table setting looked good. Senator Mueller will be here! These families with their large ranches are wealthy. I hope I won't be embarrassing Louisa. The adults can eat in the house but the children have to eat outside on the board set up on two sawhorses. It's the best we can do.

Catherine smiled at her two beautiful daughters. This one I worry about, she thought as Louisa stopped in front of her. Will she be able to settle down and be a good wife? She's always starting some new adventure, jumping from one thing to another. But smart and capable, passionate and loving. What's to become of her? Will she find a life full of meaning, a place where she feels she belongs?

"Are you ready to go, Mama?" Louisa asked.

"Yes, yes. I've been waiting a long time for your wedding day. I'm ready." Louisa put her hand on her mother's wrinkled cheek, an unfamiliar loving touch between them, wanting to say but not saying it, Mama, why did we always have to work, work, work, and never discuss what's really important? How I wish you could have loved me more, given me more guidance, and had more time just to be with me. Instead it was "Listen to Papa," "Don't ask questions" or "You think too much."

Catherine squeezed her daughter's elbows in her hands and shut her eyes. It hurt to look into Louisa's intense brown eyes. She was thinking, how I would like to make life easier for this child who is

116

curious and wanting so much out of life. But she's a grown woman now and will have to live with her own decisions. I pray she'll not run into trouble. Catherine patted Louisa's arm and then took off her bib apron and hung it on the back of the pantry door.

"Are you ready for the big adventure, ladies?" Karl called from the doorway. Louisa looked with relief at her young friend. Golly, he's become a man since I first met him. Helen's right, he'd be a great catch for Victoria!

"Is anyone ever ready for a wedding?" Louisa replied rhetorically as she slipped her hand into Karl's elbow. They had had many good times together, going to the country dances when Adam was gone and discussing the legislative events at the dinner table when Senator Mueller represented them in Helena. They were good friends.

"I'm really happy you're standing up for Adam," she said to him.

"Yep, he needs a strong arm like me to lean on, doesn't he?" Karl teased Louisa. "And Adam knew I was the only one who could get you to church and down the aisle."

Louisa drew back and regarded him quizzically. Does Karl sense all my misgivings? Or is Adam having doubts, too? Karl patted her arm reassuringly.

When they drove up to the church, Adam's Model A was parked directly in front, already bedecked with a sign, "Just Married," on the back and cans tied to the rear bumper. Louisa's stomach clenched in fear and excitement. Papa stood solidly on the cement walk with his back straight waiting for them in his black suit, vest, and tie. Karl helped Louisa down from the car and Papa helped Catherine.

Cecilia came down the church stairs with an armful of purple and white lilacs with a few pussy willow branches tucked into them. In the center were wild yellow roses. The bouquet was tied with a long, wide purple ribbon, with streamers halfway to the ground. Raymond followed behind his mom carrying a basket of corsages.

"Oh, Ceci, they're beautiful!" Louisa exclaimed as Cecilia handed the flowers to her. Cecilia pulled a hanky from her pocket and dabbed away the tears coming from Louisa's eyes. Louisa was thinking, this is better than those baby roses in the photo.

"My friend, nothing's too fine for you. I'm happy for you."

"My goodness, Raymond, you've grown a foot since I last saw you," Louisa said to her nephew. Raymond grinned revealing a couple missing teeth, happy to be noticed by the main focus of this event. He wrapped his arms around her knees.

Cecilia took a yellow tulip bedded in green ferns from the basket Raymond had set down and pinned the corsage on Catherine. There were more: a similar tulip corsage for Helen and two smaller boutonnieres of Lily of the Valley for Karl and Alois. Cecilia and Raymond then ran up the church stairs. At the top of the stairs, Raymond turned and waved at Louisa. She waved back, thinking, Raymond's such a sweet child. Maybe I'll have a little boy like him.

"Mrs. Janochek," Karl asked politely of Catherine, "May I escort you into the church and to your seat? I'll stay in front to stand with Adam. When Mrs. Janochek is settled, Helen, you walk slowly down the aisle and stand to the left of the pastor. And then Mr. Janochek, you'll be escorting beautiful, beautiful Louisa down the aisle." Karl looked at Louisa's red face and blinking eyes. "That is, when Louisa can see well enough to manage to walk."

Louisa was amused at Karl's authoritative manner, but also alarmed at how quickly everything was happening. I'm not ready. Oh, please, give me time to think. She turned her face toward the sun and wind and blinked away tears of joy and tears of concern for herself, her family, and the world. Oh God, please be with us. Time had stopped. This moment was crystallized. Louisa swayed slightly, feeling dizzy. Am I going to faint? Through a haze, Karl moved away with her mother. This is the end of existence, as I know it.

118

"Louisa, would you like me to carry Papa's Bible? You have your hands full with the bouquet." Helen is here! Louisa looked down. She could barely see the big, black Bible through the purple and white flowers. Louisa took a deep breath of the lovely lilac perfume. I'll be alright. Helen will make sure everything goes well. She nodded her head in assent. Helen stood in front of her and waited until Louisa looked into her eyes.

"Adam is a fine man, Louisa. You're doing the right thing." Then Helen gently lifted the veil from the back and brought it down over Louisa's face. Louisa could still see Helen's sweet smile through the netting. Helen took the Bible and Louisa found she could hold her mother's lace handkerchief with the bouquet nestled into the crook of her left arm. She reached with her right for her father's arm. In the new heels which she loved, Papa was only an inch taller. He twisted his head down and to the side to look at her. His mustached lip curled into a broad grin. He patted her hand resting in his left elbow.

"You've grown into a beautiful lady, my little namesake," Alois Janochek whispered. Louisa could hear the organ strains as they solemnly walked up the stairs. Is it Bach? Maybe "Abide With Me?" I love that melody.

Then the music stopped. The eight rows of people, her friends and relatives, stood and turned to look at her. Louisa wished she could sink through the floor. She looked frantically at the front of the church, seeing first the minister in his white robe, now holding Papa's Bible. Helen was beside the minister. Cecilia had placed big branches of purple lilacs on each side of the altar. The organist started Wagner's "Here Comes the Bride." Papa started forward. Louisa gripped his arm tightly, holding him back, afraid to move, unable to breathe.

All at once, to the right of the pastor, she saw Adam, his crooked grin as big as the sky, his blonde hair slicked back from his white brow marked with a red band where he was suntanned below, the brand of a working man. Seeing Adam, her fears fled and beneath her veil her face lit up with a huge smile. Why do I love this funny looking rancher? Standing a little taller and a little straighter, she took a deep breath smelling the lovely lilacs and with her eyes on Adam, she began walking slowly down the aisle, very stately, one foot with its new shoe with a strap across her ankle, and then the next step. Slowly, regally. Today, Jsem pani mama, truly. All is well.

Half an hour later, now united and together, Louisa and Adam joyfully walked down the same church stairs Louisa had recently climbed in trepidation. Their family and friends showered them with rice and wishes of good fortune. Louisa paused before the open door of Adam's Model A and looked back at her unmarried friend, Mable, and her younger sister, Victoria.

"Who will catch my bouquet? Who'll be the next bride?" Quickly, the group divided with all the unwed women, even the little girls, all on one side of the church steps. Louisa turned her back to them and threw the lilacs up over her head. She heard squeals and laughter before she turned to see that Victoria had caught the bouquet. Louisa couldn't help but glance over at Karl on the other side of the steps with the men and married women. He was laughing, but Louisa could see he was studying Victoria.

Another hour of laughter, talk, and congratulations at the house with Mama's sandwiches, kolaches, and cake, tea for the women and Papa's homemade beer for the men, and then they were down the road in Adam's roadster, with cans clanging behind them.

Their first night Adam had arranged for them to stay at Harlowton's Graves Hotel bridal suite with its round turret facing the Musselshell River with cottonwoods lining the banks, a view he thought might please Louisa on her first morning as a wedded woman. It was dusk when Adam pulled up to the entrance of the hotel. He took Louisa's arm to help her as she stepped from the auto still dressed in her lovely lace wedding gown. Then he removed their suitcases from the back. Several people who had been enjoying the quiet evening on the hotel porch were curious when they heard the clanging cans from the car and they had walked around to the hotel entry to discover the wedding couple. One man said, "congratulations," and a woman called out, "good wishes to you." Louisa, slightly embarrassed smiled demurely, while Adam good-naturedly replied, "Nothing better than an evening in May in Montana." He nodded at them as the two of them swept past the small group.

Adam led her to the lobby desk and kept one arm around her as he signed the registration book and picked up their key. Louisa led the way a bit self-consciously up the narrow stairwell to the sitting area on the third floor. Then Adam stepped out to the corner room door and opened it. He set their bags inside the door and turned to pick Louisa up. She gave a gasp. "What are you doing?" and then she laughed as he carried her across the threshold. Adam made a couple circles inside the room, swinging her around in his arms. Slowly he eased her to the floor and kissed her long and hard.

Adam reached back and shut the door. "Welcome to our first abode, Louisa." Then he took off her hat and kissed her hairline at each of her temples. Louisa swallowed hard as he unbuttoned her wedding gown, letting it fall to the floor. Why am I scared? Will this hurt? Will I be able to do whatever I am supposed to do? Does Adam know what to do? Adam kissed the bones at her neck and continued kissing down to the crevice of her bosom as he unhooked her new satin brassiere. Oh, my. Louisa was tingling all over. Wanting more of his musky smell, she started unbuttoning his shirt and kissing his neck and chest.

Adam pulled back the covers and lifted her to the bed. She felt on fire, throbbing in every cell of her body. Her mind alternated from fog to bright, brilliant colored lights. Electric sensations whirled around her as Adam touched her. Time stopped. Explosions with lightning went off in her head. Then time turned slowly, into warm, soft velvet. Heavenly. Louisa cuddled into his outstretched arm and fell asleep more soundly than she had slept in weeks. She'd never felt such peace and well-being.

When she woke, slowly opening her eyes, the sun shone into the room. Sitting in his shorts, Adam was reading a newspaper by the window. He heard her move and smiled at her as he set the paper down. She stretched, wincing a bit at a new, dull pain, and then she relaxed and smiled at him. Why had I worried?

"Would you like a bath? I went downstairs and got a couple buckets of hot water," he said.

"You went downstairs in your shorts?"

"No, silly. I wear clothes in public." Louisa laughed. How fine it is to lie in bed naked with her husband nearby. All's right in the world.

"How about bathing together?" she asked shyly.

"Even a better idea," he responded.

They bathed and dressed, and soon were ready to go downstairs to have breakfast before starting on their journey east. Adam picked up the bags and opened the door waiting for her.

"Go ahead, Adam. I'll be right down." Louisa turned to imprint the memory of the night. Now, sunlight streamed into their room and across the crumpled sheets. She wanted a tangible remembrance from this first night together. Taking out her manicuring scissors from her purse, she cut a corner from the bedsheet. Maybe the management won't even notice the tear. Oh, of course, they'll notice, but they'll forgive me knowing it was our wedding night. After holding the scrap of material to her cheek and feeling its smoothness, she folded it and put it into her purse.

Louisa and Adam Martin were "hitched." Bouncing across the ruts of the dirt roads of North Dakota and Minnesota on Highway 10, they felt lucky when they found gas for 16 cents a gallon, because often it was as high as 20 cents a gallon. Louisa had packed apples, cheese, and bread, and they had a gallon jug of drinking water they would periodically replenish. They bought groceries along the way. A couple times, they stopped mid-morning for a cooked breakfast at a roadside cafe. Adam didn't waste much time, though, in order to make 350 to 400 miles a day.

In the evenings, they'd find a tourist shack to rent for $1 and pull out their sheets and blankets from the car to lay over the mattress and springs. Usually the room included a bucket of water and a basin to wash off the dust. Out back there was a privy with lime in a bucket to toss into the hole to keep down the smell and the flies.

The flat plateau of the Dakotas surprised Louisa. She expected all the plains to have rolling hills with coulees and rims like eastern Montana. Probably easier to farm here, she thought. The fields are straighter and flatter with fewer complications for running equipment across them. Maybe boring, though! I like looking at the mountains in the distance from Adam's ranch.

"Stop!" she shouted at Adam when they got to the edge of the Missouri River.

"What's wrong?" Before he crossed the bridge, Adam pulled to the side of the road.

"It's so wide. So big. Is it safe to cross?"

"Of course," he assured her. "Hundreds of people cross it every day."

"I just didn't imagine that the Missouri would be this big."

Adam leaned back silently laughing at his funny bride. "You're a stitch. Of course it's big. Lots of water is running into the Missouri from the Yellowstone, the Musselshell, and the Milk. I can hardly wait for you to see Lake Michigan. It's like looking at the ocean."

Louisa considered the strength of the bridge and the distance from the bridge to the water. Finally, she nodded at him. "You can go across, but I'm glad I know how to swim in case anything happens."

The terrain east of the river seemed different. The land became greener. As they traveled into Minnesota, there were more trees, small lakes, and more farms marked with fences and barns. Lots of dairy cows. The beauty of Wisconsin with its hills and pine forests reminded her a bit of western Montana. And of course, all along the way now, there were towns and many more people.

The entrance to Chicago excited her, filled with noise and dust. Houses were crowded together without trees. The skyscrapers seemed taller than she had imagined. And people covered the sidewalks.

Louisa was startled when she saw so many black people. She wondered why there were so few in Montana or even in Spokane when she was there. How strange. She remembered a dance band member in the hotel in Great Falls who was black and one who worked at the Billings train depot. But this was different. Some are, well some are really, really black, like. . . a black, shiny stone. And their hair is frizzy. How do they comb it? It's not at all like the Indians or the Mexicans with their black, straight hair. Do mother's braid the girls' hair because there's no way to comb it?

I wonder how I could meet them and talk to them. If they'd talk to me. Are they like me? Of course, they're not like me; they've had a totally different life. But maybe in some ways we're alike. I'm supposedly educated, a teacher. I'm 24 years old. And I've never talked to a black person. I have a lot to learn. Louisa had never felt so much out of touch with the people of the world.

The Chicago Fair was a dollar a day to get in and 50 cents for some of the exhibits. There was so much to see; it was hard to know where to go. Even Montana had a display and of course they had to see it. The Outdoor Life Exposition had a diorama displaying the Beartooth Mountains from Fred Inabnit, who had climbed 50 peaks. "Just imagine him climbing all those peaks," Louisa exclaimed. "It would make me dizzy, plus worn out!" But secretly, she'd like to try hiking. "Adam, do you think we could go camping or hiking in the Beartooths sometime?"

Surprised by her interest, he quietly answered, "We'll see." Exerting himself against a mountain didn't seem like much fun to him after a day of milking, plowing fields, threshing grain, or stacking hay.

On their first night at the Fair they rode the midway rides. Louisa's favorite experience that night was riding the aerial tram, called the Sky Ride, across the fairground with electric lights shining below. The view was spectacular! Being above everything took her breath away.

At the end of that first day, Louisa asked, "Adam, I'd really like to see Sally Rand, the fan dancer. Do you think we could get tickets?"

"Louisa, you amaze me. Sally Rand is a burlesque dancer. She was arrested for riding nude on a white horse in the parade at the opening of the Fair." Adam took a good look at this woman beside him that he'd married. Why in the world does she want to see Sally Rand? Not that it wouldn't be a good show! I'd enjoy it, but what kind of woman would want to see a naked woman on stage?

"No, Adam, she gave the illusion of being nude. She wasn't nude. That's her trick. Besides, are you afraid of seeing a nude woman?" she teased.

"Of course not, but why do you want to see a nude woman?"

"Adam, she's very famous. This is not your usual dancer. She's talented. Sally Rand uses fans to create illusions. She's not like Mae West who only has sex on her mind. I think it'd be fascinating to see Sally Rand who is an artist and one of the main attractions at the fair. I don't want us to miss it."

"Sally Rand is not really an appropriate entertainment for you to see," Adam stated emphatically.

"But people love her, Adam. The authorities for the Fair gave her the Lincoln log cabin for her dressing room. Do you think the state of Illinois would do that for just a scamp, give her the Abraham Lincoln log cabin?" Louisa's voice rose hysterically at the end of her statement.

After a moment, not wanting a fight with his bride, Adam sighed, "Okay," but he wondered how many more arguments he'd lose in this marriage. I might as well get used to it. "Here's the deal. I'll get us tickets to see Sally Rand, but we're also going to the stockyards before we leave town." He needed to be firm with this new wife of his.

"Yes, of course, we'll see the stockyards. I saw they have a tour we could take." After a moment's pause, she added, "And how about an afternoon at the Art Institute? They say the building and the art are wonderful. I hear they have a couple of Picassos on loan. I can't image what they look like. I've read critiques about his style. Some critics think he's a terrible artist."

Adam hadn't heard of Picasso and wasn't that interested in art. But he was attracted to her curiosity and unusual passions. He knew he'd have to expand his interests to keep up with her. And to keep her from doing anything too foolish. What a week: a nude on a horse, the cattle stockyards, and a crazy modern artist. "We'll do it all, Louisa."

Occasionally, the smells and the noise of the Fair made Louisa nauseous. Adam would find cold water to drink and a bench in the shade for them to rest. And then they were off again. When they went to an exhibit on new hospital innovations, Louisa saw incubators holding real babies and she literally became faint. It's just not right to keep babies in a machine and not hold them, she thought. Still, if the machine can help save a life, it's an important invention.

There was a lot for them to see in Chicago with strange architectures, music, food, new automobiles, a wild animal zoo, and displays from all over the world. Their heads were buzzing.

"Adam, this is the most exciting week I've ever had in my life. I'm really happy we came to Chicago. I'll remember the 1933 World's Fair celebrating 100 years of Illinois statehood all my life no matter what other adventures come our way." Louisa was totally content. Adam was deeply pleased that he had been able to bring her such joy. It was a great beginning to a good and beautiful life together.

To Be a Mother

WIIG'S COULEE, STILLWATER COUNTY, SEPTEMBER 1934

No woman can call herself free until she can choose consciously whether she will or will not be a mother.

MARGARET SANGER (1879-1966)

Louisa ponderously climbed the narrow path of the coulee, a pail of water in each hand. The hot westerly wind from the afternoon sun ground dirt into her back, wet from her sweat from the effort of getting up the hill. Heavy with child, she set the water buckets down on a slab of shale, a level spot at the top of the ridge. She slowly straightened, rubbing her back, and turned to look at the view. Gazing across the fields, she saw the elevators at Wheat Basin where she first met Adam at the dance. A hundred miles further to the north, the Snowies where Charles had made his sexual advance were barely visible with wisps of clouds covering the peaks. She put her fists into her lower back and rolled her shoulders up and back. A spasm of pain ran down her spine. She cupped her hands around the bottom of her belly, gently rubbing and lifting the round form.

What have I gotten myself into? Getting married at Moore last year and then driving out to the Chicago's World Fair for our honeymoon was exciting and educational. But this? Living in a tiny shed with no running water? Hauling water by hand from the spring? Cooking, cleaning. Not what I envisioned for my life. Why did I marry? And now, a baby! Her top teeth slowly gnawed at her lower lip which was chapped. I hope I don't give birth out here. I hope we can make it into the hospital in time for delivery. But who knows?

The hot, dry wind sucked out all her moisture leaving her skin feeling like parched leather and her lips cracked. In the cleft of the small hill ranging east to west, she could see a small stretch of Lake Basin. She dipped her hand into the bucket and brought cool water to her lips and then rubbed the water up her cheeks.

Once I was beautiful. Then her heart thudded. But sinful. Guilt from the past swept over her: putting Joe into prison, not speaking out about Charles assaulting her to prevent him from possibly assaulting others, and not helping Isabella more when she had the measles. Is this my penance for my sins? Living a year in isolation? Last year it seemed like a romantic, exotic, cozy cottage with a great view. How I hate this exiled existence. Will we ever be able to get ahead and get out of here? Feeling weak, she tried breathing deeply before putting her head down between her knees.

Gaining a bit of energy, she picked up the buckets and carried the water to the unpainted wooden rectangular structure, their home. Previously, it had been a shelter for equipment for the men working in the oil field, but it became abandoned after the oil wells were drilled and local maintenance for them was no longer needed. The narrow building was all one room with a dirt floor, one small window, and no electricity or running water. The Muellers let them stay, rent-free. Why can't I appreciate the gift? She collapsed onto the bench in the shade on the north side.

Adam will be angry with me if he knows I went down to the spring for more water. He makes sure I have water every day. He's a good man. Solid. But he didn't see the need for me to wash all the baby's clothes and blanket. Hand-me-downs. Of course, I had to boil them in hot water and make sure they had no germs. She looked at the tiny garments on the clothesline. A small warm spot grew in the center of her being. I love children. Maybe having my own child will lift my spirits, give me purpose, and renew my life when I give life to another.

Taking another deep breath, Louisa stood and gathered in the garments from the clothesline. When she started to step into the house, she saw Agnes, Ella May and her children at the bottom of the hill walking toward her. Louisa went inside and quickly folded the clothes, putting them into the bottom drawer of their single dresser. Then she went outside and down the hill to meet her guests, giving each of the two women a little hug.

"Agnes, thank you for checking on me. It's good to see you, Ella May. And look at Matthew. I remember first seeing him as a newborn. And now! Matthew, you're getting strong and tall," Louisa said to the little boy.

"I'm this big," he said raising his hands above his head. "And I'm . . . ." He held up four fingers.

"Four. What a great age! And how are you doing with your little sister?" Louisa lifted Sally's bonnet to see her face more clearly. Her cheeks were pale and had mud streaks. "Have you been playing together?" The little girl nodded her head, but Matthew just stared at Louisa with his big brown eyes. He was delighted an adult was talking to him, wanting to hear his thoughts. Words wouldn't come to him.

"He's on his own most the time," Ella May answered for them.

Together they walked the few yards to the house and sat on the bench outside. Agnes, a Cheyenne, had married one of the homesteaders. They met at his training base in Oklahoma and moved to Montana after the War to End All Wars.

"I brought you pemmican, Louisa. Healthy for you and the baby." Agnes handed Louisa a small bucket. "Have a spoonful every night at supper." On top of the bucket lid, a couple small cloth bags rested.

"There's tea for you to use later. The red bag is partridge berry leaves to help speed up the birthing process. The other is wild blackcherry tea. It helps with pain."

"How thoughtful." Louisa's eyes filled with tears. She cares. She understands. Agnes patted her arm slowly, gently. Louisa squeezed her eyes to remove the beginning of teardrops and looked away at the blue sky with just a whisp of white.

"Agnes gave me some and everything went better with Sally," Ella May said quietly. After a brief silence, she added softly, "I'm pregnant agin."

Louisa's heart sank as she turned to Ella May and took her hand. Way too thin, Ella May's hair was stringy and her skin was burnt brown from the sun, dry, and cracked. She'd lost a tooth. Pregnancies were taking their toll on her. Louisa couldn't find joy in this announcement.

"I tried everythin' to keep from gettin' pregnant agin," Ella May continued lowering her head. "Jumpin' off ladders, hot baths, gallopin' on the horse. Wouldn't be so bad 'cept money is scarce and it's hard to keep kids fed and clothed."

"My sister gave me some baby clothes and I'll pass them on to you, Ella May," Louisa said.

"I'm glad my boys are grown." Agnes squinted, looking out at the vast prairie. "Been hard living up here?" She turned and looked at Louisa.

"No, no. I'm fine. . . fine. Just lonely, I guess."

"Do you feel the Spirits?" Agnes asked.

"Spirits?" Louisa was curious.

"This is Crow campground, good look-out for enemies, spring water in the coulee, good grass on the hillside for the horses." My word, how could I have missed this obvious history, Louisa thought. What I've been hating and complaining about is sacred ground. "Still the wind can get to you," Agnes commiserated.

"Wind drives me crazy." Ella May said. "That, and the work, trying to get enough food on the table. And the lack of company."

"It can be bad," Louisa agreed. "I'm glad you could come see me. I shouldn't complain. Adam's mom, comes every few days. I wish we had a telephone up here, but Mrs. Olson watches from the hill. I'm to hang out a white sheet if I have trouble and she'll call the Martins." Honestly, Louisa thought to herself, do you suppose Mrs. Olson looks out our way more than once a day? What if something did happen? I can't believe there'd be a quick response. Just a long wait while I bled all over.

"Well, it's your first. And...." Agnes started to say Louisa was old for her first pregnancy, but instead, she changed, "and there's always doubt about the first. You'll do fine. You're healthy and strong."

Oh, yeah, I'm probably strong enough, but why did I get myself into this predicament in the first place? Will I end up looking like Ella May? Sounding like Ella May? Desperate, jumping off ladders to prevent getting pregnant again?

Matthew threw rocks down the hill, but Sally clung to Ella May's knees. "How are the crops your way, Ella May?" Louisa asked.

"Frank's working with the thrashing crew. It don't appear to be a good year. Low yield. Too many grasshoppers." Louisa sighed. Not a good year. Is there ever a really good year?

"It's difficult all right." Louisa gave Ella May's hand a little squeeze. Then Louisa rubbed Sally's back. Louisa really liked Ella May. I wish I could help her, support her in some fashion. Frank was working for others, while Adam was working with his family and had a chance someday to get a place of his own. But Frank and Ella May? With few resources, it'll be hard for them to build any assets.

The women couldn't stay long. "Wait a minute," Louisa said and she went inside to put a few potatoes, onions, and carrots in an old flour bag for Ella May. "We have extra," Louisa said. The women then headed down the hill with Matthew trailing behind. Ella May was catching a ride home with a neighbor living near them who was working on the Mueller place.

Louisa sighed as she watched them walk away and then went inside to get supper on the table for her hungry working man. Louisa pulled the bones from a stewed rabbit and added carrots, onions and potatoes. She put kindling into the sheepherder's stove and got it lit before adding a couple bigger chunks of wood. While the pot of stew heated up, Louisa stepped out and scattered corn for the chickens that Louisa's folks had given them.

"Com' bossy, com' bossy." She called for the milk cow grazing in the grass near the runoff from the spring. The cow's bags were stiff with milk. Louisa put on the halter and pegged her, so she was ready for Adam to milk. The cream helped to pay for groceries. The pot of stew simmered while she mixed up the dumplings to put on top.

We're a lot better off than the Robideaus, Louisa pondered. Our home is just a roof over our heads now, really just a shack, but we're saving the money Adam is earning and we'll be able to buy something someday. Having your own land makes all the difference in the world. And thank God, Adam doesn't drink like Frank. It's a terrible vice. Frank drinks up everything he makes.

The sun was sinking below the west horizon when she saw Adam walking up the road from the east where Dad Martin had left him off. The trail to their home was rutted and washed out from the wagons and trucks bringing in the heavy loads to the oil field in the previous decade. Grass grew on the tops of the ruts. While it was possible to drive up the hill, the road took its toll on the springs and bearings. There was a risk with the possibility of a broken axle or a transmission torn out. Normally, everyone walked the quarter-mile from the main road.

Louisa was happy to see him and stepped out from the house and waved at him. Adam's heart skipped a beat and his step picked up when he saw Louisa's silhouette against the pink and orange horizon. As he reached the top of the hill, he gently tossed his burlap wrapped water jar and two dead rabbits against the house and wrapped his arms around Louisa. Louisa didn't mind his dirty, sweaty shirt and chest rubbing her own sweating, bulging breasts. His kiss was wet and hard.

"How're my lovely lady and our handsome son?" Louisa shook her head and laughed.

"I'm fine, but your son may be a daughter!"

"I'm excited to know. It won't be long."

"Too long for me."

"Well, I have good news. We should finish the winter wheat seeding by the end of the week. The threshing is also almost done. Soon I can take you into Billings."

"That's great news. A relief."

Adam gave her another hug, knowing she worried about when and how to get into the hospital and have a regular doctor for the delivery.

They quickly performed their evening tasks. Adam hung a rabbit he'd shot that day by the neck on the nail driven into a tall post. With a sharp pocketknife, he skinned the rabbits and cut out the entrails. Laying both in a basin, he poured fresh water over the meat.

Adam milked the cow and strained the milk through cheesecloth into a wide-mouthed gallon jug. Putting the jug into a pail, he trotted down the ridge and set the milk into a pool of cold spring water. Then he rinsed the bucket and filled it with water for the house.

Louisa added the dumplings to the top of the rabbit stew. She sliced the bread, set out butter and jam, and filled the water glasses. Soon they were seated by each other at the narrow table set up next to their narrow bed which Adam's brother had given them.

"God, thanks for bread and health. May You strengthen us for the days ahead," Adam quickly prayed. "More rabbits, Louisa. It wouldn't surprise me if we produced a litter of rabbits instead of a baby."

"What a horrible thought! You're not funny, Adam," she said, even though she was laughing. "I'm sick of eating rabbits, although I suppose we should be grateful for the protein."

"It breaks the monotony for me to stop and shoot them as I plow. There's plenty out there to shoot at, but maybe I've gotten carried away. And you really are a versatile cook: stew, fryer, jerky, salad, sandwiches. You could write a rabbit recipe book."

"Not my goal."

"Hey, I have other interesting news. Dad says there's a small farm down on White Beaver Creek near Reed Point that's up for sale. He'll loan us a down payment. Do you think we should look at it, see what they want for it?"

Louisa's heart leaped and her pupils got big. "Tell me more." Could we possibly move off this isolated knoll? Let it be!

"I don't know much. Just a few acres, a small house and shed, trees on a little crick. I don't know if it's fenced or what the soil's like."

Trees and a stream. Wouldn't that be something! In her mind's eye, Louisa was enchanted with the vision of a tree spreading branches over a cute little house. A house, a real house, and not this one-room machine shed. I wonder if it has running water and a separate bedroom, kitchen, and dining room. How wonderful that would be.

"Let's go look at the property on our way into Billings," she suggested. "That is, if the baby isn't demanding more immediate attention and we need to go to the hospital sooner. Do you think we could look at it?"

"I'll make the arrangements, Louisa."

"Oh, Adam, this may be a chance for our own home!" Louisa's dark brown eyes flashed at Adam. Now he'd definitely have to follow through and investigate the White Beaver Creek property! Adam leaned over and kissed his young wife.

"I'll do my best for my beautiful lady."

Life or Death

STILLWATER COUNTY, WINTER 1937-1938

*"Over the river and through the woods to Grandfather's
house we go. The horse knows the way to carry the
sleigh through the white and drifting snow. . .
Hurrah for Thanksgiving Day!"*

LYDIA MARIA CHILD (1802-1880)

As they drove the snow-packed lane, Louisa looked back at the
house on White Beaver Creek where they had been living the
last three years. The huge cottonwoods were now bare and she could
see their small, white-framed home, but in the summer, trees hid the
house from the road. The scruffy bushes along the creek were beautiful
reds and yellows topped by white frosting. The snow sifted across the
frozen ruts, although the Montana sky was blue and clear. The white
prairie sparkled in the sunlight.

Adam sang the Thanksgiving song in his monotone. Louisa didn't
mind. She loved her little family and enjoyed singing the song with
Adam. Roger, their 3 year old, laughed, clapped, and tried to sing along
as he sat between them his head nodding to the tune. Peter's eyes were
wide as he snuggled in his mother's arms, feeling the rise and fall of
Louisa's belly and chest, along with the bounce of the car. Only a month
old, Peter needed little attention as he quietly adjusted to the noise and
movement thrust at him, unlike what his older brother had been at birth.

"Well, we don't have a sleigh and thank goodness the snow isn't
drifting," Adam remarked. The power of the 1935 Ford sedan flowed

through his arms. The black surface of the car gleamed from his polishing. He hoped to trade for a new car every couple years with the upgrades in technology improving all the time. He loved new motorized vehicles.

"And here on the prairie, we don't have woods. Still it's a beautiful fairyland landscape with snow dusting the stubble," Louisa replied, feeling poetic. Then she thought of what lay ahead at her in-laws' house. "I'm really looking forward to seeing your folks. And Victoria and Karl with their new baby. I wonder if Richard and Ceci will make it down from Ross Creek. It was kind of your mother to invite them."

"The more the merrier," he said. "We'll soon find out who Mom invited. I think Eddie and Gina Mueller are both home for the holidays. I used to have a crush on Gina." Adam looked slyly at Louisa teasing her, but she didn't take the bait.

"I'd love to see them again. I liked Gina a lot. I admire her for getting her graduate degrees. But then, she's not married, so she can do that." Louisa paused. Once a woman marries, her life is no longer her own, she thought. Married women are meant to support their husbands. I wonder, though, what happens when a woman has spent so much time getting highly educated like Gina. Will she leave that behind if she marries?

Louisa's mind drifted from Gina to Karl's brother. "I don't know what to make of Eddie. He acts too smooth or, too, too, what can I call it? Maybe too sensual to be a preacher?"

Adam chuckled. "You nailed it. He has a religious notion that the world is meant to be full of love and goodness. He surrounds everyone with warm concern. But I can tell you he had some hard knocks as a kid and knows that everything isn't sunshine. He's more of a poet."

"My missionary brother, Walter, isn't like that at all. More practical, maybe because he studied engineering before being converted to the Church of God? He likes to fix things. Including people. Or do you think it's the difference between Methodists and Church of God?

"It doesn't matter. They're both good men doing good work." Louisa reddened at his slight rebuke and looked out her window. Adam paused talking while the car bounced over icy ruts. "A couple days away from work! That's what I'm thankful for." Adam almost shouted.

"Are you unhappy working at Davy Motors part-time?" Louisa turned back asking with concern.

"Not at all. I'm glad you suggested my working there. I enjoy talking to customers. You know I'm fascinated with the new machinery, the trucks, tractors, and cars. I'm learning more about mechanics. Still it feels good to get off my feet and sit down for these few hours driving out to the ranch and having a holiday."

"Your days are long with the work you do in town, and then feeding animals after you get home." She commiserated with him.

"You're doing a lot more work at home, too, Louisa, but we're saving money. We'll be able to buy a bigger place when the opportunity comes. We already have most of our 160 acres free and clear, even with the Depression."

Louisa nuzzled her nose into Peter's blankets, smelling the sweet baby smell of a one-month old. Then Louisa looked at Roger who had become quiet. The little three-year old had fallen asleep. Louisa fell into daydreaming about the boys and her life.

Roger's bright, always checking things out. Like the time when he was crawling toward the rattlesnake who was hissing at him! Thank goodness I grabbed him back before the rattler struck. Or when he fell into the creek trying to catch a fish in his own hands. If Adam hadn't been there wading into the swift water to pull Roger out, we would've lost him! It's a wonder he's still alive. But I don't want to curb his interest in the world. Roger reminds me of myself when I was little, wanting to try everything. Fortunately, he's a boy and can eventually do more and have an interesting career.

I shouldn't complain. Our house on White Beaver Creek is comfortable, close to the highway and easy to get into town. With a phone, I can communicate with family and neighbors. I'm really happy with our tidy, little place, just big enough for the four of us. A milk cow, a couple dozen cows for producing calves to sell each fall, chickens, and a garden with all the water I need from the creek to irrigate the vegetables. The last three years have been special, with Roger and Peter being born. We're a close and loving family. I couldn't ask for more.

That night for the Thanksgiving evening meal, Mary Martin opened the dining table to seat 12 adults as Eddie and Gina Mueller had made it home and came with Senator and Anna Mueller, Karl and Victoria. Richard and Cecilia had driven down from Ross Creek with their three children. Roger with his cousins, Raymond Janochek and Raymond's two sisters ate at the kitchen table. The two babies were held in the arms of the adults or laid in a nearby crib. The table held turkey, mashed potatoes, dressing, gravy, squash, pickled beets, corn, spiced apple rings, and Louisa's kolaches. Pumpkin pie with whipped cream rested on a kitchen counter ready to be served after the meal. Mary blushed from all the compliments. Or perhaps she was flushed from all the work.

On Friday, the women gathered by the living room stove to knit hats, mittens, and scarves for Christmas gifts. Gina had a new pattern for mittens which a Norwegian friend had shown her, complex, but beautiful. Louisa was determined to figure out the pattern.

The four older children went outside to play in the snow. The Janochek girls made snow angels while the two boys slid down the hill. Roger Martin was crying, trying to keep up with 9 year old Raymond in the deep snow. Karl came to his rescue, carrying him up the incline on his back and holding him on a tractor tire tube as they joined Raymond in sliding down the hill. After a couple times, the snow became packed and Roger pulled his own tube up the hill and rode down happily on his own or with Raymond.

Henry Martin invited the men to the barn to look over a colt that had been born earlier in the fall. After extolling the colt's virtues, they wandered into the attached machine shed which had a small iron pot-bellied stove already lit with wood burning. There, Adam pulled out a couple smooth planks to set up as a table for a game of poker. Henry took out a stash of cigars.

"Here, boys. Let's have a bit of whiskey to ward off the chill." Henry set up glasses on a side board, carefully measuring out the amber liquid for his guests. A good Methodist, Henry made sure drinking was done in moderation.

As they played a round or two of poker they had some good laughs, but out of respect for Eddie, they kept their jokes fairly clean. Then the conversation drifted toward current events.

"Do you think the drought down in Oklahoma is over? They're calling it a Dust Bowl!" Adam asked. "Thank God, we escaped the worst and last year's winter moisture was about normal."

"The grass'll come back. Nature is resilient. This is just part of a normal cycle," his father reassured him. "Some years are good, some aren't so good, no matter where you live."

Richard shook his head sadly, thinking of his own family barely making it year by year on the home place. "It hit a lot of families in the midwest hard. Heard hundreds moved to California."

John Mueller reminded them, "Not so different from what happened here in 1919. Our place is made up of homesteader's allotments, and your place, too, Henry. Lots of people left this area after a couple years of drought. Then with 1919 the worst winter on record and the flu taking so many, it was a tough time."

140

"But times change and we're doing well now," Henry assured them all.

Karl had other things on his mind. "But look what's going on in Russia and what Stalin has been promoting over there. I can't understand how anyone would think that the government should own ranch land. An agricultural collective is no way to run a farm. I can't imagine what it would be like to have women and children working in the fields and with everyone living in one compound. A country needs independent farmers owning their own land, like we do."

Richard agreed. "That's true. It's only by having a debt on your farm that keeps you caring enough for it to spend every minute of your life and every penny you have to keep running it until you die exhausted and broke!" They all laughed.

"Communism doesn't sound that bad to me," Eddie responded. "It's a bit like Jesus Christ asking us to share in the work and the bounties in a peaceable kingdom."

Richard shook his head and chortled, "That might work if people actually cared for each other. Only problem is, that in a place like the U.S.S.R., Stalin is a dictator killing people if they don't follow his rules."

Karl jumped in. "Yes, and then there's Mussolini in Italy. He wants to own everything, like a king. The people can't own anything. Everyone works and provides for the government, for Mussolini that is. If you don't work, you die. If you're weak, disabled, or ugly, you die. You can't argue. There's no free speech. The government controls the media. It's crazy."

"And now we have similar leaders like Hitler in Germany and Franco in Spain," Adam added.

"Who is this Hitler?" Karl asked excitedly. "Does he want to take over all of Europe? Germans are treating him like an emperor. Did you hear that 'Heil, Hitler' and the marching Armies and drums on the radio? Is there a way to control rogue countries other than war?

Surely, we aren't going to have to fight another war. Didn't the War to End All Wars settle these disputes?"

John tried to calm his son down. "Karl, you have to remember that politics swing to the left and then to the right every couple decades. We need to be patient and let these ideas ride out in their fury. Hopefully, the U.S. won't have to get involved."

Adam shook his head. "I don't know, Senator. It's bad this time. Hitler dissolved his parliament and took over the police force and army. I don't see it swinging back any time soon."

"He's positioned himself to take over my ancestral home, Czechoslovakia," Richard added.

Henry slowly nodded. He wanted his guests to enjoy the holiday. Could he lead their discussion back to light-hearted fare? "I'm with you. It's puzzling to know why Germany and Japan backed out of the League of Nations. But let's enjoy our time now. We're in a safe place. Let the future take care of itself in its own time. Here, let's have another round of bourbon." Henry violated his policy of one drink only and served them again.

That night as they readied for another big spread of food, Louisa was feeling nostalgic, wishing they didn't have to leave the next day. They couldn't extend the visit because they were needed at home to care for their animals. Louisa gazed longingly at all the exquisite extras decorating the Martin house. What a haven, full of memories and delightful ornaments. She reveled in the warmth and beauty of this well-stocked, well-maintained homestead developed over 25 years.

"Your dishes are beautiful, Mary." Louisa lightly touched the blue birds with the white breasts and ran her finger over the flowers and leaves painted with gold. She carefully placed the plates on the linen cloth with its embroidered green vines running down the middle. A big embroidered pink rose spread its petals in the center of the tablecloth.

Mary, shyly pleased with her daughter-in-law's delight told her, "They're from Japan. Henry got me this set of porcelain dishes from one of the homesteaders who left back in 1928. I'm missing a few pieces. I only use it for good. I worry the gold will rub off!"

"You've taken good care of them," Louisa replied. "They're so delicate you can almost see through them." Louisa held a cup up toward the late afternoon sunlight coming through the window and showed Victoria how translucent it was.

Gina joined in the conversation. "See on the back the plate says 'Nippon' and 'hand painted.' Nippon means Japan, but after 1921, because of the McKinley Tariff Act, they had to mark the china they sold in the U.S. with 'Made in Japan.' So we know these were made before 1921. Your set will be valuable someday, Mary."

"It's more important to me that we enjoy using them now," Mary responded feeling awkward with Gina's knowledge.

"It's amazing, isn't it, Victoria?" Louisa said. "You can see through the cup. How can anyone make dishware so fine?"

"Yes, yes, it's all very beautiful." Louisa looked quizzically at Victoria. She sounded sarcastic or discouraged or envious?

Louisa set the cup back in its saucer and studied her sister. Is Victoria in trouble? It's such an odd comment, as if she needs joy in her life. Karl and Victoria were living at the Mueller home with Anna. Senator Mueller was in Helena much of the time and the ranch was Karl's responsibility. Maybe Victoria living with Anna in a ranch house once exclusively Anna's isn't working. Louisa gave Victoria a hug, wishing she could cheer her up. Or maybe Victoria is has the blues after giving birth to her first-born. "Are you okay? Is having a newborn hard on you?" Louisa asked Victoria.

"Everything's okay, or should be. Anna's helpful. I'm just tired. Too much going on with Gina and Eddie home, too." Aha, I think I get it, Louisa thought. Victoria is living with a houseful of

Muellers! She needs some good old Czech craziness to help her with all that Swiss-Swede goodness! I'll have to figure out how to help her.

The women finished laying the table. Mary stepped outside to ring the dinner bell, calling the children and men into the house. Then Mary and Anna filled the serving dishes.

After their conversation about the world's events, the men were quiet as they came in and washed up. The children seemed subdued also. Eddie gave the blessing which was long and filled with pauses. He choked over his words. Louisa took a peek at him. His cheeks were wet. He was crying! Is it because it's our last night together? Louisa wondered. Is everyone sad now that we'll be parting? What's going on? It feels like a foreboding spirit has descended upon us.

When Eddie ended the prayer, Louisa surprised herself by raising her water glass in a toast and exclaiming, "Na zdravi!" Something needed to be done to change the gloomy atmosphere.

Her brother, Richard, with a grin raised his glass and responded with, "Dobrou chut'l." Victoria repeated, "Dobrou chut'l." Everyone broke out laughing, knowing it was some kind of good wishes, and raised their glasses with "To your health" and "Cheers." Good old Czech spirits come in handy once in a while. Louisa peeked at Victoria. Thank God, she's laughing.

At the end of the meal, Adam stood up and gave a bit of a speech. "The Thanksgiving holiday was wonderful, Dad and Mom," he said. "Thank you for putting us up and feeding us so well. I want us to remember the good times we've had this week." Everyone added their own positive appreciation about the past two days—the knitted hats and gloves that were made, card games won, the laughter of the children playing in the snow, the great food, the handsome-looking colt, and the antics of the kittens. They had much to be thankful for.

After the last bite of pie, the men settled into the living room while the women cleaned up the dishes and put the children to bed. Later they took places beside their husbands with their knitting and joined into the conversation about the previous summers' flood in downtown Billings.

"I had trouble getting to the Yegen Insurance office with water up to the car door," Henry commented. "Right down town! And the underpass was flooded. Billings definitely needs to get a better sewer drainage system."

Senator Mueller reported, "The City fathers want to develop a publicly-owned sewer facility by taxing the people. It's a new policy, taxing for a public sewer. I doubt voters will pass that idea! Nobody wants more taxes. Nobody can afford it right now."

"What about the Big Ditch? What if it overflows or breaks some day? Houses will be flooded out, too, not just businesses," Adam wondered.

"Be thankful if a city sewer system is the worst of your problems," Gina responded. "What did you think of John Dillinger shooting up the Chicago movie theater? I'm glad I'm not living there anymore. Wasn't that something?" Gina knew Chicago well having lived there while working on her master's degree.

Victoria agreed. "It was scary all right. But look. We have gun-toting, angry men in Montana. Maybe not in gangs, but there are disgruntled workers feeling they aren't getting their fair share. Wonder if we'll have a war like Europe."

Ceci set her knitting aside as she spoke passionately. "We need more police protection in this country. And more help for our county sheriffs."

"We're safe in Montana," Mary assured the two young women. "Especially out here where we know everyone. There won't be gangsters shooting people. We'll be fine."

While the rest of the world seemed in turmoil, the men agreed with Mary and were certain that everything was fine in Stillwater County. Good crops, water from springs, and no robbers busting into their homes or fascists running the country. It was midnight when the Muellers said their good-byes and left to go the five miles to their own home and the Martin family and their Janochek guests found their resting places.

After breakfast the next morning, Richard and Ceci with their kids packed their car and headed north. Adam and Louisa gave Mary and Henry a hug, sad to be leaving them and their warm hospitality. In order to save their folks a trip, they drove to the Wheat Basin store to deliver the Martin milk and eggs and to pick up a few supplies before heading home to White Beaver Creek. The store manager, Duane, was visiting with Frank Robideau, when Adam, Roger, and Louisa with Peter in her arms arrived. Adam brought in the milk and eggs while Louisa began picking out things they needed and putting them on the counter. Roger was busy studying the candy behind a glass case.

"How was your Thanksgiving, Frank?" Adam asked as he set the milk can down by the counter. "Did you have a turkey?"

Frank faced Adam as if he were being challenged. "We done okay. Misses always finds somethin'."

The door to the store opened and Larry Kuntz, the five year old whose folks ran the Wheat Basin Occidental Grain Elevator stumbled over the threshold. Dried blood covered Larry's head, matting his hair. His eyes were swollen. His jacket was covered with splattered blood. Larry limped and acted confused. Louisa gasped as she quickly laid Peter down on the counter and asked Duane for a wet cloth.

"Gad, have ya been attacked by a dog?" Frank asked.

Larry shook his head no and choked out, "My folks bin killed." There was an unbelievable silence and then Adam knelt by the boy.

146

"At the elevator?" Adam asked him gently. Larry shook his head like he couldn't think.

"Who done it?" Frank asked.

"Dunno," the boy responded. Louisa started slowly dabbing Larry's cheeks and head with the wet cloth carefully removing blood.

"I'll run over to the elevator and see what's happening," Adam announced.

Louisa nodded in agreement. "Yes, please."

Adam ran the few yards to the elevator. The previous day of sunshine had melted much of the snow, but Adam could see car tire tracks from the mud on the road leading into the big elevator doors. Those doors and the smaller side door were locked as Adam pushed against them. The sign on the door said, "Closed."

Adam ran around the elevator to the back door. It was ajar. He could see Larry's tracks leading away from the door. Adam slipped inside and waited a minute for his eyes to adjust to the darker space. Seeing the car, he cautiously moved toward it. The driver's door was open with a body lying over the steering wheel.

Adam started shaking. He choked out, "Oh, no, no, no," which echoed in the empty, cavernous building. Leaning over the body, he could see that Mike Kuntz had been shot in the back of his head. On the passenger side, Frieda Kuntz lay back over the front seat. With little light in the room, Adam couldn't tell for sure, but he thought she had been shot in her chest. He would have to move her to see where she was shot and Adam didn't want to disturb any clues the sheriff might need to determine how or why these murders had occurred. They were clearly dead.

By the time Adam returned to the store, Larry was unconscious and Louisa had wrapped him in one of the store's blankets and laid him on the floor.

"Sure enough," Adam said, his blue eyes wildly looking at each of them. "Larry's folks are dead, shot up bad, and dried blood on them. They're in their car in the elevator." Adam was breathing heavily. "Duane, call Sheriff Benjamin. Tell him the front door says "Closed" but the back door was open. I didn't touch anything so maybe there are clues as to who did this terrible deed."

"I saw some hitchhikers, strangers, on the road yesterday. Maybe they done it," Frank replied sounding frantic.

"Yeah, maybe," Louisa responded. "Adam, we need to get Larry to a doctor. We should take him to a Billings hospital." She spoke calmly with her nursing instincts taking over.

"Sure. Let's go. I'll lay him in the back seat and you can sit with him and watch him."

"I pray he'll be all right. Try to avoid the biggest bumps in the road. He's really banged up." Louisa pleaded.

When Duane put down the phone from calling the sheriff, Adam asked, "Duane, please call my folks and tell them what's happened. And the Deaconess Hospital and tell them we're bringing in a kid that's been beat up bad," Adam asked.

"Will do," Duane shouted back as Adam carried Larry to the car.

"Come on, Roger. Get in the front seat of the car by Daddy. Give our best wishes to Ella May and the kids, Frank," Louisa called out as she walked out of the store and got in the back seat with Larry.

They stayed with Larry Kuntz at the hospital for a couple hours and got home to White Beaver Creek late that night to feed the animals. The next day they telephoned the nurse who told them that Larry was in and out of a coma that first day. The doctors had removed pieces of wood from his scalp.

In a couple days as Larry healed, he remembered what happened and he talked to the sheriff. The whole story was headlined in the *Billings Gazette* and *Stillwater News* the next week. Adam and Louisa read how Frank Robideau was charged with murdering the Wheat Basin elevator manager and his wife on November 26, 1937. Frank

148

was arrested and was being held in the Yellowstone County jail with the court hearing set for December 11th.

"Can you believe Frank just stood there with us in the store waiting to see if Larry remembered him? What a cool character!" Louisa wondered.

"There's more news here, Louisa. Frank came in to buy a pickup at Davy Motor when I was there last summer. The paper says Frank was having trouble paying for it. He went to the Wheat Basin elevator to ask Mike for the cash he thought he was owed for 180 bushels of wheat stored at the elevator. But Frank owed a third of that wheat money to his landlords for leasing the land, and Mike, as the elevator manager, was unsure about giving money to Frank that might not be his. In the argument, Mike suggested they all go to Columbus to straighten out the deal."

Louisa got up from her chair and pulled open the lace curtains, watching as snow and wind blew dried leaves across the yard. Her stomach was churning. She didn't want to know what happened. But then she did want to know. The whole story was unbelievable and horrible. There we were at the Wheat Basin store, Adam, Roger, Peter, and me, with a murderer! A lying murderer trying to blame the deaths on some strangers passing through. Frank could have killed us all.

"Why didn't he kill Larry?" Louisa wondered.

"I guess he thought he had. He beat him with his gunstock. That was the wood imbedded in Larry's head." Louisa shivered. "But then when he saw Larry stumble in at the store, I guess Frank felt repentant because Larry reminded him of his own son, Matthew. They're nearly the same age. I think the boys were friends."

Of course. Dear Matthew Robideau. Then Louisa thought of her friend Ella May and her three children. How could such a sweet woman be married to such a terrible man?

149

"What will become of Ella May and the children?" Louisa turned from the window to ask Adam. "She's due to have another baby this month. Oh, Adam, this is horrible. I just remembered that Larry's mom, Frieda, was Ella May's midwife! Frank killed the woman who helps deliver Ella May's babies!" Louisa flung herself down at the kitchen table, crying, with anger rippling through her body. "This is inconceivable. What a terrible twist of fate."

Adam moved beside Louisa and put his arm around her. Her emotional outbursts amazed him. He didn't feel as deeply as she did and was confused by her reactions. She had been calm at the Wheat Basin store and now she's hysterical. Nevertheless, he felt his job was to keep her stable.

"Calm down," he consoled her, patting her arm and trying to comfort her.

Louisa turned and looked at Adam, her eyes big in horror. "Ella May's out there on the farm alone. Without a vehicle. Has anyone gone to her? She must be feeling terrible. Can I call her? Ask her what she needs?" Adam nodded. He knew there was no way of stopping Louisa from getting involved. "Wait, Ella May doesn't have a phone. Maybe Mary would go see her until I can get there to help?"

Louisa immediately rang the Martin number and explained to her mother-in-law the concerns she had for Ella May and the children.

"Yes, of course, I'll go, Louisa. I'll phone Agnes to go with me. We'll go first thing in the morning and I'll call you as soon as I get back home. We'll take some food."

The next morning, Mary packed milk, butter, and a turkey vegetable stew into a basket. She picked up Agnes who had pickled relish, bread, and chokecherry jelly. Agnes also had a handmade quilt to give Ella May. Mary took three pairs of mittens for the three children, the ones she had just made over Thanksgiving.

"I want to see Frank," Ella May told Mary and Agnes. "And then I'll go stay with my cousins south of Columbus 'til the baby comes. I'm sure they'll take me in. They never liked Frank, but I think they'll find room for me and the kids until the baby is born." Mary told her Louisa would take her and the children to see Frank at the Billings jail where he was being held and afterwards to her relatives.

Two days later, Louisa drove with Roger and Peter to the Wheat Basin farm where Ella May was living. She helped Ella May bundle up Mathew, Sally, and Dolly in warm clothes. Ella May had packed two suitcases and a box with her essential belongings.

Ella May told Louisa more of the story as they drove into Billings. "They found from fingerprints that Frank had killed a man in a holdup in 1910, way before I married him. He and his brother were in prison when Frank escaped from a chain gang. He was known as Joseph Liberty. I didn't know any of this! He never told me." What an odd name for a murderer, Liberty, Louisa thought.

Ella May went on with the story. "Frank changed his name and came west. I knew he was rough around the edges when I married him but not that he was a murderer. My dad needed me out of the house. What could I do? Frank was a good father and not a bad husband. He tried to provide for us. Drinking was his problem; he couldn't leave it alone."

"It's the downfall of many." Louisa was thinking how grateful she was that drinking was not a problem for Adam.

Louisa parked in front of the Yellowstone County jail. "I'll take the kids to the courthouse square to play, while you talk to Frank," Louisa suggested. Ella May nodded.

There was enough snow to make a fox and geese circle. "Come on, Matthew, we'll make a big circle and cut it into four big slices of pie." The four older children followed Louisa as she made the pattern. Soon

151

Louisa, with Peter in her arms, was chasing Matthew. He touched Dolly and then Dolly was trying to keep her little legs going fast enough to catch Roger. Sally slowed down, let her little sister touch her, and she was "it." They were all squealing with excitement and joy. I love to hear the laughter of children, Louisa thought. They've been so quiet the last few hours. They know what's going on. It must be really hard for them, but this is a great release. I'm glad they can be kids for a little while.

"Louisa. Is that you, Louisa?" A beautiful, young lady in a fur coat called out from the sidewalk. Louisa walked over to her. It was Isabella! Grown up and strikingly beautiful. Of course, she'd be beautiful. Of course, she'd be wearing a fur. Louisa opened her arm, greeting her old friend. They hugged with Peter squished between them, tears coming into their eyes. Louisa felt Isabella shaking, silently crying.

"Oh, Louisa, I've wanted to see you, to thank you for turning my life around, for letting me see the joys in nature, for saving my life!" Isabella stated dramatically.

"You weren't going to die, Isabella, and you were loving life before you met me."

"No, Louisa, I was too serious, not having any joy and you helped me to find pleasure. I really appreciate all you did. And this is your baby?" Louisa happily showed off 2-month old Peter and pointed out Roger. Then she explained who Matthew, Sally, and Dolly were. Isabella had read about the murders and Frank Robideau in the papers. Louisa filled in further details.

Isabella shook her head. "I should have known you'd be helping Mrs. Robideau. Is there anything I can do to help?"

"There's not much any of us can do. I'm taking Ella May to stay with cousins after she's finished talking to Frank. She's having another baby within the month. She'll have a lot to think about, other than Frank."

Isabella reached into her purse and pulled out three ten-dollar bills. "You give these to Ella May for the baby or for Christmas presents for the other kids."

"That's good of you. Will Amelia and Mr. Lewis permit this? Won't they be upset?"

"They're used to me having my own way now. Don't worry. If you need anything, anytime, Louisa, you call me and I'll try to help. I want to help. On anything."

"Thanks, Isabella, I really appreciate knowing that. Now tell me about yourself. What are you doing?"

"I'm graduating from high school in the spring. Mother wants me to go to Europe for finishing school and to study art, but I want to stay in Montana. Father wants me to study music at Eastman. I like art and music, but... well, I've been visiting the reservation with Arthur and staying at the sheep ranch in the summer. You taught me to treat people fairly. I don't know what you did, but you turned Arthur around, too. He's actually kind to his employees, not excessively generous but he does listen to their stories and problems. I'm thinking I'd like to study law, to work for justice for everyone."

"That's amazing!" Louisa exclaimed. "I'm happy for you! A woman lawyer! How absolutely wonderful." But Louisa thought it an odd career for a woman. Women are more suited to being nurses, teachers, and office workers. She'll be taking a job a man might need in order to feed his family. A woman lawyer? But Isabella would be great!

"Or the other possibility is to study journalism and be a reporter, but I'm not sure I'm brave enough to be an investigative reporter, which is what I'd like to do."

"You'll find a way." Louisa suddenly felt old. Here I am raising children instead of following an exciting career. I could have been an artist! Or a radio announcer!

"I'm planning to start at the university in Missoula next fall. They have both a journalism school and pre-law courses. Mother is disappointed I'm not going East or to Europe, but they have a Christian Science church in Missoula and I've promised to attend in order for her to allow me to go."

Louisa laughed. "Isabella, I'm pleased for you. You're an inspiration for all women! You're paving the way. It's amazing what women can do now." But will Isabella ever get married and have children? It's not possible to have a big career and still manage a home. No, it's best for women to stay home and take care of their families, like I am, Louisa concluded to herself. Still, it's fun to see Isabella exploring the possibilities.

"You started me on this path. I'm grateful. We'll see where it goes."

"And how are your parents? Are they well?"

"Father spends an enormous amount of time in the East on business matters and I suspect my parents will be moving to Boston on a more permanent basis after I graduate. Mother, of course, would enjoy going to more concerts and art exhibits."

"And you'll stay in Montana and bring concerts and art to us!" Louisa exclaimed.

"Hope so." Isabella grinned. "I want to show you my ring, Louisa." Louisa expected to see a flashy diamond like Amelia wore. Instead, she was puzzled by the nearly translucent stone with a small red center and black spots shaped like a heart on Isabella's middle finger on her right hand. Louisa held Isabella's hand and looked carefully at the ring, wondering what special meaning it had.

"Ooh," Louisa exhaled, finally recognizing it. "It's the pebble we found along the river." Louisa's eyes met Isabella's deep violet ones as they both smiled.

"I had it polished and set into a ring. An Indian acquaintance told me moss agates have special powers. They give to the owner strength and confidence to meet challenges. And, Louisa." Isabella pulled a chain which had hung around her neck over her head, took off her leather gloves to unclasp the necklace closure, and slipped a ring off the chain. "The agate was cut in half to show the pattern. I had a second ring made for you, knowing I'd see you someday. I've been saving it for this moment." Isabella took off Louisa's woolen glove and put the ring on Louisa's middle finger of her right hand.

Louisa had a lump in her throat. This gift of friendship did give her new strength and confidence to meet the challenges. With identical rings, in a sense, they were blood sisters.

Later, when she was home again, Louisa puzzled over this meeting and conversation with Isabella. Life is full of surprises, of turn-arounds, of consequences one can't imagine. Isabella is now a strong woman with deep values. And, best of all, the two of them had forged a bond. Even Arthur had become more human. The sarcastic young man had become compassionate. Will wonders never cease?

On December 11, Frank Robideau pleaded guilty and asked the judge for mercy, saying he was desperate for the money owed him so he could get the pickup for his family, not wanting to leave them isolated. Without a jury trial, the judge pronounced Frank Robideau guilty of a double homicide and sentenced him to die by hanging on January 15, 1938 in Columbus, Montana.

On the evening of December 24, Ella May gave birth to a baby boy. A midwife and Ella May's cousin assisted her. Jimmy, a mechanic from the Davey Motor Ford repair shop stopped by with a gift of two warm blankets, a soft flannel one for the baby and a big wool one for Ella May, and candy for the three children.

"I met Frank when he came to buy the truck," he explained. "I'm really sorry for what happened. It's a tragedy." Jimmy seemed to be intrigued by the new birth and asked to hold the baby. His big hands with grease imbedded under the nails and in the work-worn cracks engulfed the small form wrapped in the new pale blue flannel cloth. Fascinated with the baby, he stayed much longer than he had intended and became acquainted with Matthew, Sally, and Dolly. With Isabella's money, Ella May had bought oranges, apples, cheese, milk, and bread for the older children and her cousin spread out this Christmas Eve feast for all of them. Ella May had also purchased for each child new stockings, shoes, and a coat.

"Mama, it's bu-tiful." Sally stroked the arms of her red plaid coat and did a little dance, turning in circles. The grown-ups laughed at her antics, pleased with Sally, the gifts, the evening. Matthew pranced in his new high-topped shoes.

"They're a little big, but you'll grow into them in no time." Ella May remarked. "You need them for our trip."

"Where ya going?" Jimmy asked.

"We need to start a new life in a different part of the country when I get strong enough," Ella May explained. "I can't bear the gossip. All the constant talk about Frank and how awful he is. I want to be rid of all these bad feelings."

Before long, the family was worn out from the birth, the talk, and the excitement of the gifts. Jimmy, the unexpected guest, could see it was time for him to take his leave.

The next few days, everyone in the county talked about the hanging. Adam wanted to see it. "It'll be a major event in the history of our state," he argued with Louisa who was adamant against him attending the gruesome spectacle.

"Why do you want to see Frank die? Why shouldn't Frank just stay in jail?" Louisa asked.

"I want to see an end to this. I need to see justice at work. I feel directly involved. I was at work when Frank came in to buy the truck.

I was the first one to find, to see Mike and Mrs. Kuntz...dead. I want to see Frank hang." Adam found it difficult to talk with Louisa. She was a strongly opinionated woman.

Louisa stood her ground. "No one deserves execution. Death should be a natural process, not one determined by other men. Frank could repent and become a better man. It's not up to us to stop his soul-searching."

"But if we lock him up, he might escape like he did before and kill again."

As their argument continued, Louisa revealed to Adam details of the trial of Joe Jacob where she accused Joe of killing Karen Jones, her hope that Joe would not be given the death sentence, and her lingering fear of what might happen when he is released from prison. The story details shook Adam. His own dear partner was nearly killed and then had to face her assailant in a courtroom. And now to live with the fear of his release.

"The fear of Joe leaving prison and taking revenge on me is a risk I have to live with," Louisa explained. "I don't think it justifies executing him."

How could she forgive Joe and be begging to save Frank's life? It didn't make sense to Adam. How could she feel differently than what he felt? Adam couldn't understand her.

"Anyone who watches Frank die is participating in another killing, approving of taking the life of another human, condoning murder by the government." Louisa pleaded with Adam, her brown eyes dark with sorrow.

"It's not murder," Adam countered. "It's legal to take the life of someone in order to defend yourself or the innocent ones around you."

"It's not moral for us to kill a person when the person is locked up and unable to defend himself." Louisa strongly stated holding onto her values.

"Punishing a killer shows to future generations that killing is not right!" Adam argued.

"Not by killing again!" she shouted.

Their argument went on and they never came to any agreement. In the end, no one, not even Louisa, could keep Adam from meeting Karl at the Atlas Bar in Columbus on the evening of January 14. Hundreds of men gathered there and flowed into the street as they waited. The "Galloping Gallows," a nickname for the platform with the hanging apparatus sent around the state to execute people, was set up a couple blocks away from the bar at a warehouse.

While a few carloads of men came from Billings and other parts of the state, most of the men lived in the area, had known Frank and liked him. They nervously retold the tale about Frank being Joseph Liberty in New York, escaping a chain gang, and changing his name. It was difficult for them to believe that the man they worked beside in a threshing crew or had a drink with at this very bar was a vicious killer. Each had his own personal story of some exchange he had had with Frank. A couple of the men who'd had too much to drink were shouting and shoving each other. They were quickly pulled out of the bar into the alley and doused with a pail of water.

After midnight, a man stepped into the bar and shouted, "Sheriff Benjamin and the prison car has arrived at the warehouse." Adam and Karl left the bar to wend their way through the crowd, trying to get closer to the gallows. Adam knew several of the men and nodded to them. He noted there were no women present.

The street, once snow packed, was now slushy with the mass of boots softening and melting the roadway. In the cool, dark night, the steady breathing of the men warmed the air, enveloping them into one body. As a packed herd, they crowded together, each to find their place to witness the hanging, a couple hundred inside and several hundred more spreading out in a large arc from the warehouse doors where the stark outline of the hangman's noose could be seen. The men were utterly silent at 1:10 a.m. as Sheriff Jack Benjamin led Frank to the steps of the gallows. The clump of Frank's boots echoed out into the space as he slowly climbed the 13 steps. Frank stood for a couple minutes with the noose hanging beside him looking around at his neighbors.

"Any last words, Frank?" Sheriff Benjamin quietly asked. There was not a sound as all the men strained to hear what Frank might say.

"Well, goodbye, boys," Frank said. A black hood was placed over his head followed by the noose. Sheriff Benjamin snapped his fingers and the body dropped through the opened hole. Frank Robideau was dead at 1:27 a.m. January 15, 1938.

Ella May and Jimmy, the Ford mechanic, married in April. With Matthew, Sally, Dolly, and baby Frank, they moved to Spokane in Jimmy's new pickup.

The Tree of Life
MOLT, 1938-1939

I think that I shall never see
A poem lovely as a tree.

JOYCE KILMER (1886-1918)

With a sense of deep satisfaction, Louisa looked over her table loaded with golden crisp fried chicken, fluffy mashed potatoes, smooth gravy with not one lump, new tiny carrots from the garden, perfectly baked buns, and pickled beets. Adam's parents, Henry and Mary, had driven over from Molt to be with them at their White Beaver Creek home this sunny Sunday in late June. Henry gave the blessing and then the family relished visiting as well as the food. Best of all was her angel food cake, Adam's favorite, with fresh strawberry sauce and whipped cream on top. At the end of the delightful dinner, her father-in-law complimented her cooking which pleased Louisa immensely.

As Louisa began picking up the dessert plates, Henry said, "Mary and I have a proposal we'd like to discuss with you both. Do you think the dish washing could be held off for a bit?" Louisa's heart started thumping hard and fast. *A proposal. This sounds serious. Something momentous is happening.* Her hand shook and the dishes she had picked up rattled for a minute.

"Yes, of course, I'll get these dessert plates off the table and serve the coffee." Louisa hurried into the kitchen with the dishes and picked up the coffee pot from the stove.

"Roger, you may go play in the sandbox," she whispered to her son after she had served coffee. He climbed down from his chair stacked with pillows and ran outside. Louisa watched from the window to see him settle into the sandbox in the shade of the big cottonwood. Peter was having his nap and hopefully would sleep another half-hour.

"I'm offering to sell the ranch to you, Adam." Louisa became intently alert as Henry continued. "We've built up a nice-sized acreage, the perfect size for a single family, but not big enough for both of our families. Our early years were difficult as homesteaders, losing Mary's sister and our baby during the 1919 flu epidemic, and then the drought in the '20s. But we survived and prospered with help from our neighbors, especially the Muellers. You boys helped, too, and I appreciate that."

"What will you do, Dad? The ranch is your whole life," Adam asked.

"We want to move to California to be closer to your Aunt Margaret. I hate to admit it, but feeding the cattle in the winter is getting harder for me. And for the place to be profitable, we need to keep it diversified by planting some acres to both wheat and barley. The continued, year-round, chores have worn me down. I'm not a young man anymore. It's time to move on and let you take over."

"Billy told me you were thinking of selling, Dad, but I didn't believe it," Adam responded. Louisa sat up straighter. What? Adam knew this was happening but didn't tell me? Why would he keep such news from me? Oh my gosh, maybe he didn't want me to know.

Henry nodded his head. "I talked to your brother about taking over but he says he has more than he can handle on his own place. He bought quite a large spread and he seems happy there. And his wife likes their house." Adam was thinking, why didn't Dad come to me first? Didn't he think I could run the home place? I've always wanted to run it. What was Dad thinking? Was it because I was traveling before I got married? Didn't he think I could settle down? Dad's the one who wanted me to go to California and help Aunt Margaret so it's his fault I wasn't home working. It hurts to think he didn't ask me earlier, or didn't talk to us kids together. And why doesn't Bill want to manage it? Does he know something I don't know?

Henry went on. "You seem happy here at White Beaver Creek, but I know it's rocky and there's not enough land to support a family. It must be difficult having to work in town, too."

Louisa was too stunned to comment. She looked out the window at the willows along the creek which flowed gently down the ridge into the Yellowstone River. A flock of geese rose up from the water. As Louisa watched, she mused, I love the variety of birds I see every day as they follow the waterways, maybe all the way to the Missouri. It's green right now but even in the winter the house is huddled in this swale, safe from the blizzards and cold storms. I can't imagine leaving this beautiful spot.

She sighed. I don't want to go back to that dry, windy, God-forsaken ranch on the open prairie. So few trees. No water. I will not go back! No. No. Please Adam, say "No." Louisa looked sternly at Adam, hoping she could catch his eye and let him know of her strong desire to stay put.

Adam was looking down at his coffee cup, nodding his head slowly. I've often thought I'd like to manage the ranch and Dad's right about this place, he was thinking. Not enough land to run a decent herd of cattle. We've improved the property, though, and could make money selling it.

"Yes, you're right, Dad. Tough to make a living here." Adam paused and looked at his father. "I'd need an agreement with you for some kind of extended payment."

Louisa's voice cracked as she said, "Adam, the children... Roger'll need to go to school, and, and distances to schools are so great at the ranch." She could scarcely breathe. This is a nightmare. How can he make this decision without even talking to me!

"We can figure that out when the time comes." Adam responded calmly, still not looking at her.

"We'll be happy knowing you and Louisa are there," Henry added. "We've always wanted to keep the place in the family. It's a great place to raise your children, our grandchildren."

Louisa was fuming. Adam didn't even look at me! Does anyone care about what I want? I want to travel, learn languages, and go to art museums and concerts. Now we'll be tied to the land. The only purpose in life I'll have is taking care of Adam and the kids. Oh, God, I want more. Yes, I know my duty: to support Adam and his needs and raise our kids. But, please dear God, I don't want to go back to the ranch. Why did I fall in love with this guy! Why does he love the ranch? Can I change his mind?

"Do we have enough money to buy the ranch and still operate it?" she asked bluntly in front of her in-laws, trying to get Adam to face her. "I'm not sure this is a good economic decision. We need to think about this." I have a realistic argument. It might even be a winning one.

"Selling this quarter-section will give us a good start toward a healthy down payment. We can start by getting yearlings and build our herd slowly." Adam sounded knowledgeable and reasonable as he considered Louisa's comment. Adam had been thinking about this possible transition for a long time. He was surprised to hear that Louisa had been thinking about the economic difficulties of moving back to the ranch, too.

Henry pulled out some papers from his jacket. "I've written out a contract draft for you to look over. It has a deed for the buildings and that section of the land. I've included the equipment and the milk cows. You can lease additional acreage from me for the time being with an option to buy when you build up your equity. Take a look and see what you think, Adam."

Louisa studied Adam and Henry, looking from one to the other with her heart in her throat as Adam read through the papers. They have it all figured out. They've probably had this figured out for years, even before I came along. I'm just an unimportant appendage. Why didn't I understand this is what would happen before I married Adam! Her hand shook as she took a sip of coffee and set her cup back in the saucer. I knew. In my heart, I knew.

Adam, feeling a gut instinct of needing to include Louisa, gave a little speech. "We've lived through the worst economic times ever. The Great Depression, the drought, grasshoppers eating every sprig of grass, and the coldest winter of my lifetime in 1936! But last spring was different. Rains came back. Grasshoppers died. The country's looking good again. We can get a good price for this place here and have a fresh start on the home place."

"I know you'll do well, Adam." Henry encouraged his son.

Louisa sat back, her anger slowly dissipating. She saw she'd lose this battle. It was foreordained. I did know this would happen when I married him. Maybe Adam's right. Maybe this is our opportunity for economic advancement. And my place is by my husband, no matter what the cost to my own needs or desires. She rose to get the coffee pot from the kitchen to refill the cups. Mary followed her to the kitchen.

"We're leaving the furniture, linens, dishes, and condiments," Mary told her. "I'd like you to have those beautiful Japanese dishes you admired at Thanksgiving, for you to keep as your own. A few beautiful things will help you through the hard days." Louisa turned and looked into the eyes of her mother-in-law. Does she know what I'm thinking? She knows how difficult it is for a woman to live out there! Did she once feel like I'm feeling? Mary took Louisa's hands and gave them a little squeeze. Then Mary picked up the coffee pot from the stove.

164

"Let me serve the men their coffee and I'll be back to help wash the dishes," Mary said. Louisa put on her apron, put water on the stove top to heat, and started scraping the dishes.

By the middle of summer, the White Beaver Creek place sold. The two families met at the Yellowstone Bank in Columbus where Adam signed the papers to borrow money, and buy Sections 30 and 31, the home buildings, and to rent the other land. Henry then took them out for lunch at the Stillwater Café to celebrate. After lunch, Adam, Louisa, and Roger gave Henry and Mary big hugs before they got into their car. "Don't grow up too fast, Peter," Mary said as she kissed the little boy in her mother's arms. The young family stood waving good-bye for a long time as Henry pulled out in their packed car and headed west for California.

The next day, neighbors helped Adam and Louisa load their belongings into the farm truck which Karl had brought. Then, with Karl driving the truck and Adam driving the car, they drove the 50 miles north and east to the ranch on the prairie.

The morning was exciting and exhausting with Adam dreaming of huge expectations and Louisa nervous with anxieties. Adam had already moved his farm equipment to the home place. Since the house was furnished, it didn't take long even in the hot summer heat for Karl to help Adam unload their personal clothes, kitchenware, and mementos into the house and the tools into the barn. By late afternoon, they had finished unloading and Karl left for the Mueller ranch, five miles away.

A wind picked up towards dusk. Louisa felt the rapid drop in temperature and her stomach turned over. She could smell the rain even before it hit.

"Roger! Roger! Come in," Louisa called to the little boy who was swinging in the tractor tire hanging from a tree by the kitchen door. The wind had already picked up so much that she didn't know if her voice reached him. Roger ran in, just before Adam did with the screen door banging behind them as they entered. Adam firmly shut both the screen and back door.

"Make sure the bedroom window is closed, Louisa." Adam strode into the living room and shut the window and the front door while Louisa lowered the window in the bedroom. Louisa picked up Peter from his crib and went to the living room window to watch the storm with Adam and Roger. Rain came in heavy sheets. Then a ping sounded, and more and more pings, pongs, and bongs started pounding the roof. As they watched huge, fist-sized hail bounced in the yard. Adam started to put his arm around Louisa. Before he could do that, there was a large crack and they jumped back from the window as hail stones as big as baseballs shattered the window and ripped through the lace curtain.

"Oh, my God," Louisa shrieked and hugged Peter close. Adam drew Roger into the group, his big arms surrounding all of them as hail kept pelting down outside as Adam watched. Prayers rose from the family circle with Louisa begging, "God, oh, God, please stop the hail. Please keep us safe. Stop the wind. May your Almighty Power stop the hail and the wind."

All at once, the wind and the pounding ended. Light rain continued to fall, a pleasant sound after the terror. Adam relaxed his tight grip on Louisa and Roger. Shattered glass and a puddle of water were at their feet. Roger reached out to pick up one of the large hail stones.

"No, Roger, it might have glass. We need gloves." Adam held his son back. He looked through the torn curtain, seeing a pink streak of light already showing from the sunset behind the veil of rain, now nearly gone. He shook his head in disbelief. Adam went to the kitchen, got the broom, dustpan, and bucket and went back to clean up the mess.

Louisa took Roger's hand and led him away from the broken glass and into the kitchen. There, holding Peter, she also clutched Roger and rocked back and forth, moaning.

"Mommy, want to see." Roger pushed himself away from her. "Go see the ice stones?" Numbly, she nodded and he ran to pull open the back door. Roger laughed as he picked up hail stones and then dropped them when he found them to be so cold.

In the eerie evening after a light supper, Louisa put the children to bed and looked out in the summer darkness toward the barn where by moonlight she could see Adam checking the damage. She closed the door to the bedroom, something she had never done in her old home, lay on the bed, and wept. Exhausted, she was asleep when Adam crawled into bed beside her.

In the rising sun the next morning, the ground looked like a desert with the grass beaten down into mud pits. Broken tree branches and leaves were strewn across the yard. The few trees surrounding the house had bare branches, looking forlorn as the heat from the sun now hit their trunks.

Adam brought in the milk pails and announced to Louisa, "We're selling the milk cows." Louisa nodded in resignation. Is this the end? Does this mean we're leaving? How can we make a living? Where will we go?

"I'll call Karl and see if he can help me haul them to the auction yard. We should get good money for them. The milk cows are in good shape. But the hail took our grass for the immediate future. It'll not come back in the August heat and there's no way we can afford to buy and feed the milk cows hay now in the summer. The few yearlings we kept when Dad sold his herd should be okay and able to find grass in the coolies. We'll buy a few bred cows this fall and get into a cow-calf operation. I've milked enough cows in my life. We'll keep one cow for our own milk." Adam strained the milk through the cheesecloth into the glass gallon jars. Louisa turned her back on him, putting Peter in the high chair, so he wouldn't see the tears in her eyes. She was thinking of how she was hoping Adam would want to leave the ranch now after this disaster. *I guess not. Oh, how I wish he didn't love this place so much.*

"Roger, get in your chair," she said more sharply than she meant to do. She swiped at the hair in her eyes and in the same movement wiped away teardrops. *How am I going to bear up? I don't want to stay here!* She dished up the oatmeal for the children, adding cream, raisins, and brown sugar for Roger. Then she dished up Adam's oatmeal as well as the eggs, bacon, and toast she had made for him. He washed his hands at the sink and sat down to eat.

Into the third spoonful of oatmeal, he asked her, "Aren't you eating?"

Louisa wiped her hands in her apron, poured Adam and herself each a cup of coffee, and sat down at the other end of the wooden table. "I'll eat the leftovers," she softly answered.

"You've got to eat, Louisa. We have to keep our strength up. It's no time to get weepy. There are dead turkeys out there that I think you can skin and salvage the meat. They were too dumb to get under shelter like the chickens. Once the fields dry, I'll see if we can put some of the damaged wheat up as hay. Probably not; it looks pretty beaten down into the mud but you never know. See what you can salvage from the garden. Potatoes and beets should be OK. Maybe there's cabbage leaves for you to cut up for that great sauerkraut you make."

Louisa nodded and looked out to the back yard at the tree stripped of its leaves. A single leaf hung on a low branch, a couple more, further up. *Life will come back, but it will be so long, too long.* A wave of anger rose up from the bottom of her stomach. *This is not what I want for us. What right does he have to make us stay in this desolate place?*

"Adam, let's back out of this deal. Your dad'll understand." She tried to keep her voice steady. "Let's move to Billings and you can get a job as a mechanic or in some agriculture business. You're smart; there are lots of possibilities. The kids will be able to go to good schools." I'll be able to have friends, not this isolated life.

The chair tipped backward, banging, as Adam stood up. "I never took you to be a quitter, Louisa. Now is the time for us to show some backbone. To stand up to adversity. To show what we are made of. And we are going to succeed at running this ranch. We may be starting at the bottom, but WE WILL SUCCEED." The last three words were spoken slowly and loudly. A pronouncement and a promise.

Roger had stopped eating and looked up at his dad and Peter started whimpering, his lower lip quivering at the harsh sounds.

Louisa's brown eyes blazed at him with anger. "And at what cost to your family? Why do we have to suffer as you succeed," the words flung at him, "and you prove you are such a GREAT MAN."

Adam studied his spit-fire wife as he gently patted Peter's head and rubbed his cheek soothing him. Adam had quickly cooled with her criticism. Very calmly, he said, "Louisa, you're the one to make me a great man. You're the reason for all of this. If I succeed, it'll be due to your support. Don't turn away now. We're a family. We can do this." Adam picked up his chair and sat down again. He picked up his toast, buttered it, and went on as if everything had been settled. "Roger, we'll need your help today, so eat a good breakfast. You're a strong boy. You can help your mom by bringing the dead turkeys to the house. Do you think you can find the dead turkeys, put each of them into your wagon, and bring them to the back door?"

"Yes, Daddy."

"They might be heavy."

Roger held up his arm to show his muscle. "See."

"I know you can do it. You're a good boy." Adam patted Roger on his back.

Louisa picked up the spoon and fed Peter some oatmeal. All right. She'd make him a great man. She had lost this skirmish, but the battle wasn't over in her mind. This was no place to raise a family.

The hail storm, the worst the county had ever seen, was five miles wide, right across the Martin land, and it took out every acre of wheat Adam's dad had planted. While there would be a small amount of insurance money, it was a terrible loss. Other neighbors hadn't been hit nearly as badly. The hail storm passed by the Mueller's place entirely.

The phone lines were repaired quickly and Louisa was relieved to hear from her sister, Victoria, later that day. Since it was a party line, they didn't talk long because Louisa didn't want the neighbors to gossip about their huge hail loss. The near-by folks already knew from Adam's call to Karl that they were selling the milk cows. Victoria invited Louisa and the family for Sunday dinner and Louisa accepted saying she'd bring a turkey casserole. Since they lived close, Louisa was hopeful they'd be able to see Victoria and Karl and their baby, Johnny, often.

Louisa talked herself into thinking more positively about their future at the ranch. Maybe we can stay long enough to clean up this mess and have the place looking good again before we move. During the hot August days, Louisa started hauling pails of water to the shelterbelt trees that her mother-in-law had planted years ago. They were still alive and a few leaves hung here and there on the branches.

After the hail storm and Louisa's gloom, Adam realized he needed to think about ways to keep Louisa happy. He suggested they go to the Midland Empire Fair in Billings in August.

Louisa and Roger had a grand day as they went through the exhibits, ate hotdogs for lunch, and watched the animals as they were being displayed for prizes. I can embroider as well as the blue ribbon prize winners, Louisa thought. And bake a cake and decorate it, well, maybe not as well as the grand prize winner who had frosting with elaborate roses. Still, it was satisfying for Louisa to know that she matched up to some of the best homemakers in the county.

"Look at the paintings, Roger. Do you think you could paint an antelope like that?" she asked her son, thinking about how she loved the sketches, sculptures, and watercolors. And especially an oil painting of an iris. Louisa hoped Roger would take up art or music.

"I like the plane," he told his mother as he pointed to an airplane model. "I make a plane," he announced with confidence.

"That would be wonderful! Adam, do you suppose there's a store that sells patterns for building model airplanes? And where would we find the proper tools?"

Adam laughed. He was happy Louisa had her old enthusiasm back. "I suspect I have what he needs in the shop at home. But you know, Louisa," he whispered in her ear, "He's just a little kid. It won't look like much."

"Big things come from small beginnings," she replied.

Adam tousled Roger's dark head of hair. "You like airplanes? Would you like to see a real one?"

"Yes! Yes!" Roger grinned his approval.

In a low voice, Adam commented to Louisa. "You know airplanes aren't safe. Cars are safer. I wish Roger was more enthralled with automobiles. I could teach him a lot about cars." Louisa smiled to herself. Sons don't always follow the loves of their fathers!

Adam went on. "You know, Louisa, we haven't driven that new road on 27th Street up to the airport. It might be fun to take a gander at the city from the top of the rims before we go home. Roger can see how large airplanes really are."

"Yes, let's do it!" she enthusiastically agreed. Something new, something exciting. Maybe we can ride in an airplane someday. She sighed. Maybe I can survive this ranch life after all, as long as there is something educational once in a while. Hope rose in her once again.

That fall, Victoria invited Louisa to the Happy Homemakers Club that met at the community hall in Molt once a month. At first Louisa wondered what she could learn from other farm women, but they had surprises for her. As they shared lunches, Louisa tasted new foods like enchiladas and she got recipes for making them. At her turn, she taught them how to make kolaches. That fall they crocheted toys for an orphanage and designed holiday table decorations. Louisa realized she needed to buy a stouter needle for her Singer sewing machine in order to sew heavy winter coats for the children and denim trousers for Adam with material that she had thought was too thick to sew.

The group invited speakers to come to their gatherings. An accountant spoke about household budgets and a veterinarian described animal diseases. Since Senator Mueller died, Anna had become more involved in the Party and Anna invited legislators to explain bills that would be introduced.

In the company of these honest farm women who shared with her their own frustrations of loneliness and hard work, Louisa realized the value of being a smart, capable homemaker who could help her family and care for others. And Victoria is a hoot, Louisa reminisced one day. I didn't know how funny my little sister can be. I love these women and their quirky personalities.

By the following spring, Louisa felt she could make a life for her family at the ranch after all. While daily work was tedious, she began thinking about how she could make their home more pleasant. She put up fresh wallpaper in the bedroom, flowers with a purple background. And wallpaper with yellow and white daisies in the kitchen. I need to sew new curtains; the current ones are dingy. I wish we could get a rocking chair to rock Peter and any more babies that might come along.

Long days with no company made her hunger for intelligent conversation. They managed to get to church at Molt a few times during the winter where she could learn what was happening in the community and in the larger world. But Adam knew it was not enough. He felt Louisa's restlessness and was feeling the need for a break from work himself after the long winter. "How would you like to take a road trip for a couple days, Louisa?" Adam asked one morning. "There's only a couple cows left to calve, lambing hasn't started, and it's still too early to put in spring wheat."

Louisa brightened at the prospect of leaving the ranch for a few days. "What did you have in mind?"

"Let's go to Red Lodge for lunch and then down to Cody, Wyoming. There's a fancy hotel there, the Irma. I'd like to stay there one night and see the Buffalo Bill artifacts they have. We'd drive home the next day. We could see how the fields look south of here. I'll put the calf in with the milk cow and the chickens should be OK for a couple days."

Louisa gave Adam a big hug. He's not lost his sense of adventure! Thank you, God! It didn't take Louisa long to pack overnight bags for the four of them. Three days later the last cow had her calf and Adam put the herd out to the pasture where grass was greening again as the snow melted. He added a couple bales of hay for them to work on. With extra cups of feed for the chickens, sheep corralled where they could get hay and water, and the milk cow in a pen with her calf, Adam was sure the livestock could make it through a couple of days without him.

Louisa was slightly disappointed when she first saw the Irma. Built of river rock and sandstone with a veranda porch similar to the Graves in Harlowton where they had honeymooned, it didn't seem all that "fancy." It was old, built in 1902 by Buffalo Bill Cody and named for his daughter. Still, she was curious about the interior.

"Momma, Momma, look." Roger pulled on her dress pulling her toward a hall of taxidermy animals: elk heads with huge antlers, big horn sheep with their convoluted horns, the lovely striped necks of antelope heads, and even a fox. Animal heads just above the human eye level reigned majestically down the whole corridor.

Louisa's stomach turned as she saw this display of animal destruction. "Is this legal, Adam? To shoot and display dead animals seems immoral or primitive to me," Louisa wondered.

"Yes, it's legal. Of course it costs money to hire a taxidermist to do it properly. But every fall hunters from all over the world come here to shoot wild animals and then to display their heads in their homes. Lots of people do it. It gives one a sense of the animal's essence and strength, don't you think?"

"But the eyes are looking at us, condemning us for taking over their land, their space. When we came in to the Irma, I saw the buffalo head below the hotel sign. I wondered if I needed his permission to enter this building, like a god of some kind."

"What an imagination you have, Louisa! It's true we need to respect animals. Not so long ago, bison ruled this area, but scouts nearly killed them off. We wouldn't be able to live here if the buffalo continued to roam this area like they once did."

"The Indians were able to live here with buffalo," Louisa responded.

Adam quietly sighed and shook his head. It's tough to change her opinion. "Come, Louisa, there's so much to see." He drew his family toward the massive fireplace. "There are fossils in the rock as well as minerals. See what you can find, Roger." Louisa explained to Roger what fossils were. They had seen a few fossils of wood on the ranch, but he had forgotten what they looked like. Soon they found pretty gem stones and a fossil with a fern pattern. Adam then asked, "Are you all right having a pre-dinner drink in the bar, Louisa? I'd like you to see the cherry wood bar Queen Victoria gave to Cody in

174

appreciation of his Wild West Show. The bar was made in France and shipped here."

Louisa laughed. "You know I've been to bars, Adam." But this bar was amazing. She wondered how they could get this long and massive structure from France. The cherry wood was gorgeous. They sat enjoying their drinks and the luxury of the room as other tourists and cowboys started to drift into the bar.

Later, Louisa stood a little straighter and walked sedately when they entered the dining room with crystal glasses and solid silverware on white linen table cloths, napkins in neat pleats above the china plates. Even Amelia Lewis would approve, Louisa thought.

"I'm having a T-bone steak," Adam declared after studying the menu. Louisa studied the menu a little closer. They even serve fish, sea bass and salmon!

"The children and I will share the veal," Louisa told the male waiter. "A glass of milk for Roger, please." Now, this is fancy. But I wonder why elegant restaurants have male waiters. I'm sure women could serve as well. Louisa leaned back in her chair. She didn't remember a time when she had felt this pampered. She loved Adam for treating them well.

The next day they saw the fringed leather jacket that Buffalo Bill Cody wore. And photographs of the Wild West Show: pictures of Annie Oakley shooting her rifle, rodeo riders, and Indians dressed in long headdresses and beaded shirts. There were beaded moccasins and rifles on display, and Frederic Remington bronze sculptures of bucking horses. Louisa had not seen anything like it before. The legs of the horses and the ropes held by the cowboys seemed thin. How could Remington get such thin clay to hold together as he cast the figures? Energized by all she had seen and learned in one day, Louisa was ready to go home. Her head was buzzing.

As they put their suitcase in the car to leave, Adam said, "I think we should go home by Powell rather than go back to Red

Lodge." Louisa nodded her assent but looked at him for more explanation. "There's a man who escaped from jail who is in the Bitterroot Mountains west of here. He's thought to be dangerous. A posse has been formed to find him. Even the Montana National Guard has been called in and given permission to work in Wyoming to hunt him down."

"What did he do?"

"Doesn't sound like much at first. His original offence was poaching a couple elk, but when he escaped jail, he went on to kill a cow which is a felony offence."

"Killing a cow is a felony?" Louisa was puzzled.

Adam laughed. "Come on, Louisa, you don't know that in the west, cattle rustling is a worse offence than kidnapping a child?"

"What! Hush!" She glanced to see that Roger and Peter were playing on the hotel porch bannister, and out of their hearing range. "How do you know all this, Adam?"

"I heard people talking about it when I was checking out of the hotel and asked some questions. The word is that he also killed a ranger and a rancher who were looking for him so he's very dangerous. He's a skilled woodsman, but they think they have him trapped in a canyon west of here. I'd rather go home by the more eastern route and stay out of harm's way."

"Of course. We don't need to get involved in some shoot out."

They were quiet for the 30 minute ride from Cody to Powell, each lost in their own thoughts. They had had a good breakfast at the hotel before visiting the Buffalo Bill Cody Wild West artifacts, but it was now past noon and they were once again hungry.

"Let's get a bite to eat here at Powell," Adam suggested. "It's another 4 or 5 hour drive, but we should be home by suppertime."

The café was next door to the National Bank. When Adam finished eating, he asked, "Louisa, I'd like to see if they'll cash a Yellowstone

Bank check for me next door. Do you mind waiting here for me for a few minutes?"

"Of course not. Roger and Peter are still eating." Louisa sat back, relaxing with her cup of coffee. It was grand being served and not having to wash dishes afterwards. She loved traveling.

Ten minutes later, Louisa heard gun shots. What's going on? People in the café moved to the window to see what was happening, but Louisa picked up Peter from his chair, whispered to Roger, "Come with me," and moved to a table at the back wall. She had a vivid memory of what happens when you move toward gunshots. She started saying nursery rhymes to the kids, distracting them from the street commotion. Her heart was beating hard and fast. I wonder what's happening? Miss Jones lying across her desk in a pool of blood crossed Louisa's mind. A fear for Adam flooded her whole being.

Inside the bank, a few minutes before, Adam had turned from putting his cash into his pocket at the teller's window to face a tall, broad, blonde with wild blue eyes and the beginnings of a beard. "Go face the wall," the muscular man brandishing a rifle said to all the customers in the bank. "Hands up!"

Adam raised his hands and moved with the other four customers, one a women, toward the wall. Adam's heart was pumping. Not the right time to argue with a man with a gun. He looks tough. Adam also saw two pistols shoved in the man's belt. What can we do? Adam was realizing that this has to be the escaped jailbird, Durand. And the posse is off in the mountains west of here looking for him. We're on our own!

Adam sized up the man. A couple of inches taller, maybe 50 pounds heavier and all muscle. I don't think I'd have a chance against him. And he's holding a gun.

"Keep those hands up!" the man yelled at Adam. "And ya'll face the wall." The robber leveled his rifle at Adam.

177

"Open the safe!" the robber shouted at the two tellers behind the teller windows. "You two," he motioned to the president and vice-president at their desks, "over here with your hands up."

"You," he shouted to one of the tellers. "Open up that safe behind you."

"It's impossible to do that, sir," the young, well-groomed teller responded politely and firmly. "The safe is on a time lock and will open only at 8 a.m. and 5 p.m."

"What the hell! Let me shoot off the combination."

"It will still remain sealed," the teller flatly stated. "It's built to unlock only twice a day." The teller's hands were in the air but he was looking coolly into the gunman's eyes, with not even a tremor in his voice, just stating the facts. It was obvious that he spoke the truth.

"Well, ain't that the shits." The big man's lip curled in distain as he looked down at the teller's nameplate. "Maur-ice. What kind of sissy name is that? OK, Maur-ice," he growled emphasizing the last half of the teller's name, "ya gather up all the bills and silver dollars in the drawers and put them here." Durand banged on the teller's window with his rifle.

Adam started to reach over to the woman who had gasped but immediately stood straight with hands up when Durand twirled around brandishing his rifle around the room. "Don't none a ya git to thinkin' ya kin do somethin'!"

He turned back to the bank officers. "You, Mister Hotshot President, put your hands out where I can tie 'em up." The robber pulled out a leather string from his pocket and with the quick skill of a rodeo calf roper tied the bank president's hands together. He nodded at the vice-president who in seconds had his hands tied with another leather string in a quick knot.

"Thanks, Maur-ice," the robber crowed as he stuffed the bills and silver dollars into his pockets. "I have two more leather cords," he said

178

inviting the tellers to put their hands together and in another minute, both tellers had their wrists tied.

"Now we'll have some fun. Earl Durand wasn't meant to die without a bit of excitement. You officers march to the door in front of me and," he turned to Adam and the four others facing the wall, "you can turn now and be witnesses."

And with that pronouncement, Durand started shooting out the windows, the lights, the ornamental wood work in the bank and then out the door across the street. Adam and the other customers crouched down as gun shots whizzed around them. Durand reloaded and kept on shooting in a random rampage. Soon shots were also coming toward the bank as townspeople realized a robbery was going on inside.

"Now, our grand exit," Durand shoved the four bank employees ahead of him through the bank doorway. Almost immediately, the teller beside Maurice fell with a mortal injury.

As the teller fell, Earl Durand was in view of townsmen and a bullet blast knocked Durand back across the bank doorway. Durand, still alive, crawled back into the bank.

Adam saw Durand pull a revolver to his head. There was one last gun shot.

There was utter silence for about 10 seconds. Then townspeople cautiously moved toward the bank. With the sheriff, police, rangers, and Guardsman in the mountains searching for Durand, there was no one to take charge. Powell's citizens came closer, standing in amazement in front of the bank, trying to understand what had happened.

Adam's concern was for his family. He wrote his name, address, and phone number on a bank note pad and gave it to Bank President Robert Nelson. "I doubt you'll need my eye-witness account, but here's the information if your sheriff needs me. I have a family to get home."

Adam pushed his way through the crowd to the now empty café next door where he saw Louisa at the back table calmly playing, "Patty Cake, Patty Cake, Bake Me a Cake" with Peter and Roger. Louisa was shaking as she stood and grasped him tightly.

"Adam. Adam. Oh, Adam," she repeated. The fear of his dying dissipated. Adam started tearing up, too, as he held her and rubbed her back. He squinted his eyes and cleared them. Roger and Peter only knowing that something big had happened hugged Adam's legs, calling, "Daddy, Daddy."

Adam slowly released Louisa. "You're okay? You aren't hurt?" she asked.

"I'm fine." Adam laid a $5 bill on the table for their lunch. "Let's get out of here, Louisa." He picked up Roger and Peter and they quickly walked to their car parked down the block.

They were nearly to Frannie before either one of them could talk calmly or coherently. The children, tired out, slept in the back seat for their afternoon nap as the parents began to share their views of the horrifying event. And then they couldn't stop remembering details.

Adam felt guilty for not taking better care of his family. "We should have gone straight home. I should have known Durand might find a way back to his hometown of Powell. Of course, even the law officials didn't imagine he'd backtrack into town. Most of them are probably still out hunting him at Clark's Canyon."

"No one could have known what he might do. That's the nature of a deranged mind, or maybe in this case, a terribly crafty mind. I'm so grateful you weren't hurt. Think of the danger you were facing. You could have been killed."

"I couldn't think of how to stop Durand. His physical build was amazing, all muscle. And he was clever. I can see how he out-smarted his trackers. But that teller, Maurice, was a cool character. He just told Durand the facts about the safe on a time-lock and Durand could tell he'd met his match. Durand knew his game was up. I think that's when Durand decided to go out in a blaze of gunfire. He wasn't going to walk away with thousands of dollars in his pocket, just a few hundred and not enough to get him very far. He decided if he couldn't get away, he'd have a dramatic ending. And that it was. But in the end, he killed himself."

When they reached Laurel, Roger was calling "Potty" and they stopped for gas. Louisa changed Peter's diaper in the back seat of the car while Adam took Roger into the station's rest room.

The radio was on at the station and the conversation from the station crew was lively. "There's been a bank robbery in Powell! It's on KGHL. A Billings Gazette stringer was near the bank when he heard the first gunshots and reported it! They're still figuring out what happened!" As Adam and Louisa listened with them they learned that 17 year-old Tipton Cox had skipped school that day to hang out at the Powell Texaco station across from the bank. The owner knew Tip was a good marksman and handed him a rifle. It was Tipton Cox's shot that stopped Durand.

As they listened, Adam and Louisa glanced at each other, knowing to keep quiet about what they had experienced. Adam smiled to himself as he handed his recently drawn cash from the Powell First National Bank to the gas station clerk. A withdrawal just before Earl Durand's withdrawal, he mused.

They left, going up the Laurel canyon and as they reached Clappers' Flat, red streaks with purple edges from a gorgeous sunset lined the western sky behind the Crazy Mountains. White strata clouds could still be seen in the darkening sky. It was as if God was reassuring them that all was well. Maybe living in the country miles from your nearest neighbor isn't so bad after all, Louisa thought. I'll be happy to stay and work at home. No more pining after a more exotic life! I've had enough excitement. I'm looking forward to a few boring days.

Lambing began. It was a relief to be at the ranch where the biggest problem was getting a ewe to accept her newborn. Adam and Louisa took turns getting up in the night to check on the progress of the ewes. While tired, they were safe. Louisa appreciated the steady routine.

One night as Louisa made her way to the lambing shed she saw the outline of the tree limbs in the light of the moon. Leaf buds were starting to appear. She rejoiced at the thought that no hail storm could kill them. Our trees are going to look beautiful once again. Adam's mom watered them faithfully to get them started. Now it's my turn to maintain life on the prairie.

Diamonds are Made Under Pressure

MOLT, 1941-1945

When we long for life without difficulties, remind
us that oaks are grown strong in contrary winds and
diamonds are made under pressure.

PETER MARSHALL (1902-1949)

Louisa adjusted to the ranch routine of planting, harvesting, canning, butchering, with the complementary tasks of cooking and baking, sometimes for branding or combining crews of 20 people. She took her turn at entertaining the extended families at holidays and providing for the community celebrations of weddings, christenings, and funerals. Karl and Victoria as their nearest neighbors had become their close friends and they did many activities together.

Louisa came to accept and even like the changes in the seasons she experienced at the ranch, the bitter cold of winter and the dry wind of the summer. Best of all, she loved spring as the pussy willows down by the springhouse became fuzzy and purple. Sweet Rockets sprouted in the ditch by the road and grew nearly to her height. Louisa started her own wildflower patch by the house, carefully transplanting yucca, Indian paintbrush, bluebells, daisies, pascal flowers, and bitterroot rose.

In the fall of 1940, Roger started 1st grade at the Mueller School and Louisa became friends with the teacher, a woman she admired. Periodically, Louisa would take Peter to the school with Roger and help tutor individual students in reading or math.

As December 1941 approached, Louisa was once again huge with child. At the ranch in Montana, the thunder of war and death across the ocean seemed remote, especially when life was running smoothly with a new birth imminent. Louisa ignored world events and concentrated on providing good meals and warm clothes for her family and knitting a shawl and cap for the baby whom she hoped would be a girl.

Nevertheless, underneath the daily chores was a sense of unease. They knew it was a troubling time. Hitler had rolled across Europe, starting in Poland in 1939, then Denmark, Norway, Luxembourg, Holland, Belgium, and France. Great Britain pleaded for help with President Franklin Roosevelt who was reluctant to enter into the war after experiencing the devastation of WWI.

On December 7, the noon broadcast on the radio shouted the news: the Japanese bombed Pearl Harbor! Louisa was jolted out of her complacency. The next day they learned that twelve battleships and 188 military airplanes were destroyed or damaged and about 2,500 servicemen and 68 civilians were killed. President Roosevelt called the nation to war.

How could so many Americans be killed in one day's battle? Frightened and worried, Louisa sat by the radio in her bathrobe listening to the news reports. She moved only to get breakfast on the table and then the dishes were stacked in the sink. At noon and again in the evening, a minimum of food was on the table and dishes piled up in the sink.

The next morning when he came in from milking, Adam found Louisa once again in her bathrobe listening to the radio. He decided to take action.

"Louisa, I'll find you a room close to the hospital to wait out your pregnancy and we will move you into Billings at the end of the week."

"Will you have to go to war, to fight?" Louisa was worried and more concerned about the year ahead than the week ahead.

"I doubt it. At 34, I'm too old and they need men to stay on farms to feed the nation. The most important thing right now is for you to have the care you need when you deliver the baby. We'll deal with the war effort later after you have the baby."

"Will they be bombing us in Montana?" Louisa could not get her mind on anything except the developing war for the U.S.

"Louisa, the war is in the Pacific islands and in Europe. They won't be here next week. But you're having a baby next week and that is what concerns me. Get a bag packed and when Roger is out of school on Friday, we'll drive into Billings and get you settled near the Deaconess Hospital." Louisa stared stonily at Adam. He isn't taking the bombing of Pearl Harbor seriously. This is the worst event of our lifetime. He isn't paying attention.

Adam stood calmly before Louisa, staring her down. "Louisa, you are about to have a baby. Do you prefer to have me deliver it or will you consent to going into Billings to a hospital?"

Louisa looked down at her huge belly. Suddenly, she realized he was right. It's time to have a baby. Louisa finally turned her attention to the immediate needs of the day and week. On Saturday Adam moved her into a small rented room close to the hospital.

Before he could leave her and return home, Louisa started giving him instructions. "Remember to call Victoria if you need help with the boys. She said she'd be glad to take them. You don't have to do it all yourself."

"We'll be fine," Adam assured her.

"Promise you'll make sure Peter drinks his milk. Why doesn't he like milk anymore? And that Roger has clean clothes when he goes to school."

"Louisa, I can take care of the kids. Trust me." Adam sighed and then winked at Roger. "We men can handle a few days alone."

185

Four days later, early on December 17, Adam heard the three shorts and a long which was their ring on the telephone party line. It was Margaret at the Molt General Store relaying a message from Louisa since the rural areas still didn't have a direct telephone connection to the cities. Adam could scarcely hear Margaret with neighbors on their party line picking up their phone when they heard the Martin ring to hear if Louisa had had her baby. Adam shouted into the phone, "Will you please get off the line so I can hear Margaret?" Numerous clicks were heard.

"What did you say, Margaret?"

"Louisa is on the line. You have a baby girl! Born a couple hours ago."

"That's terrific. Is the baby healthy? How is Louisa feeling?" Adam wanted to know everything. He was pleased Louisa would have a little girl to raise and to be her companion.

After a pause during which Margaret asked Louisa the questions and got the answers, she relayed the message. "Louisa says the baby is perfect. She's pretty bald, but looks like she'll be blonde like you. Louisa is glad it's a girl so she won't have to fight in a war. Hold on." Adam waited for Margaret to hear what Louisa was saying. "Louisa said she had eight hours of labor. The easiest birth she's had. She's tired, though, and the doctor wants to keep them for a week."

"Tell her to get her rest and we'll be in to get her on Christmas Eve."

Margaret returned with "Louisa said she misses you and will be looking forward to coming home."

Adam told Margaret, "Tell her that Victoria invited us for Christmas Eve and we'll stop there to celebrate and stay over before coming home."

"And thank you, Margaret." Adam hung up the phone, elated that Louisa and the baby were well. I forgot to ask what name she was giving the baby. She said it was a girl. Oh yes, so she wouldn't have to be in a war. Healthy, that's what's important.

After Roger got home from school, he told him and Peter together, "You have a baby sister. Your mom and sister will come home on Christmas Eve."

"Santa still come?" Peter asked very seriously.

"Of course," Adam replied, thinking that Santa had already brought him his gift of a baby girl with his beautiful Louisa.

"Can we hang up our stockings tonight?" Roger asked.

"Of course," Adam replied, wondering what in the world could he put in them?

"See Mommy agin?" Peter asked in a worried voice.

"Oh, yes, she's doing fine. Mommy will be home for Christmas with a baby sister!"

That night Roger and Peter hung their stockings by the pot belly stove. In the morning they discovered something round.

"A ball!" Roger shouted. "Santa brought a ball!" When Roger pulled it out, it was a red potato. "A potato?"

"A tato?" Peter repeated.

"What a great gift," Adam said. "We can roast them for supper tonight. Or would you like to save them to show Momma when she gets home?"

That night they hung their stockings again, hoping to get a toy or candy the next morning.

"A potato again?" Roger wondered as he felt the round object.

"Tato gin?" Peter repeated.

"Let's put them in a bowl for Momma to cook for us when she gets home." Seven days later as they left for Billings, the bowl held 14 shiny, red potatoes. Roger and Peter were still waiting for Santa to bring them something more.

On Christmas Eve, the road to Billings and back to Victoria and Karl's house where they would spend the evening was dusted with snow, but clear. Adam was in high spirits as he wrapped his chubby wife and their bald baby with a blanket in the front seat and put another blanket over Roger and Peter in the back seat.

"This is the best Christmas ever," Adam announced. Louisa closed her eyes and breathed deeply. It was special to be going home, but. . .

"Yes, indeed, a great Christmas," Louisa responded, but in her heart she was feeling the weight of the war. A baby born at the beginning of a war. God save us and all the babies born this year.

Victoria had squash soup and fish balls and Anna had made fruit cake for their holiday eve celebration. Roger and Peter were relieved to find real presents under the Mueller tree for them as well as for Johnny and Susan, their cousins.

"I have a little announcement," Victoria said shyly while they ate their dessert of Christmas cookies and canned plums. "Karl and I are expecting a baby late this spring."

"Congratulations! We're happy for you," Adam actually laughed for joy. Holding his own baby girl in his arms gave him great pleasure and he was elated that Karl would soon have another treasure to hold and care for.

"How wonderful! Sarah will have a playmate her age!" Louisa added. But she worried. Will our men be home to help us? Or will they be on some island in the Pacific fighting for our nation? What sacrifices will Victoria and I have to make?

After the children were in bed, Karl invited Adam to the barn for a cigar and some beer. After talking over the weather reports, cattle and crop prices, Karl told Adam he needed help making a decision.

"I've pretty much made up my mind to sign up to fight the Japs," Karl said. "I'm in good shape for being 26. I can take on anything an 18-year-old can. I know how to handle a rifle."

Adam responded slowly and thoughtfully. "You can get a waiver, Karl. They'll need us to keep agriculture production up to feed the troops. And you'll soon have another child. Think of Victoria. She'll need you. You don't have to go." Why would he want to leave? Adam wondered. There's going to be plenty of work to do right here.

"Adam, it's my patriotic duty to go! Geez, think of the boys killed at Pearl Harbor. I keep seeing that picture in the paper of the ships being blown up. You know, I'm pretty mild mannered, but that surprise attack made my blood boil. I'm itchin' to go. What the Japs did is wrong. We haven't done them any harm."

Adam took his time to respond. He could understand how the attack on U.S. soil made Karl angry, but he pondered over Karl's reaction. Pearl Harbor upset me, too, he was thinking, but I'm more sad and worried than angry. Maybe it's because I can remember WWI men coming home. I was 12, old enough to see the injuries and depression. My mom was suffering, too, during the war, not just the soldiers. Karl is younger. He didn't see what I saw.

"I respect whatever decision you make, Karl. Still, if you stay home, you'll also be helping your country. There'll be shortages of food and equipment and we'll have to do what we can to provide for those at home as well as the soldiers. I remember from WWI, your mom and mine tearing up good sheets for bandages, cutting up our best coats for vests and gloves for the winter Army. This war will affect every single American. You don't have to go off to some foreign land to serve. Staying home and supplying food is also a patriotic act."

The two good and old friends talked long into the Christmas Eve night.

Karl announced at breakfast that he was enlisting. Victoria left the table, crying. Louisa grabbed Karl's arm trying to get him to look at her. "Don't go. I beg you, don't go." Karl drew his arm away from her and looked away. Oh my God, this is terrible, Louisa thought. Karl can't take off and leave Victoria and Anna alone here at the ranch. They'll soon have a baby to care for as well as Johnny and Susan. What is Karl thinking? "Your family needs you, Karl. Please stay home and help take care of all of us here."

Adam rose from the table and put his hands on Louisa's shoulders, trying to comfort her. "Every man must make his own decision to fight or to stay, Louisa. Our job is to support Karl and help Victoria in any way we can."

"Don't worry about my family," Karl insisted. "My mom has run this place before and she can do it again. I've already talked to my brother, Eddie, about coming home to take over the heavy workload."

"Eddie?" Louisa looked up from her tears, remembering Eddie as a soft, tender-hearted pastor. "How can Eddie help?"

"When Eddie was a kid, he did everything I do now. He knows the routine. Plus he's a fine carpenter. He can fix anything that's built of wood. Might get some repairs done around here. And maybe he'll find a preaching job here, too, which is his passion."

"We'll help out, too, Karl," Adam assured him. Louisa's stomach turned over. *Adam and Karl have decided on our families' futures. Why, oh why, don't Victoria and I have a say in this decision!*

The excitement of the children opening their Christmas presents could not overcome the somber mood of their parents. The ham dinner served at noon ending with apple pie would be the last time they'd be eating together for many years.

Louisa hugged Victoria tightly as the Martins bundled up to travel the last five miles to their home. "Oh little sister, who would have thought we would have to face such a calamity as this in our lives?" Victoria patted Louisa and gently separated herself.

"Our family will make it, Louisa. Don't worry." *Don't feel sorry for me,* Victoria thought.

Adam and Louisa reached their home late Christmas Day, just ahead of the snow storms that kept them inside for much of the winter of 1942. The national news was worrisome. Men were volunteering from Montana at a high rate. There was talk of hosting Japanese-Americans from the coast at the University, taking the place of students who were leaving to fight. It didn't make sense! But the government was trying to find ways to contain anyone who might be supporting the Japanese government and what better way than hiding them at a Montana campus! Adam kept trying to focus Louisa's attention on the work they had, to try to keep her from getting emotional over events in the news.

Louisa settled into a rhythm, feeling some contentment, rocking and singing to her baby girl, providing food and clothes for her brood, and knitting woolen caps, socks, and gloves for the troops. And then wrapping cotton strips for the American Red Cross with her neighbors.

Production and prices had been fairly stable for four years. Now with the U.S. war effort, prices for cattle and wheat were rising. Adam was grateful as rain came at the right time and he looked forward to a bumper winter wheat crop. The problem was labor. Young Montana men had volunteered and high school students that Adam usually hired to help harvest were gone. Karl, too, of course, had left.

"I'll ask Dad and Mom to come home from California to help with harvest in August," Adam told Louisa. "You and Mom can drive the trucks. Dad can run the auger and spell me on the combine at mid-day for an hour. We'll run 16 hours a day and when we're done here we'll offer to do the same at the Mueller's and help out Victoria, Eddie, and Anna."

"Who's going to take care of the kids and feed everybody if Mary and I are driving trucks?"

"Let's see if your mom can come down for a couple weeks."

"Adam, our moms aren't young anymore. Can Mary even drive a truck? Do you think my mom can handle a newborn as well as two

191

older boys? And keep everyone fed? And how do I breast feed Sarah if I'm driving a truck all day?"

"You can breast feed while your truck is dumping grain into the bin. And trust me, after raising seven children of her own, your mom is strong enough to handle our three and provide food for all of us. And I doubt my mom has forgotten how to drive a truck. Roger can help by spreading the grain in the hog barn, so the wheat doesn't heat up and spoil."

"Adam, Roger is only eight!"

"Nearly nine. Old enough to work. We could ask your dad to come, but I'm betting Alois is helping Richard at the ranch or building houses in Great Falls for the air base."

Every able bodied person in Montana worked more than full-time during WWII. They later learned that a tenth of the population, 57,000 people, more than any other state per population, served in the military during WWII. Montanans also went to the West Coast to help in the militia and airplane factories. A drop in the state population intensified the need for laborers. Labor shortage was a bitter, tiring problem for those remaining in the state to work in the fields.

There were always major projects that demanded attention at the ranch. The watering system which consisted of a pump in a shallow well in the basement of the house was in need of repair. The water was often contaminated or was so low it didn't run at all except for a few vital hours. Alois came with Catherine for several weeks the second summer to solve the water problem. Alois put the family to work to build a concrete water cistern. Louisa and Roger helped break up the sandstone rock to be used as gravel for the concrete. A windmill provided the power to pump water up to the cistern. From the cistern, water fed into the house and the barn by gravity flow. The cistern was a great improvement with a regular supply of good water for the house and the barn.

Louisa was grateful to have steady, clean water. What a gift! "Papa, I can't thank you enough," she said giving him a big hug before he and Catherine left to go back to Moore.

Alois patted her, embarrassed by her emotion. "One does what one can, Louisa. Building a cistern is not a big project for me."

Louisa turned to hug her mom, but as usual Catherine stood a bit aloof. Louisa squeezed her arms and with tears in her eyes said, "Thanks, Mom, for taking care of the kids and cooking for us." Catherine stood tall and nodded her appreciation. Louisa breathed a bit deeper, holding back her tears. Mom is tough, but so am I. Thankfully, we are making it through these difficult years.

One late afternoon in the spring of 1944, Louisa arrived home in an agitated state after shopping in Laurel for groceries. She could scarcely wait for Adam to come in from chores. He didn't even have time to finish washing for dinner before her misgivings boiled out of her. She stood at the bathroom door while he wiped his face and hands.

"Did you know German prisoners are walking around Laurel just like anyone?"

"Calm down, Louisa. Yes, I know there's a POW camp at Riverside Park."

"The kids and I were going to Wold's and there they were, two of them, getting out of a car at the curb. They had POW in big letters on the back of gray shirts. They weren't shackled or anything."

"So, what did they do? Where did they go?" Adam was amused by her excitement. He led her back into the kitchen where the children sat waiting for supper.

"They went up the stairs above Wold's to the doctors' offices," Louisa explained.

"Well, then they probably needed medical attention," Adam replied.

"Nobody was guarding them, Daddy!" Peter shouted.

"That's not true. There was another man with them. He was the guard," Roger contradicted him.

"But he didn't have a gun. They could get away," Peter announced fearfully.

"What imaginations you all have," Adam calmly replied. "What do you think they could do? Where could they run? It's a long way across the continent and the ocean for them to get home."

"So what are they doing here, Adam?" Louisa had become less hysterical.

"For one thing, they are doing us a big favor, planting, hoeing, and harvesting the sugar beet fields for very little pay. I hear they get coupons for 80 cents a day to buy cigarettes or soap. Not much for their service. We need them. I wish we could have one working for us. And they are just like us, farmers or laborers. Maybe they'll stay here after the war is over." Louisa poured milk for the children and started dishing up the fried potatoes.

"Maybe they have relatives in Laurel," Louisa mused. "There are a lot of Germans living on the south side."

"It's good to have them where there are others nearby who speak the same language," Adam agreed. Louisa sat down remembering that her mom and dad had a difficult time learning English in Montana. They often said they yearned to be back in Kansas where they could talk freely with other Czech people. I hope people in Laurel are talking to the prisoners, she thought.

"Maybe having POWs in our back yard isn't so horrible." Louisa had calmed down. "Nevertheless, I wish, I pray this war ends soon." Oh, God, let this war end. I'm sick of it.

The war effort continued with rationing of gas, tires, sugar, and nylons. Even children became involved as the war intensified in Europe. The school teacher suggested that Roger memorize the silhouettes of a Messerschmitt ME 110 night fighter and the twin-engine Mitsubishi G4M2a bomber and report it immediately if he saw one. Roger, who loved to watch the commercial air flights over the ranch, was thrilled to be assigned such an enjoyable and important task. Maybe he'd spot a German fighter! He watched the skies closely but never saw enemy aircraft.

On August 6, 1945, the United States dropped an atomic bomb on the Japanese city of Hiroshima. Three days later the U.S. dropped another A-bomb on Nagasaki. News reports later indicated the two bombings killed at least 129,000 people with thousands of others permanently injured. They read that the rationale for the bombings was that the Allies had already used conventional firebombing that destroyed 67 Japanese cities. Even with that the Japanese had refused to accept the Allies' demand of an unconditional surrender which Nazi Germany had agreed to on May 8 just after Hitler committed suicide. The final act of World War II was the bombing of Hiroshima and Nagasaki.

Louisa was distraught over the unleashing of atomic weapons that kill so many people. What a terrible outcome with innocent people dying and being injured: mothers and babies and misled men.

"How can we ever be forgiven for using such a destructive force? Will other countries be able to use these massive bombs against us? Adam, will we ever be able to live without fear of atomic bombs?"

"We'll have to meet future threats if and when they come. Just be thankful the wars in Europe and the Pacific are over. The wars are over, Louisa, and we can go back to a normal life." But we'll be living with fear of atomic bombs the rest of our life, Louisa thought. I'm relieved this war is over, but we'll never go back to a normal life.

Their dear friend Karl Mueller would be home again and the two families could once again share holidays together. Louisa was looking forward to seeing and being with Karl again, the two families being one happy unit again. They had made it through the worst of times; fighting other nations was over for them.

Gaunt and tired, Karl looked like an old man when he got off the train. He loosely hugged Victoria, Johnny and Susan. He seemed startled to see his youngest, Dale, born after he had enlisted, now 3 years old. When Adam reached out to shake Karl's hand and pull him close to him in an embrace, Karl pulled back.

"It's okay, buddy," Adam said, his eyes moist. "Glad you made it home in one piece."

Karl's eyes squinted into slits and with a low growl said to Adam, "Don't touch me." Man alive, Adam thought, he ISN'T in one piece. What has he seen and gone through? He has serious scars on his soul.

Louisa lightly patted Karl's uniformed arm and when Karl didn't look at her, she turned away to let the tears flow silently. Oh my Lord, where has our dear Karl gone? Such a sweet boy, swinging me around on the dance floor, teaching me about milking, and so much more. Karl, Karl, please come home. Sarah hugged Louisa's knees and buried her head in her mother's skirt. Something bad was happening. Louisa patted Sarah's back and reached out to bring Peter into her embrace.

Travelers swirled around the small group as the two families stood in a quandary, together physically but not united. I wish Anna were here instead of staying home to fix supper, Louisa thought. She'd know what to do, what to say to her son. Anna has experienced all kinds of tragedy, her daughter's suicide, her husband's automobile accident. She'll know how to help Karl. Victoria should get Karl home to the ranch where Anna can help him. Get Karl fed. My God, he's a ghost of himself. No wonder he's out of sorts. He's been starved to death. And let him sleep off his nightmares.

Louisa put her arm around her sister trying to comfort her. Victoria was stiff as a board and had not said a word. Her eyes were blinking in confusion. Meeting Karl this way was not what she had anticipated. In fact, it was the opposite of what she imagined. Three years apart and they were now strangers.

"We'll help you get home," Louisa said to Karl. "Anna is waiting for you with supper. A good night's sleep will do wonders for all of us. Would you like Adam to drive you and your family home and I'll follow in our car?"

Karl picked up his duffle bag and said, "I can get my own family home. I haven't forgotten where I live." He looped his duffle bag over his shoulder, picked up his three year old who he had just met, took Susan by the hand, and said, "Show me where the car is, Victoria." He walked through the depot doors to the street with Victoria and Johnny following in a dazed state.

Left behind, Louisa put her face into Adam's shoulder and bawled, "Oh God, it's awful. War is awful. Where is the Karl we know?" This is not normal. Life will never be normal again.

What did happen to Karl? Adam thought. War wasn't easy on any of us. Exhaustion. All I can think is how tired I am. Still, I experienced nothing like Karl. Wonder if he'll ever talk about what he saw or what he went through. I wonder if he's physically injured or if it is all mental.

Like so many Montana WWII veterans, Karl never did talk about the war. He just went back to work on his ranch. Karl had become serious and isolated himself from his friends and neighbors. Even Victoria became less light-hearted and distant. I've lost my witty sister, Louisa thought, along with sweet Karl. The Martins didn't see the Muellers as often as they once did.

The war, with its doubled hours of labor, had in some ways broken Adam's spirit also. He was tired of the never-ending seasonal changes of plowing, seeding, fertilizing, harvesting, feeding cattle and sheep, lambing, calving, branding, shearing, putting up hay, and marketing. Never getting a full night's sleep and not having had a vacation for years, he needed a change. With the demand for farm products, the war had given him plenty of cash. He had paid off the ranch mortgage with its increased land holdings, built a stock shed, and when he could get it, bought better machinery. The ranch was in good shape. Adam was ready for something different.

Over the Christmas holidays, he surprised Louisa by saying, "What would you say about moving to California?"

"What an idea! Are you serious? Just pick up and leave? Leave everything?"

"Yep. I'm thinking of buying land down by your brother, Alvin, somewhere north of Sacramento."

"Alvin? You don't even know Alvin." Or what a drunk he is, she thought. I have plenty of memories of him waking me up when we were in high school as he slipped into the house from a drunken spree. How could Alvin help Adam?

"I know from your letters from Alvin that he and Charley have an irrigated acreage raising rice. Your pa says they are doing well down there. It doesn't take as much work as this ranch. Can you imagine the water they must have to do that? Nothing like our dry land farming. I'm curious about their farming methods."

"What will you do with the ranch? Even though Henry died, don't you feel some responsibility for keeping it in the Martin family name?"

"Oh, I wouldn't sell the ranch. I'd like to keep it as the Martin ranch for a couple more generations. But Bobby Holden could lease it. I picked him up for temporary work from the Billings Day Labor service, but he turned out to be a hard worker."

"Have you talked to Bobby?" Once again, Louisa figured, Adam's made decisions without talking to me first.

"You know Bobby got married this fall to a good woman. He needs something better than being a hired man and he could make a good living from our place and pay us a tidy lease payment. They could live here in the ranch house instead of the bunk house."

Louisa started thinking of the good dishes she'd have to pack up and store someplace. But there wasn't much else of value.   Louisa was amazed at Adam's decision. I'm lucky to have a husband who isn't afraid to try new experiences. He knows I hated living here in the country, although I got used to it. But he's not suggesting this change for me. He has wanderlust in his soul. And not many wives would embrace this kind of change. I like adventure, too. And do I ever love the idea of warm California. But Alvin? What could Alvin teach Adam? Well, you never know. Let's see what Alvin has done.

"I like your idea, Adam. But can we find a place not too close to Alvin?"

"I was thinking of heading for Santa Rosa, it's about 50-60 miles west of where Alvin farms."

"What a beautiful name for a town. Sounds good. I'm ready to see the rest of the world. I might like California. All right. Let's do it. Do you think we'll have trouble finding gasoline for the trip?"

"We still have a few good gas ration coupons. And gas is more plentiful again. Shouldn't be a problem."

After Christmas the family packed up the Buick with essentials and drove west. While they were anxious to get settled somewhere before school started in January, they wanted to take time to see the big trees at the Humboldt Redwood State Park in Northern California.

"Adam, can you believe this? The road actually goes through the middle of one tree!" Louisa stared out the car window at the road ahead. With little traffic, Adam stopped the car and they took a picture of the car and the kids in the center of the tree trunk.

They drove on Highway 1 along the ocean, stopping on the beach. The weather and water was warm enough for these Montana children, used to playing in snow, to take off their shoes and socks, roll up their trousers, and run in the tide. The ocean is better than the prairie, Louisa thought. I can see forever and no mountain stops the view. It's quiet with the lapping waves on the beach. The view and the sound covers up the complexities and confusions found inland. I could live right here and die happy. Louisa raised her arms to the sky, breathed deeply throwing back her head, rejoicing in the sun, sand, water, and space.

Adam bought a small house in Santa Rosa. Adam and Louisa scouted around and found a few used pieces of furniture and kitchenware to set up their household for the time being. Roger and Peter started school and Sarah found a pre-school friend her age next door.

Alvin was soon invited to drive over for Sunday dinner. Louisa ran out of the house to greet Alvin as he got out of his car, astounded at what she saw. Heavens, he's taller and stouter. His hair is combed back and he has a mustache. He's wearing a suit! Is this Alvin?

"Hi, Sis." Alvin swung her around with a bear hug. "I've missed you. I miss family. I'm so glad you're here." He was nearly in tears.

"I can't believe how much you've changed." Louisa was struck by what she saw and felt.

Alvin laughed. "Well, it takes longer for some of us to grow up. I had to learn life's lessons the hard way. Papa and Mama gave us good instruction. I eventually heard those words of advice when I was a thousand miles away from home."

That day they learned how Alvin had been able to develop a rice farm near Woodland. With the Mediterranean weather, fertile soil, and plenty of water, production was high. Three rice mills surrounded Woodland, so transportation to market was no problem. Not like in Montana where wheat and cattle transportation to the coast or to Chicago lowered their net gain.

"The biggest problem the last few years was labor," Alvin said, and Adam responded with "same for us."

"Our Japanese workers, who knew a lot about rice paddies, were evacuated to Wyoming as prisoners of war," Alvin continued.

"Wyoming? I didn't know that." Louisa responded. "Were they supporting the Japanese government?"

"Heavens, no." Alvin explained. "Most were American citizens, but our government feared they'd be sympathetic to the Japanese and would somehow hurt the war effort." Louisa couldn't help but think about how Hitler put people he didn't like into prisons. Probably a few of our Czech relatives were picked up as gypsies and thrown into a prison. Were we the same? How could the U.S. do something as terrible as putting hard-working, patriotic people into a barbed-wire camp? It's not the same as the POWs who were held in Laurel. They had fought against us.

Alvin went on, "A couple of our Japanese workers have returned to us, but the war years treated them poorly." Louisa was reminded of the devastating effect the war had on Karl. I wonder if the world will ever fully recover.

"And what about Charley? You're still working with him?" Louisa was afraid to ask, but still wanted to know what happened to him.

"He's great. We're good partners. He has a really swell wife, Elsie. You'd like her, Louisa. And he has good kids that help us in the rice fields. I stay with them at their house. I've not been as lucky as Charley in finding a good woman. They're a wonderful family and I'm fortunate to be with them."

Seeing Alvin healed some of the old emotional wounds for Louisa. She was relieved that Alvin had become a warm, caring, hard-working adult. Adam learned all he could about farms in the area from Alvin. It took Adam less than a month to realize that, at California prices, land ownership was way out of his reach. He looked for a job and fortunately found one on a 12 acre chicken farm where he built chicken coops. This was not, however, what he dreamed of doing. By the middle of summer, Adam knew this scheme of his for buying land and living in California was not working for him.

"Let's go to L.A., see Mom and Aunt Margaret and then head home," he suggested to Louisa one evening. They were sitting on the porch and Louisa could see and smell the rose bush on the corner of the house. Egrets were flying overhead and she remembered the blue heron she had seen earlier in the day. She closed her eyes, feeling the warmth of the evening on her skin. When Adam couldn't buy land, I knew this day would come, but I hate leaving this lovely area, she thought with regret.

"With the lease on the ranch, where would we live?" she asked.

"We'll go back to the ranch for a couple weeks and help Bobby harvest. With nothing but elementary schools in the country, however, we've got to find a place in town before fall so Roger can start junior high school. How about Laurel? Do you like Laurel? It's close to the ranch and close to Billings for shopping and cultural events that you like."

"It's okay," Louisa slowly responded. "Laurel seems to be thriving well with the railroad and refinery." She nodded her head in agreement with him. "I think Laurel is a good choice. Laurel, it is!" Laurel doesn't have the beautiful scenery and warm weather like Santa Rosa. Still, Laurel is a lovely name for a town and has good schools. And it'll be far better than living at the ranch. Louisa was ready for a new chapter in her life.

Adam didn't have faith in his old Buick anymore, so he sold it in Santa Rosa. The family took a bus to San Francisco and then a train to Los Angeles. Adam's dad, Henry, had died during the war years, but Mary and Aunt Margaret who shared a house welcomed them and showed them around Los Angeles. Adam got a kick out of seeing how much LA had changed in the 14 years since he had worked there in his Aunt Margaret's automobile repair shop. Louisa enjoyed seeing the unusual architecture and sights of southern California. The visit was not long enough for Louisa. Too soon they were on the train to Billings.

They stayed in the bunk house for a couple weeks and helped Bobby and his wife with the harvest. Afterward they used the ranch pickup to move a few household items to the house Adam bought at 513 Wyoming Avenue in Laurel. A new family era began in town where Louisa wondered if she and the children could find friends and meaningful activities.

Hold Fast to Dreams
LAUREL, 1946-1950

Hold fast to dreams
For if dreams die
Life is a broken-winged bird
That cannot fly.

Hold fast to dreams
For when dreams go
Life is a barren field
Frozen with snow.

LANGSTON HUGHES (1902-1967)

"Gramma" Jones who made hand-sewn quilts lived next door. Next to her were the Bridgers who had two sons, one a year younger than Peter, and another Sarah's age. Next door to them were the Ficks with so many children, Louisa never knew how many. The day the Martins moved in, three of the Fick children came into the kitchen and stood watching the family eat supper. They looked hungry. Louisa offered each of them a slice of bread with butter and jam, but they shook their heads "No" and waited politely until supper was over. Then all six children went to the back yard to play.

Well this is different, Louisa thought. Neighbors! Children who hang around our house. Schools our children can walk to! A grandmother I can talk with anytime I feel like it. Groceries within walking distance. A cozy house where prairie storms will not blow it away. I like it.

Within a week, Adam found a job for 95 cents an hour at a saw mill. Neither Adam nor Louisa would be satisfied with that! Still, it was a good job and one took whatever work was available while looking for something better. Fortunately, they also had lease money from the ranch. With wheat and cattle prices at near record highs, the war years had brought a small fortune to Adam. Now Adam wanted to enjoy life after having worked long hours at the ranch during the war without the help of laborers. An 8 a.m. to 5 p.m. work schedule was relaxing!

Adam kept his eyes open for an automobile he could buy since the family was now on foot. The cars that were available to buy were five or six years old because new cars had not been made, the materials going instead to build war machinery. Adam wanted a new car, and he didn't want to be on a long waiting list.

One Saturday afternoon in early fall, at the urging of Roger, the family rode the school bus with team supporters to watch a football game between Columbus and Laurel. Before the game started, Adam walked over to see his friend and old boss, Mike Davey of Davey Motors. Mike had one new car on display. With so few cars coming onto the market, Mike did not want to sell the one he had. Adam offered him cash. With a little persuasion, Mike couldn't turn Adam down. The Martins rode home in style!

In November, having barely adjusted to the new schools and living in town, Louisa was in for another surprise. "Would you and the kids be okay if I went to Helena for four months in the new year?" Adam asked Louisa one night after the children were in bed.

"My word, what would you do in Helena?"

"Anna Mueller told me the Republicans need an assistant Sergeant-of-Arms for the legislature. It pays better than the saw mill and I think it would be interesting work. I could stay with friends of the Muellers."

"I didn't realize you were that interested in politics!" There's a lot I don't know about this husband of mine, Louisa thought. Politics! I was the one working to get Anna Mueller elected and Adam didn't stuff one envelope! Now, here he is, wanting to be in the middle of it.

"When I was young," Adam explained, "I always wondered what Senator Mueller was doing. And I wondered if I could ever be a senator. Anyway, what you read in the papers is not what happens. I know that from the stories he'd tell us. I'm curious about the process. I've heard it's like making sausage." Adam laughed at the thought of chopping up and stuffing legislative bills into pork casings.

"Hm, I can see that watching the legislators might be fascinating," Louisa said while thinking that it sounded more frustrating than fascinating. "So what will you be doing?"

"The Sergeant-of-Arms primarily makes sure only people with credentials are allowed onto the floor of the Senate or the House. Kinda like a guard."

"Would it be dangerous?" she asked. "What if bullies try to get into the chambers? Do you carry a gun?"

"No, of course not. How could it be dangerous?" Adam laughed. "Representatives themselves will make sure no unsavory characters gain entrance to their hallowed chambers. My biggest problem will be buying a suit and a couple white shirts."

Louisa started to see the advantages to this idea and responded more enthusiastically. "You'll meet new people and learn a lot. You'll probably know all the legislators before you're done." Maybe Adam will be a legislator someday. Maybe he'll be governor! Louisa started to dream about the possibilities. I could be a grand lady in the governor's mansion. I could help change policies!

"Maybe you and the kids could come and visit. Will you be all right here by yourself? Will you need the car? You should be able to get around town without it, don't you think?"

"That's not a problem. We can walk to schools and the grocery store. You can take the car. We'll be fine."

"The job is for four months and then I'll find work around here. Opportunities will open up."

"We'll be fine," Louisa repeated, not totally sure they'd be fine. Things were different in town and now she'd be without Adam. But look at all the good neighbors! I know Gramma Jones will help me if I need it. "I'm excited for you, Adam."

As Christmas neared, Adam was determined to get Louisa something she really wanted: a radio. Adam remembered the stories about how Louisa and Mable had put together education radio programs when they were students in Billings. The radio had a lot of static at the ranch, but it's a clear signal in Laurel. Listening to the radio was one of Louisa's greatest pleasures at the ranch. The radio would help Louisa through the winter days and nights. Because of the war, like everything else, radios were in short supply.

One day Adam went into Wold's Department Store to buy a radio. The clerk emphatically told him, "No radios are available."

"I wonder where I can find one," Adam said to the clerk. "I'll pop upstairs to the office and ask Mr. Wold."

Adam walked into O.M. Wold's office. There on his desk was a radio! After announcing himself, Adam told Mr. Wold, "I'd like to buy a radio."

"We have none," Mr. Ole Martin Wold, with all his department store authority said, looking at Adam over the top of his wire-rimmed glasses.

"What about the one here on your desk?"

"It's not available," Mr. Wold replied.

207

"I'll take it, paying with cash," Adam said as he opened up his wallet with a wad of money. Adam left the store with his radio.

After Louisa had opened her Christmas present, Adam laughingly told Louisa the story of how he got the radio. What brashness, Louisa thought. This is my husband? I'm amazed at his overwhelming confidence. What more lies ahead?

"I have another surprise you'll like. The lot across the street was up for sale at a reasonable price. I bought it so we could build a new house."

Louisa's mouth fell open. "What in the world!" Why didn't he tell me before he bought it? Why doesn't he ever consult with me on important decisions? Anger started building up in Louisa. She had had enough of his domineering behavior.

Adam went on. "You've told me that this house is too small with the kids bunched up into one bedroom. I agree that Roger needs his own room. And I know you'll be happier in a big, new house." Why isn't she responding? Adam wondered. I thought she'd be excited about the idea. She told me we needed a bigger house. I thought she'd be dancing all around me.

Instead, she blandly said, "I don't know what to say."

"You could design the house, or at least tell a contractor what you'd like. You like to draw. You could draw out the rooms, like an architect." He was looking at her now, studying her.

"Draw up house plans," she flatly responded.

"Louisa, you've always wanted a dream house. Now is your chance. You've told me about working with your dad building houses. You could do this!" Adam found himself almost pleading.

A few seconds went by before the words fell out of her. "Oh, my gosh, oh, yes, I could do that. I have lots of ideas about how a house should be built. When I was little, I did follow Papa around when he worked at construction. I know quite a bit about how a house is built. Adam, you're a jewel." Louisa wrapped her arms around him and gave him a big hug.

Adam grinned and hugged her back. "That's my girl. I know you'll have the house designed before I get back from Helena."

And she did. In her mind, Louisa always had a dream house. Louisa telephoned her father in early March. "Papa, I need you to look at my house plans. Could you and Momma come for Easter? Maybe Richard could bring you? I'll write a note to Ceci and invite them, too."

"Slow down, Louisa. What's the rush?"

"It's nearly Spring and the weather is good enough to lay the foundation."

"Will Adam be home by Easter? He needs to approve your plan."

Louisa paused for a minute before responding politely. "The legislators have that weekend off and Adam will be home on Saturday." Papa doesn't trust me to draw up house plans by myself!

"I'll talk to your momma. How are the children?"

"Sarah had the chicken pox last month and we were under quarantine for a week, but we're all healthy now."

"Good. Good. Your momma will send you a letter tomorrow if we can come." Alois hung up the telephone, nervous about how much all that talking on the telephone would be costing Adam.

Louisa hung the telephone on its hook on the wall. She studied her drawings of the house layout once more. What if something is totally wrong? I can scarcely wait for Adam to come home.

She looked at the clock and hurried to turn on the radio. Just in time, she heard the opening, "We give you Stella Dallas, a continuation on the air of the true-to-life story of mother love and sacrifice, in which Stella Dallas saw her own beloved daughter, Laurel, marry into wealth and society and, realizing the differences in their tastes and worlds, Stella went out of Laurel's life."

Louisa pulled out her ironing board, filled her steam iron with water, and plugged it into the wall socket. As she listened to the most recent heartache between Stella and Laurel, Louisa ironed the ruffles on Sarah's dress. Thank goodness we'll never have those kinds of problems in our family, Louisa thought. We belong to each other no matter what. Sarah will never go off and live with someone different from us. Louisa relaxed as she drifted into imagining the lives of her radio friends with crises far more troublesome than her own at the time.

Family holiday gatherings were frequent for the Martins and the Janocheks. It was normal for half the extended family to wake up at 5 a.m., drive for three or four hours, have dinner with the other family members, and then drive the three or four hours to get home late at night. As small as their house was, Louisa could find space to serve Easter dinner for her parents and Richard, Helen, and Victoria's families.

Seventeen-year old Raymond, the eldest of the next generation, took charge of his cousins who followed him down the block to the dirt lot where he set up a softball game. The neighborhood kids joined in the game with them. Lots of kids, but Raymond got them organized.

"We need two teams. Line up, tallest to shortest," Raymond ordered. "Count off, 1,2,1,2 from the tallest to the shortest and remember your number," which they did. "All the 1's are one team and bat first. Roger, you're in charge of the 1's. All the 2's come here and we'll figure out your positions."

When the littlest kids didn't know where to stand, Raymond picked them up and set them where they should be, saying "watch for the ball and when it gets close, run and catch it. Then throw it to the biggest boy near you." The girls played along with their brothers and boy cousins. Roger, who normally ignored his sister, watched the attention being showered on Raymond, and helped Sarah with her swing when it was her turn to bat.

For dinner, parents dished up the plates for their children who sat in the living room on a blanket on the floor. Louisa had made ham, potatoes, corn, beans, and a cake with lemon frosting. With their stomachs full, the children went back outdoors to play while the grownups carefully looked over Louisa's sketches for the new house and listened to her ideas.

"A clothesline on the garage roof? That's crazy, Louisa," Helen exclaimed. "What if you step back to see what you're doing and fall off the roof?"

"Do you need a two-car garage?" Alois asked. "You have only one car! And what automobile can't stand a little rain and snow?"

"Papa, you know Adam likes his car to look good." Louisa defended the garage, looking at Adam for approval. "And the boys can use the garage for their chemistry projects or whatever activities they dream up," she added, thinking of a school laboratory.

"With the attached garage you can't step out of the kitchen to catch a breath of fresh air and see the flowers," Catherine slowly remarked.

"You're right, Momma. But think how handy it would be able to step from the car to the kitchen without getting wet in a rain or snow storm!" Louisa started to worry that her family didn't like her innovative ideas.

"Your dirty clothes chute from the 2nd floor is a terrific idea," Victoria said. "That'll save a lot of running up and down stairs."

"Don't you want a basement?" Ceci asked. "Where will you make sauerkraut and store potatoes and canned goods?"

"There's a lot more cupboard space, plus there's a closet under the stairway that you can enter from the garage, like a root cellar," Louisa nervously explained.

"I've never seen a house with the sink in the hallway and the toilet and tub in separate rooms," Richard mused. "Pa, will there be a problem with the water pipes? How do you get to a hot water tank without a basement? Oh wait, where is the furnace and hot water heater, Louisa?"

"In the hallway! Easy to get to! But they'll be enclosed so you don't see them." Louisa was getting exasperated and fearful that all was wrong.

Everyone was jabbering about her design in a critical way. Louisa didn't hear any approval and certainly not a consensus on the overall project. She was disappointed. She wanted her family to love her dream house like she already loved it. It wasn't a mansion like the Lewis mansion, not by a long shot. Just a solid, well-designed house. Oh why, oh why didn't they like it?

"All your ideas are really great, Louisa," Adam pronounced into the clamor. He silenced them. "I like the design. Go ahead and explain your plan to Barney this week. I'll tell him to get started digging as soon as the ground thaws."

They all looked at Adam, astounded at his ready agreement.

Louisa breathed out a big, happy, "Yes. Thank you, Adam." His approval is what she had been waiting for and what she needed to hear. He really does love me and respect me, even after 16 years, she thought. It doesn't matter what the rest think. Adam likes it!

Louisa, ecstatic from Adam's affirmation of her, couldn't wait for the family to be gone so she could begin actual work on the new house. However, she quickly learned that waiting was a big part of the building process; there were endless decisions to be made. It was a relief to Louisa to have Adam home when the legislative session ended to help her with the construction process.

"I found a good job with the Production Credit Agency in Billings," he told her almost before he set down his suitcase. "I met the director in Helena. They need someone with agricultural experience to talk to farmers about their goals and budgets before deciding on giving them loans. It's something I'm good at. I enjoy working on financial accounts."

212

"And you're good working with people," she agreed. "Patient and steady. But you'd have to drive to Billings every day?"

"Yes, or to the farms, but that won't be a problem, will it?"

"No, I guess not." She sighed, thinking of how she had imagined driving the car for shopping, the children's activities, and church gatherings, instead of walking. "Just that there might be times I need the car."

"We'll work it out," Adam assured her. Other matters were on his mind. "I'm going to have to get some good work shoes and a couple more shirts. Never thought I'd have a job in an office. I'm to be there next Monday."

"I knew you'd find a good job, Adam." We'll soon have a new house and Adam will be working in an office. Finally! We're on our way up the economic ladder. I might get a new dress, myself, a bought one, not home-made. She dreamed once again of new dresses.

The months flew by as Louisa busied herself, making sure Adam had decent looking "city clothes" for work, the kids got to the summer park recreational programs as well as church vacation school, and in watching the new house go up across the street. She was glad when school started in the fall with Sarah in 1st grade, giving Louisa more free time to work on details for the new house.

Finally in the spring of 1948, the new house was completed. Louisa wanted an hour to herself with her dream and walked across the street to greet her creation before the family got home.

Oh, my Lord, it's beautiful. Thank you, Louisa prayed as she walked up the concrete sidewalk and steps to enter the wooden front door with its small glass inset with frosted etchings. Her pumps clicked on the wooden floor. We may need an entry rug here, she thought. She slid back the closet door on her right and hung up her coat, grateful for closets, actual closets built into the bedrooms with doors that shut with clean clothes hanging beautifully from hangers. No more cardboard armoires sticking out into the bedroom crowding the beds. Louisa gently closed the entry sliding closet door to turn and view her living room.

Oh, my gosh, it's perfect. Roysdan's furniture store that afternoon had rolled out the area carpet with its pattern of gray, pink, maroon, and floral pattern. A drop-leaf walnut table that could be pulled out from the wall and opened up to seat 12 people was set under the picture window. Mrs. Roysdan had helped her pick a mirror with a blooming desert painting on it which now hung above the dusty rose colored sofa. Louisa could see her reflection with blooming cacti surrounding her. Louisa had picked out a gray velveteen reclining chair for Adam and next to it a swinging floor lamp so he could relax and read the newspaper in the evening.

Louisa gingerly sat on the sofa breathing a sigh of satisfaction. A thin branch from a newly planted tree in the boulevard outside the window waved gently in the slight breeze bringing a sense of peace into the room, welcoming her. The scene was framed with crème colored drapes with green and rose patterns. She could imagine a Christmas tree, a big one as tall as the ceiling in the front window.

Louisa explored the upstairs with two bedrooms and their own bathroom. She was delighted with book shelves and a desk off the stair landing. I'm definitely getting a new set of encyclopedias for the children. What a great place to study.

Louisa explored every inch. Everything she'd ever wanted was there. She looked forward to entertaining family and friends. She knew she'd feel comfortable asking the preacher and the church folk for Sunday dinner. It was her castle.

It didn't take long to move all their material goods across the street to the new house. Adam arranged for friends from Molt to move into the old house on a rent-to-own contract.

Louisa wanted to keep everything perfect in this new house, so she strictly monitored the children's activities. No food was allowed anywhere except in the kitchen with a linoleum floor. Each child had Saturday chores: cleaning the bathrooms, emptying the garbage, vacuuming the carpet, scrubbing the kitchen floor, and picking up their own rooms. They mowed the lawn, picked raspberries, and shelled peas. In many ways, the new house meant more work for everyone; it wasn't easy. Louisa, however, reveled in her domain, a dream come true.

Halloween arrived; it was a big event for Laurel school children. Peter had become a ghost and Sarah turned into a witch.

"I'll go around the block with them to trick-or-treat if you let me go with my friends afterward for at least an hour," Roger negotiated with his mom. As a 9th grader he thought he was too old to be trick or treating around the neighborhood. Louisa sadly agreed, realizing how old her oldest son now was.

Louisa made popcorn balls looking like pumpkins to hand out to the children that came to their door. That Sunday night with children coming and going as goblins and goofy looking clowns, the phone unexpectedly rang interrupting the excitement.

"I have sad news, Louisa," Alois announced after a cursory "Hello." "Now don't get upset, but a terrible thing has happened. Sit down and listen to me." He could tell from Louisa's excited greeting that she would have a hard time listening to him.

Louisa stuck the bowl of popcorn balls into Adam's hands and sat down on the stool under the phone in the hallway. Her dad sounded more serious than normal. Golly, I hope Mom is all right. Louisa's heart started pounding more rapidly and a hot flash went through her body. Please let it not be Mom.

"It's about your brother, Alvin. He was working, plowing a field yesterday. He wasn't ill. He hasn't been sick for years. Charley was working nearby and saw it all. Alvin stopped the tractor, got off, and started walking to the truck when he collapsed. Charley got Alvin to a hospital right away but he died. Charley thinks Alvin's heart just gave out."

"What? How can that be? Alvin isn't that old. He looked healthy when we saw him a couple years ago." Maybe a little chubby, she thought, but in good shape. "He looked strong." Louisa sighed. She had really started to like Alvin.

"You never know when the Reaper will come, Louisa." Louisa was trying to comprehend that Alvin had died. And why would Alvin be the first in our family to go. Alois didn't rush the conversation. He was struggling with his own emotions.

"How's Momma? How's she taking it?" Louisa finally asked.

"Momma's fine, but we need you to go to California and bring back Alvin's body to be buried here in Moore."

"Oh, Papa, I can't do that. I don't know the first thing about doing something like that."

"You're the only one in the family who can do it. Richard's sorting calves to sell, Walter's preaching, Hank can't leave the store, and I'm in the middle of getting a roof on a house before snow flies."

"Why does anyone have to go? Couldn't they just, you know, couldn't they somehow, put him, put the body on the train in a coffin? I don't want to go. I have children, a husband to take care of, a new house. Papa, please, don't make me do this." God, please spare me from having to get Alvin. Everything's finally going well. I don't want this interruption in my life. And I don't know anything about making arrangements for someone who has died.

"I want him buried here in Moore, at home. There are papers to sign to get him out of California. Charley can't do it. It has to be family who identifies him and brings him home." Oh, no, this is even worse, Louisa thought. I'll have to face Charley. I hate the thought of seeing him ever again. This is the last thing in the world that I want to do. Alois continued, "You need to do this for your family." Silence. "Is Adam home? Let me talk to him."

Louisa knew Adam would agree with Alois. After talking with his father-in-law, Adam took charge. He called the train depot to get the schedules from Billings to Woodland, California and then from Woodland back to Moore. He called Charley to tell him Louisa would arrive on Tuesday evening.

Monday morning Adam fed the kids toast and jam and sent them to off to school while Louisa packed. Then he drove Louisa to the Billings depot to catch the faster train. He escorted her onto the train platform and kissed her tenderly.

"I'll miss you, Louisa, but don't worry about the kids or me. You just take care of this family business for your dad."

"You don't know half of it, Adam." Louisa's lip started to quiver. He pulled her closer to him and spoke softly into her ear.

"I know every family has its dark secrets and that you weren't fond of Alvin. I also know we grow stronger from facing what we don't know. You'll come out of this stronger, my love. I'm supporting you in all that happens." Louisa teared up. How does he know all this? He's such a good man. How did I get so lucky? She tightly hugged Adam.

Louisa sat on the train watching the rims as they disappeared. They whizzed through the Laurel railroad yards with its Round House on the side. Soon she saw where her beloved White Beaver Creek formed a crevice through the hill and was flowing to the Yellowstone River. The beautiful Crazy Mountains appeared with new snow on its peaks. She tried to relax and appreciate the scenery, but she was irritated. Men take over. Honestly. It's do this, do that. Why do I have to do what Papa wants, what Adam wants? Why can't they hear 'No.'

Louisa started to laugh at herself. Of course, I can do this. Women are capable of almost anything. I recently designed a house! I just wish we could be more in control of situations ourselves.

That's what irritates me. I'm dreading having to deal with Charley. Why did Alvin stay friends with such a corrupt person? I wish I could've told Papa or Adam about Charley. Maybe they would have agreed that I shouldn't be making this trip. But no one talks about sexual assault. And if they knew, maybe they'd just say it must have been my fault; I led him on. Only Alvin knew and now he's gone.

Louisa watched as the Yellowstone River meandered its way east to the Missouri. A few cows grazed on the bank and periodically willows or Russian olives grew in a valley leading to the river. The rural scene was peaceful and Louisa became calm.

I wonder what the next generation will be like. Adam told me that it's up to me to train Sarah to be a good housewife and to teach Roger manners. Thank goodness, Peter isn't much trouble. My duty is properly raising the kids. There's more to it, though. I want to stretch their view of what they can be. It'd be great if Sarah could be more than a housewife. Women seem to be taking on new jobs all the time, especially since the war. Maybe Sarah will run the ranch or become Montana's first female governor!

There are different careers for men, too, with new equipment. We don't have to sew our own clothes anymore or build our own furniture. You can buy almost anything. Louisa thought of Raymond, her nephew. I hope he does more than help Richard on the ranch. He's good-looking with his olive skin and dark hair. And polite. And getting married already. He could do something special.

Louisa had asked Adam not to reserve a sleeping compartment because of the extra money and because she knew she'd feel awkward using a bed in what seemed to be a public space. Sleep would have been impossible anyway as she was stewing over how to deal with Charley. Consequently, she was exhausted and cranky when she stepped off the train the next evening in California.

"Louisa, it's great to see you," a man called to her. Louisa looked at the man, not recognizing Charley with his beard and pot belly. He had on a brown suit with a vest and a fob watch chain across the front. She remembered the voice, however, calling for her on the edge of Crystal Lake, and she walked slowly toward the voice.

"This is my wife, Elsie. Elsie, meet Louisa Janochek Martin." Louisa looked down at the round-faced, rotund lady with the twinkling eyes. Louisa couldn't help but smile at this sweet-faced woman. Elsie was dressed in a dark blue suit and white blouse, with a little hat perched on wavy hair.

Elsie reached out to Louisa, cupping her elbows, drawing her close, and looking into her eyes. "It's good to meet you, dear. Alvin told us all about you and how proud he was of you. We're sorry about Alvin. What a fine man. He was a perfect gentleman. We miss him very much." Is she talking about the Alvin I knew, a gentleman, a perfect gentleman? Louisa wondered.

"You must be exhausted after your long train ride. Let's get you home for supper and a good night's rest." Louisa nearly collapsed into the warmth of this full-bosomed, angelic person. What a relief! She had Elsie to protect her and she was no longer nervous about being around Charley.

A sense of peace enclosed Louisa as she entered their house. A wonderful smell of a spicy oven dish filled the rooms. Everything seemed to be homemade and comfortable: a braided rag rug, stuffed pillows on a well-designed wooden settle, a simple Japanese print framed on the wall. Louisa remembered that they had hired Japanese-American workers in the rice fields.

Elsie showed her to the attached spare bedroom with a single bed and desk where Alvin had stayed. Louisa removed her coat, gloves, and hat. Elsie returned with warm water to fill the basin for Louisa to wash, chattering all the time about Alvin.

"Alvin was neat and tidy. Never wanted much or had much. We enjoyed having him as part of the family, so easy to be with. Alvin and Charley were such close friends. Alvin didn't leave much. You may take anything in here you like, to remember him. Come join us for supper when you're ready."

Louisa met their five children at the supper table. She was surprised when everyone bowed their heads for a blessing by Charley. By Charley! As the adults talked, the children ate quietly, and then, when given the opportunity, they asked Louisa about Montana and her children. Tears came into Louisa's eyes as she thought of her own children. Did they miss her? What did Adam feed them for dinner? It seemed natural when the older children picked up the dishes and helped their mother serve dessert.

Before she turned in to sleep, Louisa looked through her brother's room. There was a photo of the Janochek family taken in a commercial photography studio when Louisa was about six with Victoria as a baby in her mother's arms. The boys, all with suits and ties, stood in the back with Irene. Helen and Louisa had big bows holding their hair back from their faces. Momma had a white shirt with puffy sleeves. How did she keep it cleaned and ironed? And we were still living in the barn when this picture was taken! Then there was a blurry photo of Alois in a bear-skin coat standing in a snowbank, cutting wood. I remember that coat and burying my head in it. It smelled like firewood. Other than the photographs, there was nothing of significance, a couple pairs of work shoes and his work clothes hanging on nails on one wall. Louisa opened the drawer to his desk and found a dozen letters from his family wrapped in a ribbon. Under them was a small-sized Bible. It fell open to Psalm 51:11. "Create in me a clean heart, O God; and renew a right spirit within me." Louisa sobbed. Afterward, she put the photographs, letters, and the Bible into her travel bag.

The next morning, Charley drove Louisa around the nicely groomed town to take care of business. First, the funeral home.

"This may be hard for you," Charley explained, "but the funeral home needs you to identify Alvin as your brother, just to reassure the state authorities that they're sending the right body back to Montana."

"I can do it, Charley. I can see him." When she saw the body in the open casket, she was startled to see how stiff he looked, dressed in a white shirt, striped tie, and brown suit with his hands folded on his chest. This was the first time for her to see someone who was dead. Louisa touched a finger. It was cold and hard. Then she touched his cheek that had an unnatural blush on it. His face, too, felt like a carved stone sculpture. She felt little emotion. This is not Alvin. Alvin was gone. It was like looking or touching a courtyard statue.

"Yes, this is my brother, Alvin," she identified him sadly, remembering what a great reunion she had had with him when they were in Santa Rosa. Tears of regret for what might have been escaped down her cheek. She couldn't help herself. They went to the office to sign papers allowing her to get a death certificate from the courthouse and a permit to transfer the body to Montana. The funeral home manager presented her with an invoice.

"I'll take the bill," Charley told the manager. He folded the paper and put it in his pocket. Louisa shook her head, starting to protest. "Louisa, we'll sort this out later. Let it be."

"We can't let you do this. Papa would not allow it."

"Alvin has paid for it himself, Louisa. I'll explain later," Charley said. Louisa wrinkled her forehead, confused.

Next, they went to the courthouse for the death certificate and then to the train depot for passage for Alvin's body and to confirm a place for Louisa back to Montana the next day. Charley was polite, opening doors, introducing her, helping her in and out of his work truck. They had a sandwich with Elsie before they went to the bank

221

to meet with a real estate agent, an attorney, and a bank loan officer. Oh my Lord, now what? Louisa thought. She was tired and ready to get on the train to go home. Why do I need to meet these men?

After introducing the three men, Charley explained, "Louisa, Alvin and I were partners. Everything was split, half and half, right down the middle. Expenses and profits were shared equally. Land was cheap when we arrived and it has gone up in value considerably since the war. Alvin had no will." Charley now looked at the attorney who took over.

"Do you know if your brother married or had any children?" the attorney asked Louisa.

"As far as I know he never married nor had children. Charley, you'd know."

Charley assured the attorney. "Alvin never married and had no children."

The attorney went on. "I talked to your father and he said the same. Without a will, all assets and debts go to the nearest relative who in this case is his father, Alois. Do you anticipate any contest to that decision?"

"No. I agree with you. Papa and, of course, Momma are Alvin's closest relatives." So, Louisa thought, my suspicion about Charley wanting Alvin's assets is wrong. Alvin's assets and debts will go to Papa. Louisa relaxed back into her chair, her shoulders releasing their tension.

"Would you please sign this legal form confirming that Alois Janochek is the nearest living relative to Alvin Janochek?" The attorney handed Louisa a paper in triplicate to sign. With her carefully crafted cursive writing style, Louisa signed, Louisa J. Martin, in sloping, curving, feminine letters. Louisa smiled to herself as she thought, I love signing my name. I wish I had more business papers to sign.

Charley started again. "Louisa, I want to buy Alvin's share of our farming operation. We didn't have a contract, but our banker can confirm that our checking accounts and loans were joint accounts and that we both signed all transactions. Now that Alvin is...is gone, I tallied our assets and expenses, so I'd know how much I need to borrow to buy Alvin's half and send that amount to Alois." He looked at her, wondering if she were all right. She seemed dazed. "Do you understand, Louisa?"

Louisa had a headache and felt dizzy, but she sat up and tried to look alert. She wanted to understand. I don't trust Charley. Is Charley trying to steal from Papa? Did Alvin leave a huge debt? Am I getting Papa into trouble? Louisa took a sip of water from the glass they had offered when they sat down. She thought through what she had been told. Charley said the land was more valuable now. It doesn't sound like there's a debt. I need to see where this conversation goes.

"Yes, I understand. Charley, you want to buy what was Alvin's half-interest in your partnership as it's now Papa's?" she asked for clarification.

"Exactly. I asked Mr. Janochek if he wanted to keep his interest in the farm down here or if he'd prefer to have me buy him out. He'd rather not be involved in a California rice farm. Didn't he indicate that to you?" Louisa nodded, remembering a comment her father had made, but it didn't make sense at the time. "The real estate agent will show you comparable prices so you know that I'm offering your father a fair price for everything."

Charley knows I don't trust him and that I need proof that his offer is fair. What Charley doesn't know is that Adam's work for the PCA is figuring out farm values and I've learned quite a bit myself from Adam.

The real estate agent pulled out papers listing different farm locations, their acreage, crops, and total values with accompanying pictures of buildings, equipment, and farm fields. Louisa studied the figures and saw that the value of rice land in California per acre was 4 or 5 times more than range land. The sheds were high-priced, too. Papa could build a little ole shed like that for half the price or less, she thought. What she saw looked like a fair appraisal for Alvin and Charley's operation.

The banker and attorney were still in the conference room. Just to make sure she was making a correct assessment, Louisa asked them, "Do you each agree that what is being shown to me is accurate for this area?" The banker seemed a bit startled by such a question, but both of them nodded and the banker confirmed, "The values are in the right price range."

Charley looked directly at her, with his eyes beseeching hers. He politely said, "Louisa, I want to settle this today if we can and have a check drawn up for Mr. Janochek for you to take back to him. I've always admired your family and want the Janocheks to know Alvin and I . . . we've been good farmers." Charley's voice trembled. Louisa nodded at him trying to reassure him and then she sat back in her chair wondering what was next.

Charley pulled out a paper with a few figures on it and passed it to Louisa. On top it said A&C Farms. She saw assets listed and an asset total; then, liabilities listed and a liability total; liabilities were subtracted from the assets. Assets were high; liabilities were low. Louisa gasped at the result which was then divided by 2. After that came a recently penciled figure of the funeral home's expenses which was subtracted from the total of Alvin's half of the net assets. The resulting figure had in pencil: Due Alois Janochek. Louisa stared at the dollar amount. It exceeded the cost of their new house in Laurel. It was more than three years from the ranch lease. It's probably more than Papa makes in a year or two building houses.

Louisa looked at Charley, amazed. Charley was chewing on his lower lip and fingering his beard. Louisa started laughing. "You and Alvin amassed all this? Two . . ." Charley raised his hand to stop her, glancing at the men. She had wanted to say "two no-good drunken bums," but Louisa caught herself and calmly said, "You've done really well, Charley. You and Alvin."

Louisa took a deep breath, thinking this is a huge gift from Alvin to Papa and Momma. And from Charley. He's an honest man and even a gentleman after all. I'm grateful to have had this opportunity to help Papa and at the same time to resolve an old wound. She studied the assets and liabilities again and then looking at the three businessmen, she announced, "Everything shown to me in this summary seems to be in perfect order. Do you agree?"

"We do," they affirmed. The banker stood and said, "I'll get a cashier to write a check." He left the room.

"It was good meeting you, Mrs. Martin," the real estate agent said as he rose from his chair, nodding to her. "Charles, you can keep the real estate documents for your files. We have copies."

"Thank you," Charley replied and stood to shake his hand.

"I'll see you next week, Charles, to draw up your will." The attorney rose and shook Charley's hand. "Have a safe trip back to Montana, Mrs. Martin," he said with a slight bow to her. Both he and the real estate agent left the room.

Alone with Charley, Louisa let out a quiet whoop, "How could two, goofy, dry-land farm boys from Moore, Montana do so well on a rice farm in California?"

Charley grinned as he organized the papers left on the desk and responded, "Hush, Louisa, sh-sh, we're in a bank. You know Alvin could fix and build anything we needed. I could, well, I know you won't believe it, but I was good at convincing people to work with us and I could talk the language of these business types. I kept the books and we bought more land as it became available. Elsie kept us on track and off the sauce. We loved working together!" The room was dead quiet. "We were br. .bro. .brothers." Charley's voice cracked

225

as he held back tears. "Alvin loved our family. It reminded him of his own family. And he was all I had."

Louisa swallowed hard to get the lump out of her throat. Charley. And Alvin. So different from what I thought. I wasn't very good to Alvin. But Charley was.

The banker returned and sat beside Charley. "Sign here for the check, Charles." The banker then passed the check to Louisa in an envelope with 'For Alois Janochek' carefully typed on the front. "Charles, here's the loan we agreed on. You'll need to sign here." Louisa looked at the check while Charley signed the papers.

"Can you afford to do this, Charley?" she asked when the banker left. "You need to think of your family." Louisa was thinking of how much she liked Elsie and their children.

"Alvin wanted his father and mother to have an easier time. He'd want this. And my boys are old enough to help with the labor. We'll have this loan paid off in a short time."

Louisa carefully placed the check inside the envelope and into her purse. I hope I don't lose this. I'm going to have to sit on my purse all the way home.

The next morning, Louisa found herself crying, saying good-bye at the train station to Elsie and Charley. She knew she was overwrought from seeing Alvin and dealing with the estate, but there was something more to her sorrow. She truly liked this family and Elsie already seemed like a sister. She knew she'd probably never see her again.

There was much to think about on the way home. She was relieved to have the solitude of the train ride home to work through the emotional roller-coaster that she had been on. Elsie knows how to handle men. Look at how she cleaned up Charley and Alvin! She's terrific.

Louisa fell into Adam's arms when he met her at the train depot in Moore. Peter and Sarah hugged her tightly while Roger gave her a smile and muttered, "Welcome back, Ma." The Janocheks had gathered for the funeral scheduled for the next day in Moore, the first of several services they'd have in that graveyard.

Louisa gave the envelope with the check to her father that evening before the funeral. As he opened the envelope and looked at the check, he nodded his head and said, "Alvin was a good boy." He then opened his Bible, laid the envelope with the check in it, and put the Bible on the mantle. Louisa wanted to scream, "He was a drunk! A drunk, Papa. But he grew to be a responsible man. Primarily because of Charley's wife! Let's give Elsie some credit!"

Instead, she said, "It's a lot of money, Papa."

"So it is." He looked directly at her. "I'd prefer you didn't tell Adam or Momma the amount." She stood facing him, a question on her face demanding an answer.

"Ah, Louisa, I have some debts to take care of first." Louisa stomach tightened up. Bar tabs? A woman? Bad investments? "Don't worry, Louisa. Most will go to give your momma an easier life."

Louisa cried a lot at the funeral, partly for Alvin, but mostly for her father and the wayward way of men. Even Papa has some sort of hidden misconduct! I finally see how difficult it has been for Momma. She's had to ignore some fault of Papa all her life. And be gracious about it. Women are the ones who establish and keep the moral values of the nation, she concluded. It's time for me to make sure our children have good moral values that last them their lifetime.

Not long after her trip to California, Louisa asked Adam, "Are we going to church on Sunday?"

"Of course, we usually do," he responded, puzzled by her question.

"I'd like our family to join as members. And Roger needs to be in confirmation classes. Peter is old enough, too."

"OK. Sure, it's time we did that. I'll speak to the pastor. I guess I thought once we were members in one church like Molt, we're automatically considered to be members here."

The Methodist Church in Laurel was more formal than the country churches. Services were in a gray stone building with a sanctuary that could seat 100 or more worshippers. It was often full, especially for special events like confirmation. The pastor offered instruction about Christianity, the Bible, and the Methodist denomination itself. Louisa insisted that Roger join the confirmation class and with his usual wish to please his mom, he went. Peter naturally followed his older brother.

Louisa had always felt uncomfortable, even sinful, in church because her Janocheck family had dropped from the Catholic Church. She felt awkward around the Martins who seemed solid in their religious convictions and were natural at communion or baptism. How do I catch up and learn what all these sacraments mean, she wondered. I want our children to be moral and loving. I want to be more loving like Elsie. Church seems like a path to a good life. I need to learn the rules.

Louisa studied Roger's confirmation book while he was at school. She joined the Women's Bible Study, the Methodist Women's Circle, and the Women's Temperance Union. Louisa spent hours carefully reading suggested materials and trying to understand what they meant. She bought a notebook and with a pencil wrote out important scriptures that she copied from Alvin's Bible. Much of it didn't make sense to her, but once in a while a line would stick in her head and reverberate over and over, like "Create in me a clean heart and put a right spirit in me," which she and Alvin had learned as children. She could understand how cleanliness and Godliness went together and put it into practice.

How they looked at church was important to Louisa. Every Saturday night Louisa washed Sarah's hair, rinsing it with vinegar water.

"I don't like the vinegar, Momma," Sarah would complain sputtering out the rinse water as she hung her head over the sink.

"The vinegar makes your hair shine. And let's hope it keeps the lice out," Louisa calmly responded thinking of Sarah's classmates who were suspended from school for having lice. She toweled Sarah's wet hair, rubbing her head hard.

"Do we have to put it in curlers?" Sarah asked. "I'm too old for curls. None of the other girls have them."

Louisa combed out the snarls and pondered. "Well, you look good in curls. Your hair is beautiful."

"Mom, I look goofy. I'm nearly 9 and no one else wears curls."

Louisa replied, "I'll consider your request," and started rolling Sarah's hair into curls, securing each with bobby pins.

Peter was given the task of shining shoes on Saturday. Roger made sure the car was washed and waxed.

Soon Louisa was president of the Women's Circle. While preparing the opening worship services for the Women's Circle Louisa began to understand the "methods" of Methodists. I love this spiritual inventory, Louisa mused, easy to use, like reading a recipe or checking off a spelling list. Reminds me of teaching.

"A. Concerning the Lordship of Christ: Have I accepted Christ as my Savior and Lord? Have I given myself to God without any reserve?

B. Concerning Christ's Church: Am I regularly attending worship services? Do I invite friends and acquaintances?

C. Concerning My Relationship to Christ: Do I seek spiritual insight in my worship, study, and meditation, or am I content with the forms, facts, and customs of the religious life?

D. My relationship to Others: Do I place the good of others ahead of selfish concerns and personal objectives? Do I speak the truth?

E. My spiritual Growth and Prayer Life: Is God real to me when I pray? Have I read a book on prayer during the last year? Do I make every effort to be pure in my thinking and actions?"

Before every meal, they said "Grace." After every meal just like at Elsie's, the children picked up the dishes, washed, and dried them. Louisa couldn't get them to stop arguing over who washed the dishes the most often and complaining about it, but at least they were following her instructions.

The Methodists were great singers and Louisa loved singing the hymns. She was thrilled when Peter wanted to learn to play the piano. Sarah begged to take lessons, too. Louisa picked out a beautiful Acrosonic spinet piano for the corner of the living room. The Laurel High School had a highly skilled band instructor who the kids liked and soon Roger was playing clarinet and Peter took up the baritone. Both Louisa and Adam loved the music flooding their house. Adam woke Sarah to practice the piano while he shaved and Louisa made breakfast. Then Peter practiced while Sarah got ready for school. Louisa enjoyed organizing their activities and setting up a household routine.

Louisa encouraged the children into doing civic activities they weren't sure they wanted to do. She helped Roger when he became president of the Methodist Youth Group. Peter went through the Cub Scout program with Louisa urging him to get more and more badges. The more they did individually or as a family, the more Louisa wanted them to do. Roger was football captain, president of his junior class, editor of the student newspaper. Peter followed his brother's footsteps as a football and class leader. The children volunteered in many of the outside activities just to get out of the house. Still, they were good at what they did and the activities became their own source of pleasure.

Louisa made sure they had new clothes for special events. While she sewed them school clothes, shopping at Hart-Albins in Billings was a twice a year event for their dress outfits.

Louisa was concerned about what others outside the family thought of them. Therefore, she was strict with the children and

230

diligently followed the rules she thought church promoted. With her background as a Czech immigrant and the Janocheks and Martins being farmers, she was proud they were now leaders in a small town. She put her family on such a high pedestal that it was difficult for the children to meet her standards.

"Roger, you've tracked mud in. Peter, the dishes aren't clean. Do them again. Sarah, you haven't practiced today. And keep your feet off the couch. Adam, your tie is crooked. Roger, stand up straight. You're slumped over. Be proud that you're the tallest in your class. Sarah, you can't eat that cookie. You're too stocky as it is. Peter, you do look good in that shirt. Why can't you always dress like that? Take your football cleats to the garage, Roger. Hang up your coats. Mind your manners. Speak clearly. And 'ain't' is not a word."

On Sunday mornings, Adam called for the children and they settled into the car several minutes before they needed to leave for church. Together they'd wait for Louisa to join them.

"Why do we always have to sit here and wait for Mom?" Roger complained, squirming in the back seat. "I could have used some more sleep."

"She needs a few minutes to herself after getting you kids ready," Adam calmly responded.

Roger went a bit further. "You treat her like she was some sort of Queen."

"She is our Queen and you kids better treat her as such."

Very softly, Roger muttered, "She's a mean Queen."

"I'll pretend I didn't hear that," Adam said.

"She is mean, Daddy." Sarah took up the battle. "She yells at us all the time when you aren't home."

"You don't know what she's like when you aren't home," Peter agreed.

Adam sighed. "Just do as you're told."

Adam thought Louisa was doing a fine job of training the children to be good workers, just as he had learned to be a hard farm worker from his own strict dad. He was happy with the way Louisa was in control of the family and the household activities. It left him more time to think about agricultural practices, politics, and business enterprises. Adam liked his job and was comfortable. Life for him was good.

He was surprised one evening when Louisa announced, "Adam, you need to do more things with the children. You're not around much, with your long hours of checking on farms for the PCA and then going to the ranch every Saturday. The only time we see you is Sunday afternoon. You can't be going to the ranch every week. We need to start doing something fun together as a family. Roger, especially, needs his father."

Adam set his paper to the side and sat up in his recliner chair. What's she talking about, he wondered. I go to all of Roger's games and the kids' concerts. He didn't like to argue with his wife but she had gone too far this time.

"I do things with the kids. Roger often goes with me to the ranch. Peter, too. They've been a great help, Louisa. Last summer, Roger painted the garage and chicken coop. He's started driving the tractor and summer fallowing. And here at home I put up a basketball hoop on the garage for the boys and their friends to shoot baskets. I built stilts for Sarah. I go to school conferences. I do a lot with the kids."

"You could try to get a better job in Laurel, Adam. I'd like to have you home more. I bet you can find work here." Adam had worked at the PCA for five years and enjoyed traveling to farm auctions where he kept track of what sold, to whom, and at what prices. While Adam was happy, it was clear that Louisa was not content. This was not just idle talk.

232

"What do you have in mind?" He sighed.

"I saw an ad in the *Laurel Outlook* for an agricultural loan officer in the Yellowstone Bank. You could work in Laurel and we'd see more of you."

Adam laughed. "I'm not qualified for that job. They want an accountant or someone with a business degree. I didn't even make it through high school."

"Of course you're qualified with all of your work experience from the ranch and at PCA." Louisa was determined to get Adam into a better job.

"It isn't the same. I enjoy working in the field talking to farmers. They like me at PCA and I like my bosses. You've met them. You like them, too. Sitting at a desk all day doesn't sound like something I'd enjoy." Adam didn't want to tell her that the bank president, B. Meyer Harris, seemed intimidating. He was distinguished, refined, and a proper businessman. He might laugh at Adam's lack of education and rough language.

Louisa was insistent. "I'm going to the bank and get the application forms tomorrow, Adam, and I want you to fill them out. I need you here at home."

"What's going on that you <u>need</u> me here at home?" Adam sighed. "You're doing a great job."

"I'm not," Louisa answered hysterically. "I need you here." She was twisting her apron into knots. Adam kept quiet waiting for the rest of it.

Finally, she leaned over and said in a horrifying whisper, "I caught Roger smoking. In the garage. With friends who came to play basketball. I think he's been smoking a lot. I can smell it on his clothes."

Adam relaxed. A cigarette. She's upset over a cigarette. It's natural for a boy Roger's age to try smoking. I enjoy a good cigar myself. "I see," he calmly answered. "Boys will be boys."

"Not our Roger! And it's not just Roger. I think Sarah's stealing from our petty cash jar to buy candy. The children are supposed to ask for permission to take money from the petty cash jar."

Oh, gosh. How serious, is that? Adam thought. Not very. "What do you want me to do? You really don't want me to go over to Olsen's Grocery and ask Kenny and Ila to keep track of how much candy Sarah's buying, do you? Just remove the petty cash saucer for a while, if you're that concerned."

"You don't think she'd start stealing from others?"

"She's a good kid. She's not on a criminal path."

Still, Adam had started thinking, it'd be good not to have to drive to Billings or out to country farms every day. "Go ahead and get the application forms. I'll take a look at them." She doesn't understand how different the work will be at the bank, though. And if I can even do it.

"And you'll talk to Roger? About not smoking?"

"I'll talk to Roger." He nodded his assent.

Adam was surprised when he was offered the job at the Yellowstone Bank. At Louisa's insistence, he accepted it. He started walking to the Bank in the morning and coming home for lunch when the children had a half-hour off. At night, they squeezed supper in between Roger's football or basketball practices after school and Peter's evening activities of church choir, Methodist Youth Fellowship, and Boy Scouts.

A few months after he started work at the Bank, Adam surprised them at supper time asking, "How about going to the Grand Canyon this summer for vacation?" Enthusiastic shouts of excitement resounded in reply. Louisa was gratified that finally they were doing things together as a family. Trips were educational as well as enjoyable. The summer of 1950 they went to Bryce National Park, Zion National Park, Grand Canyon, and Hoover Dam. It was the beginning of yearly trips around the U.S. during Adam's two week vacations.

Life was moving swiftly. Louisa was running all the time supporting the three children in their activities: camps, swimming classes, and costumes for the Kid's Parade in the summer, band and choir practices during the school year, driving lessons, piano lessons, teaching Sarah to sew and the boys to cook. She stayed active participating in the Bank's social events and helping Adam run for City Council. The family attended Community Concerts, the Midland Empire Fair, and the Billings Western Parade. Louisa had her dream come true of belonging to a welcoming community and having a lovely home, a fulfilling marriage, and healthy children. She thought she was a good wife and mother. Maybe even as good as Elsie.

Fidelity to a Worthy Cause
LAUREL, 1955-1959

Many persons have a wrong idea of what constitutes true happiness. It is not attained through self-gratification but through fidelity to a worthy purpose.

HELEN KELLER (1880-1968)

"Louisa, can you come? Please, please come. Something awful's happened." Ceci kept crying, hysterically over the telephone. "I need you." Richard and Cecilia still lived at the home place, a four hour drive for Louisa and she wondered how she could drop all the activities the family was involved in to go see Ceci.

"What, Ceci? What's going on? Slow down and talk to me."

"I can't, I can't tell you on the phone. Just come. Please come. I don't know what to do."

"Tell me something, Ceci. Is Richard okay?"

"It's Raymond. It'll be in the paper. A terrible, a horrible accident. Oh, so awful." And Ceci burst out in big sobs. Through the staccato cries, she said, "Just come. As soon as you can."

"Is Raymond hurt?"

"It's not that. . . he did something. . . something so horrendous. I can't, I can't, I can't tell you."

What in the world? What could that sweet Raymond have done? Louisa thought. He's been married about 5 years now, and has his own children, two girls. I wonder what could be so bad that Ceci can't even tell me. But it sounds bad enough that I better go. Louisa took a deep breath and decided.

"I'll drive up tomorrow."

"Oh, thank you, Louisa." Ceci stopped crying. She blew her nose. She already sounded better. "Thank you. Thank you. Thank you. Tomorrow. Now I can face tomorrow."

Louisa rarely called Adam at the bank but this seemed important enough to let him know something was going on.

"We'll probably read about it in tonight's paper," Adam said. "And then we'll know what you can do for them."

There it was, on page 4 of the *Billings Gazette*, in the evening news. Not in big print, but it seemed like a huge Neon sign to Louisa:

Moore. Wife Shot Dead At Home. Raymond Janochek is being held in custody at the Lewistown jail pending inquiries into the shooting death of his 23 year old wife at their home late Tuesday evening. Janochek admitted guilt in the shooting, claiming infidelity by his wife. Two children, who were home at the time of the shooting, are being held in foster care. Arraignment will be in District Court on Friday.

"There must be a mistake," Louisa immediately claimed. "Raymond wouldn't do such a thing." Louisa could not comprehend how Raymond who was raised strictly with high morals would kill anyone, let alone someone he loved. This couldn't happen. Not in her family.

"Whether he did or didn't, your family needs you now," Adam responded. "It must be a shock to Richard, as well as Ceci, and to your momma."

"You're right. What must Momma be going through? I'm glad Papa passed on last year and doesn't have to see this. What would he say? I'm glad Momma is with Richard and Ceci. They can support each other. But maybe I'll ask Momma to come stay with us. What do you think, Adam? I could bring her back with me. Would that be a good idea?"

"Whatever's best for the family."

Louisa packed the back seat of the car with a box of home-canned vegetables and frozen meat from the ranch. I have no idea what they'll need in a situation like this, but at least I can cook meals for them.

It was dark when she left the house, but the sun gradually showed the shadows in the coulees. On the flat tiny green winter wheat could be seen between the golden stubble of last year's crop. All the way to Ross Fork, Louisa pondered, what can I do? What can I do? And the answer hit her, a bolt out of the blue. I'll see if we can raise Raymond's girls! They can have Roger's old bedroom with twin beds. Sarah can help them as a big sister. Oh, I can hardly wait to get to the home place to call Adam and make sure he likes my idea.

"They don't even let us see our grandchildren," Ceci said when Louisa started talking about who would care for Raymond's girls. "It's like the authorities want to shield them from us as well as from Raymond. I don't understand it. As if we'd hurt our granddaughters! Sweet, beautiful, little girls." And she started crying again.

Richard, Cecilia, and Louisa went to the courthouse to hear the arraignment. Afterward, they were allowed five minutes each to talk with Raymond individually. Richard and Cecilia went first.

Raymond was quiet when Louisa saw him. He shook his head and tried to explain. "I don't know what happened, Aunt Louisa. I was so angry when she came home with her lipstick smeared, her blouse undone, laughing at me." He tensed up and tears came to his eyes. "She'd been drinking. It wasn't the first time she's done this." Raymond then turned Stoic. "I walked out to the garage, got the rifle, came back and shot her. I wasn't thinking. Obviously, I wasn't thinking. She was in the wrong, but what I did was even worse. It all happened in a few short minutes."

Louisa looked at him, trying to understand him. He's calm. And open. Not trying to hide anything. He went on. "Maybe we could've worked something out, but she's been like this since we married. It was a bad marriage, a bad marriage. I should have divorced her, but after the little girls came, I loved them too much to leave. Now, it's a real mess for them."

"I'd like to talk to the judge to see if Adam and I could raise your girls. Would you like me to do that, Raymond? Would that help you?" The question seemed to echo from the prison cement walls.

Raymond looked down at the floor, shaking his head, as if to shove the question away. Slowly he looked up at her and said, "You can ask, but I don't think they'll want the girls with anyone in our family. A social worker already told me that Welfare never wants me to see them again." His voice was husky; he was holding back tears. "If I ever get out of prison, she said I'd have to live in another state. At least until the girls are grown. I'd upset them."

"I'm really sorry to hear that." Louisa wanted to hug Raymond to console him but the window and bars prevented that.

Raymond took a rag out of his pocket to wipe his nose. "The girls are with her folks right now. The in-laws never liked me. I wasn't good enough for them. They'll probably change the girls' last names and try to erase all memory of me. They're young enough to forget me. I'll miss seeing them grow up! I'll never see them." Raymond hung his head and with the back of his arm wiped the tears from his cheeks. "At least that's what the social worker told me. The law is on their side."

"Oh, Raymond, you don't deserve this." Louisa held back her tears. She hadn't meant to disturb him. She wanted to help.

He straightened up, took a deep breath, and went on. "I'll be lucky if they let me live. It's a capital offense, you know. The only thing I have going for me is that there are witnesses to her infidelity. The judge may have some compassion for me at sentencing. But Aunt Louisa, I know what I did was absolutely wrong, truly evil. I'll have this nightmare of that night in my mind the rest of my life. If I live."

The clang of iron doors inside the prison rang across the visitor's center as prisoners returned to their cells. Louisa knew her time was over. "Is there anything we can do? Anything to help you?"

"Just do what you can for the folks. Mom is taking it hard. And Dad was counting on me to take over the ranch, but remind him he has other children who might want the ranch. Or maybe Roger?"

Roger managing a couple ranches is not what Louisa wanted for him. We need to advance as a family, not step backward. Lordy, lordy, what do we do now? One of our most delightful, most caring family members is behind prison bars. Her heart ached for Raymond and she prayed for the future of her own children.

The guard nodded at her. Her time was up. "Raymond, remember we love you. Keep strong." Louisa pressed her fingertips to her lips and threw him a kiss. Finally, she saw his sweet smile.

That evening, Ceci and Richard talked and cried, while Louisa listened. Ceci was especially distraught and depressed. Richard, who depended on Raymond for labor at the ranch and hoped he would take over some day, struggled with the future of the ranch. The other three children, two of them girls, seemed to have little interest in farming.

Catherine was now hard of hearing, but she could hear enough to know that this tragic event might mean the end of the family home place, her first Montana home. She hated thinking of the possibility that the land Alois and she had worked hard to develop and keep might end up with another family. After all, Alois and Richard had built the house in which they were gathered. This was the original Montana family home!

"What would Alois do, what would he be telling us if he were here?" Catherine pondered. The three of them looked at Catherine. What would Papa do if he were alive? A good question.

"He'd probably start building another house," Richard slowly answered.

Ceci started to smile through her tears. "He'd ask me to make meatballs and potato salad for his work crew. In other words, get back to work."

"Yes, the future will take care of itself," Louisa suggested. "Hunker down and get through the day, that's the Czech way."

Louisa left for home the next morning as Ceci had calmed down and the family seemed ready to go on with their usual routines. Catherine decided to stay with Richard and Cecilia for the time being, but promised to spend a few months with Louisa and Adam later.

Louisa had a lot to mull over as she drove home the next day. Why were there so many homicides with guns? Montanans need guns, she thought. What would we have eaten without Adam shooting rabbits for us to survive as newlyweds? Lots of people need to shoot prairie birds or antelope for food. But why do we turn our guns on each other? Montanans are moral people, as much as anybody. Joe and Raymond were upset and angry but not crazy. In each shooting they took what they thought was justice into their own hands.

Louisa had saved her tears for Raymond for the quiet ride home. She kept blowing her nose and wiping her eyes, trying to see the road. She worried now for her own children. Had she raised them to be strong enough to resist anger and revenge? Richard and Cecilia had been great parents and Raymond had been a loving child. And yet. Could they have done more? Could she have done more? Was she, herself, guilty of not doing enough to help Raymond become a strong individual capable of handling adversity in a peaceful manner?

Louisa felt hollowness in her stomach. God, I've been a horrible aunt ignoring my dear nephew. And maybe—am I a bad mother? Help me. Help me to be kinder and not drive my children to despair. She knew in her heart that her religious obsession had made her too strict with her children. And it wasn't the church's fault. Focusing on rules was not what Jesus taught.

She and Adam had built a beautiful, safe home. But was I kind enough? Will my children imitate the few loving moments I had with them and not inherit my critical, sharp tongue? I have to have faith they'll make good decisions. Roger's married and gone and with Peter and Sarah in high school, there's not much I can do for them now.

The experience of seeing what had happened to Raymond was a rude awakening. I need to turn my life into making the world a better place. But how? What can I do? Helping other children? What is my future? What can I do? What is my path?

One Saturday not long after she had returned home from Ross Creek and seeing Raymond in jail in Lewistown, Louisa rode to the ranch with Adam, asking him to leave her at the Muellers while Adam visited with his ranch manager. Louisa hadn't seen her sister, Victoria, for several months and maybe Victoria would have ideas as to what she could do. Karl and Victoria now had four children, Johnny, Susan, Dale, and the little caboose, Dorothy.

Adam gave Victoria a hug and teased Dorothy by pulling on her pigtails before driving to his own ranch over the hill. Karl and Johnny were out in the field, planting spring barley. Dale and Susan were at Columbus setting up for the high school prom. Louisa put her arm around Victoria as they walked to the house.

Louisa couldn't help but notice how run down the place looked. The gate was broken, the sidewalk was crumbling, and the house paint was peeling. Karl had never fully come out of his depression after the war. I shouldn't be so judgmental, Louisa thought as she gave Victoria a little squeeze. Here I am wanting Victoria's advice while she probably needs my assistance.

Victoria poured them a couple mugs of coffee and they sat at the kitchen table. Dorothy showed Louisa her 4H sewing project of honey comb smocking on an apron and then went outside to play on the swing. With Dorothy out of hearing range, Louisa told Victoria about Raymond and how Richard, Cecilia, and their mom were handling the tragedy. Louisa had started to accept the situation but Victoria was in tears when hearing the details.

"How sad they won't let you raise Raymond's girls," Victoria exclaimed as she dabbed at her eyes with her apron hem. "You're such a great mother."

Louisa smiled, loving to hear this compliment, but wondering if it were true. "I would have enjoyed having little ones with us again. It's awfully quiet with Peter engrossed in his studies and athletics. Although Sarah gives us enough trouble. Still, there's less for me to do and frankly, Victoria, I'm having trouble thinking of my future. You still have Dorothy to raise, but I'm nearly done. Will getting supper for Adam and cleaning house be all there is to life?"

Victoria had to chuckle at her sister's drama. "You always wanted more out of life than the rest of us, Louisa. What are you thinking about doing now?"

Louisa sighed. "I'm not sure. We'll soon have two extra bedrooms when Peter graduates. Do you think I should take in foster children? What else could I do?" They could hear Dorothy singing as she played in the back yard and a chicken clucking over her newly produced egg.

Finally, Victoria said, "Maybe you could go back to work. Women are doing that now. You liked teaching." Louisa had a brief and horrifying image of her now padded figure and graying hair in a college classroom with young, lithe women.

"I'd have to go back to college for a couple years in order to teach now." Louisa had another argument for not going back. "And I don't think it's the right thing for me to look for outside employment when there are men who need jobs and women without husbands who need the work." Victoria nodded in agreement, thinking how lucky she was that Karl didn't die in the war which would have forced her into trying to find work as a widow.

"What about being a librarian? You took that class on the Dewey Decimal system. You probably wouldn't need more schooling. And maybe not many people want to be a librarian with their low salaries."

Louisa thought for a moment and then shook her head. "I don't know. I don't read much anymore," Louisa confessed. "I used to love reading but sitting in a library seems boring. Raising children is more challenging and more useful, don't you think?"

"Yes, I love being a mother and being at home," Victoria responded. It was quiet for a few minutes as they thought about their lives. But then Victoria started thinking of all the work she had to do. "How about helping me make some rolls? I started dough to rise this morning."

"Sure." Louisa got up and put on the apron Victoria gave her. The two sisters enjoyed rolling out the dough and shaping them into crescents. They sprinkled a few with poppy seed.

"What did you mean, Sarah's trouble to you?" Victoria was curious. She spoke softly hoping Dorothy wasn't in hearing distance.

Louisa sighed, searching for the right words. "Sarah's different. She has no interest in shopping for clothes or even keeping her hair combed. She's happy in shorts and floppy shirts. She runs with a couple of boys. They go biking or do science projects or go to movies together. It's strange, not romance, more like good buddies. And I don't know if she believes in God. She's always questioning the sermons or the Bible. Sarah's a free-thinker." Louisa paused. "I'm wondering if she's a communist."

Victoria couldn't help but chuckle at Louisa's concerns. "Sarah sounds like a wonderful human being. What you and I wouldn't have given to have that freedom as young people! Let her be. She's enjoying her teenage years and probably learning a lot from new experiences!"

"You think so?" Louisa asked. "I'm worried she's going astray. She seems to listen to our requests and then goes about doing what she wanted to do in the first place. Not like Peter who always obeys us. Keeps his room clean. Even irons his own clothes. Sarah's room has a pile of washed and unwashed clothes strewn on her bed. I don't know how she finds anything to wear. I think I do better raising boys."

Victoria laughed. "You know, Louisa, Sarah is like you: independent and adventurous. And Roger and Peter are more like Adam: responsible solid citizens. You've raised them just fine. You're good parents."

Karl and Johnny drove in from the field for lunch about the same time Adam came to pick up Louisa. The women washed their hands and took off their aprons to meet the men outside.

"You're welcome to stay for lunch." Victoria invited Louisa as they walked out the door. "I have cold roast beef to slice up for sandwiches."

"You know how worried I am about Sarah. We better get home to see what she's up to. But thanks, Sis, for being a good listener and giving me some ideas. It's been good talking with you." Louisa gave Victoria a hug and gently swept Victoria's hair back from her face. How she loved her younger sister even more now with her lightly graying hair and wrinkles forming around her eyes.

Out in the farm yard, Adam was getting a quick review from Karl on how his wheat and cattle were doing. Johnny was hanging on every word looking with pride at his dad. Louisa could see that he was hooked on farming like Karl had been. It's in his blood. Louisa had hoped for more for the next generation. Johnny was turning red in embarrassment as Karl was telling what a great job Johnny was doing teaching Dale how to raise prize 4H pigs. They all trooped to the pig shed, Louisa carefully watching where she stepped and where she placed her hands to admire the snorting, squealing, muddied hogs. Johnny hoped Dale would get a good price at the 4H fair that summer to buy more for next year. The pigs did look really good, fat and sleek.

On the way home, Louisa explained to Adam about her hope to bring other children into their home. He agreed that with her nursing and teaching background she was well prepared to take care and raise foster children.

"Are you sure, though, that this is how you want to spend your time? You like leading the women's church groups and raising money for the school band. Having kids living with us is a 24 hour a day job." Adam was wondering how he was going to fit into this mix. "I like the idea of coming home to just you, Peter, and Sarah."

By the end of their conversation, Louisa convinced him that this was what they should try. Adam as usual found a way to please Louisa. The ranch manager and his wife had been looking for an easier way for their daughter to get to school as the 20 mile round trip to school twice a day was a burden. Adam suggested to them that their daughter could stay at their home in Laurel that fall. It seemed like a great idea and the little girl lived with them for four months until Christmas. Then, for unknown reasons, the manager's wife found an apartment in Columbus for her and their daughter for the winter.

Louisa was excited when her brother Walter, who was a missionary in India, was coming back to the U.S. with the assignment of sharing his experiences with churches. He and his wife would be traveling for a year. Their two boys needed a stable place to live and go to school. Louisa offered to have them stay in their home.

"I don't know, Louisa," her brother Walter told her. "The boys are used to the English boarding school in India. Living in your home may give them too much freedom. They have already been accepted to live and study at the Montana Deaconess School in Helena."

"But that's an orphanage. A home for troubled kids," Louisa charged, her voice filled with anxiety.

Walter looked at her in surprise. He paused before slowly agreeing, "Well, I guess we could try it at your place for a while."

Sarah had a great time showing her cousins refrigerators, radios, wash machines, irons, telephones, televisions, all the technologies people in the U.S. now had and they had never seen. The oldest boy was intrigued with the engineering that went into these machines, but he didn't realize that you couldn't start taking things apart in stores to see how they worked! On the other hand, the youngest was wild with his freedom and played jokes on everyone in the family, including Adam. Their stay at the Martins lasted one month before Adam delivered them to the Helena orphanage.

Louisa was disappointed she wasn't able to provide the home that these children needed. She was ready to give up on her idea of caring for others.

Then Adam's Aunt Margaret died in California leaving his mother, Mary, on her own. Adam talked to his brother Bill and they decided Mary should come to Montana to be with family. Mary could stay with Bill and his family at his ranch for six months and then stay with Adam and Louisa for six months. Louisa was thrilled with the arrangement. While the caring of children hadn't worked out, she could care for the widow, just as we are called to do in the Bible, she thought.

The second bedroom on the main floor was made into a comfortable room for an older woman. Louisa put in new curtains, decorator pillows for the bed, and a better bedside light. Sarah was moved upstairs to Roger's old room while Peter kept his room driving to Billings where he attended Eastern Montana College, Louisa's old "Normal" college. Mary had diabetes and needed the Billings medical care services, so she stayed with Adam and Louisa longer than the original time allotted. Mary's toes became badly infected needing daily attention and eventually she could no longer walk. Louisa got a wooden back bed rest which she covered with a pillow. Then Mary could sit up in bed and read. With a tray, Louisa was able to serve Mary her meals in bed. It wasn't long before Mary died in the little bedroom on the first floor. Her death was seen as a blessing and neither Adam nor Louisa grieved for any length of time. Nursing care had been exhausting for Louisa.

Louisa signed up to become a foster home. Louisa thought Sarah needed a female companion so Ruthie came to stay. Two years older than Sarah, Ruthie was much larger than Sarah, and a year behind her in school. Sarah was asked to tutor Ruthie. The only class Ruthie passed her freshman year in high school was home economics. She could bake muffins. Ruthie turned 18 and was removed from foster care and the Martin home at the end of her freshman year.

Louisa was frustrated. Being a foster home for Ruthie wasn't quite what she wanted. There had been no notable change in Ruthie. Ruthie was pleasant, but there wasn't much intimacy with her. Maybe it's because she's older, Louisa thought. Or maybe because she's a girl, I didn't know how to respond.

Louisa's mother, Catherine, had been staying three months with each of her Montana children: Richard, Helen, Victoria, and Louisa. As she became more fragile she needed to be close to a good hospital, so she started spending more time with the Martins. Catherine never did talk much, and as she had aged and lost her hearing, she talked even less. An aid with batteries clipped to the front of her dress did not seem to help much, leaving her less and less communicative. Catherine was diagnosed with cancer. As she became weaker, Catherine dressed only in her bathrobe and slippers, coming out from her bedroom in the morning just in time to wave good-bye to Sarah from the living room window as Sarah left for school. Louisa cared for Catherine with the same gentleness she had cared for Adam's mother. It was an emotional, physical challenge, but the mothers had needed her. They had given Louisa a purpose.

In the fall while at a football game, one of Sarah's friends, called to her, "Hey, Sarah, there's an ambulance at your house." Sarah's heart started racing. With the half-time band performance over, she packed her flute in its case and ran the six blocks in the dark to her house. A stretcher with an obscure form on it was being carried out the garage doors to a black van by two strange men.

"Your grandma died," Adam told her. Wanting to get Sarah away from the hearse he added, "Go see your mother who's resting in our bedroom."

Louisa was sitting in bed in her sleeveless nude-colored nylon nightgown, propped up with a pillow reading a book. Sarah crawled into her arms and hugged her. "Oh, Momma, I'm sorry."

Louisa replied quietly, "These things happen. Grandma wasn't well. It was time for her to go." With Catherine's illness, Louisa had been prepared for death, even wanting it for her so she wouldn't suffer pain. Her mother had been distant, not giving the affection and intimacy Louisa craved. This passing was one which Louisa could accept.

She laid down her book and slowly patted Sarah who was sprawled out across her. Louisa thought about her mom being 74 years old and in poor health. It's not good to live a long time if you aren't well, Louisa mused. Momma had a hard life. I don't know how she did it. Papa wasn't always good to her. I know for a fact that he hid secrets from her. And at the end she couldn't hear at all. How sad to be isolated from others in that way. Louisa sighed. Now all our parents are gone. We have to rely on ourselves. It's difficult to face the fact that Adam and I are now the older generation.

Sarah snuggled up closely to her mother. "I love your mooshy boobs, Mom."

249

"Sarah, really!" Louisa didn't know how to respond. Finally, she said, "mooshy's not even a word."

"Well, why not? Mooshy would be a good word for describing breasts. At least your boobs are not like my stiff pointy ones." Sarah sat up straight for a moment staring down at her own small breasts. Sinking back into her mom's arms, she said, "Grandma was straight as a board, no boobs at all, and hard to hug. I don't think she liked me to hug her. She worried I'd step on her toes."

"No, I guess not." Louisa remembered the times she would have liked a hug from her mother, or even a kind word. Louisa tried to understand and explain the prior generation. "Your grandma was always reserved and quiet. It was her nature. She had a lot of work to do. She raised 7 children! And maybe she never totally understood English, so it was difficult for her to relate to others, including her children and grandchildren."

Sarah was quiet, listening silently to her mother's heavy breathing, lightly rubbing her mother's cheek.

"I know I've been strict with you, Sarah, but I hope you know I love you." There, Louisa thought, my mother could never say she loved me.

Sarah gave her mom a long, hard hug. "I know, Mom. And I love you." With a final pat, Sarah rolled over and off the bed to stand up. "I'll be in my room, Mom, if you need me. The football games aren't exciting any more without Roger or Peter playing in them. And we were losing. I wonder if it'd be a faster game if girls could play."

"Honestly, Sarah. What will you think up next! Girls playing football!" The two smiled at each other before Sarah turned to go.

Louisa went back to her book, but she kept thinking, I'm a good mother. Even with a difficult child, like Sarah. Maybe we should try being foster care parents again.

It wasn't long after Catherine's death, when the foster agency director called Louisa with a challenge. "We have a 7 year old boy who, I will not lie to you, is a problem. He's the oldest of five children abandoned by their parents who are in jail because they were the cause of a horrific car accident while they were drunk. They're in detox. That's when we learned of the kids and picked them up. The boy is a holy terror here in the orphanage and we've had to keep him locked in the coal room. We need him out of there before the state authorities get after us. I'm telling you the truth, Mrs. Martin, because I don't want to mislead you but I know you can handle him. To keep control of him, it might be helpful if you take two of his sisters with him for a few days as we work out their foster care. They're 4 and 5 years old, sweetest things you ever saw. Well, not always perfect angels but a lot better behaved than Michael. And the three are bonded. The girls seem to keep him calm. But it's up to you. Whatever you can do will help. Are you willing to at least meet him?"

"Of course!" Louisa responded and she and Adam were at the orphanage the next afternoon. When Michael was pulled, really yanked, into the waiting room, Louisa's heart melted. He was thin with unkempt, straight hair which fell across his blazing brown eyes that defied anyone and anything. He reminded her of a rat caught in a hole, ready to bite and escape. His desperate look touched her heart. He'd barely been introduced before two little girls scampered into the room, the smallest one running to hug his waist tightly and the elder one grasping his arm. Immediately, a big grin spread across his face and he stood a little taller. Louisa straightened in response.

"There you have the little family tableau, Mr. and Mrs. Martin," the orphanage director announced a bit sarcastically.

"Patty and Danny?" Michael asked, his dark eyes searching the director's face.

"You don't need to worry about your youngest siblings, Michael. They're in good homes. Babies are always easier to adopt out," the director responded.

"They're gone?" Michael quizzed.

"The quicker you forget them, the better off you'll be." The director spoke harshly to Michael and then in a half-voice to the Martins, "Michael was caught stealing milk for them. He could have been locked up."

Louisa gasped and closed her eyes. Adam put his arm around her, fearful she might faint.

"If you can take all three for a few days, we'd be grateful," the director went on. "We have several families interested in the girls, but we have paperwork. Just a few days." The director's eyes were pleading, "Please."

The Martins went home with three thin, disheveled, poorly clad waifs. Louisa set to work scrubbing them, feeding them, and finding clothes that fit. Michael kept his eyes on Louisa all the time as if she would do something mean to his little sisters. But he didn't cause her any problems. Just doing as she told him. Louisa was transformed herself as she spoke quietly and explained everything gently, fearful that she might set him off into a tantrum if she were not careful.

The director was true to his word and in the following week, he arrived to remove the girls and take them to different foster homes. The littlest girl would be in a home in Laurel where Michael could see her often. The other girl was going to a family in Conrad, Montana.

Starved and sullen, Michael needed to be surrounded with care and good instruction. Louisa was determined to make amends for his early years. But he didn't seem interested in new clothes or even the special dinners she made for him. Adam gave him a ride on a horse at the ranch, but Michael seemed more excited by the baby kittens in the barn. He seemed to like plants; together they picked out ivy for his room. Eventually, they brought in one of the barn cats.

Michael's needs were so great that he filled her every moment. He wasn't necessarily "bad" but he didn't seem to understand "normal" living patterns. Michael was often late or wouldn't come when she called for him. He didn't seem to know how to socialize or make friends. Louisa had her hands full trying to figure out how to help him adjust his behavior as she tried to meet his emotional and physical needs.

One day Sarah arrived home furious at him. "He stole my transistor radio and took it to school saying it was his," she complained to her parents. "I found out from one of his classmates. I worked hard to earn enough to buy that radio and I don't appreciate him taking it from my room and pretending it's his. He needs to be taught a lesson."

Louisa took Michael to his bedroom and sat him down for a talk. She was still a bit frightened of him, fearful he would either erupt in a surly rage or, on the other hand, simply walk away from them. She didn't want him on the streets and her being seen as a mother who couldn't control a child. And she truly wanted to help him. She sat on his bed and took his hands in hers as he stood in front of her.

"Do you understand why Sarah's upset?" she gently asked him, trying to get him to look at her.

"I took her radio to show my friends. That's all." He was staring at the floor.

"Did you tell them it was yours?" He shrugged. "Sarah says you stole it. Do you know what stealing is?"

"Sure, I know about stealing." They both were thinking of the times he stole food for his younger siblings so they could survive. After a moment of silence, he added, "It wasn't stealing because I returned it. I didn't break it." He looked back at her, his eyes defiant. Louisa's heart constricted and she lightly squeezed his hands. She understood him and she wanted those eyes to deepen into love.

"Michael, when you want to use something, you can ask me. Or ask to borrow whatever you want from the person who owns it. But you must not take anything that hasn't been given to you." After a quiet moment, he nodded.

"And now, a hard thing to do." She stopped talking wondering how to broach the consequence of his action and then plunged ahead. "You must tell Sarah you're sorry. Can you do that for me, Michael? Sarah needs to know that you did not mean to take her radio without her permission."

Michael snorted. "She would never have let me have it."

"Maybe not. But maybe. You could have told me and we would have worked it out. Please tell her you're sorry." She felt herself pleading. She badly wanted him to understand right from wrong. Michael shrugged and then finally nodded his acceptance.

Louisa found herself loving this child maybe more than the love she had for her natural born children. In short order, one night as they were lying quietly in bed, she asked Adam if they could adopt Michael.

"Sweetheart," he responded with exasperation, "I was hoping after Sarah graduated, I could quit work and we could travel. Wouldn't you like to be free of the responsibilities you've had? Wouldn't you like to see the world? Europe, South America, India, Hawaii?"

"Michael really needs us, Adam. No one else will adopt him. You know that. He'll be passed from one foster home to another. He's too old to be adopted by others." Louisa rolled on her side to put her arm around Adam, praying he'd open his heart. "And I love him," she whispered.

Adam pushed her away from him, sat up, and turned on the bedside lamp. He looked directly back at her. "Louisa, you just turned 50. You really want to spend the next 12 years raising another child? One who is going to take <u>a lot</u> of work?"

Louisa's eyes filled with tears as she rolled back flat on her back. She stared at the ceiling afraid to look at him as she said slowly and solemnly, "Yes, Adam, yes." What does one do after the children are gone, she thought. I'm worth nothing without giving to others. And while I love Adam, he does not need my help anymore. My parents are gone. My sisters and brothers and my children do not need me. Michael needs me. And while I love to travel, Michael's life is more important.

Adam shook his head and stood up looking down at her and in his most authoritative voice said, "I'll be honest with you. I do not want to adopt Michael. I do not want that responsibility." The tears ran down Louisa's cheeks as she moved across the bed and threw her arms around him to cling to him. He stood erect, staring into the dark corners of the room. Raising kids was not his life's task. What was he to do? He loved this woman but. . . he wasn't about to be shackled with this burden.

As the minutes ticked by, her tears ebbed and she quietly explained, "Adam, I think this is my purpose in life. Raising Michael is what I'm meant to do. He needs us and in many ways, I need him, too."

Adam was caught. He heard her. She had her own destiny apart from his. She went on more forcibly, "Michael will be my responsibility, Adam." And then she stood and looked at him. "You don't need to parent him like you have the others. Just stand by me if I need you." She paused. "And join me in signing the adoption papers."

He took a deep breath. He had never been able to deny her anything. "All right." He nodded. "We'll adopt Michael." Louisa started to put her arms around him in relief, but he held up his hands to stop her. "Stop. Now listen. You'll need to accept whatever decisions I might make for my own future, too. I don't know what my next move is but whatever it is, you'll follow me. We'll do it together, as a family, just as we always have. But Michael will be your responsibility, not mine. And the two of you will follow my lead."

Louisa was relieved that Adam had accepted her proposal. And what could he possibly mean to do that would be difficult for her to follow? "I can do that. It's a deal." She held out her hand and he formally shook it. And then they found themselves hugging, trusting each other.

Adam was successful in the bank, working in the field at farmers' auctions and advising farmers on loans, but also learning accounting, budget, and investment strategies. He edited a weekly bank newsletter which became popular due to the jokes he always included. Nevertheless, the seven years in the Bank seemed long and Adam was restless.

"Louisa," he asked one evening not long after this bedroom episode, "once Sarah graduates this spring, what do you think about moving to southern California?"

"Moving? Permanently?"

"Well, not totally. For a vacation and to see what we think. We'll go in the fall when Sarah starts college and stay in California at least through the school year for Michael's sake. You've been working hard taking care of our mothers, arranging for their health care, and then the funerals. Then the foster children, along with raising Sarah. We need a good long vacation."

"We just received permission to adopt Michael."

"Of course, I agreed, and he'll come with us. They have good schools in California."

"What would you do?"

"Walk the beach for starters. Maybe study the stock market. Figure it out and invest."

"What about this house?" This house I designed and we built together, she thought. Her heart sunk. I hate to leave it. "Would we sell it?"

"Let's ask Peter if he and his wife would want to move in, pay rent, or they could start paying toward a down payment on it if they want to buy it. Since Peter's been working at the bank, it would be easier for him to live here rather than living in that apartment in Billings."

"You have it all figured out." He's always three steps ahead of me, Louisa thought. But I like his idea. Walking the beach. I love the ocean. I wonder. "Can you find us a place to live near the beach?"

"I bet I can. Should I start the search?"

In the fall they took Sarah to the university in Missoula and headed for California. Adam had found a rental at Laguna Beach where Michael attended third grade at the only California elementary school with a playground on the Pacific Ocean. Michael often forgot to go home after school as he built sandcastles on the beach by his school. Adam, too, was building his own sandcastles in his mind. A nine month vacation was all he needed before his energy was restored for a new adventure.

Possibilities in Ordinary People
HELENA, 1960-1964

Democracy is based upon the conviction that there are extraordinary possibilities in ordinary people.

HARRY EMERSON FOSDICK, (1878-1969)

While walking the beaches on the Laguna Beach peninsula, Adam schemed about his next step in life. Before talking to Louisa who might talk him out of his idea, he wanted to make sure he had the details worked out. He called Peter who with his family was living in their Laurel home.

After inquiring about Peter's wife, Judy, and their baby boy, Stanley, born in December, Adam was ready to talk business with his son. "Peter, when Michael's school is out this summer, I'd like to move us back to Montana. Is there any chance we could use the upstairs' rooms at the house for a couple months?"

"You're always welcome, Dad. What's going on? Are you moving back permanently from California? Do you want the house back?" he asked hesitantly.

"No. No. A deal is a deal and the house is yours. I'm thinking of running for Secretary of State and your mother won't be able to be on the campaign trail with me all the time. She and Michael need a place to stay while I campaign."

"Wow! Running for a state office! Good for you, Dad. It'll be an honor to have our house as your campaign headquarters. What about

Michael? Will he be able to adapt to moving back again? It might be hard on him to keep changing schools."

"He won't be a problem. I don't expect you to take on the responsibility of Michael. He'll be with Louisa. He'll be fine."

"Whatever you want, Dad. Tell me the details as they develop. Judy and I support you all the way. I'm excited for you." And as the conversation came to an end, "Say 'hello' to Mom and Michael for us."

"Will do. Thanks, Peter. I knew I could count on you."

Adam now had to deal with Louisa and he tried to see things from her point of view. He knew she loved living in California in the winter, escaping the snow and cold. But I think she misses Montana. My one concern is what to do with Michael for the summer while Louisa and I campaign. Well, he's Louisa's "project." I know Louisa wanted to have something important to do but that doesn't stop me from having my own interests, does it? It's time to move on. She agreed to follow my lead.

That evening Michael was building a city with garages and bridges with domino blocks and cards while Louisa and Adam were watching the evening news. There had been interviews of presidential candidates with Nixon and Kennedy seeming to be the preferred ones for the two major parties.

"Kennedy's a Catholic!" Louisa exclaimed. "I thought we had a separation of religion and state. How can he become president? Won't he be influenced by the pope and follow the Pope's edicts? Will we all become Catholics?" She was remembering her father's battles with the Catholic Church, his anger over their policy of paying "obligations."

"Our constitution will protect us from any laws favoring one religion, Louisa. That's not a problem. But Kennedy may not be the best choice for president for other reasons."

"I wish Eisenhower could run again. It'll be terrible if we have a Roman Catholic president," Louisa responded regretfully.

"We have to hope the people have the good sense to not elect him," Adam replied. There was a pause. "Maybe we need to work harder for the Republicans to make sure Kennedy doesn't get elected." He leaned toward his wife. "Remember the other day we were wondering what we might do if we went back to Montana? You didn't want to go back to the ranch. And I wasn't sure what I could do. I have an idea. I've decided to file to run for Secretary of State in Montana. No one in the Republican Party seems interested in taking on the Democrat. I'd like to give the people a choice."

Louisa looked up at him from her mending in quiet wonderment and thinking, I should not be surprised. He's reading and watching political news summaries every night. He's good at meeting people and knowing how to work with others. This could be an amazing adventure. Then she noticed Michael had stopped his building project and was watching them.

"Just a minute, Adam." Louisa reached over to turn the TV down and spoke to Michael. "It's time for bed, Michael. How about taking a bubble bath and then having ice cream. Would you like that?"

"Okay," he said and dutifully started packing up the dominos into their little metal box. "Can I have chocolate sauce?" He looked at her with his winning smile.

"Sure." And to Adam, she said, "I'll be back," as she turned the TV back up and left the room to get Michael into his evening routine.

"What are you thinking?" she asked breathlessly when she was back. Whatever he has in mind could be exciting.

"No one is challenging Frank Murray, the current Democrat Secretary of State. There's only a slight chance anyone could win against him, but I'd like to try. Citizens should have a choice."

"I totally agree. What does a Secretary of State do?"

"Most of it's paperwork, but important work, like making sure the election process is fair and accurate, keeping track of businesses and licensing them. I would be an administrator with a staff that already knows what they're doing."

"You'd be terrific. You know a lot about business."

"I've learned a lot about finance this winter at the library. I know I could handle an office with a big budget. And I know something about politics from being on the Laurel City Council. The deadline is next Tuesday and no one else has filed. I can't let the last day pass without filing."

"Next week? Are you telling me we need to be in Helena by next week for you to file?" Honestly, what miracles does he think I can perform: packing and getting transfer letters for Michael from his school. . . in a week?

Adam laughed. "It's not that bad. I wrote and got the application form and filled it out. All I need to do is mail it with a check to the Republican Party Chairman and he'll walk into the Secretary of State's office before noon on Tuesday and hand it in, if no other Republican has come through and applied to run."

"Okay. And then?"

"With no one in the Republican Party running against me, it's a sure bet I'll win the primary. But we'll need to leave for Montana as soon as Michael's school is out and start campaigning seriously for the November general election."

Louisa studied her ambitious husband. There's so much more to him than just the farm boy I married. This is what he meant when he asked that Michael and I follow him in whatever he decides. I want this for him, too. And for me. Just think, he might be Secretary of State. She smiled remembering her childhood dream of being a grand lady.

"I know it doesn't make sense," he added. "There's no logic to this. I'm just asking you to go along and see where this goes. We can always come back here in November if I don't get elected."

On the way back to Montana, they stopped at Irene's apple farm in Twisp, Washington. Michael had a great time with Irene's grandson who was about Michael's age. Adam talked to Louisa, then to Irene, and then to Michael about the possibility of Michael staying with Irene and her family for a few weeks, maybe a month? A couple weeks? Both Irene and Louisa were worried about this arrangement. Michael was devious at times. But I need a rest, Louisa thought to herself. I didn't realize how much energy it would take for a 51 year-old-woman to raise an eight-year-old child. I want to take care of Michael, but, oh, I'm so tired.

In Laurel, Adam and Louisa became guests in the upstairs bedroom of their old house. They started working on campaign travel plans and designing brochures and posters. They decided the poster should have a picture of Adam with "Vote for Adam Martin" at the top of the poster, "Businessman-Rancher" at the side, and underneath his picture, "Secretary of State — Integrity in Government — Not Politics." They had 500 posters printed and gave them to the Republican campaign organizers to distribute throughout Montana.

Louisa was energized. Designing flyers, editing Adam's speeches, and going with him to rallies was fun. She loved the carnival in Lewistown with a man dressed as Lincoln. Adam was dignified, yet friendly to everyone. I can learn a lot from him, she thought. And, indeed, Louisa became quite adept at small talk and greeting strangers graciously. People seemed to like her as well as Adam wherever they went. I can do this, she told herself. I enjoy campaigning with Adam.

Peter and his wife Judy with baby Stanley in her arms joined Adam at a couple rallies in Eastern Montana. The crowds enjoyed seeing the grandbaby. Sarah handed out pamphlets at the State 4H Fair in Great Falls with her dad. Roger, however, was at a Mississippi Air Force base; he, Karen, and his children were the only family members unable to be part of the exciting, exhausting campaign in Montana. Adam was proud of being introduced with potential Governor Nutter at events, and being with him shaking hands and greeting people all over the state. Balloons, red and white streamers, white-frosted cupcakes with bitty flags stuck into them were standard decorations at the gatherings along with the loud brass bands and speeches shouted out across the heads of the audience. Hearing retired Governor Aronson, the "Galloping Swede," was a special treat as he joked with the crowd and his Republican friends.

On one of his campaign swings into western Montana, Adam met Irene and her husband at Spokane to pick up Michael. Adam took Michael to a couple rallies, but it was obvious to Adam that Michael was bored as he spent most of his time looking for trouble in back of the buildings. After that, Louisa and Michael spent most of their time in Laurel. By August, all was not going so well.

"Dad, this isn't working," Peter reported to Adam. "Mom criticizes us for feeding Stanley processed baby foods instead of mashing foods. She thinks we need to scrub the kitchen floor every day as Stanley learns to crawl. We can't do things Mom's way. And we're afraid to have Michael with the baby. Michael likes Stanley, but he doesn't know how fragile a baby is."

"I understand," Adam responded. "I'll make some other living arrangement. We'll leave soon. Thanks, Peter, for the support your family has given. I appreciate it."

In a couple days Adam sat down with Louisa and told her, "I found a three bedroom house to rent in Helena. It's two blocks from the Capitol. We can move in now at a reasonable price through the end of December before the legislature comes back into session. You can get settled and enroll Michael in a Helena school for fall. If I win in November, we can stay there with an increased rental fee. If I lose, we can go back to California."

Louisa was relieved as living at the house she designed but no longer hers, was not easy for her. "That sounds good, Adam. I'm tired of living out of a suitcase." The rental house at 408 Washington Drive had some furniture and appliances. It didn't take Louisa long to fill in with the rest of their basic household needs.

She registered Michael for fourth grade, filling in application forms and the necessary papers to get his Laguna Beach reports sent to Helena. Within ten days, the school secretary called Louisa and asked her to make an appointment with a teacher to meet Michael.

"Is anything wrong?" Louisa asked.

"They need some initial testing to see where to place Michael," was the response.

Louisa and Michael went to the school for his appointment with a teacher. Afterward, Louisa was asked to talk with a school counselor. Louisa left Michael in the hallway while she went into an office with a young looking woman. "We'd like to place Michael in third grade," the well-groomed woman announced immediately.

"But why? He went through third grade in California and passed satisfactorily." Louisa was puzzled.

"The California school standards are less stringent than ours and he is at third grade level for reading and math." As young as she was, the counselor was firm. How horrible, Louisa thought, I'm a teacher. I should've been aware if Michael was behind. Louisa remembered the afternoons in California when she and Michael fed bread crumbs to the ducks in the lagoon. And picked lemons from the ever-bearing lemon tree together and then made lemonade. I should have spent that time tutoring him!

"I should have been tutoring him," she guiltily repeated out loud. Louisa was embarrassed. Our children have always been the smartest in their classes. What does this counselor think of me having a child that didn't do well!

"It's no fault of yours, Mrs. Martin," the woman responded. "The California schools are just not like ours. Michael has excellent cursive writing. But he'll be a lot happier if he's in third grade where he'll be able to understand the math lessons and may be ahead in some areas, rather than being behind and struggling in basic curricula."

"But is he behind mentally? I mean, is he. . ." I don't want to say 'retarded.' But is he? She'll think I don't even know my own child! I need to explain. "Michael is adopted, so we don't know his mental capabilities." It sounds like I'm apologizing for him. Or making excuses for myself.

"I have no doubt that Michael is capable of learning third grade material and keeping up with his classmates. He just needs proper instruction and time to adapt to a new school. We look forward to having him here." The counselor sounded as if she were ending the conference. Then she saw the tears in Louisa's eyes who was thinking, I didn't pay enough attention to Michael last winter. What was I doing? Enjoying the 'vacation' from hard Montana winters. And now, helping Adam campaign. I abandoned Michael! But I love him so much. I want him to do well.

The counselor leaned toward Louisa to console her. "Michael needs a little extra attention at the start of school. We'll provide that. Don't worry. He'll do fine." She handed Louisa papers with the room number where Michael would go when school started and stood. The interview was over.

Louisa walked out of the room slowly, solemnly trying to process the news. Michael was looking at pictures in a Smithsonian magazine in the school hallway. He's a dreamer, different from our own kids she was thinking. But he's my responsibility and I'm determined to do my best. Attention and love. All he needs is attention and love. Oh, Michael. How horrible that you have to repeat a grade.

"Michael, we can go home," she spoke softly. He put the magazine back on the side table and stood. He had grown in the last year, but he was still small for his age, several inches shorter than Louisa who was also short. He had a cowlick in his dark, straight hair. Louisa reached out to try to pat it down. Her heart went out to him; she felt pity and sadness for this small waif. "They think you'll do better if you repeat the third grade," she told him nearly in a whisper.

He shrugged his shoulders, unconcerned. Michael looked at her with clear dark eyes. "That's fine, Mom." Louisa's breath caught in her throat. I love being called Mom. And I think he loves me. He's different from the other children all right. Doesn't even care if he has to repeat a grade. Happy just to be with us. Louisa was grateful for his quiet acceptance.

The November election day came quickly. It wasn't a surprise when Adam lost the election to the popular Frank Murray. At the Republican election headquarters where they had been waiting for the results, the shouts and cheering were overwhelming when Nutter was announced as the governor. I think in some small way, we helped Nutter win, Louisa thought. More people were drawn into the Republican Party in Montana because they could see what a fine man Adam is. I wish Adam's father, Henry, were alive to see what a great man Adam has become. I wish we could do more in politics, but this is the end. We can stay in Helena at least until Christmas vacation. And then, who knows? Maybe back to California for the rest of the winter. It would be good, though, if we could stay here and Michael could finish third grade. He's doing well this fall. He's really learning a lot. The school counselor was right.

Louisa noticed Governor-elect Nutter whisper into Adam's ear. Adam nodded and they smiled at each other and shook hands. I wonder what that was all about? A parting joke?

266

Louisa learned later that evening that Nutter was going to recommend Adam to become the State Examiner-Superintendent of Banks. He would have 26-30 employees who audit state banks, Savings & Loans, Credit Unions, school districts, universities, cities, counties and government departments each year. It was a four year appointment and they could settle into living in Helena. Adam readily accepted the challenging offer.

Adam, along with other department heads, was sworn in for his position at the Capitol, February 6, 1961. It was a huge moment for Louisa. Legislators had arrived from all over the state in early January and many would be watching as the department officials were sworn into their offices by the Associate Justice Wesley Castles of the Montana Supreme Court in the rotunda at noon.

A podium had been placed in the middle of the floor where the Montana seal was laid in tile. Folding chairs were set up on the north side and other people would be able to watch the ceremonies from the steps leading to the House and Senate Chambers. People were also gathering in the circular balcony overlooking the event. Louisa saw an empty chair in the second row behind Mrs. Nutter and Mrs. Babcock, the wives of the governor and lieutenant governor.

"Hello, Louisa," Maxine Nutter rose as Louisa made her way to the empty chair. "Have you met Betty Babcock? Betty, this is Louisa Martin whose husband, Adam, will be the Bank Examiner."

Mrs. Babcock greeted her warmly. "It's good to meet you, Louisa. We admired how your husband ran his campaign."

Louisa was radiant. "Thank you. I'm delighted to meet you." These women are young and look absolutely eloquent! They're very well dressed. Louisa pulled in her stomach and nervously fingered the pink bow on her blouse as she sat down. I should have a red or white blouse to go with my blue suit. I'm not looking patriotic at all. Golly, I feel like an awkward farm girl at a formal prom. I need to relax. Relax!

She studied her surroundings, wanting to remember this moment forever. The sun, shining through the colored glass windows, filled the three-storied hollow space with a golden glow turning the wooden beams into a burnished bronze color. This is where Adam would be anointed. It does make me feel like a duchess at court. Louisa laughed at herself.

Voices hummed around her. Once in a while she heard someone call out a name in a greeting. The click of the high heels of busy secretaries hurrying across the tiled floor added to the feeling of anxious excitement.

Louisa looked for Adam gathering with the other officials in the hallway leading to the governor's office. She breathed a sigh of relief as she spotted him, standing to the side and back of Nutter who was shorter than Adam. Adam was distinguished in his new dark gray suit, a color complementing his hair. His white hair lends a sense of authority to him. With his slim body and standing straight, he looks young.

In the midst of the muffled noise as conversations echoed in the capitol dome, Louisa daydreamed. I'm sad our parents have passed on and can't experience this moment with us. I wish our children could be here, but they're all busy. It's amazing how far we've come, from farming to a position in the state government. I don't think Adam could have done it without me. Without my nagging to get off the farm and then my encouragement to work at the bank, we would never have made it this far. Still, politics was his idea, not mine.

Louisa was startled with the announcement, "Please rise for the entrance of the flags." With the scraping of chairs the crowd stood to place their hands over their hearts as Montana National Guardsmen marched in with the U.S. and Montana flags and set them on each side of the podium. Tears came to Louisa's eyes as they said the pledge together and sang the Star-Spangled-Banner with a trumpet accompanying them. I can't imagine a better life than we now have. I'm going to do all I can to help Adam and serve Montana. Louisa thus made her own commitment as she witnessed Adam and the other government officials swear to uphold the constitution of Montana.

As the weeks went on, however, Louisa struggled to find her place in Helena. At Parent-Teacher meetings, the other mothers thought Michael was her grandson. Republican Party meetings were intimidating because the members were a decade younger and most of them were well-versed in political activities with husbands working at the Capitol or with the legislature in previous years. I don't fit in, she thought. They have children in high school and ours are in college or out of college, except for Michael. I don't have anything in common with others. When Adam was home in the evening, she listened politely to his adventures of organizing his office and overseeing his employees, but her heart wasn't with him. She concentrated on feeding Adam and Michael well and keeping their rental clean.

Her main duty became keeping Michael out of trouble. He was struggling with Montana classmates; he seemed to be picking out bullies as friends. Louisa started picking him up after school and making sure he had games to play with at home. She talked Adam into allowing Michael to have a kitten and Michael found pleasure in playing with and teasing the cat.

St. Paul's Methodist Church was older and bigger than the church in Laurel, but Louisa found it comforting to attend their Women's Christian Service programs as she knew a couple of the Helena women from her earlier work. Church activities once again became a major part of her life and a comfort.

Six months into Adams' new job, on June 14, 1961, the *Great Falls Tribune* headline read "Martin Lists Hindrances to Good Government." The article went on to say: "Speaking at the County Clerks'

Convention, Martin claimed, 'Politicians whose every decision is based on what there is in it for themselves hinder progress in Montana. A growing government debt in which we have reached a point of diminishing returns poses the question of whether the taxpayer can continue to carry the load. Too many decisions are made by the state's legal departments for political reasons, by compromising, by being silent, locking the door after the horse is stolen, and decisions with a greater concern for the villain than for the injured victim.'"

Louisa saw the *Great Falls Tribune* article when she took Michael to the library and she bought a copy at a newstand to bring home. The news article worried Louisa. I'm embarrassed for him. How can he face his office workers? What does the governor think? Adam'll be fired!

"Adam, look how awful the newspaper is treating you," Louisa said as she showed him the article that night. She sat in her living room chair and watched him as he read.

"I'm doing my job, Louisa, and the newspaper report is factual," he said as he laid the paper on the floor beside him as if he was done with it.

"Aren't you concerned with how government leaders will respond to your speech?" Louisa asked.

"The battle has just begun. Gov. Nutter had good proposals to improve fiscal responsibility in Montana, but it was defeated in the legislature. Nevertheless, those of us in Nutter's administration will try to get all government employees to be honest and the budgets balanced. Don't fret. It's like a good ride on a bronco at a rodeo. I'll stay on and I'll win." Adam turned back to the portfolio he was reading.

Louisa sighed as she picked up her mending. She didn't know enough about the situation to offer any suggestions. But her stomach was churning.

The grumbling about the Bank Examiners' office continued, much to Louisa's dismay. She tried to keep their home happy by controlling Michael's noise, feeding Adam well, and making sure they all had clean, well-pressed clothes. She kept their rented house tidy allowing her to feel comfortable in inviting visitors from Laurel to stay over when they visited Helena.

Adam found Sarah a job writing out big game licenses for out-of-state applicants at the Fish & Game Department that first summer. Sarah and Adam walked the two blocks together to the Capitol complex each morning, enjoying this time together. Sarah described the long coffee breaks they were allowed at the Fish & Game and asked him why his agency kept coffee breaks to 15 minutes. She had heard various staff members complaining over the inconsistencies in the departments.

"We're hired by the people of the state to work, Sarah. Not to have coffee. A 15 minute break is long enough. You be sure you stick to that time limit." Dad's tough, Sarah thought. He's different. But state workers seem to admire him. Golly, maybe he'll change the whole atmosphere around here. Sarah made sure the breaks she took were less than 15 minutes and she was often at her desk alone. Her fellow workers found her strange.

With Sarah at home for the summer, Louisa thought it would be a good time to invite Peter and his family for a weekend. She talked Adam into getting reservations for a Lake Holter boat ride through the Gates of the Mountain and for a picnic on a weekend in August. Then, Adam invited his top staff and their families, too. Louisa's idea of a family gathering turned into an office celebration.

On Saturday night they saw "The Bad Seed" presented in the Brewery Theater, a factory-sized beer company that had been abandoned and revitalized as a cultural center. The play was a hilarious spoof of murder, mystery, and comedy. Louisa wondered why Peter and Sarah were laughing hilariously in tears and bent over from their laughter. Are they laughing about me as the mother passing on bad genes to her little girl who is a murderer? Surely, it has nothing to do with us? Have I lost my sense of humor? Adam is chuckling. Even Michael is laughing. I'm too serious! I used to be fun. Are they laughing at me? What's happened to me?

On Sunday morning, the Martins attended the St. Paul Methodist Church where the well-known and well-loved Rev. George Harper gave the sermon. After church, Louisa started feeling good again. This weekend was great, even more than I planned, Louisa thought. I'm pleased I was able to get Adam to laugh and to think about something other than business.

By October, Montana newspapers were printing articles about Bank Examiner Adam Martin with headlines like: "Martin Warns About Illegalities," "Martin Says Butte in Trouble," "Officials Snub Martin Views," "Martin Cites Silver Bow Finance Crisis," "Silver Bow Can Return To Financial Solvency," "Martin Asks Politics Be Divorced From Legality of County Pay Raises," and "Problem of County Officials' Salaries 'One Big Fat Mess' State Examiner Claims." County commissioners were after him from all corners of Montana.

Louisa was worried. "What can we do to stop this media attack on you, Adam?"

"Nothing."

"You aren't concerned?"

"No. Truth will win out." He put down his newspaper and changed the topic. "How about helping me plan a Christmas party for the office? I'd like to have it at Jorgenson's with a steak supper and some entertainment. We'll pay for it, not the government. It'll be a family party. I was thinking of asking Sarah to play and lead the singing of Christmas carols. Will you be willing to give the grace, a blessing before we eat?"

Louisa was astounded. She wrapped the dishtowel she was carrying around her arm and sat down across from him. What's happening? Nothing's going right. I thought this year would be grand. Instead I can't seem to make friends, I think my children are laughing at me, Michael is starting to fall behind again at school, and counties are publicly criticizing Adam for the way he's doing his job. And all Adam is thinking about is an office Christmas party. Maybe I worry too much. But still. . .I'm his wife. And I'm worried for him.

"A prayer? Adam, they'll laugh at us. I want them to like us. They'll want liquor and light entertainment like a dance. Not singing Christmas carols. Not having prayers."

Adam was adamant. "We'll offer them a family dinner. I won't serve liquor. I don't want to spend my money on booze. But they could buy their own drinks if they like from the bar. I'm not opposed to that if they need a drink. These are good men, Louisa. They travel all over the state and do a great job under adverse conditions. They walk into banks or counties unexpectedly to see the account books and they aren't loved for that. I want to show them and their families my appreciation. I want to give them a meaningful, enjoyable Christmas party. It'll be fun for all of us."

Louisa shook her head and sighed, thinking I don't think this will help him at all. Nevertheless, it's my duty to support him to the best of my ability. Instead she said, "Of course, Adam, I'll be honored to give the blessing for the meal." But in her mind she thought maybe no one will even come.

Louisa was surprised as she met and greeted more and more of Adam's staff and their wives, some of whom went first to the bar to order drinks which they brought to the tables decorated by Louisa with evergreen branches, red ornaments, and white ribbons. The tables were filled. No one was missing! Adam was in his element with Louisa, Sarah, and Michael at the head table with him. After clinking spoons on the water glasses to get their guests' attention, Louisa stood and led them in a short and simple Grace. As his employees ate their salads and waited for their prime rib, Adam welcomed them and began entertaining them with puns.

"A washerwoman, annoyed by the cars on a dusty road soiling her clean clothes, posted this sign on each side of her washing: 'Drive slow—big washout ahead.'" Adam's employees politely chuckled at Adam's big grin.

"Here's one you'll love. Don: Found a new house? Dick: We've stopped looking—the appraiser's description of our own house seemed to be just the place we were looking for." Adam slapped his thigh in laughter and his guests started chortling along with him, enjoying Adam as much as his puns.

"Sales Manager: To whom do you attribute your success? Salesman: To the first five words I utter when a woman opens the door, namely – 'Miss, is your mother at home?'" Adam's employees now started laughing out loud as Adam wiped his eyes having laughed so hard.

"Any little tomato who knows her onions can go out with an old potato and come home with a couple of carats." By now, the entire group was laughing, even Louisa. Adam was hooting and really enjoying himself.

"It seems that every time we meet an attractive gal, either she is married or we are." Louisa rolled her eyes, as everyone else howled in appreciation.

"My workers, my friends and families, I appreciate you." Adam was smiling but he had become a bit serious. "This is just for you, a quote from William Feather. 'What makes the contest so uneven is that certain people have brains and are willing to work hard.' That's you! Brains and working hard. You did a great job this year cleaning up financial improprieties in many parts of the state. Here's another quote I like from Bob Carroll: 'No one ever lost anything by doing a little more than he was expected to do.' Keep up the good work, fellas! I hope you enjoy your steak. During dessert, Sarah will play a few Christmas songs. Feel free to join in singing with her. Eat, sing, enjoy yourselves. Merry Christmas and Happy Year to each of you."

Adam's workers enjoyed the party which reminded them of earlier years when they gathered with family to celebrate the holidays. Louisa was reminded of their own Thanksgiving and Christmas parties at the home place in Lewistown or the Molt ranch.

As they left the party, Louisa kept thinking, families don't get together like we used to do. Neither Roger nor Peter could make it to Helena. But this was a great party. Many of Adams' workers thanked me for my blessing! It's amazing they care about such an old-fashioned custom. I'm happy I could support Adam in this small way. How they laughed at Adam's jokes and clapped and sang with Sarah. Adam knows how to make people feel special. These are educated men, most of them have college degrees in business or accounting and still, they appreciate Adam. Maybe they don't know he didn't graduate from high school. I'm proud of Adam and maybe I helped him and gave him the confidence to succeed.

At home after the party, Adam asked Sarah, "What did you think of Orville?"

"Orville? Which one was he?" Sarah tried to remember which of the suited up men was Orville.

"He's the short accountant from Bozeman. Smart man. Single." Sarah raised her eyebrows, thinking, I remember now, a chubby red-faced guy who laughed too loud.

"I liked Jerry. Didn't you like him, Sarah?" Louisa asked.

Again, Sarah pondered and looked back at her mother questioningly. "Who was Jerry?"

"You know the man who got up to sing the carols with you. He looks like he'd be fun to be with." Oh, yes, Sarah thought, the awkward one who had the wrong rhythm. I get the hints. . . an accountant or an attorney as a husband. Boring!

In the mail the next week Adam and Louisa had a little Christmas card from the office with an original poem:

We think he's tops among bosses,
This Superintendent of Banks,
And he does his job quite often
Without the people's thanks.

But we appreciate him,
And we take this time to tell,
We're glad he heads our office.
P.S. We like his wife as well.

Louisa was thrilled with the note. His office staff loves Adam. They like me! Adam knew what to do. He's a great man. Louisa was relieved. Everything was going well for Adam at his office and that was all that really mattered.

Just a month later at the end of January, the state was reeling from tragedy. Governor Nutter and four other state employees were killed in a small airplane crash. Tim Babcock took over as governor. Adam respected his new boss and Gov. Babcock also liked Adam. Nothing changed for Adam who kept trying to get counties, universities, and banks to follow the law and do the right thing.

Later that year on November 7, 1962, the *Montana Standard-Post* out of Butte-Anaconda reported in an editorial, "Now it's Beaverhead: Martin Hews to the Line." They reported, "Beaverhead County, we note, has received a scolding from the office of Chief State Examiner

Adam Martin for 'procedures contrary to Montana statutes.' The point here, as we see it in the light of what has been done by the state examiner's office in Silver Bow County, is that predominantly Republican Beaverhead has not been a beneficiary of favoritism from Martin's office because it is Republican."

It was reported that there were 79 state banks, one state trust company, and 43 national banks. State and National bank resources were over $1 billion dollars for the first time in their history. The State Bank Examiner was putting the fiscal balance sheet of Montana in order.

Adam is vindicated, Louisa thought. Hopefully the worst is over for him and we can enjoy our years in Helena. I wish I could feel as confident as he does. He's grown over the years we've been together. He's extremely competent and attractive in many ways. But who am I? Where do I belong? A dark shadow was hanging over her that she couldn't shake.

"Adam, Michael's not obeying me," Louisa confessed one night. She couldn't pretend to herself any longer that she was doing a good job in raising Michael. "He goes to friends' homes after school instead of coming home. He's not doing his homework. You can see at dinnertime that I can't get him to eat vegetables. I don't like to bother you, Adam, because you're working hard, but I'm worn out. I can't take it much longer."

Adam nodded in sympathy. He had seen the disagreements between the two of them. "I'll talk to him and see what I can do." Adam found out fairly quickly that Michael was bored with them as parents, especially since they were nearly a generation older than most of the parents of Michael's friends. Adam and Louisa's friends were in politics. Gatherings with them tended to be serious discussions of state policies rather than light hearted social events with other children Michael's age to play or talk with. Adam could understand Michael's viewpoint.

A couple weeks later on a Saturday Adam said, "Let's take a ride after lunch." They rode north of town about six miles into the Helena valley where houses were surrounded by one to five acre plots. They turned onto Munger Lane, a narrow street with a ditch and trees on the side. Two houses before the end of the lane, Adam pulled into the driveway before a sprawling, modern ranch-style house. On one side was a fenced pasture with a tack room.

"Let's look around and see how we like it. If you like this place, it's ours," he told Louisa and Michael. Louisa and Michael looked wide-eyed at each other and jumped out of the car to explore the property. Another car pulled up and a real estate agent opened up the house. Louisa walked in and turned in a swooping, slow circle taking in the large glass windows on the south side, fireplace on the west, and wooden beams above. A counter separated the living room from the kitchen area and bedrooms were on both sides of the main entry area. This is a far better house than the one I designed, Louisa thought. Newer, of course. She looked at the garden plot out the kitchen window. Just like my mother said, you need to be able to step outside the kitchen and smell the flowers. This is perfect!

In the meantime, Michael was outside noticing the dog kennel and a small shed for horse tackle. I'm betting Dad will let me have a horse and a dog, he thought. Maybe Mom'll calm down and not be yelling at me all the time. He looked down the lane and saw a couple boys his age riding bikes. Yes, this might be all right.

That spring Michael found a mongrel dog that he loved. He named him Pal. The horse came a bit later, and because of its pretty copper color, Michael named him Penny. Along with Pal and Penny came friends who also loved animals. At the end of the lane, there was a pond that entertained the boys with toads in the summer and ice-skating in the winter.

The house was large enough that Louisa could invite her friends from church or those in the Republican Women's Club to hold committee meetings or have dinners together. She felt honored when she was invited by Rev. George Harper to be on the Board of the Montana Deaconess School, the very institution that had taken in Walter's children when he traveled the U.S. as a missionary. The Board immediately voted to have Louisa as their secretary.

Gradually, Louisa felt like she belonged in Helena. Still lonely without her older children or her siblings nearby, she became satisfied with gatherings with working friends. She realized the culture was changing and since Adam's and her parents had died there didn't seem to be a reason to get their families together.

Louisa was asked to help with the Montana Territorial Centennial Ball on May 26, 1964. And its Adam's birthday, she wanted to shout. He'll be 57! What a great way to celebrate his birthday. She readily accepted the job and was thrilled to be a part of organizing the event. Past governor J. Hugo Aronson came as well as a Broadway singing star, John Hickman. Abraham Lincoln had appointed Sidney Edgerton to be the first territorial governor so it seemed appropriate to have Lincoln present! Louisa arranged for Mr. and Mrs. John Taylor of Kalispell to attend as they enjoyed dressing up as Mr. and Mrs. Lincoln.

"Gala Centennial Ball Termed Huge Success" headlined the *Helena Independent* when it was over. Louisa had helped make it a success and she patted herself on the back.

"You look beautiful in the picture in the paper, Louisa," Adam remarked after he read the news article. "You are beautiful. I'm one lucky husband." Louisa gave him a big kiss grateful for his compliments and encouragement.

"And I'm a fortunate wife." Life was finally going well.

Before the election of 1964, they flew with Michael to Boston to visit Roger, Karen, and the two grandchildren. Louisa and Adam hadn't seen them for a couple years with the Air Force keeping Roger busy. And Adam, too, seldom had time for family vacations.

"We're happy to see you." Roger greeted them when he picked them up at the airport. "We're lucky you could get away with your activities in Helena."

Louisa was excited see the rush of activity as they moved to the car. "Being here has been a wonderful opportunity for you," she exclaimed to Roger as he put their suitcase in the trunk. "It's amazing the Air Force selected you to get a MBA from Harvard."

"Right, Mom, it's amazing." Roger responded slightly sarcastically, as he shut her car door and got into the driver's seat.

Louisa was in her own dream world. I can scarcely believe it. We have come a long way as a family! Our son is a Harvard business graduate student! I wish Papa and Mamma could see this. What would they think of a grandson at Harvard! From Czech immigrants to Harvard. Then it hit her that Roger had taken her remark poorly. "I didn't mean. . . I meant I'm proud. . ." but Roger was pointing out Boston sights to Adam.

Louisa studied the people on the streets. She wondered if Arthur Lewis was still living in Boston. I haven't heard from Isabella in years. Maybe she's here. I'd like to shout out to them, "My son's at Harvard!" Even Arthur might finally find me to be acceptable! It's hard to be humble when I'm proud of all we've done as a family! Life certainly has its surprises. Roger as a little boy on the ranch loved watching airplanes overhead, and that led him to the Air Force and Harvard business school.

"Isn't the river beautiful, Michael?" she exclaimed as they crossed the Charles River, thinking what a marvelous opportunity for him to see one of the first cities in the U.S. Glancing at him across the back seat from her she saw that he had his nose in the comic book which she had allowed him to have to entertain him on the airplane. She sighed.

At dinner that night, Louisa was quiet as Roger described the campus and his classes and Adam shared his experiences as bank examiner. Louisa admired the lovely place settings, the furniture and lamps realizing that Karen with her home economics degree had skills in homemaking that she didn't have. Once again Louisa rued her immigrant, impoverished background. She watched in embarrassment as Michael in a T-shirt with his hair hanging in his eyes shoved down his food. In contrast, the two little grandchildren sitting on booster seats, the girl in a darling pleated skirt and the boy in a button-down shirt, ate mannerly. I don't even know them, she thought. I could have spent more time with them instead of raising Michael. Why didn't I? The oldest grandchild was born the same year we adopted Michael. Instead of accepting the role of grandmother, I opted into raising another son. A shiver went down Louisa's back.

When they were home again, Louisa didn't have time to dream about Roger's successes or mull over her own past choices. Gov. Tim Babcock won his reelection in November and given the great success of the Centennial Ball earlier that year, Betty Babcock asked Louisa to help with the Inaugural Ball. Louisa was inspired to make this the greatest Ball ever. Always good at organizing, Louisa worked with six other committee members to hire a band, rent a hotel for dancing, get caterers, and print the Inaugural Ball invitations. As she worked on the project, Louisa was delighted to meet new people. She became a network center for introducing people to each other and getting them involved in the Republican Party's activities. She finally felt like she belonged in Helena. Working with her husband to build a better democracy was what she was meant to do.

Rough Places into Level Ground
HELENA, 1965-1968

I will lead the blind by a road they do not know, by
paths they have not known I will guide them. I will
turn the darkness before them into light, the rough
places into level ground. These are the things I will do,
and I will not forsake them.

ISAIAH 42:16

In the whirlwind of entertaining political leaders, Louisa seldom had time to think of herself. While rushing to get her grocery shopping done, she froze when she heard "Hello, Louisa" from a voice she remembered all too well. The man who greeted her had a receding hairline and red, slightly graying hair slicked back into a pompadour. Her eyes widened and her heart started pumping fast and hard. Joe Jacob! Taller, bigger, older. Louisa, ready to run, glanced backward down the aisle. Another customer was there. Would she help if Joe hurt her?

"I saw your picture in the paper working on the Inaugural Ball." Joe sounded friendly. Louisa kept her cart between them. Feeling faint, her knuckles turned white as she clung tightly to the cart handle to hold herself up. The image of black and white hexagon designs on tile blocks swirled around her. Had it been 40 years? Slowly, she started breathing again.

"Joe? Joe Jacob?" Louisa choked out his name. Swallowing hard, she pulled herself together and found her voice. "How are you?"

"I'm working for an engraver. I probably made most of those name plates you see on legislators' desks. In prison I was one of the best, making license plates." Joe laughed. "It gave me experience for engraving metal." Louisa slowly nodded. She was at a loss for words, having feared this moment for years, imagining it, wondering if it would be her last day on earth as he might seek her out to get revenge. She had no idea of what to say or do. Louisa unconsciously reached her hand up to touch the scar at the base of her hairline back of her ear. Joe watched her.

"I'm sorry, Louisa. I was angry at all women, not you in particular." Louisa nodded again, trying to hear and to understand. "I was good as a nurse, really good, but I wasn't accepted. I was a man in a woman's world." Anger was still in his voice. Louisa could connect with this statement remembering her own feeling of rejection at the hospital as a too young, poor Czech from central Montana.

Louisa noticed he had green eyes as he looked at her, questioningly. She had forgotten how green they were. Or had she ever seen them? Joe frowned and then looked away. He wanted her to say something, but what? Does he want me to apologize for him shooting me?

Joe shrugged and started to turn down the grocery aisle away from her. "See ya around."

Louisa started breathing normally again. "Joe, wait." But when he turned back to listen to her, she still didn't know what to say. She had feared this moment for so long and here it was. She was now looking at one of her biggest fears in life straight in the face. This man had tried to kill her. She needed closure.

"I didn't belong there either," Louisa finally choked out. Her life flashed in front of her. "My life changed, too, from that moment." Maybe I would never have been a teacher, maybe I wouldn't have met Adam, she thought. "But everything worked out." A customer passed by them both as they stood frozen. Finally, she said, "I'm sorry about what happened to you, Joe." She had always regretted having to name him as the shooter.

Joe smiled. Louisa had never seen him smile. It was what he wanted to hear, her remorse, or perhaps her forgiveness of what he had done? She realized she had wanted for years to see Joe, even tell Joe that everything was okay. Her spirits lifted as she realized she had met one of her biggest fears in life and was now fully alive. It's over. It's truly over. I saw him. I can live freely. Their eyes connected and Louisa smiled back at Joe.

This time when Joe turned, he gave her a little salute and said, "Take care, Louisa." As she watched him saunter away she wondered if he had ever met her nephew in prison. Maybe not, it's a big place. Still, both were there for homicides. But that was their life, not hers.

Louisa felt lighter, freer after her accidental meeting with Joe. A dark cloud had been lifted from around her shoulders. Trying hard to be perfect and in control was no longer necessary. As if I could have changed anything, she thought. The past is what it was. I no longer need to fear anything, not what happened, not what may happen, or what others think. I can live in the moment without the rules I've been putting on myself and my family. Look to the future!

Still, it was a bit of a shock when Sarah called to announce she was leaving her job in Missoula and traveling to Texas to marry a high school classmate who had been drafted and now based at Fort Sam Houston in San Antonio. Louisa stood beside Adam at the telephone listening to every word. While Adam in his usual calm manner talked to Sarah about the condition of her car and the possibility of driving through snow, Louisa's mind buzzed with questions: how did the two get together again and how did she know this is "the one" and why wouldn't Sarah want to have a big wedding in Helena or Laurel? Adam then said, "How about if your mom drove down to Texas with you? It might be safer for you to have her along as an extra driver."

"Okay," Sarah responded easily. "I'll be home to pick her up at the end of the month. Tell Mom I love her. Thanks, Dad, for your good advice." Adam slowly hung up the phone and looked at Louisa.

"You heard?" he asked. Louisa nodded.

"How can she do this? No wedding announcements, no dress, no reception, no church? My only daughter." Louisa was obviously disappointed.

"She's always had a mind of her own. Maybe like her mother," he teased. Silence. "We can still do some of those things."

"You're right!" Louisa's voice rose in excitement. "I'll find a pattern for a simple but smart looking dress. White linen. I think I can make it in two weeks. What do you think?"

"I think you better see what Sarah thinks. But I bet she'll be happy with your gift."

"I think I'll make myself a new dress, too. Oh, Adam I saw the most beautiful gold brocade fabric. And let's buy them a set of really nice cooking pans which every family needs and what I wish we would have had early on. Once they're married, you can put an announcement in the paper. Our friends will want to know." Adam nodded and smiled at his wife's excitement and her acceptance. She wasn't going to stew over Sarah's announcement. Louisa smiled back at him.

"Thanks, Adam for asking Sarah to take me to Texas with her. It'll be an interesting ride. Could you fly down for the wedding?"

Adam shook his head. "Too much going on at the office. I trust you'll represent us well. You can fly home and tell me all about it." He paused. "You're taking this well, Louisa."

"I'm learning."

A few weeks later her wisdom was tested. Louisa pondered as she lay in her motel bed, her third night in San Antonio. There had been no mention of a wedding. Sarah was spending her nights at the cute apartment Dan had set up for her above a single garage, just a block off the base. And is Dan spending his nights there, too? Was Sarah going to end up being a dalliance, a paramour for an Army man?

Louisa remembered the long years she waited before Adam was ready to marry. While Sarah and Dan had known each other since first grade, they may need time to get better acquainted as adults. Maybe they shouldn't rush into marriage. I wish Sarah and I had talked about these details as we drove down here. What did we talk about? Nothing important, obviously. Well, I never talked about love or sex or marriage with my mother either. But Adam and I weren't living together before we got married. I don't like the idea of Dan and Sarah doing so. What can I do? Should I intervene? Insist on their marrying before living together? They're grown-ups. I can't control this. Dear Lord, give me guidance.

The next morning as she sipped on her coffee in Dan's apartment, Louisa casually announced, "I planned on leaving Sunday, but if you're not getting married, I can stay and help you find a place in Austin, Sarah. I'm sure you can find a job at the university or the capitol." The room was silent. The young couple looked at Louisa. While Louisa didn't say it out loud, her message was clear.

Sarah then looked at Dan. He slowly smiled and Louisa thought she heard him mutter, "Ah, a shotgun marriage." What she did hear from him was, "Sarah, I need to meet a friend at the courthouse to transfer ownership papers for my car since we can use yours. Do you want to come with me?" They were soon gone.

Saturday at noon, Louisa carefully pinned into Sarah's hair the circle of lace that Sarah had made out of Louisa's wedding veil. There were no flowers for the bride, but Dan had bought an orange, pink, and red corsage for his mother-in-law. To Louisa, it looked outrageous on her gold brocade dress. Dan, however, wanted to be an artist. Maybe the clashing colors were an artistic expression? Or did it mean something else?

Sarah and Dan both cried during the brief ceremony. Oh, goodness, have I done the right thing? Louisa worried. Why are they crying? Perhaps this marriage was not meant to be. Nevertheless, Louisa dutifully signed her name to the wedding certificate as a witness along with Dan's one friend who came to stand by Dan.

At the airport the next morning, Sarah kissed her mom and whispered, "Thanks, Mom . . . for everything." Early sunlight through the bay windows softly encompassed the hug of the two women as they said goodbye. Louisa was relieved. Sarah seemed grateful for her interference. And I can return home to Adam knowing Sarah is safely launched.

The responsibilities of being a mother never ends, Louisa mused during the weeks that followed. It's difficult to know what to do and what guidance to give to a child's growth patterns. Being a good parent is the toughest job in the world.

"Louisa, you're chewing on the pencil again," Adam complained. Louisa took the pencil out of her mouth and studied it as if it had offended her. She was having a hard time concentrating on the simplest matters. . .even a grocery list.

Louisa thought and prayed about Michael a lot. She couldn't figure out how to help him. She loved him deeply and she knew he loved her. Michael was the only child who'd say, "Love you, Mom" as he'd leave the house. But he doesn't follow my instructions at all. It's like he's forgetful or doesn't think. She mulled over his behavior. Sometimes he's rude to the point of being aggressive. He has everything a child could want, a good home, playmates, animals. We take him on trips. We give him freedom to be with his friends. Maybe he was so badly damaged before we adopted him that he can't recover. Oh, Lord, I don't know what to do. She was chewing on the pencil again before she realized it.

"Adam, I can't take it anymore." She had Adam's attention. "I try to be a good mother to Michael, but nothing I do is working. He's not like our other children. He acts politely when you're home, but..." Does she dare tell Adam that she's afraid of Michael, her own son! "He's stronger than I am. I love him . . . but . . . ." She was almost crying; she was trying not to cry. "I have to admit that sometimes I'm afraid of what he might do."

"I thought it might come to this," Adam responded. He moved to the table where she sat and put his hands over hers. "You've been a good mother. Don't ever doubt that. You've done all you could." He rubbed her arm and looked into her deep brown eyes. As always, Adam was prepared for this moment. Sitting beside her, he told her, "I have an idea. One of my bank examiners told me about a high school military academy in Minnesota. Boys are given uniforms and military training and at the same time continue their high school subjects. He'd be in a dorm with other boys, but under strict supervision. The school has an excellent record of helping young boys. What do you think? Should I look further into it as a possibility for Michael?"

The relief on Louisa's face was his answer. "Oh yes. Find out if they'd accept him. And then we'll see if he'd be willing to go."

"If we decide that's what's best for him, he'll go," Adam firmly responded.

Michael went to St. John's Military Academy for the fall semester of his junior year. He came home for Christmas feeling very smart, dressed in his blue-gray wool uniform and shining black leather shoes. He enjoyed how the girls on the plane admired him and how well he was treated by the plane personnel. That was a great Christmas.

But by spring Michael was through with the academy; he didn't like it enough to go back his senior year. When he first arrived home that summer, he was popular with the kids for having had such a different experience. Michael had acquired a few military behavior codes and spoke a bit more politely to his parents and other adults with his "yes, sir, yes, ma'am." It raised Louisa's hopes that Michael might be able to get a high school diploma. They didn't force the issue of him returning to the military academy and hoped they would make it to seeing him graduate.

Adam helped Michael get a summer job painting signs for the Montana highway department as a way to learn to work for others and at the same time to have his own spending money. He seemed to like the job, being outdoors with workmen who joked with him. It helped that he was away from the house and his parents most of the time.

That summer the Republican Central Committee chair for Montana telephoned Louisa to ask her if she'd be willing to be an alternate to the Republican National Convention in Miami Beach on August 5-8. A chance to visit Miami? Of course.

"But why me?" she asked the Republican chair. "Wouldn't you rather have Adam? He's more active in the Party."

"You've done a lot of good work, Louisa. And, to be perfectly frank, we're trying to build our base with women participants. Betty Babcock recommended you and she'll be going."

Louisa started planning her convention clothes. She had a favorite pink suit she had worn to bank examiners' events. But Betty Babcock destroyed that idea.

"They'd like us to wear red, white, or blue dresses or suits, Louisa," Betty told her. Louisa put the pink suit back in the closet and went shopping for a red suit.

The store clerk told her, "The red looks lovely against your dark skin tone," but Louisa thought the red made her look green. What can I do to look patriotic? Louisa sewed herself a white cotton dress and bought a red, white, and blue scarf. She could also use the scarf with her blue suit. She bought white shoes, a darling hat, and gloves.

Louisa read the papers far more diligently than her usual perusal trying to retain all she could of state and national issues. She thought about the presidential candidates and tried to settle in her own mind whom she would support if she were called upon to give her opinion.

As Louisa and a couple Montana delegates entered the lobby of the Miami Beach Convention Center, they could choose buttons: "Nixon, He's the One" or "Draft Reagan." Louisa thought the one for Rockefeller was ironic, a tiny button with only his name. Definitely not who he is! Nixon should win this time, Louisa thought. I like him a lot. He's better known now than in 1960 when he lost to J.F. Kennedy. I especially like his wife, Pat. A nurse in the White House would be great! And they have raised beautiful, talented daughters. But I also like Nelson Rockefeller and Ronald Reagan. All good men. I'm glad I'm only an alternate and can enjoy the convention without major responsibilities. Louisa decided to get all the buttons, pinned them onto her white dress, not claiming allegiance to any one candidate for the time being.

When Louisa turned around, her Montana acquaintances were gone as she was swept into the Convention Center with the crowd. The massive space and noise overwhelmed her. She'd never seen anything like it. There must be thousands of people under this one roof. The noise was deafening. A band was playing and people were shouting to each other over the music. Louisa stepped to one side of the aisle to clear her head. How do I find where I'm supposed to go? This is worse than being lost in a prairie blizzard. Help! Help! And she laughed at herself. She spotted a man with a big STAFF name tag and she waved her arms to get his attention.

"Montana," she shouted at him. He pointed to the left and front of the room. She pushed her way through the crowd to eventually find a seat with the Montana delegation.

The convention got heated as Nixon chose Maryland's Governor Spiro Agnew to be his vice-president. After Martin Luther King, Jr.'s assassination earlier that spring, there had been riots in Baltimore. Agnew had invited Black religious and political leaders to the state house. Agnew thought his Republican administration had done a lot for the Blacks with new programs and he complained that the Blacks hadn't done enough to support the state's projects. A group of delegates in the convention hall walked out in disgust as they heard Agnew's biting comments.

Louisa remembered how surprised she was watching an elegant Black woman on television on their trip to Detroit for a bank convention the previous year. The woman spoke with clarity about the lack of opportunities for Blacks in the city. She outlined the reasons for riots around the country and emphasized the need for quality education for Black children and the need for more support for all Blacks, even those who are doing well. Louisa agreed that schools should hire more Black teachers even when students were White.

I had never seen a wealthy, beautiful Black woman before, Louisa mused. She was right. We can't expect Blacks to immediately change the situation by themselves when they've lacked education and opportunity. Maybe opposing racial integration is okay, she thought, as long as Blacks have educational programs that are equal to other schools. We need to stand in favor of strong schools for all children, Black and White. And for the American Indians in Montana. Why can't we get along? We need to keep finding ways to work together. Agnew isn't right, but I'm not going to walk out of the convention! What are those delegates thinking? They should be supporting all these fine Republican national leaders!

Nixon was nominated on the first ballot with 692 votes. Nelson Rockefeller had 277 and Ronald Reagan had 182. In his acceptance speech, Nixon stated: "When the strongest nation in the world can be tied down for four years in Vietnam with no end in sight, when the richest nation in the world can't manage its own economy, when the nation with the greatest tradition of the rule of law is plagued by unprecedented racial violence, when the President of the United States cannot travel abroad or to any major city at home, then it's time for new leadership for the United States of America."

Louisa stood, clapped, and yelled "Nixon, Nixon, Nixon" with the rest of the crowd. Nixon will be the best president we've ever had, she thought. He'll get this country back on the right track. What a joy it has been to belong and support the Montana Republican Party. She went home rejuvenated as a strong American patriot.

Everything seemed calm that fall as Michael started his senior year at Helena High. One day the school called to tell Louisa that Michael hadn't been attending classes. Adam gave him a stern lecture and Louisa made sure he was up and going to school every morning, but he didn't make it there or if he did, he didn't stay. He was soon expelled. Louisa felt dismayed and discouraged. She'd tried so hard to help him get through high school.

Before Louisa had a chance to help Michael figure out the next stage of his life, they had a call from the police telling them Michael was arrested and in jail for stealing motorcycle parts. They knew Michael and a friend had been repairing motorcycles, an activity that seemed constructive. But now this! Louisa was heart-sick. Her son was a high school dropout and a criminal. She immediately called and cancelled her committee meetings and her weekly Bible study, not wanting to face anyone while her stomach was churning and she couldn't keep her mind on anything for any length of time. She watched the clouds drifting by outside their living room window trying to find inner peace. Adam went to the station after work and paid the bail money to get Michael out of jail.

Adam was concerned for Louisa and calmly approached her that evening as she was making supper. "It's time to let Michael go, Louisa. He's 18 and has the right to make his own decisions about his life, whatever it may be."

Her dark eyes flashed as she angrily shot back at him, "He's been arrested for stealing!"

Adam remembered the many times over the years when Michael had been accused of stealing from family and from neighbors. Adam thought, after having to steal milk to feed his baby sister when he was only five, he never got over it. Not an excuse, but an ingrained reaction.

He tried to reason with her. "We've tried to show him that stealing is not right. You've taught him right from wrong, Louisa. The church also taught him moral values. We've done our best. He has to choose for himself now."

"He doesn't think. He can't choose. Friends talk him into these crazy, illegal acts." Louisa was chopping furiously on the garden carrots and tossed them into a pan of boiling water.

"Yes, and maybe he'll have to continue to learn the hard way, the legal consequences of illegal acts," Adam commented matter of factually. Louisa paused in her chopping, laying down the knife, remembering Joe Jacob, Frank Robideau, and Raymond Janochek. All men she had known that ended up paying for their serious illegal acts. For murder, she thought, far worse than stealing.

"I pray Michael doesn't do something foolish and end up in prison." Louisa turned to her job of breading pork chops for supper.

Adam put his arms around her, nuzzling her neck. "Louisa, don't let this sour you. You've given Michael a good foundation and he has some admirable qualities. Just keep your loving, hopeful spirit."

With tears running down her cheeks, she turned into his arms, flour from her hands flying around the room and onto his shirt. He held her tightly until the tears ebbed.

Two weeks later after he had paid for the stolen parts and the court fee, Michael sauntered into the living room where Adam and Louisa were reading. He waited for them to look at him, leaning back on the doorpost, and then he announced, "I'm leaving tomorrow to go to Idaho." Louisa exhaled a sharp breath and started to get up, but Adam reached across the lamp stand and placed his hand on her arm, firmly holding her back.

"You have someplace to stay?" Adam asked his son calmly.

"A friend."

"Do we know this friend?" Silence. "And how are you getting there?" Adam continued conversationally.

"You know Rob. We have motorcycles. I fixed mine. Not from stolen parts like you think."

"We know you paid your fine to the judge. And I'm glad your motorcycle is working again. Do you suppose you could give us the address of Rob's family?" Michael didn't respond. Louisa wondered, doesn't Michael want us to know where he's going? Or maybe he doesn't know the address? Adam continued, "Could you call us when you get there? Your mother will worry otherwise. You can reverse the telephone charges."

Michael looked at Louisa and she thought she saw a shimmer in his eyes. Maybe he still cares for me, she thought. I want him to care for me. Even with all the fights we've had, I still care for him. What joy he brought me as a little boy. And now he's a good-looking man. He's a man. Adam's right. I have to remember that Michael is an adult. I'm no longer responsible for him.

"I'll call you, Mom," Michael agreed. Then he turned and left the room. It was months before they heard from him. And that phone call was to tell them he had joined the Marines. Louisa tried to put Michael out of her mind, but he was always there, and in her heart as well as her mind.

In November Nixon won the White House, but in Montana, Republican Governor Tim Babcock lost to the Democrat Forrest Anderson who had been the attorney general. Adam would be leaving his position as State Bank Examiner in January as the governor made his own appointments. Their adventures in Helena were over. Political and parental involvements ended at the same time. Retirement for Adam was real this time and for Louisa as well. Louisa was grateful they had made it over the bumpy trials they had been put through. The rough places had been made smooth.

Living on Momentum

AROUND THE WORLD, 1969-1985

We live on momentum—if you stop you are finished.

SMEDLY DARLINGTON BUTLER (1881-1940)

"Whooee," Louisa was laughing as Adam swung her around in an allemande left, then a right and left grand. This is great! We're back dancing just as we did at the Wheat Basin Community Hall where I first met Adam. It must be the gypsy blood in me. I love dancing.

"Ladies, left hand star, allemande your partner, dosado to a right hand star. Star promenade." The caller kept them moving. Louisa held up a corner of her blue and white lace dress and let her crinoline underskirt swish. Her soft shoes kept her light on her feet. So what if I get out of breath! I can do this!

"Right and Left Grand circle.... California twirl... and promenade."

When a break in the square dance came, Adam escorted Louisa to a folding chair against the wall at the Senior Center. "I'll get us a cold drink," he told her as he wiped his brow with a handkerchief.

"What a night!" Louisa said to a dancer beside her. "I'm happy to be back in Oceanside. No responsibilities. No children to worry about! The ocean breeze and beautiful sunsets."

"We're the same, enjoying retirement. Glad the years of work are over and we can relax," her new acquaintance agreed.

"But there is so much more I want to do." Louisa was alive with energy. "We're hoping to travel. I want to see and explore the world!"

The slightly rumpled gray-haired lady nodded slowly and looked at Louisa. "Where will you go?" she asked politely.

"Well, my brother, Walter, and his wife are missionaries in India. I'd love to see them and the Taj Mahal. Can you imagine? I've heard it's the most beautiful structure in the world." Louisa's eyes were dancing with excitement.

"It would be wonderful to see the Taj Mahal," the lady replied wistfully. "Yes, indeed, if you have the means to go."

"Adam's been checking out tour groups for next fall. We'll go back to the ranch in Montana for the summer first and help out. But, in the meantime, I'm glad we can spend our winters in southern California. I love the ocean and the warm sea breezes."

"We're happy to be here, too. But you're fortunate to be able to travel. I wish we were healthy enough to travel overseas but I don't think it's in the cards for us."

"Well, Adam's only 62 and I'm 60. Neither of us has ever been sick. You're right, my friend, you're right. We better travel now when we can."

Louisa was the happiest she had ever been with no responsibilities and Adam was content, walking the beach and studying the stock market. Many mornings Louisa didn't even dress until nearly noon. In the afternoons she'd take her own little walk down to the pond where the birds gathered. They would come to her when she threw them bread crumbs. She began checking off the names of the different birds she saw, searching through the book for the ones she didn't know. Eager to learn more about the world she lived in, she started with these beautiful creatures living around her.

They returned to the ranch for the summer, a pattern they'd follow for the next couple of decades. But that fall, Peter took Louisa and Adam to the Billings airport for a trip around the world. Adam was impressed with the 360 passenger Boeing 747 airplane.

Transportation had changed a lot in his lifetime. Before they left the U.S., they took a 35 mile Greyline Boat tour around Manhattan Island. Adam was amazed at the economic vitality that lay in those few acres.

From the Kennedy airport they flew to Heathrow, toured London briefly, and then flew to Paris. From Paris they took a three week bus tour through France, Belgium, the Netherlands, Germany, Switzerland, Austria, and Italy. After their tour group flew back to the U.S., Louisa and Adam enjoyed a couple days in Rome before flying to Bombay, India to visit Walter and Pauline.

"Europe is different from what I imagined," Louisa mused as they sat at a busy café sidewalk sipping morning cappuccinos. Adam had a small smile on his face as he sat back, watching the Italians walking by them. After a few minutes, he became aware that she had spoken and he sat up and looked at her.

"How so?"

Louisa smiled then, too. "You like it here, don't you? You seem relaxed."

"Sunshine, flaky croissants, and heart designs on our cappuccinos. Who could ask for more?"

"Well, you'll find me strange then because I miss the flat, empty plains. Europe is full of purple mountains, green hills, and tidy rock-lined roadways. Mother Mary icons in brick cubbyholes and red geraniums in pots seem to be at every door. And then there are the mammoth, dark cathedrals full of gold vessels, marble statues, stained glass windows, bronze doorways, and pipe organs or string quartets playing Baroque music. It's overpowering; it's too clean; it's too civilized." She sighed. "I miss the Wild West."

"You do surprise me."

"On the other hand, Italians are too laid-back. It bothers me that they close their businesses at 1 p.m. and go home for three hours. Even the tourist spots are closed. All we can do is take a nap ourselves in our hotel. An ambitious American would definitely stay open and take advantage of the extra shoppers he'd have for three hours."

Adam laughed. "Louisa, you are a conundrum. Italians love eating lunch with their families, just like you wanting us to eat together. And you yearned for art, music, literature, and gracious living all your life and here you are finding out you don't like it after all. You like space and hard work! The ranch!"

Louisa laughed, too. "I wouldn't go quite that far. I do admire the European practicality in their clothes. Women wear sturdy shoes, not these heels where we twist ankles. And teens, too, wear leather shoes, not tennis shoes like American kids."

"That may be because that's what's available or affordable." Adam was quiet for a few minutes as he continued watching the flow of the pedestrians in front of them. "We live at a very exciting time. Just 50 years ago we were plowing with a team of horses and now we're flying around the world. Before radio and TV we were waiting two days for newspapers. Now news is instantaneous. Corporations are global. Soon everyone will be wearing tennis shoes, jeans, and eating lagsne."

"You mean lasagna?" Louisa intervened, pronouncing it correctly.

"Right. Whatever it was they served last night. It was good, wasn't it? Still, keeping cultural identities seems important to me."

"Oh, Adam, it's fun to talk with you. I totally agree with you. By traveling we can learn about other cultures, but still keep our identity as Montanans."

"I'm sorry we weren't able to travel to your ancestral Czechoslovakia. It was too risky and our travel agent didn't recommend it."

"I know. That's okay. I didn't want to go there with the communists tightening their control. It was great hearing Dvorak's 9th Symphony in Vienna, though. I'm glad we had a chance to hear that wonderful music by a Czech composer. We're having really marvelous experiences."

A day later they flew into Bombay, India to be met by Louisa's brother, Walter, and his wife, Pauline.

"Oh, thank you for remembering the hairpins and safety pins," Pauline, exclaimed as Louisa pulled them from her purse. "It must seem silly to you, but it's these simple pleasures common in the U.S. that I miss the most." Both Walter and Pauline were dressed as the Indians dressed in white wrap-around cloth. Pauline immediately put a hairpin into her bun to catch a loose lock. She's very attractive, Louisa thought as she felt the sweat under her brassiere. The Indian sari must be much more comfortable in this humidity.

Walter immediately took charge of their luggage and the events of the day. He took them for a tour of the city and his church. He introduced them to friends and then took them to their home. They had supper sitting on the floor which was awkward for Louisa. She began to relax when she pretended they were at a picnic. Strange, though, to have a maid serve you at a picnic. They chatted about family events before turning to the political turmoil and student unrest in India.

"Who knows where Mrs. Gandhi will lead us with a war with Pakistan and a friendship pact with Russia?" Walter asked rhetorically. "India is changing."

"I saw children begging," Louisa mused. "Why aren't they in school? Don't the parents work and provide for them?"

"Parents often train their children to beg; they're so poor," Walter slowly replied. Then he added, "Did you see how many of the begging children are crippled?"

Louisa nodded her head in concern. "Oh, yes. Yes."

"Some parents break the legs or arms of their children to make them better beggars," her brother told them.

"What? That's terrible! Outrageous," Louisa responded. "Can't you stop them from doing that?"

"One must survive." It was quiet as they ate their dal and rice. "It's a different culture. We understand their problems." Louisa was chagrined as she absorbed the idea that families might be completely opposite of what she valued. How could this be?

Walter then said, "Maybe you'd like to meet some mothers, Louisa. I was wondering if you would speak to our women's group tomorrow morning and tell them about your work."

"What could I possibly tell them?" Especially after what I saw today, she thought. "I obviously don't know their situation at all. What would they want to know from me?"

"All families are not financially strapped like those with children on the street. The women you'll meet are similar to you. Christians in India believe St. Thomas, Jesus' disciple, came to India after the Lord's crucifixion and resurrection. He remained here to preach the Good News. Indian women today control their households and work to get food and water for their families, not unlike the women in Jesus day. And not that different from many women in the U.S. They believe the living Christ works with them as they lead their families. In India, women usually do not work outside their families, although that's changing. Tell the women about your family and what you do to serve your community. I'm sure they'd like to know more about your life. They are curious about Americans."

Everyone around the table was quiet, waiting to see what Louisa would say. Then Walter added, "And maybe you could ask them about their lives, too."

Louisa stared amazed at her brother. He wants me to learn from them. But does he actually believe I could teach them something? What would that be? Then Louisa remembered Elsie and how she "saved" Alvin and Charley. She thought of her own mother, quietly going about a long day's work of supporting her husband and family. Or I could tell them of the suppers the church women serve after

301

funerals. The Indian women probably do the same. Is that what he means? Or maybe I could tell them about the Intermountain Children's Home which was the school where Walter and Pauline's children had lived. Or could I talk about influencing their government for better policies? Supporting a law for not breaking the legs of children to make them better beggars! Do I dare even say such a thing? I suppose there are things I could share and no doubt there are many things I could learn from them.

"I guess I could meet with them."

"Good. We'll have an interpreter for you."

The next day Louisa was given a chair in an otherwise small barren room at the church with only a cross on the wall. Twenty attractive women in saris were sitting on pillows on a carpet beneath her. A few were as old as Louisa but they were slender and lithe. Really gorgeous. Louisa had on a cotton green and white sheath dress while many of the women beneath her were dressed in gold or wore gold jewelry. They shimmered. Yet here I sit above them like a grand lady. What do we have in common? Husbands. Children. A faith.

"Let's begin with prayer," Louisa said, and all dutifully bowed their heads. Louisa begged God to be present (mainly for herself) and to fill minds and hearts with love. When she opened her eyes, she saw Adam, Walter, and Pauline had left. Alone but surrounded by a sweet presence, Louisa began to speak. Having an interpreter slowed the process down, allowing Louisa to think clearly about each phase of her life.

Louisa told of her Czech parents as babies coming to the U.S., their marriage, how they built a home on the Montana prairie, about Papa's farming and constructing houses. She told of her own life as a nursing student, a teacher, and a farm wife. She described her four children. Finally she mentioned her work with the church, the children's home for orphans, and working to support good government.

Suddenly, Louisa had an epiphany. She realized she had wanted to be perfect, to live an unblemished life, to be some grand lady, sitting above everyone else. At the same time, I wanted to belong, to fit in with others. I don't want to be the pani mama above others, she thought, I want to be respected by others and belong equally with others within a community.

"I've always loved children," she said thinking of the little beggars on the street and her voice wavered. She looked at the beautiful, attentive women quietly absorbed in what she was saying. I want to belong with them. "We, too, are children, children of God. No matter who we are, where we live, or where our ancestors come from, we belong to each other using our gifts to serve others," she finally choked out. I've always been on the border to belonging, never quite there. Until today. One of the Indian women bowed toward Louisa with her hands in a prayer position, acknowledging her statement of unity with them. Others did the same as tears leaked out of Louisa's eyes. Then they talked, sharing stories about their children and their prayers for their families.

After Bombay, Adam and Louisa went to Agra where the Taj Mahal was built. As the sun moved across the building, the reflected colors changed. Louisa stood transfixed as the light transformed the building into interlocking colors of beauty. They were told the Taj Mahal was built by Shah Jahan to show his love for his wife. It reminded Louisa of how deep her own love was for Adam, but also how deeply she truly loved everyone in the world.

As they sat on the granite bench before the rectangular pool leading to the Taj Mahal, Louisa remembered her own conversation years ago with her mother and she asked Adam, "And you love me?"

Adam put his arm around her, "You don't know how much I love you? I can't build you a Taj Mahal, but I hope together we built a good life."

"It has been a great life. I love you, too, Adam. I'll never forget this moment." Louisa was content. She belonged with a prince.

The next decade found Adam and Louisa spending every winter in Carlsbad, California where they walked the beach, square-danced, and participated in the senior center activities. They helped build floats for parades and rode on floats as "old-timers." In his seventies, Adam washed dishes at the senior center for "the old folks," he said. They took their many guests to Knott's Berry Farm, Disney Land, and Lawrence Welk's restaurant.

In the summers they went back to the ranch which Adam had given to Roger, Peter, and Sarah. Adam bought and set up a mobile home because the ranch house was used by whoever was operating the ranch. Louisa built flowerbeds and enjoyed transplanting the local prairie cacti and wildflowers into her yard. Adam repaired fences and buildings and helped where he could with haying and harvest. Friends and family visiting them at the ranch would have a tour of the ranch, the barn, and the cistern. They'd have picnics, feed bum lambs, or help with a roundup or branding when it was that time of year.

It was difficult for Louisa to return to the ranch, but that was Adam's home place, his roots. Louisa was still lonely there. They exchanged dinners with Karl and Victoria every summer, but their earlier, tight connection no longer existed. Their lives had gone in different directions. Louisa missed her Laurel and Helena friends. She wished her grandchildren would visit more often. Adam regretted that he no longer could manage the ranch and have control over the way things were being done. What Adam and Louisa preferred to happen at the ranch, did not always happen.

Nevertheless, their homes in California and Montana were open, welcoming places, and friends and relatives came for short visits. Adam and Louisa also spent time going to different states to visit friends and relatives whom they hadn't seen for years. They enjoyed renewing old relationships.

They continued to travel. On that first world trip they also visited Kathmandu, Nepal; Calcutta, India; Bangkok, Thailand; Hong Kong, China; Taipei, Taiwan; Tokyo, Japan. Another year they took a seven nation tour of South America. They had two trips to Mexico and a two week cruise of the Caribbean. They went to Hawaii. They went on an Alaskan cruise for their 50th Anniversary with Roger and Karen. At age 76, Louisa with a granddaughter and several grand-nieces visited China after Nixon opened up that possibility. By the time it was too difficult for them to travel and their momentum had wound down, they had been in all 50 states, revisiting several of them many times, and they had traveled to 30 nations.

Louisa's dream of traveling with Adam had come true. Approaching the end she was continuing to discover the meaning of belonging.

Into the Unknown

BILLINGS, 1992-2002

*When we walk to the edge of all the light we have and
take the step into the darkness of the unknown, we must
believe that one of two things will happen. There will be
something solid to stand on or we will be taught to fly.*

PATRICK OVERTON (1951 -)

"Go, Broncos, you can do it. Go. Go," Louisa was shouting at the TV screen when Adam walked to the side of the console.

"Roger, the Broncos are winning!" she shouted at him. She looked up at Roger and thought, he looks upset. Oh wait, it's not Roger. Who is it? It's Adam. I can't hear what he's saying. Oh dear, where's that button. Ah, here it is. Louisa shut off the volume on the TV remote.

"What were you saying? I couldn't hear with the TV on." Louisa fussed with her hearing aid earpiece and tried to concentrate on what he was saying.

Adam looked directly at her and spoke slowly. "Peter was on the phone. He can't come tonight, but will try to make it later this week."

"It's difficult when things change," she agreed.

He wondered what she was talking about. Was she thinking about Peter or was something else bothering her? "Sweetheart, I need to talk to you. Is the game over?"

Louisa saw the commercial on TV. It wasn't a game. What game was he talking about? "I think it is." She shut off the TV.

306

"Do you remember we moved to this duplex six years ago when it got too hard for me to do much good working at the ranch?" Louisa nodded. "Lately we talked about moving again because it's too hard to do the yard work and the house work. Well, I've been waiting for an opening at Sage Towers and they have the perfect room for us on the 9th floor with a window looking at the rims. We can watch the airplanes land."

"Roger will like that."

"Yes, when Roger visits us, he'll enjoy seeing the planes." He needed her attention. "Louisa," he said sternly. He got her to look at him. "We need to start sorting, so we'll have fewer things to move."

Move. Are we moving back to California? Louisa wondered. I'd like to be by the ocean again. But we'd have to leave this place. "I like the rose bushes we planted."

"The roses are beautiful, Louisa. It was a great improvement when you decided to plant roses in the front of the duplex." She's gone again, he thought.

"And the bluebirds and chickadees. They're so cute."

"The bluejays are really unusual," Adam corrected. "We're lucky they like our feeder in the backyard." Adam sighed. Could he get her attention? "Louisa, could we sort the curios tonight, these here in the cabinet? Look, we have two Chinese Cuisinart vases that you bought in China. Do we need both of them?"

"I like the blue one with the red flower."

"But we could give the brown one away?"

"Okay." Aha, Adam thought. She made a decision.

"What about this music box platter we bought in Switzerland. It's scratched on top."

"Can I turn it on?" He's looking at me rather sternly. "And then you can have it." Now he looks happier. She nodded her head to the Swiss Alpine tune as he handed her a Japanese doll. "What a pretty doll." She fussed with the brocaded costume.

"Louisa," Adam called her back to the task on hand.

"Yes?" Louisa started humming. He's watching me. He wants something. She thought about what it might be. "Could we give it to a grandchild?" she asked tentatively.

"The grandchildren are grown. Maybe for the great-grandchildren. You're doing great, Louisa. You wrap those things up in the newspaper and I'll bring in boxes from the garage."

When he returned with the boxes she was still playing with the doll. Adam sat with her and started wrapping up curios and placing each in the appropriate box, most to be given away. Later Adam heated a can of soup and got out crackers. As they had their light supper, Adam tried to explain, "Do you remember last winter when you had the shingles, those bumps that gave you a lot of pain?"

"Oh, that really hurt. I felt very sick. They had my medicines all mixed up."

"We're both starting to have health problems. In our new place, there's an alert bell you can pull if you need help and someone will come to our apartment to help us."

"But you take good care of me! I don't need someone else." Then she understood. "Oh, Adam, you aren't sick, are you?" Louisa looked at him intently. She couldn't see that he had changed at all, still tall and strong and good-looking.

"I have problems. My ticker isn't working well and there may be a time you'll need to call for help." Louisa set the cracker she was nibbling on down on her plate. Her eyes filled with tears. "The doctor said I need a heart valve replacement."

Louisa nodded her head. I know what he's saying but I don't want to hear it. He thinks I can't understand but I can. I need him. He can't be sick. She started pinching her finger hard concentrating on the pain it was causing rather than the pain he was causing with his words.

"Everything's in place, Louisa. Roger has our will and my obituary and funeral plan. I want you to write your obituary," he told her firmly.

He's speaking to me like I'm a child, Louisa thought. Am I a child? Nothing makes sense anymore. An obituary? What's that? Something about dying. But I'm not dead. And I don't want him to die. She shook her head and looked at him crossly.

"I don't want any more." Louisa shoved her bowl and plate away in frustration. Adam picked them up along with his own and started running water to wash the dishes.

"We won't need dishes," he said to her matter of factually. "Maybe a couple plates, bowls, and a saucepan. We'll be eating two meals a day in the dining room with everyone else. If we have company for cake and ice cream, we can use paper plates."

Adam was able to make their last move to Sage Towers with little difficulty. Peter used the ranch pickup and he and Stanley moved the couch, bed, desk, table, and chairs in one trip. The boxes fit into Adam's car. They had few possessions by then, having moved often.

After the move, Adam had a serious talk with his doctor about the possibility of a heart valve replacement. The doctor gave him a 50% chance of making it through the operation. Adam didn't think those odds were very good. He opted to have a pacemaker inserted instead which would help keep his heart steady for a couple more years. Adam was determined not to end up in the hospital. He typed up a little note which he kept in his shirt pocket. The note read: "If you find me unconscious but alive please deliver me to Sage Towers and call my doctor (and he put the address of Sage Tower and the number of his doctor.) If I am no longer breathing, please call the Michelotti funeral home (and he gave the phone number of Michelotti.) DO NOT TAKE ME TO THE HOSPITAL."

Louisa easily fit into the routine at Sage Towers. In recent years, she had never had to cook or clean as Adam was doing most of it. All she had to do was pull out crackers and cheese for supper because they had breakfast and lunch downstairs. There were plenty of people to talk with in the common area. She loved to put puzzles together and watch TV. She enjoyed having friends and church folk visit and then writing cards to those they seldom saw. At Christmas time, she and Adam would hang the cards from yarn around the living room. As a couple, they enjoyed Bingo night and the occasional movie downstairs.

Once in a while, they'd go to church or for a short drive. Most of the time Adam preferred not to drive so he walked to the broker's office or the grocery store, both only a few blocks away.

Adam was eventually diagnosed with congestive heart failure and was given hospice care at Sage Towers. Louisa enjoyed the visits of the nurses and the male counselor. Such a nice man to visit us every week, she thought. He's just like a son. Sometimes Peter visits, too. Do I have daughters who visit us? She tried to remember but no one came to mind. Adam lays out my pills in a little plastic box. He's so helpful. He takes good care of me.

When friends came to visit Adam, Louisa was delighted with the gifts of fruit and bread they brought. She didn't worry about not remembering their names as they knew her and Adam well. And since she was always the life of the party, they enjoyed her stories of the leaves turning red and yellow as she looked down on them from their window or the snow falling out of the dark sky in the evening. When she forgot, Adam would help her.

"When Helen was here last week," she would start to tell a story about her sister. Adam, sitting next to her on the couch, would take her hand and interrupt saying, "It wasn't last week, Louisa. Helen was taken from us a few years back."

"Oh yes, Helen was beautiful and smart! We had fun playing poker with the boys. She'd win all the money and they'd be so upset they'd grab their leather coin bags and walk away!" Everyone would laugh at Louisa's tale. It didn't matter when it actually happened. Louisa could sit quietly, basking in their company's amusement and approval of her. It didn't seem like Adam was sick at all.

The time came when Adam had trouble walking and a wheelchair was brought for him. They used it to go down stairs via the elevator for their noon dinner. Louisa would pull the rope buzzer for help to wheel Adam. As his legs and feet swelled, Adam became clumsy and Louisa needed to help him getting in and out of bed. His bathrobe became his daily dress. Louisa didn't seem to notice the changes. Peter and the hospice worker were coming often. She was thinking, how lovely it is that they are coming to see me. I enjoy having visitors every day. They are attentive and concerned for me. They help Adam, too. And we're getting flowers and more and more chocolate! How fun this all is.

Sarah came one evening when Louisa wanted to go play bingo downstairs. "Go ahead, Mom. Do you know the way? I'll stay with Dad."

Louisa looked at her strangely. "Of course I know the way."

Sarah and Adam were playing dominos when Adam quietly said, "It won't be long now."

Sarah looked at him, questioning him, "Why do you say that?"

"I can no longer do the figures," and he showed her the scribbled notes he had made for their scores from their game. "I was always good at adding columns." Sarah lightly patted his hand, amazed at how calm he was in anticipating death. She looked at him, wanting to ask, wanting to know more.

"I've had a great life and there's nothing more I can do. Eighty-nine years is enough. It's time to go." He added, "I don't think it'll be long before Louisa comes with me."

"I agree," Sarah responded. "She's dependent on you. I don't see how she can keep going without you." They continued playing dominos for a few minutes without using the score pad. "Dad, do you want me to stay with you and Mom? I can sleep on the couch."

"It would be good if you could do that. Your mom is going to need help."

It was a difficult week for Sarah, Peter, and Roger. Adam quickly declined and Sarah ended up sleeping with him, her arm over him to keep him from rolling off the bed while Louisa thought it fun for her to camp out on the couch. Peter couldn't handle being around serious illness. He had always been the major one caring for them when they were relatively well, but he was relieved Sarah could be there as Adam failed. Peter, though, was the one who knew which doctors to call, when to bring in the hospice workers, and which family and friends needed to be called. He started organizing details of the funeral most of which Adam had previously dictated.

Toward the end, Adam could no longer eat or talk. He'd pull out the catheter and as he had lost a lot of weight, Sarah could easily support him, nearly carrying him to the bathroom. He soon quit sipping water. By then, Roger was with Sarah helping her and they would slip ice into Adam's mouth every hour so he'd receive some moisture. When they asked the hospice worker if that helped Adam, the man shrugged his shoulders and then quietly explained, "You're just prolonging his life." The brother and sister looked at each other and stopped giving Adam ice.

Adam died in his bed with Sarah by his side. Sarah stepped out to the living room to tell Louisa, "Come with me, Momma. Dad's gone. He's no longer breathing." Louisa calmly sat on the edge of the bed. Adam looks peaceful, she thought. He's no longer big and strong. He's small. I've seen death before. I know death. Adam has died. He's with all the others. So many others. She tried to remember their names.

Within minutes Peter had called in the wives and grandchildren, several who had flown in earlier to say goodbye to Adam. They gathered around Adam's bed. Peter gave a prayer and they sang "Amazing Grace" and Adam's favorite, "Out Where the West Begins." Most of the family was still there as the mortuary bagged Adam's body and wheeled him out on the gurney. Roger, as executor, was telling the family that Louisa would be well cared for.

The funeral was at the Grace Methodist Church where the pastor sang at Adam's request, "Home on the Range." There was a large number of people attending, even a carload from Helena. Louisa greeted people. She thought she was handling everything very well. Adam would be proud of me. I can do this.

No one else in the family realized how physically and emotionally strong Louisa really was. She surprised everyone by living another six years after Adam died. In the second year, Peter moved Louisa to an assisted living facility close to his home. There, Louisa particularly enjoyed having ice cream in the afternoon. They both liked the dining room with its linens and fresh flowers. Peter was being treated for kidney failure and had started dialysis. Having lunch with his mother in the quiet setting comforted him. Louisa's room was close to the entrance and looked out at flowers along the walkway. Louisa would converse about those flowers as if they were intimate friends.

"Look at what I've done," Louisa said to Peter one day. "Isn't it beautiful?" Peter looked at the picture puzzle with mountains in the background and flowers in the front, with many pieces shoved into a space that didn't fit.

"Indeed, it's beautiful," Peter agreed while in his heart he was sobbing for his mother's decline in motor, visual, and mental abilities.

"Could we save it?" Louisa was happy with her creative endeavor.

"Yes, I'll ask Stanley to glue it to a board. Would you like that?" Peter hugged Louisa as Louisa nodded yes.

Peter organized a 90th birthday luncheon for Louisa in a small room off the dining room with many of the family there. Sarah, Victoria, and Karl came as well as April, Sarah's daughter, with her baby. Louisa couldn't remember who April was but it didn't matter. Louisa held April's baby and looked into the startling blue eyes reminding Louisa of someone.

"I love babies. She's so cute," Louisa said and she tried to rock the bundle.

April laughed saying, "He's a little boy, Grandma."

Louisa wondered, whose baby is this? Maybe it's mine. Maybe I can keep her. Louisa moved back forth, rocking in her dinner chair as she held the baby. Suddenly, the baby pouted and Louisa pouted in response. Oh dear, she's crying. They're trying to take her away from me. Oh, I don't like crying babies anyway. Louisa closed her eyes shoving the baby away.

Who are all these people? They're singing and looking at me. I know that song. I used to sing it. Happy. Happy. Louisa clapped her hands in rhythm. They are looking at me and laughing. Louisa smiled in delight. They like me. "Blow out the candles, Louisa." Lots of fire and light. A fire. It burned my finger. I don't know what to do. Quit pushing me forward. I don't like fire. Ah, the flames went away. Oh goody, sweet tasting goo. I like that. She kissed the frosting, letting it spread on her lips and nose. People around her were laughing and she smiled.

Peter was unable to recover from his disabilities and a few months later he died. Roger flew in from Seattle and took Louisa to the funeral, holding her tightly as they walked down the aisle to the front of the church, packed because Peter was well-known as a real-estate agent. Look at all the people, Louisa thought. Black coats. A blue coat. A yellow shirt. All dressed up. Are we in Helena? I'd like to touch that lady's hat. Maybe I can. No, he's holding my hand too hard. He even

314

has an arm around me. Who is this anyway? I don't think he's Papa. I love the pretty flowers. Music! Is it time to dance? No, I'm to sit. That lady smiled at me. And I smiled back!

After the funeral, Roger visited with Louisa. She was not in a conversational mood. Roger picked up a children's book to read to her. Louisa paid close attention. A story of a princess, like me, in a long flowing dress. And they love her. A grand lady. Louisa clapped her hands when Roger got to "The End."

Not long after that, Louisa woke on a summer morning with the sun coming in through her window. Oh, the sun is so bright. It's warm. Louisa took off her nightie and walked from her room to the entrance door which opened automatically. She wanted to be in the sunshine. She kept walking to a bench. Not too cold; not too hot. It feels good, the sun on my arms, my legs, and belly. Louisa shut her eyes. She could hear a meadowlark. Just like in the country. Where was that? Where did we live? It had sun and birds and trees. I think I liked it there.

"Louisa, here's your robe. You need to put on your robe." Who's this lady? I don't think I know her. Louisa frowned. I like it here. I like the sun on me. I don't need a robe.

"Let me help you stand and I'll put your robe around you." Louisa was quiet. Everything's ruined. Louisa held up her arms and the care taker helped her stand, put her robe around her naked body, and led her back to her room.

Sarah had a call that afternoon from Roger, Louisa's power of attorney. "We need to move Mom into the locked Alzheimer's Unit down the hall from where she is now," he reported. "She was walking outside naked."

Sarah laughed. "I'm not surprised. I figured something like this was bound to happen fairly soon. I'll see if Stanley can help me move her bed and the couch. Thank God for Stanley. Did the administrator give you a deadline? When do we need to move her?"

It was easy enough with Stanley's help to move Louisa one more time. There wasn't much left of belongings: her bed, a bed stand, an easy chair, and a few clothes. Louisa seemed unaware of the move and was content in her new quarters.

On the wall above her bed, Stanley hung two of Louisa's favorite black and white photographs: the Taj Mahal and Ronald Reagan who Louisa insisted was her husband. The family agreed that Ronald Reagan with his cowboy hat did look a bit like Adam.

Her one request to guests now was: "You'll take care of Michael, won't you?" Over and over. Roger was with Sarah one day when Louisa frantically was asking them to take care of Michael. Sarah finally promised, "Yes, Mom we'll take care of Michael," but she noticed Roger holding his hands up shaking his head, No. Sarah was thinking we'll probably never see Michael again. He hadn't contacted the family much after serving as a Marine gun runner in Viet Nam. When was the last time we saw Michael? Not at Dad's funeral. Maybe at their 50th Anniversary party. I think he was there, hm, 20 years ago?

At the very end, Louisa was no longer talking much. Often, visitors found her with her eyes shut and not responding. Louisa only livened up to watch the cat walking through the unit. Louisa would reach out to touch it, but the cat knew he was there only for his looks and would escape her touch. Sometimes Sarah would walk with Louisa outside to see the flowers planted along the walled patio. Smelling and touching the flowers brought Louisa pleasure.

At mealtime, Louisa sat quietly with eyes closed and folded hands. A very nice time to rest. Why do people keep putting food in my mouth? Louisa wondered. Maybe if I just keep my eyes shut and not look at them, they'll leave me alone.

After she broke her hip, and had a pin put in, Louisa wouldn't cooperate with the physical therapist to gain strength to walk. I do not want to walk, she'd say. "No. No," she'd shout to the CNA and the therapist, but they kept trying to get her up and walking. Until they gave up trying. They sent her back to her Alzheimer unit which fortunately took her even in a wheelchair. Louisa could walk and would use a walker when she wanted. She simply enjoyed being wheeled about in a wheel chair. Was she in physical pain? She didn't report pain.

She was, however, in mental anguish. "Shoot me!" she shouted at Sarah one day when she came to visit and wheel her mother around. "You should shoot me. Shoot me. I want you to shoot me." Other residents looked at them as Louisa yelled her demand. Sarah wheeled Louisa back into her private bedroom and shut the door hoping the rest of the residents would not understand what Louisa was saying.

"You gotta shoot me! Take care of me! Shoot me! Shoot me! You need to shoot me. What's wrong with you? Shoot me." Sarah wondered how she could calm her distraught mother. A gun, Louisa thought. I need a gun for someone to shoot me. Where is a gun when I need it? Why doesn't this lady get a gun? Why doesn't she shoot me? People get shot by guns all the time. I know.

Epilogue

BILLINGS, AUGUST 17-18, 2002

To live in the hearts we leave behind is not to die.

THOMAS CAMPBELL (1777-1844)

Sarah picked up Roger from the airport the day before the memorial service. She was nervous and blabbered. "Everything's ready, Roger. April made a beautiful memorial packet tied with a ribbon with Mom's picture on the front. She drew a bird that goes with Mom's letter to us and then there are Mom's favorite poems. Stanley is reading scripture and his children are singing and reading poems. I'm playing 'The Swan' for a prelude. I couldn't learn one of the "Hungarian Dances" before tomorrow. But Mom loved both of those pieces. The Methodist pastor's been great about letting us do whatever we want. The only thing left is whether you and I talk, and what we say."

"I'd like to say something," Roger replied thoughtfully.

"Do we tell the truth or do we remain pleasant?"

Roger chuckled. "Let's tell it like we see it: the truth, but as pleasantly as we can."

"You're one tough son ... of a Louisa!" Sarah said. At that, Roger laughed outright. "She was a bit ... shall we say ... difficult at times." He changed the subject. "Do you think anyone will show up?"

"Oh, yes, we've already had sympathy cards and phone calls from all over: church folk, Dad's political and banker friends, the Molt community, the square-dancers, the Laurel crowd, the Janochek

318

cousins, and Muellers. There are cards from strangers—a Joe Jacob with a beautiful calligraphy script and then someone who says she was Charley's widow, but who was Charley? A card with a large memorial gift from Montana Supreme Court Justice Isabella Lewis. How did Mom know her? Do you know? Mom had a lot of friends it turns out. And then there are Peter's friends and my own. My new intern, Diane, even brought sweet rolls for us."

"Did you get ahold of Michael?" Roger asked.

"Yes, he's in Spokane, staying with friends, but he claims he doesn't have money to come for the funeral. I'm disappointed."

"We could've paid his way from Mom's estate." Roger was in charge of the estate.

"I told him we'd pay his way, but I don't think he wants to come. It may be more difficult for him to lose Mom than for us. Oh, did I tell you, we're having a reception in our backyard after the memorial service? And will you be here on Monday for the family service at the graveyard? It was funny, years ago, Mom and Dad's argument over whether her ashes should be placed at the head or at the feet of his casket."

"Mom would definitely want to be at his head," Roger pronounced.

"And I want to save some ashes to spread on the California coastal waters as she asked: being part of the wind and water, you know."

"Good idea. Yes, I'm staying until Tuesday. Karen will be coming tomorrow morning and staying until Tuesday with me. Our kids won't be here, though." He sighed. "I'll be glad to get through the next three days."

Twenty-four hours later, Sarah and Roger greeted Louisa's family and friends at the church. People they hadn't seen in years showed up, many from Stillwater County. Sarah was reminded of her dad's old joke, "If you don't go to other's funerals, they won't come to yours." Sarah knew her parents had been to the funerals as well as wedding dances of many of these families. Still, for a 93 year woman to have this many acquaintances at the end of her life is amazing.

At the funeral, after music, scriptures, and Roger's kind remarks, Sarah took a deep breath and stood to talk.

"Thank you for coming to remember Louisa. We want to hear your stories about her and hope you can come to the reception in our backyard. Louisa was special and obviously meant a lot to many people.

"We were told that as a child, Louisa would often repeat, 'Jsem pani mama,' which meant something like "I'm a grand lady." Louisa was a grand lady, gracious and kind, a welcoming hostess and a terrific organizer. I often thought she could have been president of the United States if she had been born a century later.

"Our father, Adam, loved her. Really, he adored her no matter what she did. She was a teacher and helped Adam with his language and English, although she could never get him to pronounce 'drought' correctly. It was always 'drouf.' Nevertheless, Louisa inspired Adam to become more than he thought possible and he did a lot of good for Montana as a result.

I loved my mom. However, as her child, I felt I was in a wolf pack. She was the wolf mother who snarled at us if we went outside her boundaries. She'd nip at my heels to bring me back. Inside the pack, it was warm and safe. But if we stepped outside, she was cold and frightening." Sarah saw one of the Janochek cousins shaking his head, wagging his finger at her, shaming her. Sarah thought she had said enough.

"Louisa wanted to belong, to be loved, and to do the right, moral, and good thing for everyone. And so she did. I suspect I'll learn more and more from her, even now after her death.

"I hope you'll have time to read the poems Mom loved and the letter Mom wrote to us a decade ago for this memorial before she was overcome with dementia. We know that Louisa lives on through each of us."

From the Memorial Service Handout

October 6, 1992
To my loved ones:
Do not mourn my passing—instead, celebrate the happy "gift of life" which
was mine. Each day Adam and I thanked God for our four wonderful
children, their spouses, and all of their offspring which made our last years
joyful. Nothing in this entire world is as precious as an innocent child.
So many new discoveries and inventions came during my lifetime—and
that will continue if man-kind will learn to live in peace and harmony
with one another.
May each of you continue to live to the fullest, according to God's will.
My love, always –Mom

Living in God's love by Albert W. Palmer
All this day I am going to be a child of God.
His love is round about me.
Underneath are the "Everlasting Arms."
I am going to be honest and true, in all events of life;
And I believe that to those who love God, all things work together for good.
I am going to rise above all worry, fretting, fear and hatred–
And live in an atmosphere of spiritual serenity–
Behind all that comes, God's love and wisdom will be present to strengthen
and sustain.

From the Sanskrit, a specific request of Louisa.
Look to this day!
For it is life the very life of life...
For yesterday is already a dream,
And tomorrow is only a vision:
But today, well lived, makes every yesterday
A dream of happiness, and every tomorrow
A vision of hope.

It was late that night when Sarah and Dan were able to shut the door on their guests. "The Janocheks sure like to talk," Dan remarked tiredly as he put his arm around Sarah.

"A Czech tradition," responded Sarah, smiling as she thought of the stories she had just heard about her mom.

"Do you want a glass of wine and a few minutes to wind down before we hit the sack?"

"You go ahead and go to bed. I have a couple of things I need to do." Sarah gave him a quick kiss on the cheek and went to her small office space to open her laptop to the Word program. She turned on the desk lamp and began typing:

```
A Grand Lady
Chapter 1.  The match lit easily. The flame
flared up and bit her finger. Louisa tried to
take the match in her other hand, but instead
the match dropped to the ground. The fire came...
```

Postscript

On the Border of Belonging is a fictional biography of my mother born March 29, 1909 in Lost Springs, Kansas. Louise Pospisil Leuthold lived primarily in Montana with numerous winters in California. She died August 14, 2002 in Billings, Montana.

Louise's father, John Pospisil was born in Bobat, Czechoslovakia, September 3, 1876; her mother Josephine Navrat was born March 19, 1883 in Prague. John's family came to the U.S. in 1880 when he was 3 years old; Josephine's family came in 1884 when she was 1. The families settled in the Bohemian Colonies in Kansas. John Pospisil, as the eldest in a Catholic family of 12 children, was expected to be the priest. Instead, he married Josephine and they moved to central Montana. As with many immigrants, learning English and understanding the American culture was not always easy; adaptation struggles continued into the next generation, my mother's generation.

Events in this book are often true with dates and descriptions reported from primary resources. I used the actual names of historical figures. I've recorded where my parents lived, the years they were there, and imagined their reaction to major events in the 20th Century.

I'm thankful for friends and family who encouraged me to complete this second historical novel, especially my Laurel classmates. Shari Pyke and my brother, Ken Leuthold, read early drafts and offered excellent suggestions for changes. I'm deeply grateful to Susan Lubbers who edited and pruned the final draft. Thank you, Jean Albus, for allowing me to use your intriguing photo on the front cover. My husband, Paul, is a special gift in his steadfast love for me throughout my starts, stops, and stumbles over the years. I appreciate the skill of Peter Tolton in book design and layout.

As I wrote, I became aware that this telling of Louisa's life brought me closer to understanding my mother, what her life meant to her, and how she shaped my life. I hope that if she were alive, Mom would enjoy this herstory as an entertaining life adventure similar to her own.

Also by Betty Whiting

Becoming

Anna Mueller, a Swiss immigrant, becomes enmeshed in the politics and community events of Montana from 1908 to 1936. With her older, adventurous husband, Anna learns to overcome the obstacles of living in a new, sparsely populated state where men dominate politics and home life. Set primarily in rural Eastern Montana, this stirring account tells of one family's encounter with homesteaders, women's suffragists, deaths, oil development, KKK, and the Sedition Act.

For more information or to order books contact
bettywhiting@bresnan.net